MW00577011

REVELATION IN THE ROOTS:
EMERALD ISLE

NANCY FLINCHBAUGH

ALL THINGS
THAT MATTER
PRESS

Revelation in the Roots: Emerald Isle
Copyright © 2021 by Nancy Flinchbaugh

This is a work of fiction. Any resemblance to actual individuals, living or deceased, is purely coincidental. While certain locations are real, all events occurring are solely the product of the author's imagination.

ISBN: 978-1-7377671-5-2

Library of Congress Control Number: 2021952941

Cover art by: Margaret Olsen

I dedicate this book to all those who work for peace, encourage listening across differences and work to build a more just society. My prayer is that this book will encourage all of us to be bridges across our divisions into a better, more compassionate future for all.

Acknowledgments

As I think back over the five years during which this book took shape, I am so grateful for the many people and experiences of my journey.

In Ireland, I would like to thank Sister Mary Minehan of the Solas Bridhe Retreat Centre and Hermitage in County Kildare and the staff at Corrymeela, a Christian peace center in Northern Ireland, particularly Sean Pettis, who helped with Irish history and retreat strategies.

For editing, I am most grateful to my writing coach, Kathie Giorgio of AllWriters' Workplace and Workshop; my husband Steve Schlather; high school friends Cheryl French McKinney and Mark Henry (who edited for political bias); and Deb Harris of All Things That Matter Press for her belief in my book and her painstaking final edit.

I extend appreciation to Everyday Democracy for their leadership in conducting democratic dialogue and to the Shalem Institute for Spiritual Formation, for their leadership in Christian contemplative practice. I've learned so much from both organizations

I'm grateful to many authors listed in the Bibliography who have informed my understanding of Ireland, Irish spirituality, genealogy, and racial divisions in the United States.

Finally, I extend appreciation to the City of Springfield, Ohio, my coworkers, and the Human Relations Board for fostering dialogue about race, celebrating diversity, promoting conflict resolution strategies, and furthering fair housing, during my time there from 1994-2021.

IN THE BEGINNING

The leprechaun dusted off his coat with a feather, shined his shoes with a leaf, and prepared to report for duty in the Miami Valley of the Americas. Today he would follow his people, answering St. Brigid's call. He gazed into the heavens, waiting for a ride. In his enchanted forest on the Emerald Isle, a rainbow materialized just about every morn' when the mist lifted off the land, greeting the sun for a new day. He cherished these sacred moments when dewdrops and light spread colors across the sky. Ah, here it came now.

Síochán jumped aboard the rainbow and sailed up to the top of the arc, wondering what the journey would hold. Hovering over Earth, he smiled with anticipation, knowing that St. Brigid and the Lord Himself were always up to something good. He snapped his fingers and let the colors carry him across the waters. He released himself into the experience, sliding down the rainbow into the valley where the Miami Tribe once lived. Finally, he plopped down into a bed of leaves beside a large gold pot, tended by a wise and familiar woman, who hovered over her cauldron and greeted him with a smile.

"Ah, there ye be, Saint B," he said. "Síochán, reporting for duty, ma'am." With a jump, he leaped up, shook off the leaves, and perched himself on the branch of a nearby bush. "And just what might have ye up your sleeve this good day?"

Over the years, Síochán had marveled at the ways Saint B sparked humans into the possibilities of their lives in her mission projects. So he enjoyed coming along and helping out when invited.

St. Brigid poured water into the large gold pot in front of her and added some herbs from her bag. Lighting a fire beneath the cauldron, she said, "The people continue to struggle here in America. Once they came searching for food and work, fortune and hope. They found all that here, and more. Yes, they found their pot of gold." She slapped the side of the pot and continued, "But sometimes they grab too much. Sometimes they forget they once were lowly indentured servants, building railroads and struggling to survive as immigrants. Sometimes they turn downright ugly."

A large Black woman sauntered into the clearing beyond Síochán's perch. "You got that right, Saint B," Grand MaMa drawled.

"Got a whole lot of ugly going on these days in this U.S. of A. Is that why you called me down?"

St. Brigid nodded. "I'm no stranger to the ways of the people. I've seen it all, lived it all, loved them all, and they keep doing it. Now we've got a division going here bigger than the oceans Síocháin and I just traversed, we do. We've got a people divided and we've got work to do."

Grand MaMa laughed. "What makes you think you gonna bring these people back together now? After all these years? Mm, mm, mm. What kinda magic you think you gonna stir up in that pot of yours? That take some doin', I tell you. I been around these parts long enough to tell you, that's some work."

Síocháin rolled up his sleeves. "I've got the magic covered, Grand MaMa. You've got the love and the wisdom, and Saint B's the bridge between us all. Never doubt the possibilities. When Saint B sets her mind to something, she serves up a feast, she does. I've been a-watchin' her roll it out, one generation to the next."

Brigid leaned back her head and let out a laugh that echoed into the heavens and resonated among the trio gathered. Then she said, "I'm giving us assignments for now, and we can put our heads together later and check in. Síocháin, you get the widow, Abigail. Help wake her out of her grief into a new adventure with her friends, the MAMs. Click your fingers. Help her rekindle the spark of her life. A little romance might do.

"Grand MaMa, I want to you to be checkin' in on Welby, that great-grandson of yours. If you've told him once, you've told him a hundred times he's got that gold inside of him. He needs you now to help him get away from those drugs and find his future.

"And I'll be taking Reagan. Life brought her down, so I must build her up. She's quite a lovely young woman, but she took some wrong turns with those pain meds, like too many in this land. But Reagan's got a future. They all do. We're all bound up in this together."

With that, Saint B extended her hands to Grand MaMa and Síocháin. In their circle of three, she began to sing, "Blest be the ties that bind." By the time she got to the second phrase, Grand MaMa's voice weighed in, offering a resonant alto to Brigid's soprano. Honey flowed into the valley as they sang out, "our hearts in Christian love." And then Síocháin joined in with his robust tenor pipes and the three sealed the deal, finishing off the verse, "The fellowship of kindred minds is like to that above."

PROLOGUE

Marcus Welby to the Rescue

His mind raced beyond his body as he crafted his steps to the prize. He perused the blueprints of the Fossil Fuel Kings headquarters, tracing the path to the center. For inspiration, he coated his nose with some coke and took a few snorts. Then he went to smoke a joint for one last time.

Flying high, he tap danced through his plan to set his people free. Tomorrow, he would live out the true meaning of his name. Welby would become Marcus and the healing of the nation would begin. Black Lives Matter? Hell, yes. He'd go down in history. Blow up the Fossil Fuel Kings headquarters and kill off some of those white kings holding the nation hostage with their billions. Sacrifice a few of them for the sake of the future. Someday, they'd write a rap song about him, their savior, the bomber who set them all free.

Nancy Reagan to Save the Day

"Ace Steele! Ace Steele! Ace Steele!" The cheering filled the stadium. Reagan stood on the stands behind the dais, waving a "Women for Steele" sign, cheering after every sentence for her candidate for president, the handsome, broad-shouldered leader who bellowed to the crowd. When he stopped, she let go and started chanting again with the rest of them. "Ace! Ace! Ace!"

Finally, a man had come to lead the nation back into the good old days. Finally, a politician who would make America better for the people again. "We won't let the Muslim terrorists into our country. We will deport the criminal Mexicans. We will keep our streets free of crime, locking up those no-good ghetto dwellers," Steele announced.

Yes, Reagan thought. *This is the man for the job.*

Reagan looked at her watch. Time for another pill. She reached into her purse and found the bottle, those little pain pills that kept her going. She took two for good measure to get her through the morning and help her prepare for her evening shift at the hospital.

She shook the bottle, hearing them rattle, and knew there were only two left. Almost out, but she knew just where she could sneak a few more, to keep her going for another week.

"Ace Steele! Ace Steele! Ace Steele!" She joined the thunderous crowd yelling for her man, hoping for a new day.

Abigail Listening

Abigail heard a voice. She craned her neck to listen. She missed her late husband, who often came to meditate and pray with her in the mornings. *Okay, I'm going crazy*, she thought. But, no, now the voice spoke quite clearly. She picked up her pen to write.

"Ah, the Emerald Isle. Such a classic, such a beauty. There, the mist rises off the bern in the early mornin' and the cock crows a new day. The landscape grounds the soul of the people, it does. There, the wells hold mysteries, waters deep from the earth. There, the people know how to tell a good story and celebrate. At night, the pubs come alive with the fiddlers and the singers and the drone of the bodhran. Ah, my lassie, yes, such joy there, but also such sorrow. The British stole our land, the rich enslaved the poor. But God always spoke to us, through the land, and then through Saint Patrick and Saint Brigid. So many starved when the potatoes failed. Those who could, escaped to America. Others died. Some of us were left to tell the story. Listen, my dear, and I'll tell ye. Aye, just listen."

Abigail looked up. The room lay quiet now. She reread the words. Had she invented this imaginary friend to ease her pain? She closed her journal and stood. She would pretend that didn't happen. A lot of people dreamt of traveling to Ireland, but her people came from Switzerland. Why did Americans fixate on St. Patrick's Day and the Irish? She didn't get it.

CHAPTER ONE
LAST DAYS

Welby Out

Welby shuffled around his cell. Today he would leave. After five years of doing time for drug possession, he felt dragged down, spit upon, and used up. His aunt had talked him into a halfway house called Sun Power up in Ohio.

He hated leaving North Carolina. Get away from your old crowd, she'd advised. Hell, what old crowd? Half his buddies had overdosed already and most of the others were still in the joint. But he sure as hell wanted to get out—and stay out—of prison; maybe going to a new place would help.

When he'd first come to the joint, he'd focused on getting back to his plan. Then he began to wonder. The fossil fuel industry seemed hell bent on destroying the USA—and life on Earth, for that matter—with their mad grab for profits. But after five years of pondering possibilities, he knew blowing up the headquarters of an oil company probably wouldn't change anything at all. And could he really say Black Lives Matter if he planned to take his own? Why sacrifice his life to make a statement? They'd just rebuild, bigger and better, and not skip a beat. Maybe his life could have a different purpose. But what?

When he really thought about it, God had dealt him a big favor in that highway patrolman who pulled him over, conducted an illegal search, and sent him to prison for marijuana and a little bit of coke. Unfair as hell, yet in the end, it gave him a second chance. If he proceeded with his plan and killed people with his bomb? No way he'd ever get out of prison again. So damn lucky, really.

The guard threw a bag of clothes into his cell. "Marcus Welby Jones! Your day has come. Get dressed," he barked.

Welby listened to his name. *Can I be a real person again?* He didn't see a whole lot of hope. Grabbing the bag, he pulled out his blacks, still fragrant with the cologne Adriana loved so much. Hell, she'd dressed him up in these threads before life came crashing to a halt. His senses transported him back to her apartment. No woman for five long years. Why start now? Where did she go? Dropped him quicker than a smack when he went in the slammer.

He fingered the silky shirt and smoothed the shiny pants fully capable of showing out his gluteus maximus back in the day. Now? He stretched the shirt over his battered chest, feeling like a lamb leaving the slaughterhouse. After being beaten up, abused, and hung out to dry too many times to remember, he had learned to fight here. He had to give it that.

The tattoo on his belly told it all. "You die."

Who dies? Fossil Fuel Kings? Himself? Hope for tomorrow?

All dead. All dead. All dead.

Welby stepped into the soft pants and, with a hard thrust, pulled them on, zipped up, and sat. Welby out, headed for the Sun? Directing a few choice words to his aunt, he grabbed his head, bowing it between his knees. He should be happy. But really?

Reagan Free

The shrink perused her chart and said, "Nancy, are you ready to go?"

"My name is Reagan," she said. After three months of rehab, they still didn't get it. How many times had she explained her dad named her after Nancy Reagan, but not to call her Nancy? When she turned sixteen, she'd gotten rid of that stupid name for good. She chose her middle name, Reagan, and no one had dared call her anything else ever since.

"I'm sorry. That's right," he said. "Reagan, are you ready to leave now?"

Reagan scowled. Her mind raced over her situation. How to navigate a way through this new problem called her life. "Do I have a choice?"

"We've done all we can. We offer ninety days. You're on probation now. The judge sentenced you to a halfway house for a year. It's called the FARM, Farming and Restoring with the MAMs, in River City, Ohio. A group of ladies started this project to help women trying to kick their addictions. Or you can go to the Ohio Reformatory for Women in Marysville, if you'd rather. It's your choice."

She studied the floor, tracing the tile designs with her eyes while considering her path. She looked up, frowning at the man. "That's no choice."

Abigail's Angst

Abigail Wesley turned down the covers and slipped into bed. Alone. She shivered, snuggling up to the little Ecuadoran blanket she kept between the sheets during the winter. She missed having her husband beside her at night. After forty years of marriage, sorrow didn't evaporate just because three years passed. She wondered when the ache would leave. She wondered how to find happiness again. Sunday, her friend wanted to introduce her to a man. *Why did I say no? Why did I turn down Mike when he asked me out last week?*

She propped herself up with a pillow and grabbed her gratitude journal from the nightstand. In her grief group, they recommended taking time each day to give thanks. For months now, she took time every single night. Some days, she thought perhaps she glimpsed light entering her vision with the practice, but the darkness still overwhelmed her.

The state of affairs in the USA and the world didn't help her general sense of angst, either. As a Quaker, her big cause through young adulthood had been working for peace. Standing up against the nuclear arms race, speaking up against guns, speaking for building bridges across cultures and divides. Now she glanced across the room to a framed photo of the Great Peace March her husband had organized in earlier days. That was Jon, always so kind.

Well, the nuclear arms race seemed to be resolved for a while. With international agreements, even though the threat lingered, for many years it had felt like the nations of the world agreed they didn't want mutual assured destruction. But now North Korea kept bragging about intercontinental missiles and their nuclear capacity. She shivered.

Gun control? She laughed. Didn't win that one. *How many guns do we have for every person?* She forgot the statistic. At least three, if she remembered right. Then NRA. Crazy Americans, thinking the right to bear arms meant every person needed ten guns in their house. Violence. Why such violence? Jesus said to turn the other cheek. Jesus said to love. *How do we call this a Christian nation?*

Bridges across cultures? After the Civil Rights movement in her early years, sure, there were new laws and society progressed. But now, almost fifty years later, the plight of many African-Americans remained infuriating. When her Magnificent and Marvelous Book Club—the MAMs—did a round of reading about injustice to African-Americans a while back, she began to get depressed. They read *The New Jim Crow*, learning how the War on Drugs put more people in prison, so that the USA now had the highest incarceration rate in the world, and more Blacks were in prison than there used to be slaves. They read *The Warmth of Other Suns* and learned about the great migration from the South, where African-Americans never could have bona fide economic opportunity, into the North, where suffering continued. They read an *Atlantic Monthly* article, "The Case for Reparations," which provided the statistical data to show the injustice after injustice heaped upon African-Americans in the history of the country. They read *Just Mercy* and she began to realize just how jacked the criminal justice system could be for people of color.

And now, after eight years with President Alejandro Rosales, the first president of color, seemingly ushering in a new era, here came Ace Steele with his racist allies. Black Lives Matter? Oh, yes. But not really.

The great divide seemed to be splitting the nation in half, or maybe the more appropriate representation would be the one percent versus the ninety-nine. Between the Republicans and Democrats, the government appeared stalled out, unable to govern, unable to solve the huge problems facing modern society The Republicans struggled to repeal President Rosales' work, couldn't come together to get anything done, but were still quite capable of convincing their base and the Steele supporters they had the best interests of hard-working Americans in mind.

The Democrats couldn't craft a message to counter the money machine and right-wing agenda, even though she believed they really cared about the ninety-nine percent and were the ones who wanted to create a better country. The division made her dizzy. The rhetoric crowded out decent dialogue. Both parties seemed better at criticizing each other than doing anything constructive. She reached over to the nightstand and grabbed the dove Jon had carved for her one Christmas. She fingered the soft grooves, yearning for him, yearning for peace.

Taking a deep breath, she fingered her gratitude journal. She couldn't shake the presence of that amorphous black blob hanging in the center of her chest. That heaviness gathered weight as she considered the political problems of her time. And the environment, her pet project in her later years, seemed to be losing the battle as well, with Steele and his quest to dismantle the EPA and environmental regulation and deny climate change.

Some days, she took solace that now, at sixty-three, she knew her days were numbered. She wouldn't write it down in her gratitude journal, but there were days when she wanted to join Jonathon on the other side. Some days, it got very hard to pray. *How could God let this happen? How could we let this happen? What do you want me to do? I have no idea anymore.*

Gratitude. Right. Okay. She began to write.

1. Thank you for a warm house and this incredible alpaca blanket making this bed cozy.

2. Thank you for my grief group that connects me with others suffering like me and lets me know I'm not going crazy, but just very

human, coping with the loss of the love of my life.

3. Thank you for the MAMs and for everything I learn in the books we read.

She'd been trying to figure out her own family tree recently, so was glad they were going to focus on that as well.

4. Thank you for the progress we've made with our triple bottom line businesses of the FARM and Sun Power House. Yes, thank you, God. So amazing. You are still working here in River City.

5. Thank you for Thomaseena's success and her upcoming marriage to Jose. Now another triple bottom line business building the solar industry with a healing salon right here in our community.

She smiled, thinking back over the MAMs project to start an organic re-entry farm for women in recovery. She closed the journal and placed it back on the nightstand.

As she turned off the light, she continued her prayer of gratitude in silence. *Thank you, God. Thank you for Thomaseena's healing. Thank you for your love. Thank you for my life. Thank you for hope. I know you're not finished with me yet, and we've still got work to do together.*

She wrapped up again in the alpaca blanket, sensing God's love holding her tight, closed her eyes, imagining Jon's body beside her again, and faded into sleep.

CHAPTER TWO
THE FARM AND THE SUN
POWER HOUSE

Abigail and the MAMS Read Roots

Abigail headed over to Molly's house for a night with her favorite friends, the MAMs—the Magnificent and Marvelous—Book Club. Tonight, they would begin an exploration of genealogy and roots, Molly's idea. Molly chose the first book: *Roots*.

After Abigail's husband died, she searched for her place, alone in the world. For a while, she worked on her own family history, but put it aside. Now she looked forward to talking genealogy over with the MAMs. It was such a popular subject these days. She came early to help Molly prepare.

"What can I do to help?" she asked after Molly let her in.

"Well, I need to check the cookies in the oven and get some wine from the cellar," Molly said. "Here, you can put these M&Ms into a bowl and get some wine glasses out of the dining room cabinet." She looked at her watch. "We have plenty of time. Now that I'm retired, getting ready for the meeting doesn't stress me out anymore. I feel so blessed to have recovered from breast cancer. I feel like I have a second chance at life. And I love you guys," Molly said.

As Abigail opened the M&Ms, she reflected on her life with the MAMs. She smiled, thinking about how happy they all were that Molly'd survived breast cancer. She lost a breast, but she seemed to be just fine now. Abigail knew the MAMs helped Molly through that difficult journey. For years, they'd met monthly as a book club, but when they went on an archaeological adventure to Turkey a few years back, they really became a team. Then, when they launched a halfway house called the FARM for women and formed the FARM board which also birthed the Sun Power halfway house for men, these women became more than her friends. They were family. They were community. They were her tribe.

Molly emerged from the cellar with the wine and said, "Can we talk? I'm still trying to figure out how to introduce this book."

"Okay," Abigail said. "What are you hoping for tonight?"

"With all due respect, I just don't think that white people ever quite get the African-American journey. You don't have the bondage and indecency of human slavery in your psyche and family tree. You can't really know what life is like for African-Americans, even in this day and age. I'm glad you were willing to read *Roots*, but astonished that you didn't read it years ago. Maybe this book will help you understand me and what my life was all about."

Abigail nodded. She knew just enough to know she didn't really understand the Black experience. She wondered how Molly felt, being in a book group with all white women. Abigail felt glad Molly'd found a way to talk about it with this book.

"I have to admit, being the only African-American MAM, I often feel a little weird, meeting with all you white women once a month. You answered my call for a clandestine Romance Readers Anonymous club way back then, so I just decided to live with it. As our friendships grew, the color issue faded to the back. We try to understand each other."

"I appreciate that," Abigail said. "We do try. But we don't quite get what it's like to be African-American, I agree. So you're hoping *Roots* will help us understand a little more?"

"Yes, Alex Haley and *Roots* created a major revolution in the African-American community when I was younger. I read it when it hit the bookstore. I felt an immediate shift. I started a quest to discover my *own* roots. Learning to own my past and my African roots helped me focus on the good of my people in the midst of the evil of slavery."

"I see that," Abigail said. "So what do you want to do tonight?"

"Well," Molly said, "I'll start by asking for all of your reactions. Then I'll tell my story. I know this is a long book. Do you think everyone read it?"

"I doubt it." Abigail laughed. She hadn't finished the book. Feeling embarrassed, she changed the subject. "Well, if not everyone reads it, that's not always a bad thing. Remember what happened that night we came to discuss *In Search of Paul* by John Dominic Crossan?"

"Oh, yeah. We focused on wine! Then Jane said we should go dig up Thecla, the woman on the cover. How could I ever forget?" Molly laughed too.

Abigail flashed back to that fateful night that led them to Turkey after their religion professor member, Katharine Long, wrote her college roommate, Ursula Goodtree, an archaeologist with the University of Michigan, who then wrote a grant to take them all to Ephesus. So amazing that they actually found first-century scrolls in a cave overlooking Ephesus and broke open new debate on the book of Revelation among the Bible scholars. Once again, Abigail reminded herself that not reading the book could be a good thing. But she hoped Molly wouldn't take it personally.

Molly kept laughing and asked, "Whoda thought?"

Abigail replied, "You never know what'll happen with the MAMs."

Jane arrived next, announcing, "I brought us a bottle of vino from my recent trip to Italy. Want me to open it?" Jane, their rich MAM with the resources and the time, seemed always to be exploring some foreign land in between their monthly meetings.

"Sure," Molly said. "I'm ready for some wine myself. A long day over at the FARM, learning how to plant. I am not a farm girl, for sure. Good luck turning my brown thumb green!"

Soon, Sallie knocked. Sallie Quisenberry, a retired kindergarten teacher, had been Abigail's college roommate at Earlham College. Their friendship grew through the years. Abigail really loved Sallie and, after Jonathan died, it felt better to have a friend from way back. She felt real proud of Sallie when she turned over a new leaf by mentoring women in prison and helping out at the FARM. And sometimes Sallie wrote a letter to her congressperson about addressing climate change; not bad for someone who didn't take much interest in politics.

Priscilla knocked quietly and came in, dressed to a T with her high heels, shiny black pants, and pearly white blouse. Their conservative Christian member tried often unsuccessfully to keep their group on the straight and narrow. She told them she prayed for them every day.

Finally, Katharine Long came in, apologizing for being late.

"You're fine," Molly told her.

Over at Mainline College, they kept Katharine busy with committee work. She seemed to be always working overtime, between her excellent teaching in their religion department, connecting with students, writing journal articles, and performing administrative chores at the small liberal arts college in River City. Abigail knew she tried to make it on time.

Molly served drinks as they came in and gathered in the living room. And then she asked. "So, what were your initial impressions? What did you think of *Roots*?"

An awkward silence followed. Sallie looked at Jane. Jane went for another glass of wine. Katharine looked at the floor. Priscilla sat with her hands primly folded in her lap, a slight smile on her lips. Abigail's eyes darted anxiously around the room.

Finally, Sallie broke the silence. "Well, it was eight hundred and ninety-nine pages, you know. Molly, that's a lot of reading for us old ladies." She laughed nervously and put her hands on her belly, leaning back. "When do you think we have time for that?"

Jane brought the wine bottle back from the kitchen. "Refills, anyone?"

Molly looked around and blurted out, "Did *anyone* read the book?"

"I started," Sallie said. "But I needed to clean my house for my friend who came to visit from England. And then I visited someone in the hospital and went to the prison and ...."

"How far did you get?" Molly asked.

Sallie looked down at her book and opened it, trying to find her place. She looked up. "Page fifty-three?" She laughed. "Well, I started. I read a summary online, too."

Katharine said she did skim it in college, for an English class. Jane said she'd looked at comments online and watched some of the mini-series. Priscilla said she got to page one hundred and fifty.

Abigail worried Molly might be getting upset, but honestly felt less guilty to learn the others hadn't read it either. She should've told Molly earlier, but now reported, "I read a few chapters, then I read a summary online. I planned to read it all, but life got in the way."

"Really? Nobody read the book?" Molly said. "Come on. This is my story. Why didn't you read it? This isn't fair. You read the other books. Don't you really care about Black history, about me?"

Abigail grimaced. "No, Molly, no. I'm sorry. I do think your history is important."

Sally chimed in, "Yes, Molly, I'm sorry, too. I should have made time. It's not that your history isn't important, it's my time management issues. You know I've got problems."

A heavy silence hung in the air while the MAMs looked anywhere but at Molly, who glared at them. Abigail took a drink of water and then Katharine said, "We're sorry, Molly. Will you forgive us?"

Molly glanced around the room slowly and said, "I'll think about it."

Jane said, "I'm sorry, Molly, too, but remember, the last time we didn't read a book, we ended up in Turkey. Maybe I should take you on a trip in search of your roots. Then we can write our own books on our roots. We'll make it up to you, Molly."

Priscilla piped up. "Ireland! Let's explore my Celtic roots. It's on my bucket list."

Suddenly, Abigail remembered the Irish voice in her living room. But she came from Swiss Mennonite stock. "Could we go to Switzerland?" she asked

"Let's do Ireland. I've got some of those ancestors, too," Jane said. "And England."

"Norway and Sweden," Katharine said. "Would you take me

there, Jane?"

"West Africa, the Sea Islands, South Carolina," Molly said. "You buy the ticket. I'm in!"

"Holland and Germany," Sallie said. "How about a three-week European cruise?"

Jane laughed. "You think I'm just made of money, don't you?"

"I don't call you money bags for nothing." Sallie laughed.

Jane said, "Well, I need to save money for a rainy day, too. Never know what the stock market will do next. I might be able to spring for one or two trips."

"Could we take the residents of the FARM and Sun Power?" Molly said. "I could write a grant. Roots are important. That could help our re-entry people find themselves."

"We should not read our books more often," Sallie said.

Molly interrupted. "A great idea, but, first, we need to discuss *Roots*, and maybe for two more months, so you all have time to read it. This story is partially my story. It's important to me. I want you to read it and understand what these roots mean to me. Being a descendant of slaves plays havoc with your psyche."

"Okay, Molly, I gotcha. I'll try to read more of it, but I'm not making any promises I'll get through all eight hundred and ninety-nine pages," Sallie said.

"But really, don't you have to get over that? Isn't it time to move on?" Jane asked.

"It's not that easy, Jane. One time, I went to a Reiki person at a peace conference who called herself an African healer. She told me that all the African-Americans she works on have grief issues in their heart chakra. We still carry the pain of slavery in our bodies. I want you to really understand our experience. The African-American men and women who move into our halfway houses are also living this pain in their broken lives."

Abigail nodded. "I think she's right. We white folk don't quite get it. We sometimes assume because the laws protect against race discrimination now that discrimination's all a part of the past. It's simply not true."

"Thanks, Abigail," Molly said. "You're right. And it helps when we learn about our roots in Africa, and, in my case, among the Gullah people in South Carolina. Then we learn about the good there, too. We learn that we are a strong people, connected to the earth, and with a long lineage of wisdom that spills into this generation. That makes a big difference for me."

The MAMs often listened to short videos to hear their authors up front and personal. "Okay, guys, I found a YouTube video of the *Roots* author," Molly told them. "Listen to Alex Haley talk about why he wrote this book." Molly turned on her flat screen TV, already connected to her laptop. She moved the mouse over the little triangle to start the video and used the remote to crank up the volume.

They listened to Haley, and then to Molly a little more, and the hour and a half passed quickly. At the end of the evening, Katharine suggested they just spend one more month on the book. "You know, Molly, a lot of people felt that Haley could have written a shorter book. Another month will give us more time. You can understand without reading every word."

"I know what the critics say," Molly said. "Rambles on, could've been cut in half—"

Sallie interrupted, "What do you say? Should we plan some trips?"

"Let me work on it," Molly said. "Next month, *Roots* again. Try to finish, okay? In the meantime, I'll look for grants. I love this idea."

Leaving Molly's, Abigail felt happy. Planning the future felt good. She hadn't gone to Turkey because of her hip replacement. This time, she could go along. Once again, she considered that Irish voice in her living room. Maybe this was a God thing. Perhaps something amazing was being planned for the MAMs and their re-entry people. She could only hope.

Sunshine Labor

Welby sat back and listened to the lady. Yesterday, he'd arrived at Sun Power House and already they wanted to turn him into the gardener. His aunt had said he could learn a trade, become a licensed electrician, and learn to install solar panels, but manual labor? Really? So much for becoming a doctor. Hell, being a Black man in America meant one thing: you were going down. In a few minutes, he'd be digging. Came all the way from the slammer, from his home of North Carolina, to become a slave tending Buckeye soil? He didn't like dirt. Got too many whuppings for not staying clean as a little boy to have anything to do with it.

His mind raced back to his roots, those good roots by the ocean on Eagle Island, North Carolina, where he was born. There, they'd tended him well. First his mama, until she died, but then Auntie and his uncle, with Grand MaMa always looking on. He chuckled, remembering his days in church, up in front as the child prodigy preacher. They'd loved the way the amens flowed when he got on a roll.

His aunt and uncle were schoolteachers in nearby Wilmington, but he always got to stay back on the island for the summers. Well, until he turned eleven and his father called him over to Raleigh. Said he wanted him to get some schooling, but really all he wanted was for Welby to provide childcare for his babies with his new wife. His aunt and uncle tried to fight it in the court, but his dad could talk a good line, and paternity won out in the end. Welby had to cook, change diapers, and be at the beck and call of those three little ones, while his father's wife, Mabel, took to the bottle and drugs. When she died of an overdose, and his dad went to prison for selling drugs, the kids got adopted. By then, his aunt and uncle had moved over to Raleigh themselves, and they gave him a place to rest his head while he finished up high school. In Raleigh, he got his schooling, but he also learned how to hook up with some bad dudes. Water under the bridge, all water under the bridge.

"Okay, men, today we're going to learn about roots. Have you ever thought about how a plant grows? Have you ever looked below the surface?" The slim white-haired lady named Abigail looked at him directly. "What do you know about roots, Welby?"

"*Roots*, that's the name of a book, ma'am," Welby shot back. "That be about a man tracing back his story to Africa. That be about Kunta Kinte. That be about me."

"Yes! I just started reading that book. About family roots, right? About transplanting roots on foreign soil? Quite a story," Abigail responded.

Her answer surprised Welby. What did a white lady know about the Black people's story? And why was she reading an old book like *Roots* now? She shoulda read it years ago.

Welby kept his thoughts to himself. *Roots*. He remembered watching the mini-series and reading the book in high school. He thought about his girlfriend at the time, how they got it on during that "homework" session on the couch, watching, when his auntie wasn't home.

Abigail rambled on, interrupting Welby's meandering thoughts. Used to always get hit with a stick when he didn't listen. Welby quit daydreaming and tried to focus on her words.

"Roots are important to both people and plants. Today, we're going to plant roots and prepare this perennial garden for spring. This should have been done last fall, but we didn't get around to it. A few warm days here in February thawed the soil. Better late than never.

"Plants need the sun and the water above ground to grow, but if they don't have good roots, they will not thrive. Root systems carry them through the winter. A good perennial garden can last for decades, if well-tended. Some of these, I divided and brought from my garden at home. These hostas and lilies came from my husband's family, way back.

"So it's special for me to have roots of my husband's ancestors giving beauty each year, even after he's gone. We're going to dig them up, separate them, and take some over to the FARM and plant a garden there. You'll be taking the ladies flowers, men. Once spring begins in earnest, they'll grow up and bloom out both here and there. If you take good care of roots, you can cultivate beauty and share it with others."

Real special, Welby thought. White people had time for this mess. Back where he came from, they only grew stuff to eat. Well, mostly. Suddenly, his great-grandmother's face popped into his mind's eye, front and center. There she stood, looking straight through him, like only she could do. Never met anyone who could read him the way that lady could. What a woman ... his mother's grandmother, the Grand MaMa, as they liked to call her. And if she wasn't telling him to get down on his knees and start digging to help her transplant some ... damn. Roots. She told him about roots. Now he heard her once again.

"You got good roots, boy. And you're going places. Now, you just hear me out. You'll have people tell you that a little Black boy ain't worth nuthin'. But don't you believe them. I can see it in your eyes. I can see it in your heart. I can hear it in your voice. You goin' be somebody great someday, and I don't want you to listen to them white people telling you anything different. 'Cause you got good roots. You go way back to Africa where the original people came from. And you go way back to the Gullah people who got transplanted against their wills, but, nevertheless, they put their roots down here in the islands of the South and they grew strong to birth me and my chilluns and then your mama and her cousins and now you. So don't you never think you aren't somethin'. You're going to be great. Now, help me get these plants ready for winter, boy."

He remembered standing there as a little boy and saying, "Yes, ma'am." What she expected, what he learned to say.

Grand MaMa kept right on talking, not paying him no mind. Or was she? "When you look at the root, it's real ugly and dirty and you think it's got nothing on it. And sometimes, you're going to look in the mirror and think you're as sorry as this here root. But don't you believe it. You got good roots. Just watch. This here root's going to grow up to be a beautiful lavender lily next spring. And this one's going to branch out into a beautiful green and white hosta and send up a shoot into little purple flowers. Just look at those flowers, and you remember. Just look in the mirror and you remember. That brown skin of yours got some strong roots, and you're goin' to grow up and blossom and be great. Marcus Welby Jones. You goin' be all that."

Where did that come from? He hadn't thought about Grand MaMa for ages. All that stuff about roots? Did his mind make all that up? Without drugs, so maybe he was going crazy.

Abigail continued. "The root of each plant is a little different, and you'll see that the roots start sending off shoots to begin a new plant." She dug some out and showed up a little bit of new growth. "When you separate them, you must include the little shoots, and then you'll be good. If you don't separate them, they may outgrow your garden. We'll dig these up, split them in half, and take some to the FARM. The rest, we'll plant here to make a nice spring garden."

Fortunately, she pulled out some gloves, so he didn't have to get his hands dirty. And she kept on teaching them real nice-like how to do the job, and she made him feel like it was something important. And Welby found it interesting. Even though he'd studied science hard in high school, he'd never really looked at a plant root before.

She got him thinking about all sorts of things. When they took a break, he started looking at the trees in a new way and thinking about the roots that must extend underneath them. It got him curious to look at pictures of roots for different plants. And it made him wonder if these here hostas and lilies could really grow up and show out their beauty because of care for their roots.

Was Grand MaMa right? Did he have good roots? Was it just a matter of nurturing what he was born with? Powerful thoughts for such a little bit of time of messing in the dirt.

Farming Time

Reagan scowled at her tiny bedroom in the FARM house. It was smaller than her bathroom back home. She felt cut off from her people, living with a bunch of poor folks. She cared for these kind at the hospital, but liked to keep them in their place. Although she believed in helping others, she looked forward to moving into nursing management so she wouldn't have to do the dirty work.

But what now? Would Daddy let her into her trust fund? He'd kicked her out after college. "Learn the value of hard work," he said. So she worked her butt off, and he just laughed when she complained. "My daughter will not be a spoiled brat," he told her.

Didn't he see how hard she worked, double majoring in nursing and art? She loved art, but art programs get cut from local schools when finances get tight. So she chose nursing to pay the bills since Daddy insisted on her working. She had the brain to do pre-med, and part of her always wanted to be a doctor, but she thought that would just be a little too much work. Yet she did like to help people. She could put feet on her Christian love every day and earn some money in the process, and keep her father happy.

Not her fault that drunk driver hit her head-on her senior year of college. He messed up her face. They plunked her down into intensive care for a week, followed by a slow rehab process, delaying graduation. The plastic surgeons reconstructed her beauty, but the agony took its toll. For months, she lived off pain meds and, by the time she recovered, she was hooked. All the doctor's fault. She should sue him. Look what he'd done to her life.

Reagan finished her degree the next year, finding it so easy to get that doctor to keep on writing prescriptions. She sailed through her final semester, nursing boards, and into her first year on the job. By the time the doctor finally cut her off, she was working in the hospital. Convenient then to help herself from the meds drawer, keeping her little habit going. She doctored the drug counts, making it all look straight, until the head nurse caught on. Reagan denied it. A few days later, the police came in and arrested her. So much for her nursing career.

Now what? Any way you looked at it, she screwed up badly. When she really thought about it, she knew she now was one of those poor, sorry people she used to hold her nose about. But Jesus would rescue her. She knew it. She could pray.

"Reagan." A knock interrupted her inner soliloquy. "Time to go work. You up?"

"Yes," she yelled back. "Okay, I'll be down in a minute." She pulled on jeans and a sweatshirt, then stepped into her old sneakers. Didn't they know she needed her "me" time to survive? She could tell them a thing or two about how to run this place.

Why couldn't Daddy let her come home and relax after rehab? Or pull some strings and get her nursing license back. Maybe if she wrote him a letter? Why did he send her brother Dean to pick her up after rehab, though? Surely, he'd rescue her soon.

Reagan strutted into the dining room. The room got quiet. "What's up?" she asked.

"In the future, please be on time," Gloria said, punctuating her directive with a frown and a glare. She opened the door to the outside. "Let's go, ladies. The seeds await."

While the FARM house women followed Gloria across the yard and out past the barn to the greenhouse, she told them, "Today we're going to plant our first seeds. February in the greenhouse is the spring of indoor gardening."

Reagan rolled her eyes and impatiently checked her watch, noticing the date. February 10? They'd set their wedding date for February 14. Tyler wanted it to be perfect. She did, too. All planned out, guaranteed to be the biggest event in the history of Celina, Ohio.

Her face fell. Those plans had tumbled into oblivion with her arrest. Tyler had never returned a single letter.

She tried to concentrate on Gloria's lecture about planting and caring for the seeds, but her heart roamed light years away. How could she survive a whole year of this? Did they think they could make her into a farmer? Not a chance.

Reagan's face carried a scowl as she followed the directions, poking tiny seeds into the dirt. How had her life come to this? Organic farming was just a foolhardy attempt to stroll down memory lane. No, she invested her earnings in modern agriculture, engineering new crops for the masses, growing Daddy's portfolio, and her inheritance.

CHAPTER THREE
DAY-TO-DAY OPERATION - MARCH

Reagan on the FARM

Reagan kept trying to learn the routine of this place, working in the greenhouse, preparing the fields for planting. In the evenings, they went to AA and NA groups. She learned she wasn't alone in her problem with pain meds. They called it "The Opioid Crisis," with thousands dying from overdoses. Maybe she'd lucked out after all.

On Sundays, Reagan enjoyed the break. During orientation, they'd told her, "On the Sabbath, no work. We go to church, come home and fix dinner, and then you can do your own thing. Take up a hobby or invite your family to visit."

But on this Sunday, they needed to prepare for an evening open house. *So much for a day of rest*, Reagan thought. The house manager assigned cleaning chores. She grumbled, but then worked quickly so she could paint in her room before supper. Most of the women in the house would be leaving soon. For her? Just the beginning. For the past year, the FARM, an organic farm and recovery home for women, had housed quite a few women turning over a new leaf. Reagan knew Thomaseena, the first resident, had passed through the program with flying colors and the others would graduate soon as well.

Reagan finished up her chores and hightailed it to her room for some alone time. She quickly set up her easel and paints, then stared out the window. Doing art always made her feel good. Ever since childhood, her daddy supplied her with paints and an easel. He displayed her creations around the house and in his office. He called her Rembrandt, and she longed to become a successful artist. During college, her instructors liked her work, but her nursing degree put food on the table. And in the desert of rehab, they didn't give her paint. Maybe afraid she'd sniff it or something. Fortunately, at the FARM, they encouraged creativity. When Reagan mentioned painting, the social worker, Tiffany, brought her supplies for her craft. Feeling grateful, she fingered the empty canvas and considered possibilities.

She decided to paint a miniature of the farm. Choosing a canvas, she picked up a pencil, sketched the house, then added the greenhouse and the solar panels that fueled the irrigation system and the electricity for the buildings and their house. She envisioned a sunshiny day with a brilliant blue sky and some fluffy, puffy clouds.

Perhaps they would hang her creation downstairs. Yes, she liked that idea. At home, her paintings graced every room. She finished off the sketch and opened her new acrylics. She dipped her brush into light blue and felt her heart come alive as she slipped into the creative zone. Forgetting her plight, she focused on capturing the beauty of her new home. Art transported her to an airy and light place. She painted away, oblivious to time, whistling into her afternoon.

Sunday at the Sun, Welby

On Sunday, the men at Sun Power House went to church. Not an option, just part of the routine, they told him when he checked in. As Welby headed up to his room now, after lunch, the whole morning church experience tugged at something inside of him.

He'd resisted goin' in the pen. He held out long and hard. He gave up on God years ago. How could there be a God after what happened to his people? Not the God of those KKK members going to church on Sunday and killing his people at night with their white robes, pointed hoods, and guns. He couldn't believe in a God of those white pigs, targeting Black kids, or a God of the rich farts excluding people of color from their neighborhoods. They made sure their children had all the good schools. In the neighborhoods where Blacks lived, they were more likely to go to jail than to college.

In the pen, he'd just finished reading *The New Jim Crow.* That laid it all out, pure and simple. The reason America locked up so many Black men? Those racist politicians engineered the whole thing. They'd invented a new scheme when they couldn't keep Black people in their place no more. Out with the lynching, in with illegal searches and seizures, watering down 4th Amendment protections. They armed local police with federal grants and sent one million Black men to jail. Welby knew that's what happened to him. That day he got pulled over, driving his truck on a mission? Racial profiling. He had his truck under control. That officer had no right to go through his glove compartment. Back then, Welby didn't know his legal right to refuse an illegal search. He *did* know Black men got shot for standing up to a police officer. Yep, he was six times more likely to go to prison than the white men.

On the other hand, he realized that officer had also stopped him from doing something more serious. Occasionally, he thought about shaking the guy's hand, but then he'd slide back to thinking about the injustice of it all.

Sometimes, the anger inside of him boiled over. Maybe that's why the church service that morning had reached down into his heart. He stayed away because he knew, he knew the message. He didn't want to forgive and forget. He didn't want to love, to hope, and to dream again. Once he'd thought maybe life would change when he got out. He'd heard former President Alejandro Rosales talking about opportunities for re-entry people, but once Ace Steele got elected? No hope left. But that preacher man told a whole different story. Welby just didn't want to listen.

But there he'd found himself, forced to listen to that message once again. And sure enough if he didn't hear the same thing he heard every Sunday of his life as a young boy: "You can't let their hate reduce you to evil. If you choose hate, then they got you. If you give up on love, they steal what God gave you in the first place. If retaliation is your choice, then you're just as bad as them."

Now his Grand MaMa came back for the second time in one week, telling him, "You are better than that, Welby."

Could this place be haunted? Why did his Grand MaMa decide to show up from heaven right now? Wait, he didn't believe in any such stuff. No God, no heaven.

"Welby, you just listen here. You got yourself too big for your britches. Who do you think you are? You no better than them, if you gonna shut your God out of your life because you got on drugs and made some mistakes. Don't you go blamin' them for what you done. They may be racists, but you were brought up to be better than that. Now, you cut that out and you get down on your hands and knees and you confess what you done right now. I've had enough of that hard head of yours trying to think you got the right to go bad on me."

Welby shook his head, sat down on his bed, put his hands on his ears, and put his head between his legs. He heard a knock. Thankful for the interruption, he jumped up and opened the door. Skelly handed him a phone. Putting it to his ear, he heard a familiar voice: Aunt Rosie. Did Grand MaMa put her up to this? His thoughts shouted, "WTF"? But he kept his mouth closed and listened. He suspected a conspiracy coming down. Not the first time.

Aunt Rosie yelled into her phone, "Marcus Welby Jones, that you?"

"Yes, ma'am. It's me. Good afternoon, Aunt Rosie. How ya doin'?" Welby slipped into his polite self and braced himself to hear what came next.

"Now, Welby, I been a-prayin' for you every night, and I want you to know that we're expectin' good things from you now. Everybody can mess up a time or two, but then it's time to get your ducks in a row. You know my mama always said you'd be great, and we're still a-waitin'. Now I hope you're doin' everything they tell you to do, and you're being a good boy."

"Yes, ma'am. I'm being a good Black boy. Ain't that what it's all about? Behaving for the whites so they can put us down? Don't you know they got me digging in the dirt up here, making up some perennial garden? What kind of a place did you think you were sending me? Just because it's Ohio don't mean a Black man goin' get a better rap. Aunt Rosie, I want to come home." He sat down on the bed and looked out the window, waiting for her reply.

"Now, Welby, you just been there a few days. You gotta give this place a chance. They can make you into an electrician. You can come back down here and help us go solar. But first you got to get a decent job and make sure you ain't goin' back to those drugs. You be better than drugs, Welby. Your mama always wanted you to be a doctor, you know."

"Marcus Welby to the rescue! Come on, Aunt Rosie. This stupid name she gave me? How could I forget her plans? But what's the deal? She knew a little Black boy from the poor side of town's not being no doctor. Why didn't she give me a Black man's name?"

"Welby, you just stop talkin' like that right now. You know your mama wanted the best for you. That there's called aspirational. She wanted you to dream. She wanted you to believe. She wanted you to be great. You may not be doctorin' people, but maybe you'll be doctorin' houses and turning them into solar systems for the future. Now, you get this right."

Welby started pacing as she talked. He steamed, but heard her loud and clear. He should make something of himself. He had a good head on his shoulders. Hell, he could have been a doctor, at least according to his high school biology teacher. Deep down, he blamed the white man instead of trying. He looked at his big Black hand, wishing he weren't so dark. Then he corrected himself. Ain't nothing wrong with dark Black. Didn't he always tell others that?

"Welby, you there?" Aunt Rosie yelled at him again. He could imagine her sitting there with her Sunday clothes on; probably still had that little pink hat pinned on her head.

"Yes, ma'am, I'm here. I'm listening. You got anything else? How's everybody doing?"

She replied to the point. "We're fine, Welby. But this ain't about us. It's about you. And you're the one I'm prayin' for. Now, you just be good and do right. I'm going to call you next week to check up on you again. You better have something to tell me then. You hear, boy?"

"Yes, ma'am. Loud and clear, Aunt Rosie. Thanks for calling. I guess I'll be talking to you again next Sunday then. You take care of yourself."

26

When he hung up the phone, he thought a little bit about Aunt Rosie and Uncle Clem. They raised him up like their own when his mother died when he was a little boy. Uncle Clem had died of a heart attack a few years back, but that didn't stop Aunt Rosie. Always a rock. He knew that couldn't be easy for her. Really, he appreciated her.

Then, for the first time in a long time, Welby thought about his father. Welby had hated his life in Raleigh when he babysat his drugged-up, alcoholic stepmother and her children. He'd never been so happy in his life as when that sorry woman died from an overdose and then his dad messed up and went to prison. When the children got adopted out by a nice family and he got to go live with his aunt and uncle. After he went to prison himself, he considered writing his father. Maybe someday.

Welby looked at the clock and realized he needed to get downstairs to practice. He hadn't told his aunt about the jazz band. She didn't need to know everything. He might be upset to be up here in Ohio, but picking up a saxophone again promised to be a moment. He went downstairs and smiled to see the Mabra men setting up for the show.

"Welby," George called, "we got you a saxophone. You're going to do your thing."

"I ain't picked up a saxophone for years. Hard tellin' what will happen," Welby told him.

"Second nature," George responded. "It'll come back. You'll see."

Welby picked up the sax and tried a few notes. *Must be a good one,* he thought, as he played a line or two of "When the Saints Go Marching In."

He looked around the room. George grabbed his bass guitar. The policeman, Tom, held a trumpet, and the attorney man, Leo, sat behind a drum set. These big men looked more like professional football players than jazz musicians, but they seemed ready to rock it out.

For the first time, Welby watched the house really come alive with the quartet of Black men doing their thing. He soon discovered that George and Leo had some pipes. As they got cooked up, he felt the saints marching up and down the walls and all around that living room. George and Leo closed out with an incredible jazzy duet that gave Welby goose bumps. He started tearing up, and wiped them off quickly, hoping nobody noticed.

But that didn't seem to matter because they kept right on going, playing and singing their hearts out, belting out songs from church and the bars, songs Welby knew like the back of his hand from earlier days. As he played, he felt something shift. He felt an opening. A light went on, feeling like his soul came back. A smile started deep inside, though he kept that to himself. He didn't want them to know something monumental had just happened.

"What a Wonderful World." Leo called the next song, and they were off, chasing that tune, trying to revive Satchmo, bring the spirit of Louis Armstrong into the Sun Power living room. As the tempo slowed way down, Welby could see himself strolling down the street, happy, along with the lyrics, shaking hands and saying, "How do you do?"

After an hour, Leo called for a break and Tom started talking. "Our dad was the preacher man," he said. "We took up instruments in middle school and he had us playing in church every Sunday. We didn't have a choice, but we had fun. We don't play much anymore, just for special occasions. Hey, we're real glad you're joining us. You do a good job on that saxophone. You can keep it for now and practice when you have time."

George looked at his watch. "We better pack up and get over to that open house. You good, Welby, to play along? If you don't want to go public with us yet, that's okay, too."

"I'm good, man. Yeah, I'm good," Welby said. He actually loved playing the sax and, with an audience, he enjoyed it even more. "Lookin' forward to it, yes."

As quick as they came, they collected their stuff and disappeared. Welby put the sax away and carried it up to his room for safekeeping. He felt lighter and almost happy. He chuckled on the stairs, realizing he hadn't felt this good for a very long time. Maybe he could hope again.

Celebration

Reagan put all her paints away and considered her work. *Not bad,* she thought. *Impressive, really.* She took off her jeans and looked through her closet for some nicer clothes for the open house planned for the evening. Always important to make a good impression. She wondered if she might just take her new painting down on the easel and display it in the great room. Perhaps someone would commission her to do more. Make money on the side? Yes.

She pulled out her journal to write. Someday, her memoirs would be hot. After her daddy died, she planned to publish them all. The life of the rich and famous always sold.

She needed to capture this place in words so no one would forget what they put her through. Spellbinding stuff. She ventured to write just how she felt today, but someone rapped on her door.

"Reagan, come down! The shindig begins now." She recognized

the voice. That chubby little lady, Sallie. She heard a chuckle. "Do you hear me?"

Sallie always seemed just a little bit silly, not very refined like the people in Reagan's circles. Reagan had learned to be more proper. She closed her journal and opened her door.

"Hi," she said. "It's good to see you." She extended her hand to Sallie.

Sallie batted away her hand and laughed. "You don't have to do that. We're past formalities. It's time to party!"

"Sallie," Reagan said, "could I ask you a question?"

"Sure," Sallie responded.

Reagan motioned to her finished painting. "I just painted this picture of our place. Could we set it up downstairs for the open house?"

Sallie exclaimed, "Wow. That's amazing. I love it. Yes, yes. Let's do it!" She added, "You take the painting. I'll bring the easel. Let's go."

Together, they walked down the stairs and into the great room, where the organizers and the residents were finishing preparation for the evening. Reagan held out her painting to the group. "I practiced my favorite hobby this afternoon," she said. "This one's for all of you."

"Amazing," Starletta, the tall Black resident, said. "You got it goin' on, dear." She reached over to give Reagan a full embrace.

Reagan pulled back, not used to such easy familiarity. Hugs weren't exchanged frequently in her household. "I'm glad you like it," Reagan said.

"*Muy bella*," the small dark woman, Maria, said. "*Que bonita*."

Then the little white woman, Clementine, came up and looked at it closely and drawled in her slow southern voice, "Reagan, you painted our place. So beautiful. You're a regular artist"

Sallie said, "Let's display it here by the fireplace, so everyone can see it today at the party." She put down the easel and Reagan placed the small picture on it. They all stood back and looked at it together. "This is perfect for our open house. Amazing art by our new guest."

"Thanks," Reagan said. "I always wanted to be an artist. I *am* an artist, actually. But I'm a nurse for a living." Or I was a nurse.

Then the other women placed the food out on the dining table. The door opened and in came the Sun Power guys. Several of them were carrying instruments.

Molly welcomed them and then introduced them. "Reagan, this is my husband, Tom, and his brothers, George and Leo. They're on the board for the FARM, but today they're going to be our entertainment." She laughed and continued. "Hey, everybody, I want to introduce you to the newest member of Sun Power House, from North Carolina,

Marcus Welby Jones, call him Welby for short. He'll be playing saxophone with the Mabra Music Men, the Three M's, a little group they started way back when."

Welby raised his hand with a crook of his index finger, nodded, and made what looked like an attempt to smile, but Reagan couldn't be sure.

While Molly went on to introduce Welby to all the other women in the house, Reagan tried to size up this big Black man. He looked to be over six feet tall and had a sturdy frame. Handsome? Perhaps, if you liked your men dark. She never did. Could never wrap her mind around how some of her friends fell for the Black football players at her college. She kept her tastes carefully within her own race. She'd been taught better. Weird, his hair looked red. *Do Blacks really come with red hair?* Nervously, she fingered her scalp. Her own red roots would be growing in soon. She preferred living life as a blonde.

She watched him nod to each woman in turn. She didn't like the way his eyes seemed to move from top to bottom and back. His face lit up when one lady gave him a thumbs up. She could tell he appreciated her beauty. *They might make a good couple*, she thought. *But he might be a little too old for her*. He smiled at the others, but then she heard her name. What? He seemed to have a snarl on his face now. *What is his problem?* She knew she was easy on the eyes. Didn't he know she was the homecoming queen of Middleton High?

Reagan snarled right back. What kind of mess was this Black man? How many cops did he kill? Just what was wrong with America. Black men made the country unsafe, killing each other and blaming the cops for all their problems. She was so happy when Ace Steele got elected president. Law and order, in the process of being restored.

Reagan stayed far away from Welby but did enjoy his music as they started playing up a storm, and had to admit he looked pretty darn good for a Black man. She felt in her element, greeting guests, accepting compliments for her painting. She loved all these do-gooders coming to bless them. They were her kind.

Soon the music stopped, and Molly became an emcee, leading a short ceremony to talk about the house. She explained how the FARM helped women in recovery find new hope and connect with the earth.

"Thank you for coming to celebrate our first anniversary," she said. "We've already had one graduate and soon several of these ladies will be finishing up their year as well. We are so proud of them, staying with the program, attending the AA groups, pitching in here, doing their best."

The people clapped and a man came up and introduced himself as the mayor of River City. "You are doing great things here. I can never thank you enough for helping these women get their lives back together. I'm proud of the FARM and Sun Power House. Together, you are forging a new model for re-entering citizens. While, all across the country, people are trying to figure out how we can solve the opioid crisis, you're doing it here, one person at a time. When I go to conferences, I brag about you all. Congratulations on completing your first year."

Molly said, "Thanks, Mayor. We're trying really hard. It's not always easy."

Then some other people talked and more applause. Reagan watched a young couple holding hands and suddenly she thought about her ex-fiancé, Tyler. Now that 'd written her off, she needed to get busy and find a new Mr. Right.

The band kept right on playing, and people kept right on eating and chatting, and Reagan kept trying to avoid Welby by staying away from the band. But every now and then, she caught herself checking him out, and one time, his eyes met hers as he blew on his sax and their eyes locked and she felt him looking into her soul and she couldn't stop looking. But he broke the gaze and she turned away, too. What had gotten got into her for that moment, she had no idea.

CHAPTER FOUR
EXPLORING GENEOLOGY AND DNA - APRIL

Abigail and the MAMS

Abigail perused her DNA reports one last time before going over to Molly's for the MAMs Book Club. She'd never known about the Mediterranean and Irish blood. She remembered again that thick Irish brogue she'd heard in living room the other day. She reread her journal and his words. *Was that an ancestor speaking or did I make it all up? So strange.*

Since her husband died, she struggled some days to get out of bed. As a child, they'd called her Sunshine. She lit up rooms and brought smiles. As Jonathon's wife, she became optimist to his realism, even pessimism sometimes. Now that her parents and husband were gone, she didn't quite know how to shine anymore. She gazed into nothingness. Her eyes lingered on the dip his body once created in the cushion of his easy chair. Empty space. She felt alone, no longer sure who and what she had become.

The widowers in town tried to woo her. They remembered who she once was. They sought Abby, the life of a party, the belle of the ball, the happy-go-lucky spirit who planted the downtown gardens and frolicked with glee during concerts in the park. Fred took her out one night, but brought her home early when she turned every conversation into a lament about Ace Steele's denial of climate change. Harvey whisked her out for a night of dinner and dancing at the senior center, but, after one waltz, she collapsed in tears, missing Jon. She couldn't be that Abby now. Loneliness hurt.

With a new hip, she moved around better. At least she could garden again. When she helped out at the FARM and Sun Power gardens, she felt more alive. She kept involved in some environmental organizations, and she loved the MAMs. She looked forward to the evening, imagining some of her friends would find surprises in their DNA, too. She couldn't wait for Molly to reveal their surprise.

A few minutes later, she knocked on Molly's door. "I'm here, Mol," she yelled.

"I hear ya, I hear ya," she heard Molly reply. "I'm a-comin', I'm a-comin'."

It was rare for Molly to slip into that southern dialect, but every now and then, she did.

"You sound like one old mama comin' up out of the fields after putting in a day's work, sista," Abigail said.

"Yes, and now I's got to wait on youse white folk. Never a rest for the like of me," she said and then laughed. "Mm, mm, mm. Now that takes me way back."

"Where to?"

"Oh, you know, my people. Even though I grew up in Ohio, my mama came from the Sea Islands of South Carolina. She told us stories about the Gullah people and their days of slavery, She talked about life on the island after the Civil War. Her family tried to make it share-cropping, then crabbing, until the factories shut down and they came up North for work."

Someone knocked at the door, announcing the arrival of the rest of their group. Molly served up water and tea as Priscilla, Jane, Sallie and Katharine seated themselves and began to chat. Ever since their book club beginning, Molly opened her house each month and played hostess.

When Molly finished serving, she sat and began. "And now, ladies, Abigail has an announcement to make. I think you'll be pleased."

Abigail stood.

"You don't have to stand," Sallie said and started laughing. "It's just us."

Abigail laughed, too. "But, yes, I do need to stand. This is big. Actually, I think Molly should be making the announcement. It's all her doing."

"No, you started it," Molly said. "Go ahead."

"No, I didn't," Abigail replied. "Who chose the book *Roots*?"

"Okay, okay. You two, quit bickering about who did what. Just tell us. Tell us together if you must," Sallie said.

Molly laughed. "Okay, I have an announcement to make. Because of Abigail's suggestion," she paused and pointed her finger at Abigail and said, "This is all because of her, just so you know." She laughed again and continued, "I took up Abigail and her idea to write a grant to take our group homes on some trips. I wrote one to a federal re-entry program, and I also wrote one to the Cole Foundation, with a special cover letter by our graduate, Thomaseena Cole, soon to be Martinez. And guess what, ladies? I got every penny I requested. Pack your bags. We're going to Ireland, the Sea Islands and the Ivory Coast and maybe more."

"I don't get this," Katharine said. "Are you sure you can take the people from the houses on these trips? Wouldn't that be a violation of parole? Would they run?"

Molly piped in. "Actually, Katharine, we did get permission already. The Federal Re-Entry Commission approved this as part of a research project. Tiffany decided to work on her Ph.D. She'll be doing research on how this impacts the re-entry folks."

Sallie said, "You've got to be kidding me. Under the Steele White House?"

Abigail responded, "Well, no. Our three-year grant was approved under the Rosales Administration. Our local parole board has already approved the plans, with guidelines."

"You think of everything," Priscilla exclaimed.

"Thank you," Abigail said.

"And I don't have to fork over a dime?" Jane asked.

"Well, remember, you agreed to spring for half the costs of air fare. Not cheap, but you don't have to foot the entire bill." Molly looked at Jane with a nervous smile. "Are you still in?"

Jane smirked. "Just how much are we talking about here?"

"Well," Molly answered, "with the six of us, plus we're taking George and Tom Mabra along to manage the guys on each trip, and we'll take two FARM women and two Sun Power men on the overseas trips, although not necessarily the same ones, that makes twelve. We'll take a van to the Sea Islands, so you're off the hook there. But for the Ireland trip, I'm figuring about a thousand dollars a person, and for Africa, fifteen hundred. We're talking about thirty thousand total, but your share is only fifteen."

"That's pocket change for you, money bags," Sallie joked.

"Right," Jane said. "You have no respect at all for the wealthy, do you?"

Sallie stood, raised her hands high above her head and bowed toward Jane. "I adore you, Queen Jane. Thanks be to you for a royal blessing on your subjects. All Hail Jane."

"Oh, sit down," Jane said. "I guess I can use the interest from one of my accounts. Tax deductible, right?" Then she smiled. "We have ways of making it work for our bottom line. Don't feel too sorry for me. But, Sallie, you can bow again."

"Not on your life," Sallie said. "But thank you, Jane. I appreciate your generosity from the bottom of my heart." She tapped her chest and laughed.

Molly interjected, "Yes, thank you, Jane. We are truly grateful. Right, ladies?"

The MAMs nodded and Abigail picked up from there. "So, ladies, tonight, we have your DNA results. In a couple weeks, we'll get the FARM and Sun Power members tested. Clear your calendars for our first trips in October and February, after the harvest, before spring farming."

"Do you have the dates already?" Priscilla asked.

Abigail said. "Not yet, but soon. I'm working with a travel agent. Katharine, you're still teaching. Can you get off? And Priscilla, will they let you take leave?"

Katharine laughed. "I'm actually on sabbatical next year. I'll do research on our trips."

Priscilla frowned. "I'm not sure. Ireland, for sure. I'll see about the others."

"Do you know if our re-entry folks have DNA from these places?" Jane asked.

"Well, no, but it's certainly a well-calculated guess. Among white Americans, the percentage with Irish background is second only to those with German. Among African-Americans, a high percentage trace their roots to west Africa, and the Sea Islands—well, that's mostly descendants of slavery. So it's fairly certain we'll get the matches we need," Abigail explained.

"Isn't it a little risky to take these people on long trips? What if they run away?" Priscilla asked again. "Don't they need to go to their AA and NA meetings? Is this safe?"

"I've had a conversation with the parole officer," Abigail told her. "We agreed to monitor them with ankle bracelets, new cell phone chip technology. Beyond that, we MAMs will watch the two women and share rooms with them. They won't be alone. George and Tom will be one-on-one with the guys. We'll be monitoring twenty-four seven. Not quite as fun as our other trips."

"And I've checked into AA in Ireland; plenty of meetings there. When necessary, we can have our own. George is a leader. But, certainly, we need to do some more planning." Mollie said.

"Could we get on to our DNA now?" Katharine asked.

Abigail laughed. "Who read our book for tonight, *Genealogy Online for Dummies*?"

Sallie responded, "Abigail, it's boring. Put me to sleep. Let's see our DNA."

Katharine said, "I read the book. Some of us are getting a little too lazy. If we're going to be a book club, we need to read our books. I liked it. I had no idea that genealogy is such a big thing. I'm getting the bug. I know over half of Minnesotans like me track themselves back to the Vikings. I already started my free account on a site I found." When she told them which site it was, Molly smiled.

"Me, too," Molly said. "I used this book with the grant to check out online resources we can order. Guess what, ladies? You all will receive a free year of membership in that exact site. But you'll be able not only to interpret your own results, but also to help our re-entry folks interpret theirs."

"This sounds like fun," Katharine said. "Thank you, Molly, for getting us started."

"Abigail," Molly corrected.

"Molly." Abigail laughed. "Okay, enough of that. I give up. Here you go, but wait." She passed out the test results. "Let's open the envelopes at the same time."

"Like Christmas," Sallie said.

"Yes," Abigail said and then instructed, "Okay, one … two … three … open!"

The women tore open their large white envelopes and pulled out their personal reports. Silence filled the room as they studied their results.

Molly reached out for a cookie from the coffee table and leaned back on the sofa. "Well, well, well," she said. "West African, Ghana, a little Ivory Coast. Wait. What's this?"

Abigail leaned over, looking at Molly's finger on Europe and read, "Ten percent British Isle? Maybe you have a wee bit of Irish blood in ye, lassie."

"Nobody ever told me that," Molly said. "Probably means some white plantation owner raped one of my ancestors." She looked down, running her finger over the map. "Hard to believe, isn't it?" Her finger lingered over Africa, then crossed across the water to the American south. "I wish I could get Henry Louis Gates to do my story. There's so much I don't know."

Katharine reported next. "I'm not as boring as I thought. The Vikings, for sure, but also western European, maybe German, Native American, Russian, and Irish. Wow."

Sallie laughed. "No, you're never boring, Katharine." She leaned back into the easy chair and rested her hands on her belly. "I knew I came from Dutch stock, short people with funny names, sixty percent of my DNA. But I'm Japanese and Irish, too. Could I find some lost cousins?"

Katharine said, "Yes, but I'm not going to tell you how. Read the book, Sallie."

Priscilla turned her DNA map out so everyone could see. "Well, I never. My family never talked about the past. They settled in Appalachia. Life was harsh, so they didn't talk about it much. Sure enough, I've got the Scottish, Irish, British blood going on, thirty percent of each, and then some Dutch blood, too. We're cousins, Sallie. And then, according to this, I'm five percent West African DNA. Could that be true? I don't look it, do I?"

Abigail responded, "No, your blonde hair and blue eyes surely don't show off your African roots. What a surprise!"

"But," Katharine added, "there were certainly African-Americans in West Virginia where your people lived. A lot of mixed people. Perhaps someone passing as white married your ancestor? Maybe one of your ancestors owned a plantation and hooked up with a slave?"

Priscilla exclaimed. "Oh, heavens, I hope not." She paused. "Does this mean I'm Black?"

"Yes, Black like me." Molly laughed. "You got one drop and we claim you, cause those white racists disown you now. Whoda thought? I'm Irish and you're Black. Oh, this is precious. Welcome to the family, sistah." She stood up and extended her hand to Priscilla.

"Oh, my. Oh, my," Priscilla said. "I don't believe this. Could this test be wrong?"

Molly stood with her hand out but Priscilla didn't take it. "Okay, so now your true colors are coming out? You don't want to be my sister?"

Priscilla looked up and took Molly's hand. "Right, we're sisters," she mumbled.

Abigail could tell Priscilla didn't like this news, not one bit. She began to wonder what sort of racist attitudes Priscilla might be keeping to herself behind that smile.

"Could it be a mistake?" Priscilla asked again.

Abigail shrugged. "Always possible. But I saw you label and seal the tube yourself."

"Yes, I know, I know," Priscilla said, fingering the map of this new revelation.

To change the subject, Abigail turned to Jane. "What did you find out?"

"Amazons, Spartans, and Russians," Jane said. "I always knew I came from some strong stock. But I wish I'd known about my Amazon DNA when I went to Machu Picchu. Maybe one of my guides was a cousin. I should get with President Steele on my Russian background. Maybe he'd help me develop some business opportunities over there."

"You wouldn't," Sallie said. "Jane, really. You can't trust the Russians."

"Oh, I don't know," Jane teased. "Aren't you always saying to love your enemies?"

"Okay, okay," Abigail said. "No politics tonight. Here are my results. I know I've got Swedish and German blood with my Mennonite background, but look: I'm Irish, too. No one ever told me. And twenty percent of my DNA looks like it came from around the Holy Lands. I need to learn more. Maybe I'm related to Jesus!"

"Did you really believe the *Da Vinci Code*?" Katharine asked, laughing.

Molly pointed at the clock. "Ladies, it's nine o'clock. We're running late. I promised Tom we'd shut down on time. He wants me to watch TV tonight."

Abigail looked at her watch. "Oh, I'm sorry. But one more thing. Turn to page forty-four of *Genealogy Online for Dummies*. This explains your test report and how you can find out more. Check in to the website before our next meeting," she said. "For our grant, do your homework. In a few weeks, you need to help our re-entry folks do the same."

"And don't forget," Sallie said, "I picked the book for next month. *America, Your Roots are Showing*. And you better read it." She put her hands on her hips and looked around the room.

"You're scary," Abigail said. "Thank you all for coming. We're off to a good start. Now go home and get your accounts started. I'll email you sign-on information. Remember, you can use the entire site for a year, free. Have a good evening."

Abigail picked up her own DNA results, tucked them away in her tote and said her good-byes. She felt right happy as she headed to the car. Could she be Jewish or Muslim or both? Her Irish blood really piqued her curiosity. Perhaps she'd find some answers on the trip for herself. For the first time in a long time, she felt curious, looking forward to the future.

And then her thoughts traveled back to the Irish voice that she'd heard in her living room just a few weeks back. Could the Emerald Isle hold answers not only for her own life, but for the future for America? What could they learn there? Where would they listen?

Genealogy 101 with the FARM and Sun Folks

A few weeks later, on a rainy Wednesday night, Reagan watched from the back row while the MAMs filed into the great room of the newly constructed FARM house. After a tornado destroyed the FARM house last summer, Sun Light Industries built a house as a demonstration of the newest solar technologies available. The house included this great room for big meetings and meals. Large picture windows opened out onto the fields in the distance. Here, in this newly designed space, Reagan felt like she was participating in an Andrew Wyeth painting. She admired the house and the architectural effect. Tonight, she looked forward to a program, Genealogy 101. She knew all about the topic and hoped to enlighten them soon.

A moment later, the men from Sun Power House sauntered in. Reagan checked them out as they filed down the center aisle and seated themselves up front. She was happy she'd arrived first, to keep an eye on them. She watched them strut their stuff. She noticed them glancing around, probably looking for the FARM women yet to arrive. *Eat your hearts out*, she thought.

First came Welby. Bad stuff, that man. She tried to ignore his muscled frame, but nevertheless, her thoughts lingered there. Once again, their eyes connected and her heart seemed to take a leap. She looked away, focusing on the others. She eyed the white guy they called JT, covered in tattoos, all over his face and arms, and, she supposed, probably on every other part of his body as well. She'd nicknamed him Joe Tattoo the first time they met. She didn't mind a well-placed tattoo. In fact, she'd gotten a Celtic knot herself on St. Patrick's Day a few years back, just above the crack at the top of her buttocks. With Tyler, she'd planned marriage tattoos. Fortunately, they weren't getting those until the night before the wedding, so she didn't need to get that zeroed out now. But the whole-body tattoo approach she found distasteful. She looked on to the next guy, Antonio. A scrawny mutt of some sort. Probably Mexican, not sure what else. He looked rather gross with those broken teeth. Her eyes moved on to the smooth African-American guy, Max. One to watch, she knew. She'd seen him hit on one of the FARM women at the last meeting. She could read his kind like a book that told her to watch out. He was the type who could talk a woman into bed with his hands behind his back, and before you knew it, he'd be heading out to find a new lay. Then she smiled at the good white American, Charlie. "Let the good times roll," he'd told her the first time they met, and then winked, promising her America would be all good again soon. A fellow Steele supporter, for sure. She could enjoy this man, with his muscled arms and well-sculpted body.

She placed him on a motorcycle, on a hunting expedition, and in a bar, two-stepping her around the floor. A bad boy, but damn good. But as he sashayed to a chair, her eyes roved back to Welby to take a final look. Damned if he didn't just turn to look at her at the same time and give her a wink. She fumed.

Now the other FARM women started arriving. First the African princess, all petite and with perfect makeup, strutted in on high heels, with her jeans and glittery top. She pouted when she looked at the men in the front row. No doubt she'd gotten all gussied up to be eye candy for Max, but, with his face to the front, he didn't even notice.

Next to arrive, the Appalachian one, so hard and so young. Reagan knew she'd gotten hooked on drugs very early on down in Kentucky and kept getting her children taken away. She might match up with Antonio. They both need a new set of teeth, Reagan decided. She couldn't help it. You gotta have nice teeth to make it in this world. Behind her strolled that sweet young pale thing with the beautiful long brown hair and petite body. *She'd do okay*, Reagan thought. And, finally, in walked their newest recruit to replace Thomaseena who moved out a few weeks ago: Zorastria, a biracial mama that Reagan couldn't quite figure out. One moment, she seemed street, the next, high vocabulary rolled off her tongue like she belonged in a graduate school somewhere, defending a thesis. No, she just couldn't figure this woman out, but she also knew she felt disturbed when Welby'd given Zorastria entirely too much attention at the last gathering. Not jealous, just upset they broke the rules. She would never fall for a Black man herself and the Black women had told her she better not.

Reagan thought about their no dating rule. Why did their house manager keep scheduling these meetings with Sun Power House guys? First they created a virtual nunnery. Then they bring over the monks? For what? Guided temptation? Really. She wanted to tell them this would only lead to disaster. But, truth be told, she'd like a little disaster herself. She'd love to go on a spin with Charlie. But then she stole a look at Welby from behind, admiring the way his gluteus maximus filled up the chair. What was she thinking? No one would ever catch her hooking up with a Black man. No, never. She looked again, focusing on his broad shoulders. She closed her eyes and leaned back. Damn if his face didn't pop up right behind her shut lids, so she opened them up again.

Abigail started the meeting, but then the doorbell rang. Molly went to open it and, sure enough, if the new recruits didn't show up all of a sudden. "Welcome, come have a seat, ladies," she told them. "We'll do introductions later, right now Genealogy One-O-One is about to begin."

Reagan knew some new women were coming in, because four women were finishing their year at the house and moving on, but she didn't know it would be so soon. They looked quite scruffy. No proper female friends for her in that bunch.

Abigail started again. She explained that Molly had written a grant to help them explore their DNA. "Roots can ground you," she said. "Think about a tree. There's so much you can't see. A tree sends its roots deep down into the soil and gathers water and nutrients to keep it alive. Did you know trees often have as much below the surface as above the ground?" She showed a picture of a tree and its roots.

Reagan thought she could paint that.

Abigail continued. "And, you know, each of you have a family tree. Perhaps you have no idea of the people who came before you, but researching your roots can help you get a sense of your people and their history, and a stronger sense of your own self."

Molly got to her feet. "For African-Americans, a lot of us don't know a big part of our history. We were brought here on slave boats, and knowing the past is hard. We were sold like chattel, and our families were broken apart on the auction block. But, with DNA testing and genealogical sleuthing, we can learn a lot. Have you watched Henry Louis Gates?"

Reagan raised her hand. "Finding Your Roots?" she asked. "Yes, I watched that. They find out all about the families and also the DNA."

"Right," Molly said.

Then Abigail said, "We have two speakers tonight from our local historical society. First, Mrs. Dellapina will tell you about the resources they have in our local archives. Then, Mr. Thomas will discuss DNA testing and what you can learn from the DNA. Afterwards, we'll collect your saliva and send your specimens away so you can learn about your own roots."

Now Reagan smiled. For her sixteenth birthday, her mother had wrapped papers showing her how she could become a card-carrying member of the Daughters of the American Revolution and the Children of the Mayflower. Reagan loved her pedigree. Now she would also see her pure DNA. She perked up. When the time came to spit into the tube for the DNA, she filled it up in record time. Finally, something to look forward to in this stupid program. She could hardly wait.

When all the DNA was gathered, they ushered the women out first, leaving the men sitting up front. Reagan didn't like their crowd control technique. She wanted to talk to Charlie. Tiffany had warned they'd be limiting male-female contact between the houses. Looked like they'd begun. *Damn*, she thought.

Getting Down to Business - Welby

Welby pulled out some jeans and a T-shirt from his dresser, trying to manufacture energy to face another day. Since he'd moved here, he felt cut off, isolated, lonely. He'd never lived up North before, but being all alone, that was nothing new. Not much different here than the slammer. For the five years he'd spent cooped up in that God-forsaken place, he dreamed about freedom. Yes, dreamed about good southern fried chicken, grits, and shoofly pie, sultry summer nights with a beer and a lady, and some smooth jazz blending into the air.

Instead, he wound up in a virtual monastery called Sun Power. No alcohol, no drugs, no ladies, just those FARM women, but they were enough to keep the tension alive in his groin. He tried to block them out now.

Last night, he'd spit into a bottle for those crazy women. He hadn't wanted to do it. What right did they have to take his DNA? What about the privacy law? He now knew that police officer had no right to search his car, either. What was it with these white people?

But then Grand MaMa interrupted his thoughts. "Now, Welby. You stop that kind of stinking thinking right now. You got strong roots. Didn't you hear that Black sistah last night? You got an opportunity here to discover your real stuff. You got strong genes. Look at those ancestors of yours. They built a lot of wealth for the white man, and don't you forget it."

Welby shook his head. Maybe he needed a shrink. Grand MaMa, really? She needed to quit haunting him and let him get on with his life.

The voice came back. "No, sir. I'm not going anywhere, Marcus Welby Jones. You gonna be a great man. I intend to keep tellin' it and hauntin' ya until ya be believin' it, too."

Welby could actually see the old woman sitting in the corner chair talking at him and then she winked. He ran out of the room. He did not do ghosts. And he was not about to go from prison to the psych ward. "Not on your life," he muttered under his breath. "Leave me alone."

But as he scooted downstairs, damned if she didn't yell, "Marcus Welby Jones, I'm goin' turn you over my knee if you don't start respectin' your elders. Now you listen to me, boy."

Marcus ran pell-mell into the wall at the bottom of the steps. He rubbed his forehead where it smarted while walking on toward the kitchen. He kept shaking his head.

Max started laughing at him. "You okay, man? You look like you seen a ghost."

No way Marcus wanted anyone thinking his marbles were rolling out. "No, man. Just shakin' the sleep out o' my eyes. What they got for us today?"

"Career counselor, aptitude testing, laying out our options," Max said. "What you wanta do with your life, Welby? I bet you want to be a doctor, huh?"

"Right, bro," Welby responded. "Marcus Welby comin' to rescue you." He grabbed Max by the arm. "My mother's dream, not mine. She some kind of crazy, you know?"

"Not a bad plan, really," Max replied. "You could do worse."

"Right. Who be wantin' an ex-con for their doc?" Welby asked. "Let's keep it real, Max. You know how many dark-skinned, American-born doctors we got in the USA?"

"Sounds like you've given this some thought then?"

Welby laughed. "Back in the day, yeah, man. Who don't dream when you's a chile, surrounded by all those big mamas tellin' ya you can do anything? Right. Be all that, boy. But then reality hits between the eyes with a two-by-four. You know what I'm talkin' about."

"Hey, man, I know we got it going uphill, always. Ain't easy for a Black man, but what do you want? You just got a second chance."

Welby shook his head, poured himself a bowl of Lucky Charms, and added some milk. Not much luck in his life so far, but he wouldn't mind reversing that trend. "I forgot how to dream," he said. "Maybe I never knew how."

***

Later on, when the career counselor asked them to come up with a new dream for their life, Welby sneered. His cynicism ran deep, and he knew it. The American Dream in this country sailed high for white people born with a silver spoon. The people he knew? Spent their lives sucking on plastic. He wasn't about to run circles around them anymore, trying.

But the next day, the man returned with the aptitude results. Welby managed to get a little surprised, almost excited. There in black and white, the paper told him he had the aptitude to become a plumber, an electrician, or a physician. He thought it must be a mistake. Back up in his room, he kept reading it over. And then, damn if his grandmother didn't come back.

"Mmm, mmm, mmm. Marcus Welby Jones. Now, you goin' make somethin' out of yourself or not? God gave you the brains to do somethin' big and you know it. Now get down on your knees and give God thanks and apologize for squanderin' all that good you got goin' on."

Welby tried to shake it all off. He refused to go crazy. He went back out, but she just kept right on, while he hurried downstairs, trying to put some distance between them.

"Now, boy, you listen to me," she yelled down the stairs.

No way in hell was he talking with a dead lady. "No, ma'am," he muttered. *Oh, my God, I'm talking with her already*, he thought as he hurried to the basement workout room. Nothing that an hour of weight-lifting couldn't solve. He'd sweat her voice right out of his brain.

But later on, an electrician arrived to start training them on solar panel installation. He talked about his trade, asking if anyone wanted to be an apprentice. Welby raised his hand, surprising himself. And much later, Grand MaMa came back right after Welby got comfortable in bed. "I'm real proud of you, son," she said from her chair in the corner. "Now, you get yourself a good night of sleep so you can hunker down and start learnin' that electrician job."

He did a doubletake and the chair was empty. If she wanted to haunt him, he guessed he'd have to grin and bear it. But perhaps she could tell him a thing or two about his family tree. Next time she appeared, he intended to ask. For now, he rolled over, closed his eyes, and went to sleep.

CHAPTER FIVE
YOUR ROOTS ARE SHOWING - SUMMER

Hot Fun in the Summertime - June with Reagan

As summer descended on River City, the FARM house became a beehive of activity. The second summer proved a success. The fields' bounty not only kept the refrigerators full, but also created an impressive vegetable stand at the Saturday morning farmers market in town. Reagan enjoyed getting out to sell their harvest and flirt with the locals. A steady stream of customers kept them smiling and chatting. They did enough complaining and grunting working in the fields during the week, but they were proud of their produce at the market. Reagan even started selling her paintings on the side, developing a reputation among the town folk.

The last Saturday in June, they packed up their lettuce, spinach, tomatoes, and cucumbers early. Reagan threw in a few of her recent miniature paintings before they left for town. She tried to pull the group together, now that she was the "old" one. With the first residents now graduated out of the FARM house, she kept trying to adjust to the new gang. She identified the most with Marcia Treehouse, the motorcycle mama who had an Ace Steele tattoo across her thigh. They laughed into the night about the election and cheered on the new president as he started bringing change in DC.

Then there was Nikki Bond, the white singer in a backup band, who had purple hair with yellow roots. She liked the pain killers, like Reagan, but beyond that, their paths parted. Nikki dropped out of high school to hit the road with a band. Now Reagan thought she looked like thirty going on fifty. Washed out.

They'd gotten a voodoo mama, Artemis Goodson, as well. Blacker than night, this jive-talking drug queen and proud prostitute was a sight to behold. She jolted Reagan out of her comfort zone.

Then came light brown Zorastria, still an enigma to Reagan. What a name. Was she an astrologer or something?

Reagan could write a damn good book about her year at the FARM. But for now, she concentrated on the country road and the morning ahead.

When they arrived at the farmers market, Reagan supervised the set up. She put Marcia and Artemis in charge of bringing the stuff out of the van. She helped Tiffany with the table, and then put Nikki and Zorastria in charge of setting out the produce. Zorastria seemed to have an artistic streak, laying out the food in an attractive way. Reagan looked across the road to the Sun Power men setting up their booth. She spotted Charlie, looking good, filling out that muscle shirt. The guys were laughing and seemed to be having a good time. She tried to avoid catching Welby's eye and to ignore how easy he continued to be on her eyes.

George Mabra called, "Hey, Reagan, I need your help."

"What can I do for you, sir?" Reagan asked, working to make a good impression.

"Well, we're kicking off our advertising booth for our solar business. We hope to persuade the townies to convert their houses to run on energy from the sun. See our displays from Sun Power Industries and pictures of projects we completed after the tornado last summer? I've been training our guys to promote the values of converting to solar and closing the deal. Molly thought you and the other ladies could be their first customers. How about you come over two at a time?" he asked. "Having activity at our booth might attract others."

Tiffany responded, "Yes, George, I'll send them over, one or two at a time." She signaled to Reagan. "Why don't you and Zorastria go first?"

Zorastria perked up at the mention of her name and led Reagan across road to the Sun Power booth. Reagan glanced around at the variety of vendors. The aroma of coffee filled the air at the Fair Trade stall. She read a colorful sign announcing Plants for Sale at a booth filled with green growing things. At another, bushels of fruit lined the ground. When they walked up to the guys' table, she heard George tell Welby to take the lead

"Good morning, ladies," Welby started. He flashed a smile and gestured toward their display. "We've got a deal for you. It's time to go solar. Convert your house to solar, get a tax credit to cover your costs, and then receive income by selling the extra. Can we sign you up?"

"Yes, sir," Zorastria said, reaching out to shake hands with Welby. Welby grabbed her hand. They shook and didn't let go, while Welby looked into her big black eyes.

George broke them up with a laugh. "Okay, you can break the handshake now. Good job, Welby. Not bad at all," he said. "You sealed the deal."

Not wanting to be left out, Reagan asked, "Are you all really trained for this? I thought you just got out of prison." She knew she sounded a little snobby, but she had the pedigree.

Welby flashed a smile again. "Actually, a solar electrician supervises our projects, but I'm takin' some online classes and gettin' fixed to be his apprentice. Been shadowin' him once a week. My brain ain't fried after all. Seems to be soakin' up the solar solutions quite well." He gave Zorastria a look-over and she spread her lips into a pearly wide smile back.

She whispered to Welby. "Meet me over at the porta-potties in ten?" She glanced nervously at George, who was otherwise occupied, so she added, "Quiet, Sugar."

Reagan rolled her eyes at Zorastria and bantered back to Welby. "I feel uncomfortable having men just out of prison coming into my house. How can I trust your kind?"

Welby didn't skip a beat. "Yes, ma'am, I can see that you might have reservations, but we are bonded and on the straight and narrow now. We're going to church every Sunday and AA five times a week. You gotta give us a chance. We won't disappoint."

Reagan laughed. "You almost got me believing you there, Welby."

"What's not to believe about me, honey?" Welby asked. "George prepped us for people like you." He gave her a hard look. "What are you ladies up to over at the FARM these days?"

Zorastria replied, "Just getting dirty, pulling weeds, picking produce, but it's not all bad."

"What 'bout you, Reagan? Are you learnin' a trade over there?" Welby asked.

"I'm already a nurse, Welby. I don't need a trade." She hoped that put him in his place. For emphasis, she stuck up her nose, but that just seemed to egg him on.

"Oh, baby, I'll call you for some nursing next time I got a sore back. Oh, yeah."

When his eyes met hers, an electric current pulsed through her entire body. She turned her head, telling Zorastria, "We better go back now. The market's filling up." Then she abruptly walked away, but not before Welby got in the last word.

"I'll be waitin'," he said, drawing out his words like thick molasses oozing out into the morning. Reagan wasn't sure if he intended that for Zorastria or her. She was not about to let any Black man find a way into her heart. Her daddy would disown her. She knew better. He might forgive her drug problem; he struggled with alcohol himself. But if she tried to bring home a Black man? That would never fly. Let alone what Daddy thought, she kept her distance from Black people. Weren't they always causing problems, playing the race card when they failed in school or got involved in crime and drugs? Why didn't they concentrate on doing the right thing, studying, and earning a decent living? And then here's Welby, a downright criminal. No way she wanted to get involved with a no-good Black man with an attitude.

Reagan returned to her station and concentrated on selling produce. Her miniature paintings went quickly, as did their organic greens. After a little bit, Zorastria asked to go to the porta-potties. Reagan's eyes wandered over to check on Welby, but he never left his post. Perhaps he really didn't have time to slip away. Their booth swarmed with people all morning. Reagan felt just a little bit glad he never made it over to the porta-potties.

Soon they were packing up to go home. George sent Welby and Max over to fill up a box of leftovers for Sun Power House. Welby kept making eyes at her and asked, "When can I come over for my massage, Nurse Reagan?"

Reagan watched Zorastria flinch. Tiffany frowned. Reagan just laughed. "I don't have my nursing license right now, so I can't practice. Sorry, Welby."

"That's okay, I'll be waitin'," he said again and then heaved a full box of produce up onto his shoulder. "Thanks for helping us out, ladies. We'll be mighty busy with all the deals we closed this mornin'. Got about ten contracts and ten more estimates to make."

"Way to go, men. You some kind of sales people," Zorastria flattered them, batted her mascara-heavy eyelids at them, and then sealed it off with a pearly grin.

Max and Welby smiled back. As they went toward their truck, Welby walked slowly, deliberately, strutting with pride. Yes, he knew how to stir up a woman, but not her. Instead, she told Zorastria, "That bad boy is all yours. You go for it, girl."

Tiffany frowned. "Nobody's dating around here, Reagan. Stop that talk."

Reagan responded, "Lighten up. Where's your sense of humor, Tiffany?" She climbed into the van without waiting for a reply. What a trip, these rules, this place.

The MAMs, the FARM, and the Sun, Exploring Roots - July'

In July, The MAMs scheduled a barbeque to release DNA results and announce travel plans. Abigail orchestrated the event. She asked the FARM women to cook the meal and they laid out an impressive spread, with juicy burgers, homemade fries, and homegrown corn on the cob, served up with their own organic tomatoes, lettuce, and onions. The Sun Power men topped it off with mouthwatering blueberry and strawberry pies, ice cream, and whipped cream.

"De-lic-ious," Jane yelled. "Maybe we should open a restaurant. Who grilled these burgers?"

Zorastria smiled proudly. "That would be me." She placed a hand on her hip, shooting a smile at Welby."Nothing like a good burger on a warm summer day. My daddy taught me well."

"And who did these pies?" Jane asked, smacking her lips.

Max raised his hand. "I supervised the blueberry ones, like my mama used to make."

"Thank her for me, Max. And the strawberry?" Jane asked

Welby walked over to Jane and placed his hand on her shoulder. "My Grand MaMa baked the best pies in North Carolina. Sold most of them on a stand by her house. People came from miles around. She passed on the family secrets to me. Nobody beats her pies."

Abigail noticed Reagan's eyes get real big and Welby give her a wink. What kind of sparks were these co-ed events creating? How could they keep that from turning into fire? As they launched their plans, she hoped it wouldn't blow up in their faces. Maybe they should have stuck with a focus on the businesses and recovery. She worried if they might be making a mistake with the Roots Project. Would the information really be all that helpful or important to these re-entry people while rebuilding their lives? She certainly hoped so. She made a mental note to talk about co-ed issues at the next board meeting.

"Okay, folks," she told them, "time to take this party inside for the big reveal. Come find out what's in your DNA."

The women started clearing off the tables. Then the men helped, carrying the leftovers inside, while the setting sun cast an orange glow over the backyard. Abigail felt goose bumps as she watched them work together. She was proud of the FARM women and Sun Power men. She was proud of the MAMs as well, for launching these projects in the first place. As the light slipped down into the western sky, she felt a new day preparing to rise among them.

Once inside, she fired up her laptop, projecting a map of the world on the screen. "Now, before you open your envelopes, I want to show you an example of what to expect. These are my results," she said. "See the colors of countries where my ancestors originated? Down here, they show percentages. See how Ireland is colored? I always knew that. And I suspected German. Sure enough. See the western European?" She pointed to the top of the map. "Up here, they colored in Scandinavia, maybe my Mennonite roots. But here's a surprise, for me: the Mediterranean at twenty percent."

Abigail followed with Molly's and Priscilla's maps. "Molly never knew she had Irish DNA. And Priscilla didn't know about her West African heritage. So many discoveries," Abigail said.

Reagan raised her hand. "My roots go back to the American Revolution and the Mayflower. I've got papers. My ancestors helped found this country." She turned her nose up.

Abigail searched for something positive to say. "Well, quite the pedigree then. Did your mother join Daughters of the American Revolution and Children of the Mayflower?"

"Yes, she did, and I can, too," Reagan said.

"Good for you," Abigail said. "That might show up in your DNA, then. Sallie, would you pass out their results? Drumroll, please. Are you ready for this?"

Welby started banging on the table while Sallie distributed the envelopes. Abigail laughed. "Thanks, Welby, for the drumroll. And now for an exciting announcement. We've received a grant to take you to explore your ancestry. If you have roots from Ireland or West Africa, you may be in luck. These are like lottery results. Some of you will win a prize: a trip to Ireland, the Sea Islands, or West Africa. You may open your envelopes now."

The tearing of paper ensued. Soon they were calling out the names of their countries of origin. Abigail cut them off. "Raise your hand if you have West African DNA," she instructed.

Hands fluttered up. She looked around. She'd been expecting hands from Max, Welby, Zorastria, and Artemis, but Antonio and Reagan raised their hands also.

"This can't be right," Reagan said. "I'm not Black."

"Oh, yeah. Honey, you got some black blood goin' on," Welby shouted out. "Black like me." He poked Max, who was sitting next to him, and laughed.

"Welcome to our world, sistah," Zorastria said.

"Yeah, we'll take you in," Artemis said. "We ain't stuck up. We take whoever."

Priscilla turned to Reagan. "Me, too, dear. We don't look like it, but we've got African blood. Hard to believe. My results say I'm three percent. What about you?"

"This is a mistake," Reagan said. "Ten percent? This is wrong. Could I be retested?"

"Hmm," Abigail said. "We'll have to think about that. How many have Irish roots?" Marcia, Nikki, Reagan, Antonio, and Charlie's hands shot up. More slowly, Welby raised his hand.

"You're not Irish," Reagan blurted at Welby.

"Come look, Reagan," Welby replied. "We're cousins. Ooh, baby, come on over here."

"How can he be Irish?" Reagan asked.

Molly answered. "Our people did a lot of mixing, Reagan, mostly without consent. Think about it. Three hundred and fifty years of slavery in this country. Those slaves belonged to white plantation owners. If the white boss wanted a Black woman, he took her. I've got Irish DNA, too, Reagan. And that white DNA is no better than Black. We're more alike than you ever knew."

"Are you telling me I won the jackpot? A trip to Ireland, the Sea Islands and West Africa?" Welby said. "Is this my lucky day?"

Abigail replied, "Maybe, Welby. More on that later."

Welby looked at Reagan. "Woohee! Cross your fingers for a free honeymoon, baby."

Abigail noticed Reagan's temper flaring; it was evident in her eyes. She watched Reagan clam up, reading through her results, turning the pages back and forth.

Meanwhile, Abigail asked for others to share their results. By the end of the evening, they knew more about their origins. Quite a few were surprised. Abigail thought the event was a success as she watched them looking at the map of the world with new eyes, and told them so.

"Next time, we'll start working on our family trees," she said. "We'll have a lottery for Ireland, our first trip in October. We'll be drawing from Charlie, JT, and Welby from Sun Power House and from Reagan, Nikki, and Marcia.

For the Sea Islands in February, since it's in the States, we can take more of you. We'll be taking Antonio, Max, and Welby from the SUN, and Reagan, Artemis, and Zorastria from the FARM.

West Africa will be decided later. You'll be packing your bags soon. Get ready for an adventure with the MAMs. I promise a good time for all." Abigail signed off for the evening, smiling as they went their separate ways.

Reagan Considering Her Origins

Reagan hurried upstairs with her DNA results. They made absolutely no sense at all. She wanted to call her mom and scream. She wanted to poke a finger at her dad. What business did he have being in the KKK? Was that ten percent from her dad or from her mom? Did they know? She wanted to call up Henry Louis Gates and volunteer for the show. That would make her father madder than a bull in a hornet's nest. She laughed.

She'd thought she had things all figured out. Her parents taught her she was better than those poor, good for nothing Blacks. Oh, some were okay and would try to get ahead. Some even graduated from college, but the rest? Lazy fools who deserved to be locked up and put away. Black Lives Matter? Not if they shoot up policemen and break law and order. She agreed with Ace Steele. Put them in jail if they can't behave.

But then she thought about the Black women in the house. She knew one of the earlier women grew up getting abused, but once she got a second chance at the FARM, she created a small business. And another one was a straight A student, headed for law school once she finished college, now that she was back on track. Reagan mulled over the conversation she'd had with Zorastria the night before. Zorastria told her that her mama was smarter than a whip, but they wouldn't let her go to college, and she ended up wearing herself out working in a factory and dying at fifty-two. She remembered Artemis crying her eyes out at the AA meeting the night before when she talked about how her daddy killed himself when she was eight because a white man said he stole something and fired him, and he just couldn't figure out how to take care of his family without a job. And then Welby's smile popped into her mind and she felt her body getting warm. She remembered those smooth sounds emanating from his saxophone.

When life confused her, she liked to escape into her fiddling. Too late at night for that, so she settled for number two, her art. She got out her pencils and paints and set up a canvas. She wanted to paint herself. But what would she look like now? She didn't know.

She picked up a pencil and started sketching. The paper came alive as she outlined her head. First, she imagined her face, with some shadows she'd never noticed before. She would include those dark places, she decided. Ignoring the clock, she began to fill in the lines.

A Hot Night of Jazz with Welby – August

By the time August rolled around, Welby felt grounded in this new place. He enjoyed studying at night and following the electrician around once a week. He absorbed his new trade quickly, although becoming a bona fide electrician would take a while. Now the others looked to him for direction when they installed new solar panels.

Away from the temptations of friends and partying every night, and with the help of the NA and AA groups, he seemed to be turning over a new leaf. The Sun Power House thrived as well. Between the farmers market sales booth and the word-of-mouth reputation, their solar business gathered speed through the summer. Due to required church attendance, Welby felt that good ole Spirit seeping into his heart. Once again, he found himself singing and clapping, like the rest of them at the church on Sundays with the Mabras in town. He didn't tell Aunt Rosie, but he even went up for an altar call last week. He felt as good as new, just like when he first answered the Lord's call in his church back home. Slowly, he began to hope again.

Not to say his old anger didn't boil up from time to time. Watching the news scared him real good. Ace Steele and the rest of the millionaires running the country now? Already, they set about to abolish the EPA. Steele chose a racist attorney general and a white supremacist for his right-hand man.

Now they were deregulating the financial institutions. And he knew from experience that all that law and order jive talk was just their political code for putting more Black men in jail. He felt powerless over the changes coming under the guise of taking America back again. *How stupid do they think we are?* Dumb enough to elect Steele, he guessed.

Dwelling on politics didn't help his new life, so he tried to put it out of his mind. Here, surrounded by people trying to encourage him to make it in this world, he wanted to focus on the positives and turn off all that negative thinking.

Tonight, they were invited to the FARM house for an evening of fun. He grabbed his saxophone and started down the stairs. When the ghost of Grand MaMa called after him, "You go, boy!" he laughed and called back over his shoulder, "Yes, ma'am." And then, on second thought, he turned back up the stairs with a question. "Grand MaMa," he asked into the air, "do we got Irish ancestors? They say I got that goin' on in my DNA. You know 'bout that?"

"Oh, baby, you never heard that from me, but since you done went and asked, story goes my great-grandmother be workin' in the master's house and he took liberties with her, if you know what I mean. He was an Irishman, I'm told. You don't see that much in most of us, but they say my grandmother came out all white and didn't turn dark 'til she put on some months. And that's where you got that red hair, too. Yes, it's true, Welby."

Did she really just say that or was he making it up? He shrugged. Blood don't lie. So he guessed maybe he was an Irishman after all.

Welby enjoyed playing his sax with the Mabra Music Men. They practiced every Sunday now. Today, they'd strut their stuff for the FARM house celebration. The women who'd graduated from the program were coming back for a barbeque and square dance and hoedown, a regular hootenanny. He knew a lot of townies would be coming out to wish the women well.

When they arrived at the farm, he eyed a full spread of an outdoor party, just waiting for the guests. The FARM women were putting on the finishing touches. He focused on Reagan, who was carrying out a platter of condiments. Sure did like the way her hips swayed from side to side, and he copped a look at her backside as she leaned over to put that tray on the table. Mm, mm, mm. He smacked his lips. He imagined putting his hands on her and then imagined her bending over just a little further. She turned around real quick, shooting him a reprimanding glance. Shouting out "back off" without sayin' a word. No doubt she got some good African blood in her. She bristled up real good, like the Black mamas he knew and loved all his life. Maybe they had a future after all. He winked at her, which made her even more mad. He laughed out loud and went over to join the boys in the band. Nothing he liked better than a challenging woman. Three trips from now, he'd have her in the bag—and hopefully in his bed. Just dreaming about it would give him something to keep him going on these lonely nights.

The music carried him into another realm. He pierced the silence of the night with soulful melodies from his horn. Together, they created a mood of celebration. Passing the leads around, they poured out their hearts into familiar tunes. Louis Armstrong, Kenny G, even a John Legend thrown in here and there. When Leo and George started singing "Glory" from that movie about Selma, they did Common and John Legend real proud. The applause got louder and louder with each number. And he enjoyed the reality of this integrated environment. He spotted some of his new friends from the Black church he attended with the Mabras, but just as many white all around, all applauding really hard. Never saw this intermingling where he came from.

From time to time, he searched out Reagan. She worked the crowd like a politician, offering handshakes and smiles as she made her rounds. She displayed some of her artwork to honor the graduating women. He watched her explaining the pictures. The only time she didn't smile was when he caught her eye. Then she'd close her mouth, make a face, and turn away, giving him yet another view of her beautiful behind, almost causing him a situation.

Hootenanny with Reagan – August

When the time came for the hoedown, Reagan joined in to help ready the FARM for celebration. After a long summer, she looked forward to this breather, a time to welcome back the summer FARM graduates. Four of the women who'd been in the house when she arrived had all moved on. Two settled into an apartment in town and still joined in once a week on their meetings. One moved back home and planned to start college in the fall. The other one reconciled with her husband. Reagan had heard that once he started going to AA and NA groups, he quit abusing her, and she'd felt safe enough to move home and take care of her three children. Reagan burned some midnight oil, making paintings to celebrate each of them and their new lives.

Zorastria helped her carry the paintings out under the tent, placing them on easels for display near the head table. For one of the graduates, she'd drawn a full-length portrait of the woman in all her glory, looking over her salon. Images of Black hands massaging, fixing hair, and painting toenails and fingernails surrounded the portrait, fading into white space. For the Mexican lady, she painted a scene her serving food to her children and husband. She dubbed it "La Mesa de Madre Maria," and even wrote the words in on the edge of the wood on the table, hoping perhaps the woman would choose that name for the restaurant she planned to open and manage soon. For the Kentucky lady, she showed her walking out of the hills into the dawn, with a river scene in the foreground. Reagan wanted to demonstrate that she came from Appalachia into River City, rising like the sun into a new day. And finally, she created a likeness of the African princess, with a stack of books in her arm, walking onto the college campus, headed toward a professional life, now with heels and a suit, with her family looking on with happy faces. Reagan felt proud of her pictures, but even more proud of the transformations they represented. She began to appreciate the place called FARM and hoped she could find new life here as well.

She noticed the band setting up in the corner of the tent, but tried to avoid that area, however much Welby seemed determined to draw her over, with both his gaze and his physique. The smooth jazz sounds emanating filled the summer air, helping create a magical mood to the late afternoon. She might suggest that her daddy hire them for some of his political events.

When the people started to come, Reagan forgot all about Welby. Well, almost. Except for when he caught her eye every single time she turned around. She tried to ignore him. She focused on working the crowd. Her daddy'd taught her well. She wanted to help the FARM. She knew their financial supporters were there. She walked around, greeting and massaging egos and thanking people for coming. She bragged on the graduates as she showed off her artwork, easily working in talk of the life-changing experiences that happened on the FARM. She pointed at her art subjects as she explained, "This lady went from turning tricks for her john to opening a business with another graduate. This mother overcame her drug addiction, her husband quit drinking, and now they're both working together to open a restaurant soon. This graduate took a job in town, hoping to get her children back. And this one will be attending college in the fall."

She smiled and told the truth, and that brought smiles to the faces of the supporters. She only hoped the new women—herself included—would fare as well.

When they began to take their seats for the dinner, she turned around and saw her daddy at the reception table, talking with Jane. Her face turned red. She hadn't expected him to be coming, but couldn't forget her manners. "Daddy" she yelled as she hurried to his side. "Good to see you."

He reached out and enfolded her in a big bear hug, whispering, "My baby girl."

She took a moment to compose herself against the anger that coursed through her. How could they invite him without even telling her? Over the years, though, she'd learned to put on a good face, so she tucked her anger away. Still, the FARM should know better.

Was that a tear in her daddy's eye? Impossible. She showed him to a seat, sat next to him, and asked, "What are you doing here? Who invited you?" She checked herself, and added, "I'm glad you came." Inside, she felt disappointment. She really didn't want him back in her life so quickly.

"Oh, your leaders invited me. A fundraiser, you know. They're not stupid," he said.

Reagan shuddered but didn't want him to see how she really felt. She didn't skip a beat. "Okay, yes. I'm sure they can use your money, a lot of it." She laughed and then turned serious. "So how are you, Daddy?"

"Missing you, baby girl. Your mother and I miss you very much, but we're glad you got some help. She wanted to come tonight, but she's been under the weather. She sends her love and told me to bring you back. Are you ready to come home now?"

Reagan looked at her father and blinked. She'd expected his forgiveness, but not so soon. She realized he didn't have a clue about recovery and the work she must do.

"Not yet, Daddy," she replied. "I am healing. And they take real good care of me."

"If the tabloids get wind of this, they'll have a field day. I think you should come home *now*," he said.

"I'm just not ready," she said. When she'd come here, all she wanted was to go back home. And the only thing standing in her way had been her father. But now that he'd given her what she wanted—like he had all her life—she discovered she wanted to stay. She had no idea how she could explain that to him when she couldn't even explain it to herself. She glanced around the room, wondering what the others might think of her visitor. Her eyes stopped on Welby. Darn if he wasn't giving her a look, raising his eyebrow in unspoken question. She turned back to her dad and took another bite.

Her dad changed the subject. "So what do you think of our new president, Ace Steele?" he asked. "Finally got our man in the White House. Ain't he something?"

"Yes, Daddy. He's awesome," Reagan replied. "Clearing the way for our businesses to move into the twenty-first century. I watch the news and smile. He does it all for you, right? We got a new Supreme Court justice. President Steele is protecting unborn babies, rebuilding our military to keep us safe, and making America work again for the people. Yes, a good time for our country, for sure."

Jane and Priscilla walked over to their table. "Pleased to meet you, Mr. Brown," Jane said, extending her hand. "We're so glad you wanted to come tonight to support the FARM. It means a lot to us and to Reagan that you're here."

Inside, Reagan felt her anger building again. How could Jane possibly know how she felt? And why were they using her family to get more money for this place? Shouldn't they be respecting her privacy? Her dad took it all in stride, carrying on like the good politician he was.

"So glad you invited me," he replied. "And glad to support this place. My wife and I do appreciate you helping our Reagan here. Means a lot to both of us."

Reagan grimaced, trying to hold her emotions inside. She looked around the room and felt embarrassed. She didn't think any other parents had shown up.

When Jane and Priscilla left, up came Charlie and Welby. "Who's this, Reagan?" Charlie asked.

"My father, Mr. Brown," Reagan responded. "Daddy, meet Charlie and Welby."

Her father extended his hand to Charlie first, but she noticed him frowning at the tattoos on Charlie's arm and he broke the contact quickly, and then gave Welby a perfunctory shake. Reagan could tell he didn't really want to meet her new friends, but, always the gentleman politician, he kept it cordial. "Pleased to meet you, Charlie, Welby." He gave them each a nod.

"A nice daughter you have, sir," Charlie said.

"Easy on the eyes," Welby contributed.

Reagan grimaced, wondering what would come next. But her father laughed and said, "That she is. I'm so proud of my baby. I came to take her home."

Someone called Charlie and Welby away, but before he left, Welby turned to her, cupped his hand around her ear and whispered,

"Reagan? No. Don't go, baby. Don't go."

Reagan glanced nervously at her father. Had he heard that? She frowned at Welby, but he was already walking away. Reagan's anger threatened to erupt, but she held her tongue. Her father ignored the look on her face and said, "What are you thinking, associating with this riff-raff? I can get your nursing license back, you know. I talked to a friend. Your mother and I want you home. Tyler will come around. Come on, let's get you out of here."

Reagan didn't want to leave. Maybe the other FARM women weren't her best friends yet, but they were growing on her. She remained seated and told him, "No, Daddy. I'm not ready. I need to get better. I'm sorry. Tell Mommy I just can't leave now."

Her father stomped out, not even saying good-bye. Reagan felt the tears coming. She jumped up, ran into the house and up to her room, slamming the door. She threw herself on the bed, letting the tears flow, feeling her anger at the FARM board, and also at her father. Why was he so mad that she chose to stay? Why did she choose not to leave with him? And then there was Welby. She let it all out, sobbing into pillow.

***

Half an hour later, someone knocked on her door. "Reagan, are you okay?"

"Yeah, I'm okay." Reagan recognized Tiffany's voice. Opening the door, she confronted the other woman, asking, "Why did you invite my father? You should have consulted me. Just to get money? Really?"

Tiffany hesitated. "He called last week to ask how he could help. I referred him to Jane, the board president. She invited him." Tiffany looked regretful. "I'm sorry. I didn't know about it. You're right. We shouldn't have done that. We should have asked you first."

Reagan frowned. "You can't treat people that way. You should *not* invite family members without asking your residents. You have no idea what might be going on. Not a good idea." She looked down. "He tried to talk me into coming home. Is that what you want?"

"No. You know we don't want you to leave. And you're still here."

"Yeah, I need all of you. I want to stay with the program. He didn't like it," Reagan told her. "My dad's into politics big time. He's afraid the tabloids will find out where I am and have a field day. I know it's the egg on his face he's most concerned about."

Tiffany gave Reagan a hug. "I'm glad you stood up to him, and I'm glad you're still here."

"Did he actually give any money?"

Tiffany nodded. "Yes. Ten thousand dollars. Very generous."

"When did he do that? He stormed out without saying good-bye."

"Oh, he dropped that off at the reception table when he came in," Tiffany explained.

"Well, that's something then," Reagan said, drying her eyes.

"But are you okay? Do you still want to play for the hoedown?"

"Oh, my gosh, I forgot all about that," Reagan said. She looked in the mirror. "I'm a mess. Let me fix up my makeup and I'll be down as soon as I tune my violin."

"Good, I'll tell them you're on the way."

Five minutes later, Reagan ran down the steps. When she stepped into the barn, the place sizzled with energy. Some people were learning a new square dance. Her new friends were laughing. She wondered who'd gotten Welby for a partner. But, no, he stood with the band, a banjo in his hands. He gave her a big smile when he caught her looking. She walked up to him asked, "You play the saxophone *and* the banjo?"

"Ever since I was a little boy," he replied. "We've been passing a family banjo down for generations. Never quite sure if they lyin' to me or not, but they be sayin' it came all the way from Africa. Story goes they brought an African banjo player along on those slave ships to keep the spirits up of those sorry souls, even though they kept their bodies all tied down." He stopped talking and laughed. "My family likes to tell a good tale. But this banjo, George bought me secondhand. He told me to practice my strummin' so I don't forget." He played a few notes and winked. "I hear you win fiddling contests. Just aimin' to keep up with you, darlin'."

In one breath, slave ships, in the next, a compliment? Reagan frowned and looked away. She did not want to think about slave ships and that kidnapping and how they stacked human beings like animals. She knew the history, but never heard it first-hand. She'd never had to think about it while face-to-face with someone whose actual family history it was.

Welby's big eyes seemed to read her soul. "You okay?"

"That whole slave ships thing upsets me," she tried to explain.

"It's okay, baby. It's okay. That's water under the bridge. That was then. We're here now. Let's have some fun," Welby said. "We've been waiting for you."

The square dance caller stopped and signaled to the band leader. The other fiddler called, "Old Joe Clark," and played the first round. Reagan followed. The string bass and guitar players picked up. Welby strummed along. Reagan lost herself in the music, but every now and then, she caught Welby smiling at her. And every now and then, she smiled back. The music carried her into a place of deep joy. She watched Welby twang his strings, matching her bowing note for note. She fiddled away, absorbing the happiness now filling the night.

The pace picked up just a little with each dance. The people swung their partners and did allemande around the square. Her fiddle sizzled in the hot August night, tearing through the melodies she knew so well. With a smile on her lips, her heart danced. She realized that, more than anything, she felt happy to be playing with Welby.

Right before the last dance of the night, Abigail and Molly took over the microphone. Molly said, "As you know, we'll be heading to Ireland in October, and we have room for two women from the FARM and two men from Sun Power House to go along and explore their Irish roots. Drum roll, please," she motioned to her brother-in-law, Leo Mabra, on the drums.

Leo hammed it up while Abigail drew the first name out of the hat. "Welby!"

George punched Welby in the arm. "Way to go, bro. Looks like we'll be traveling together." Welby smiled.

Abigail drew another name. Leo started up the drums. "Reagan," she yelled.

Welby gave her a wink and whispered so quietly that Reagan was pretty sure only she could hear, "Oh, yeah, baby. Let's go to Ireland."

Abigail drew two more names and announced "Charlie and Nikki," as well.

Reagan watched Charlie's and Nikki's joy and felt her own deep inside.

The caller started to explain the final dance. George called, "Irish Washerwoman." She lifted her violin and started her bow dancing on the strings. Together, in perfect lockstep, she and Welby closed the night with the music of the Emerald Isle.

CHAPTER SIX
THE EMERALD ISLE - FALL

Exploring Irish Roots – Preparation with the MAMs, the FARM and the Sun - September

On a warm night in early September, Abigail hosted Irish Night at the FARM. She planned the night to focus on the Emerald Isle and consider the history, the lives of their ancestors, in order to set the stage for the upcoming trip. She invited everyone going on the trip, which included the MAMs, George and Tom, Welby and Charlie, and Reagan and Nikki.

They gathered on couches and chairs in the living room. Abigail waited for them to get comfortable, then asked, "What do you know about Ireland and the Irish?"

"Absolutely nothing," Welby blurted. "Well, wait, I know people get wasted on Saint Patrick's Day. I think this whole Irish thing is an excuse to drink."

"Absolutely," Nikki chimed in. "The Irish are all about partying."

"Let the good times roll," Charlie said and laughed. "That's what I say."

"But we're trying to stop drinking. So why would you take us there?" Nikki asked.

Abigail said, "There's more to Ireland than drinking. Granted, it's home to some famous breweries, Guinness and Harp. And some Irish people have a genetic predisposition to addiction. Some of you, probably. But that doesn't mean that all Irish are drunks, or that you can't rise above your genes. Indeed, you are all doing just that.

"Ireland is also a very spiritual place. When Saint Patrick came to Ireland, he brought Christianity to the Celts, who practiced an earth-centered religion. He built on that, so you'll find a nice earthy aspect to their faith. I really like that about Ireland."

"I like the music and the dancing," Reagan said. "I hope I get to play my fiddle in Ireland. Can I take it along?"

"Yes!" Abigail replied. "Did any of you see 'Riverdance?'"

Several hands went up. Reagan exclaimed, "Five times. Loved it."

"Irish dance and music certainly have a following these days," Abigail said. "Now, let's watch 'Travel, Ireland.'" As she turned out the lights, she said, "Think about what interests you."

Welby's Ruminations

As the room went dark, Welby considered his options. He sat a little behind and beside the chair where Reagan sat. He calculated the distance to be about five feet. Could he bridge the gap, inch his chair closer, quietly? It couldn't hurt to try.

An aerial view of the island of Ireland filled the screen. Waves all around. Could he finally learn to surf? Maybe not in October. Green, lots of green. Then the camera zoomed in on a festival, with loud music and dancing. Welby coughed and inched his chair toward Reagan.

What was it about her? Why was he so attracted to his opposite, a white woman? Never dated them and his aunt had told him, "Don't you go bringing any white stuff around here."

He knew Grand MaMa didn't feel that way. Maybe because she knew all along about their Irish roots? But why did she take that secret to the grave?

He knew most Black women didn't want their men going white. No, they wanted them for themselves. He smacked his lips. Those Black women, the cream of the crop, often with a mouth on them, knowin' how to keep a Black man in his place. No, sir, he mused, they weren't about to let the good Black men up and leave for the white ladies. But, since he wasn't a good Black man anymore, maybe they wouldn't care if he switched up? But why even think Reagan would ever want him? Maybe not, but he had a feeling she already was starting to look his way.

Watching a fiddler on the screen, he remembered how Reagan'd made her bow dance on the strings the other night. She'd fit right into this scene. Could Irish music be genetic, he wondered. Was that the origin of her talent? Of his?

The room filled with a loud honking sound. Now a tugboat guided a large cruise ship into the Dublin harbor. He took the noisy opportunity to slide his chair a little bit closer toward Reagan. Those boats came all the way across the ocean, but he just had a journey of a few feet to Reagan. A short distance in this room, but a huge divide, between his Black skin and her freckled pink, between his Southern experience and her Northern front, between his humble beginnings and her silver spoon. What was he thinking?

But he'd always liked a challenge and didn't mind that the conquest would take some time. He felt his patience, always with him. Growing up in the South, he'd learned to take it slow.

The voice on the documentary outlined the massive exodus during the potato famine. He thought of his ancestors, uprooted from their homes, sailing to America. His DNA results had created a whole new dialogue within. He'd always imagined that Atlantic passage tied to the bottom of a slave boat. Sometimes, he could feel it in his psyche. Somebody once told him that lodges in the body, passed from one generation to another. But here were his other ancestors starving, getting on a boat and setting off into the unknown. His stomach rumbled.

Images flashed of another harbor, New York. Another loud honk and he scooted his chair just a little further to the north. He laughed at himself quietly. He might arrive before the end of the show. Reagan turned her head at his noise, but then turned back to the screen.

They showed Ellis Island, people checking into a new country, and a map showing where the Irish settled, how they spread throughout the new country. He saw the green springing up in North Carolina. His ancestors? The slave owners? Reagan's people?

As the show switched to a scene of dancing in the streets, clapping filled the room as the dancers kicked high. Welby scooted over just a little bit more. Only eighteen inches separated him from the woman of his dreams. He stretched his long leg out sideways, looking for a reaction. She looked down at his leg, then up to his face. Was that a smile or a frown?

He slipped his foot out of his sandal and gently stroked the top of her ankle with his toes.

On the documentary, the music got louder and then a boat whistle sounded and there were people talking, walking off a boat. In the midst of all of that, Reagan reached over and swatted his calf firmly, the sound muffled and unheard with all the commotion on the screen.

Oh, baby, he thought. *Okay, if you want to be that way.* He took his foot back, slipping it into his sandal, just letting it rest and pretending he hadn't transcended the divide, as he leaned back and watched the show.

His people had come a long way, all the way across the Atlantic. The Irish and the Africans came together in America and now history was about to repeat itself. *Not yet, Reagan, but soon.* Sometime in that long, dark past, the Irish and the Africans mingled and got it on. He reckoned they would again.

Reagan Considering

Reagan was happy to learn a little more about Ireland. She remembered traveling there several times with her parents. Memories flashed before her: the crowded streets of Dublin, the picturesque seaside at Galway, Blarney Castle and shamrocks in the Druid's garden, monastic ruins, green grass, tombstones and steeples. She remembered Brigid's Well. She couldn't quite believe she would soon be going back—and with Welby. She still couldn't figure out what it was about him that called to her.

The screen filled with a hometown Irish celebration. Reagan focused on a fiddler, remembering playing with the Irish dance troupe back home. Then her thoughts traveled to the barn dance and Welby's large hands cradling his banjo. She remembered him strumming those country tunes, making the runs with her, and matching her bow steps until their music just seemed to fade into the night, together, strong, dynamic. At the time, Reagan had wanted to cry out, but, instead, she let her joy ease out of her soul onto her fiddle strings. She looked at Welby and back at Ireland. *Tell me he's not part of my DNA. Please, God?*

She distracted herself by thinking about what she wanted to see in Ireland. St. Brigid's Well ... other wells, holy places, going back to earlier times. Jesus offered living water, met the woman at the well. She thought back. She'd visited the Catholic Student Center with her friend while in college. She wondered how women decided to become a nun. She'd like to meet an Irish nun. She wanted to visit an Irish church, not just the ruin of a monastery this time. Where had that come from, she wondered. She couldn't remember the last time she'd gone to church, but now, something was drawing her back.

A boat honked. She looked at New York harbor. Damned if Welby didn't just scoot his chair over toward her. She glanced at him, then back at Ellis Island. Yes, she'd swear he was moving his chair. She remembered finding some family names in the book at Ellis Island when they visited New York. The Mayflower, the American Revolution, Ellis Island—a variety of folks made it possible for her to be here. Did Welby have a name in the book there as well? She bet he never saw it, if he did. He'd seemed surprised to learn about his Irish DNA.

Thinking about Welby made her remember the country's great divide and that Welby lived on the other side. She remembered Ace Steele on the campaign trail, saying he would make America good for African-Americans, too. If people would just give him a chance, she thought he'd get America going again. She enjoyed the guy. A mouthy blue-collar fellow in the White House. Yes. So outrageous. She liked outrageous.

She almost cried out loud at the unexpected touch. She looked down to see Welby's foot sliding up her ankle. Her eyes met his, locked, danced, and let go. She looked around to make sure no one was watching and, just as the sounds on the documentary got louder, she swatted his calf and he pulled away. Who did he think he was anyway?

She looked back at the screen, and they were at Blarney Castle. She remembered that place so well—maybe because she'd been there five times.

She did not want Welby, but Tyler? All of a sudden, she remembered what her father had said. Did Tyler really want her back? If so, why didn't he call? Could she go back to work, reschedule the wedding, and see all this as just a little blip in the road? Why had she insisted she needed to stay? Did she really need this year to get clean?

Reagan looked at Welby. He winked. *The audacity of that man.* She frowned back and returned her attention to the screen. The film seemed to be nearing an end as the announcer summarized the various attributes of Ireland. "This Emerald Island, home to ancient astronomers, to the Druids and their earth worship, to Saint Patrick and Saint Brigid, an earthy Christianity, to starving people of the potato famine who migrated to a new land. This green land now a travel destination for so many where dancers kick high and fiddlers keep the night alive, where ancient and contemporary mingle, and tourists go home happy with new Irish eyes."

She kept her eyes on the screen while her heart danced light years away into a dream world where she and Tyler could be one. *E Pluribus Unum.* Out of many, one. The United States, the people all one, back together again. Perhaps she'd get her fairy tale ending after all.

Abigail interrupted her thoughts. "Okay. What did you like? What do you want to see?"

"The Blarney Castle," Reagan said. "Could we spend the day there? We could kiss the Blarney Stone, and they have so many gardens. The poison garden, the native garden, shamrocks, a druid's stone, the witch's stairs, fairy houses. A very fun place. I've been there five times."

"Guinness Brewery," Charlie said. "Let the good times roll."

Abigail laughed. "I think we'll skip the beer, Charlie. What else?"

"The wells," Reagan said. "I want to visit the holy wells and talk to some nuns."

"Can we go surfin'?" Welby asked. "I noticed there's a lot of coast, it being an island and all. I always wanted to surf. I like the beach. Can we go to the beach? Go fishin'?"

"Wish they all could be California girls," Charlie sang. "I'm with Welby." Then he started singing again, "Everybody's surfing, surfing USA."

"I'm scared of sharks," Reagan said. "That's salt water."

"My grandmother has a cousin who lives in Kinvarra. Could we go there?" Nikki asked. "She runs a restaurant and hotel. Maybe she'd treat us all to a meal. Can we go to President Steele's ancestral home? You know he's got good Irish DNA, just like us."

"Nikki, I didn't know. Are you a 'Woman for Steele,' too? I had no idea," Reagan said.

"You bet, baby," Nikki assured her. "He's my rock. Irish roots, just like me."

"Just like former President Alejandro Rosales," Welby added, and gave Nikki a smirk, as if he knew he could get her goat. "'He's got a hometown in Ireland, too, you know. Yep, just like us."

He's one bad ass, Reagan thought. Steele, of course, but Rosales? Both with Irish roots, just like her and Welby? *E pluribus unum*. She never thought about it that way before. She laughed and said it out loud. "*E pluribus unum*, out of many, one. That's our national motto, you know? Let's make America good for all people again."

"No, no, you don't," Welby said. "No, let's not. I mean, when was America ever good for African-Americans?"

"That's not what he means," Reagan said. "We can be good, all together. That's what President Steele means."

Welby Out

Welby didn't let on he agreed, but he again thought of getting her alone and they'd be all together again, just like that. Yes, and that would be so good. Isn't that what she kept talking about?

Abigail closed the evening out with an Irish blessing. "May the road rise up to meet you," she said. "May the wind be always at your back. May the sun shine warm upon your face; the rains fall soft upon your face. Until we meet again, may God hold you in the palm of His hand."

Okay, God, Welby prayed. *Could you let me do the holding and you take care of the sun, the rain and wind? I promise to take real good care of her.* As he imagined putting his body close to Reagan's, he looked over and gave her a wink.

"You be good now, Reagan," he quipped. He rolled his eyes and laughed again and went out the door, just imagining. He would see her again in his dreams tonight.

Destination Ireland, with Abigail and the MAMs – October

The days flew by on Abigail's kitchen calendar, and soon it was time for their big trip. They caravanned to the Dayton airport on a cool October afternoon. Abigail drove the van, loaded with the MAMs, Nikki, and Reagan. Behind them, George and Tom followed in an SUV with Charlie and Welby. Abigail felt a little nervous, hoping things would go as planned. She couldn't help thinking about everything that might go wrong. How would they keep the women and the men separate at night and even during the day? What if someone wandered off? What if they got drugs or started drinking?

In Dayton, they boarded the airplane for La Guardia, and by five p.m. they arrived in New York for a short layover before the transatlantic flight. As they waited for the second plane, Jane gave the group advice. "Now this flight takes seven hours and fifteen minutes. You figure that will take us to three-fifteen in the morning our time. But Dublin is six hours ahead of us, so add six hours and that puts us down in the ground in Ireland at nine-fifteen a.m. So try to sleep on the plane. Tomorrow will be rough, but we'll keep you up with activity. You'll feel weird. They call it jet lag. You'll feel much better if you get some shut-eye now."

Abigail had planned the airplane seating well, with the women in the first two rows, and the men in the back. It would take a little over an hour to reach New York. At La Guardia, they'd be able to eat, switch planes, and then board the flight to Dublin.

Abigail and Sallie were seated together in two seats on the left side of the plane; Abigail with the window, Sallie on the aisle where she could get up and roam more easily. Abigail knew Sallie tended to get antsy. Her recent diagnosis of attention deficit disorder explained a lot.

"How are you doing?" Abigail asked her good friend.

Sallie gave her thumbs up. "Good to go. Glad to be with you. This will be very cool. I've never been to Ireland, you know."

"I'm looking forward to this, too. A long time since I've traveled. Not since ...."

Abigail stopped, not wanting to start complaining about her loss again.

Sallie nodded, gave her a compassionate look, and tilted her head, as if she understood. Then she said, "I haven't left the country since our archaeological expedition in search of Thecla." Sallie laughed. "I think this trip will be a little more tame, don't you?"

"Tame? No, don't think so. With Reagan, Nikki, Charlie, and Welby? I just pray it all goes well."

"Yes," Sallie said. "I hope we have many revelations about our roots and a fun trip." Then she closed her eyes. "I'm beat. I'm going to try to sleep, if you don't mind."

"No, no. Go right ahead," Abigail said. "I want to sleep, too."

But she couldn't. She felt the ache in the center of her chest that never quite went away. That grief quashed some of the enthusiasm she held for the trip. In the middle section, Priscilla sat reading a book, in between Reagan and Nikki. Katharine and Jane, over on the far right, seemed to have their eyes closed already. As Sallie began to snooze also, Abigail leaned back and sighed. The last time she went to Europe, her husband came along.

The stewardess dimmed the cabin lights, so Abigail reached up to turn on her personal light, trying not to wake Sallie. She pulled her journal out of her satchel. She wanted to reread the words of the little Irish man who'd visited her back home. She thumbed through the pages, then began to read. She could hear his thick Irish brogue clearly.

"Ah, the Emerald Isle. Such a classic, such a beauty. There, the mist rises off the berm in the early mornin' and the cock crows a new day. The landscape grounds the soul of the people, it does. There, the wells hold mysteries, waters deep from the earth. There, the people know how to tell a good story and celebrate. At night, the pubs come alive with the fiddlers and the singers and the drone of the bodhran. Ah, my lassie, yes, such joy there, but also such sorrow. The British stole our land, the rich enslaved the poor. But God always spoke to us, through the land, and then through Saint Patrick and Saint Brigid. But so many starved when the potatoes failed. Those who could, escaped to America. Others died, and some of us were left to tell the story. Listen, my dear, and I'll tell ye. Aye, just listen."

She felt some enthusiasm return. Her husband had loved to travel. He'd want her to enjoy the trip. She laughed. Who was this voice? Could it be a long, lost ancestor? Or had she made it all up in her mind? Did God want her to have a good time on this trip as well? She laughed out loud, then covered her mouth. "Just listen," he'd said. What would she hear?

She closed her eyes, praying silently for God's blessing on their travel. She asked for open ears and a listening spirit. She prayed that her grief would lift. She asked for the joy of the Irish to infuse her soul somewhere along the way. After praying for herself, she imagined each person in their group enfolded in the light of God, praying for blessings and learnings on them as well. Finally, she closed with the Lord's Prayer, before falling into a deep slumber.

When they touched down in Ireland, the morning was already in full swing. The MAMs had a full day planned. Abigail explained after they boarded their tour bus, "Today, we explore Newgrange, and learn about ancient Ireland. Then we're off to Clonmacnoise to learn about the monasteries. We'll stay at Nikki's grandmother's cousin's hotel tonight. Tomorrow, we'll do the Cliffs of Moher and then head down to the Dingle Peninsula for a tour and a visit to an Irish pub for Irish music. The third day, we head east, to Cork. In the morning, a sunrise cruise and a visit to the Blarney Castle. After that, we'll head up to Glengarry and another monastery before stopping at the Holy Well retreat center for the night. Finally, we'll make a quick trip to Dublin before our return flight. And now, I'll let our tour guide take over."

Abigail handed the microphone to the guide, smiling at the red-haired man with freckles and a ruddy complexion. He looked to be a bit older, with just enough meat on him to be substantial, without being chubby. She blushed, realizing she felt attracted to the man. His eyes twinkled, and he gave her a wink as he accepted the microphone and began his spiel. Abigail felt her heart flutter and then laughed at herself. What was she thinking?

"The top o' the morning to you, mates," he said. "Welcome to Ireland, the friendly Isle. My mother named me Patrick, after our patron saint, and my dearly departed wife's name be Brigid, our saint for the lassies. But call me Seamus, like my father did, and everybody else, evermore. Never a saint, this one. My papa knew that. Long before the saints, the Irish knew all about the heavens and the earth. You'll see, today. We're heading north to the Boyne Valley, we are. Just a short hop, ninety minutes now to Newgrange, and ye'll learn all about the ancients.

"Now Dublin be the capital city of Ireland, ye know, home to half million people, with over a million souls in the greater Dublin area. Ireland only has four million total, so, ye see ,a quarter of our people live right in and around Dublin. A little place, compared to your country, we are. At one time, eight million people lived on our little island, before the potato famine. People were starving during that bad time. Many took a boat over to America. Ah, we'll talk more about that as the days go by.

"In the Boyne Valley, our archeological sites teach us that the ancient Irish studied the heavens, knew well the phases of the sun and the moon. Look up to the screen and ye see a map of this region. We call it High Man. Do ye see the man there with a bow and arrow, just like Orion in the sky? Did the ancients create a constellation on the ground to match the stars, or did modern men let their imagination get the best of them? Can't say for sure, but who among us doesn't look to the stars for visions? And we Irish are dreamers, this we know.

"Now sit back and watch this film and then maybe take a nap, and I'll have you there in no time. The Gaelic name for road is cow path, and that's exactly what these roads once were. Not very wide, but your mate Seamus here will get you through without a scrape, I do believe."

Abigail enjoyed the cheerful guide, who seemed like a very nice man. She followed his advice, leaned back and relaxed into her seat, as "The High Man" video began.

CHAPTER SEVEN
HIGH MAN AND NEWGRANGE

Welby and the Ancients

Welby stretched his long legs out into the aisle. "You like bus rides?" he asked Charlie.

"Not so much," Charlie said. "Unless we're talking cheerleaders in the back of the football bus on the way home from the game, if you know what I mean."

"How can we get these women in the back?" Welby asked.

"Exactly," Charlie said. "We've got seven days and six nights to solve the problem. Ah, happiness, soon." He grinned as he made a woman's figure with his hands.

Then the tour guide started talking about Ireland. Welby listened. A screen hanging from the ceiling illuminated and speakers broadcast the narration throughout the bus. Welby watched the show, learning about the High Man, the Irish Orion, and the ancient sites, dating back as far as 12,000 years BC, although the Newgrange sites date to 3,200 BC. These ancient people knew the phases of the moon and the sun and built these amazing places all lined up with the solstice. He knew down south, his people connected to the Earth as well. His Grand MaMa read it like the back of her hand. She used a simple sundial and sometimes talked to Welby about the shadows of the land. Welby hadn't thought about that for a very long time. After he went to live in the city, he didn't pay much attention to the earth at all.

The names of the places etched into his consciousness: Dowth, Knowth, Hill of Tara, Loughcrew, County Sligo, and Newgrange. When the documentary ended, he felt sleep coming on. Next thing he knew, Seamus announced, "Wake up! Newgrange!"

Welby lumbered off the bus and monitored the ladies, looking for the special one. Then he maneuvered his sorry jetlagged self in her direction. Most of the group looked a little ragtag. He guessed that happened when you traveled all night on a plane and stepped off into morning when you should be in bed. Looking out the window, he could see green farms in every direction.

They stopped at a little building and were led inside. He walked right up behind Reagan as they entered a room for a video introduction. He slipped down on the bench beside her and smiled. Maybe this wouldn't be so hard after all. But then George came and sat right next to him before the lights went out. Darn. Not much chance for fun with surveillance like that.

The video explained how Newgrange lines up with the winter solstice. Once a year, sunlight completely illuminates the center of the ancient building. They conduct a lottery to see who gets to visit on the few days this phenomenon occurs.

He looked over at Reagan and smiled. She glanced back. Was that a smile forming on her lips? Checking on George, he reminded himself to be discreet. He focused on the screen, learning about the ancient Irish .

Reagan at Newgrange

Reagan glanced at Welby as he leaned against her. For a moment, the warmth of his body radiated all along her side, spread into her center and then out to her head and her toes. But then she caught herself. She pushed him away and asked George to move down, giving her more room on the bench.

She focused on the screen. 12,000 BC? She knew the Bible says the world was created in 4,000 BC. Where did they get 12,000 from? Did the Irish government make all this up to help the tourism industry? Rather impressive, even if misguided. But how could they say these structures were built before the Earth began? Maybe they were just wrong on the dates. Obviously old stuff, unlike anything she ever saw. Okay, now they said Newgrange was built in 3,200 BC. Plausible.

The film ended. She sat up straight and noticed Welby hanging his head. She laughed out loud as the lights came on. As they were ushered out. Welby stayed right behind her, bumping into her, until, thankfully, George stepped between them. Once outdoors, they walked single file across a swinging bridge through the woods. She inhaled the crisp October air. Although she'd read the temperature in Ireland remained moderate throughout the year, today seemed on the chilly side. The fresh, cool air helped keep her awake. She turned around, looking back at George and Welby. Welby caught her eye and gave her a thumbs-up. She frowned and tripped, starting to fall.

Welby came up behind her, catching her and lifting her back up. She felt a jolt of electricity pass between them. Startled, she laughed and said, "Thank you. I'm okay now," a signal to let her go.

George said, "Good save, now let her go. Hands off."

Reagan walked on ahead. She admired George's ability to smoothly stop Welby's advances. But then Welby started talking.

"Okay, but watch your step, Reagan," he said with a wink. "I'll be backin' you up if you trip again. You can count on me."

Reagan noticed Welby seemed to always have some smooth words, but they didn't quite ring true. She didn't trust him. She really liked George. But Welby? Bad news.

Reagan hurried to catch up with the group as they approached a circular area with benches and a bus stop sign. They huddled, waiting. Soon, a little grey bus pulled up and the front door opened. Reagan took a window seat near the front. Welby stopped and asked, "May I join you?"

"No, sir," she said. "I'm saving this for Priscilla. Sorry." She saw his look of disappointment, then him scrunching his long legs as he settled in behind her.

Priscilla slid in next to Reagan. The bus transported them a short distance, depositing them right in front of the Newgrange structure, which looked like a mound at first. Closer up, she saw it was actually a little building, covered with grass and lined with huge boulders all around. The tour guide explained that builders used two hundred thousand pounds of rocks that they estimated were carried seventy-five miles to this site. Rolled there on logs was one theory.

They were ushered into the building through a narrow channel. Once they reached the center, the guide turned out the overhead lights. Gradually, the room illuminated with light streams replicating the sun during the winter solstice. With no evidence of human or animal sacrifice, the guide explained it was thought that the small bowl built into the wall might have served for a form of ancient baptism.

The guide continued, "There's much we don't know, but we believe the people were astronomers, builders, and farmers. They studied the heavens, aligning the building with the winter season. An amazing architectural feat, and still leak-proof after thousands of years."

Listening Circle at Newgrange with Abigail

When they boarded the little bus to head back to the Newgrange Visitors Center, Abigail sat up front, next to their tour guide, Seamus. She needed his help. Pondering the Irish voice who'd visited her back home, she decided listening should be an important part of their trip. The voice had said, "Listen and I will tell ye." The MAMs had once walked the Living Vine Labyrinth at Abigail's church to listen, after reading books about environmental issues. Molly's revelation during that experience had called them to create FARM. She wanted to try some other spiritual practices in Ireland.

She watched Seamus, considering his weathered face as he relaxed into the seat beside her, looking so comfortable in his skin. Once again, she noticed a twinkle in his eye and knew there was something about this man. "Seamus," she said, "do you think we could take a few minutes for a listening circle in the visitors center before we head out?"

"A listening circle, eh? And what would that be? What kinda space do ye need to listen?" Seamus chuckled. "You Americans, always something with ye. Aye, always something."

"I want to give everyone a chance to react to their experience at Newgrange. I brought along journals. I thought I'd give them about ten minutes to journal and twenty minutes to share. As we explore our Irish roots, everything we see is part of our DNA. I want them to reflect on that."

"We have a tight schedule today," Seamus said. "But I can spare thirty minutes." He winked at Abigail. "You probably want chairs in a circle, eh?"

"Yes," Abigail said. "Thank you, Seamus." She looked at him and felt something tugging on her heart. It felt strange to feel an attraction like this. Since her husband died, she'd really had no interest in men. She couldn't imagine herself with anybody but Jon, although opportunities had presented themselves. No one could take his place, but she didn't like being all alone.

Five minutes later, they were seated in a little room in a circle. Abigail started by saying, "We want to listen to our experiences. See what comes up for you. Everyone gets a journal. Write your name on the front cover. Bring them along each day."

On cue, Sallie passed a journal and a pen to each person. She laughed when she came up with one extra and said, "I guess this is for you. Surprise!" She handed it to Seamus.

"Okay," Abigail continued, "I'm going to put on some music. You have ten minutes to write your first entry. Write whatever you've been thinking as you arrived here and visited Newgrange. Consider what does Newgrange teach you? How does this connect to your DNA?"

Abigail turned her attention to her iPad, found Irish melodies, and turned them on, providing a quiet background for journaling. She set the timer, then began to write. She paused. When she heard a clear voice. She looked up, but everyone else seemed absorbed in their journals.

Then, over in the corner of the room, perched on a spare chair, she noticed a … leprechaun? She closed her eyes. She opened her eyes again. Yes, there really was a little man all dressed in green, with shiny gold buckles on his sparkling black patent leather shoes. He took off his top hat and bowed to her. She closed her eyes again and giggled quietly to herself. Maybe she was going crazy.

And then the leprechaun began to speak. "The top o' the morning to ye, lassie. Welcome to the Emerald Isle. I've been a-waitin' for ye, I have."

Abigail pinched her wrist, then looked around to see if others could hear him, but everyone else still seemed focused on their writing. Even Seamus scribbled away, oblivious to the voice. Abigail took up her pen and started to write as well. She wrote the words of the little leprechaun—or perhaps it was hallucination arising out of her jetlagged confusion. Either way, she listened and got it all down.

"So now, my lassie, ye've caught a glimpse of these ancient Irish ones who watched the heavens and knew the seasons well. A sight to behold, that Newgrange, wouldn't ye say? That's all missin' from your lives these days, for the most part. You just look it up on your internet and assume all the facts will be right there for ye. But back in the day, the people had to watch the sky and count the days and they had to be observant to be in touch with the changes in the planet. Their lives depended on it, they did. And yours do, too, you know. The message here for ye be to slow down, observe the earth, and learn from the past. Find your roots and they will teach you, and then you'll grow into a strong tree. Aye, that you will, my lassie."

Abigail put her pen down and closed her eyes once the voice stopped. She slipped into the silence of meditation. A few minutes later, the iPad timer startled her. She jolted awake in her seat and tried to reorient herself quickly for the time of sharing.

"Whew," she said as she turned off the Irish music. "I dozed off there for a minute. Jet lag is catching up with me. Maybe we all should take a quick nap on our ride over to the monastery. But first, would anyone like to share what you wrote?"

Silence hung in the space. "Welby?" she asked. "Any thoughts?"

"Oh, man," Welby said. "All that buildin', what you say, thirty-two hundred BC, over five thousand years ago? All that, just to line up with the winter sun for two or three days? Real deep, man. Those people were in touch with the Earth, for sure. Ain't that somethin'? Reminds me of my people back in the South. My Grand MaMa knew when the rain was comin'. Felt it in her bones."

Charlie shook his head. "I don't know 'bout that, Welby. Could all just be fake news, all set up for the tourists. How'd they make that back then? It's a good story, that's all."

Reagan piped in. "I'm with Charlie. They got their dates all wrong. They said there were people in Ireland twelve thousand years ago? No, the world began with Adam and Eve around four thousand BC."

"Yes, yes. So true, Reagan," Priscilla said. "Thank you for pointing that out. Sometimes the scientists get it wrong. We know what the Bible says, don't we? 'But do not forget this one thing, dear friends: With the Lord a day is like a thousand years, and a thousand years are like a day.' 2 Peter 3:8."

Abigail raised her eyebrows at Sallie. Sallie smiled briefly, then looked away. She noticed Katharine put her hand over her mouth. Abigail knew that Reagan came from some religious fundamentalism, but she was surprised to hear Priscilla's take on it. Well, okay, she had to admit she'd known Priscilla had that going on, too, but she'd never heard her come right out and say it.

Reagan interrupted her thoughts. "Well, fake or not, it's some architectural feat to get that little chamber all fixed up to illuminate for just a few days a year. I don't think the modern people would go to all that trouble. Maybe they thought the sun was a god or something."

"I started to write a song," Nikki said. "I need to work on it some more. Let me sing a verse for you, if you don't mind?"

"Yes, go ahead. Please," Abigail said, delighted that Nikki's creative juices had been stimulated.

Nikki shyly looked around and then she opened up her voice with power that Abigail didn't expect. Reminded her of Iris Dement, who really belted out with a southern twang.

"Newgrange, take us back to good old days. Newgrange, take us back to the sun. Ancient builders craft waterproof mounds. Makes us wonder what else they've done. Newgrange ...."

The group broke into applause and Charlie yelled, "Sing it, baby!"

"We'll have to sign you for a singing contract with the Three M's," George said.

Welby laughed. "Don't expect any money for that, honey."

Abigail pulled them back. "Thanks, Nikki. We'd like to hear the rest of that later."

Seamus checked his watch. "We be short of time. Need to wrap this up soon, we do. Okay?" He looked at Abigail.

Abigail nodded and said, "Anyone else?"

The rest of the MAMs weighed in. Molly focused on how no one really knew too much about the ancients, and how she was surprised it was built before Egypt. Priscilla thought it was very pretty. Katharine provided a little overview of the other High Man sites from the books she'd been reading, and Sallie, as usual, voiced concern about the children, wondering if they used child labor. Jane just gave the builders a thumbs up. George thought perhaps there was a message here for Sun Power House, that maybe the group needed to focus a little more on the heavens as they worked to harness the power of the sun for energy, and Tom just said he was so glad to be here and learn a little more about his wife's people, giving Molly a poke in the ribs. Finally, Abigail read what she'd transcribed from the leprechaun, but didn't tell them about the little man.

Once Abigail finished, Seamus spoke up, echoing the words that Abigail had read. "Slow down, observe the earth, and learn from the past. Find your roots and they will teach you, and then you'll grow into a strong tree. Aye, you will, my lassie." He winked at Abigail. "Pretty good, for a Yankee. Better listen to her, you should."

Abigail felt the laughter rolling off his tongue and started to laugh herself. Contagious, she thought, as the others picked it up as well. Sounds of merriment filled the room. She actually felt a sense of deep joy, what she'd prayed for on the plane. Something magical was unfolding.

Seamus interrupted the fun. "Okay, we must be on the bus in ten minutes. Use the facilities if you want but make it quick. Our tour begins at the monastery in ninety minutes. I'm going to have barrel down that cow path to get you all there in time. Let's go."

The group broke up with everyone moving toward the restrooms, but Abigail lingered behind to connect with Seamus a little more. "Thank you, Seamus," she said. Their eyes met and again she felt something surging within. She smiled, and he returned it with his baby blues sending energy into hers. Then she was off to the restroom herself, but inside, her heart kept right on smiling. She hummed the old Irish melody, "When Irish eyes are smiling, they'll steal your heart away." *Oh my, do I need a good night's sleep. First the leprechaun, and now this?* She hurried to join the group on the bus.

CHAPTER EIGHT
THE MONASTERY, KINVARRA, AND
CLIFFS OF MOHER

Abigail and the MAMs – Celtic Spirit

Abigail arranged for the MAMs to sit together for a chat on the way to the monastery, to give them time to discuss a book called *Celtic Spirit* by Jeanne Crane they read in preparation for the trip. "So, this book is like us: a tour group doing the Emerald Isle," Abigail started out. "I bought this at an Irish festival where I met the author and heard her speak. I asked if the story was real. She said no, but combined experiences from several Irish trips. What did you think?"

"Well, I enjoyed hearing about the various sites," Sally said. "It motivated me to read on, knowing I might soon be walking up to some of these places."

"Yes," Molly said. "I hope we have some of these spiritual experiences she talks about."

"Thin spaces," Katharine said. "She describes thin spaces where the veil between heaven and earth is closer than usual. A glimpse of the other side." Katharine smiled as she explained, "My husband and I once took a tour of the sacred wells of Ireland."

"Were the wells holy?" Priscilla asked.

"Well, that's a deep subject," Jane quipped.

"Living water is biblical, you know, Priscilla," Sallie said.

"But what did you think, Katharine?" Priscilla asked.

"Well," Katharine said.

"Yes, the wells." Jane laughed.

Katharine laughed, too. "Okay. You know here in Ireland, the people always felt a connection to the earth. Dating back to megalithic times with Newgrange, they knew about the solstice. In later times, the Celtic religion was also very earth-centered. If you think about a well, it's rather mystical and magical to think that water would come up from the earth and help sustain life. Back then, that gave them a spiritual significance. Sallie's right, too, Jesus talked about living water. Patrick used their beliefs to teach about Jesus. The wells are holy places."

"Will we visit any wells?" Sallie asked.

"Yes, yes," Abigail said. "Any first impressions, Jane? Priscilla?"

Priscilla said, "Well, the tour guide seemed a little off in la-la land, if you know what I mean. Do the Irish really believe all that new age stuff?

Abigail noticed Seamus looking back at them, catching her eye through the rearview mirror. She asked him, "What do you think, Seamus?"

Seamus' eyes twinkled and he began to respond. "Ah, you Americans want to get us all figured out, I know. But we be a little bit of this and a little bit of that. I'm not sure that you can quite sum us up. Saint Patrick, he's our holy man. And Jesus, he's our Lord. But we also believe in the spirit of a place. Our poets will tell you our landscape has a soul and our pub singers will tell ye almost anything. Don't try to put us in a box or we'll find our way out and be dancing across the room before you notice. Now, let me drive the bus." He grinned at them, and Abigail was fairly sure his wink was meant for her.

Katharine spoke next. "Most scholars would say that, yes, much of the original Celtic spiritual traditions were interwoven within the newer Christian ones. For example, Saint Brigid was a character within Celtic lore first. Later, a Brigid started a religious order of nuns. With time, the stories became interwoven. Sometimes it's hard to tell them apart."

"Thanks, Seamus and Katharine. Always nice to have a native guide and a professor along," Abigail said. "I was intrigued about the book the one guy was reading, *Anam Cara: Soul Friend*. So I checked that out of the library and brought it along. I love this book. It's written by an Irishman and really lifts up the Celtic aspects of their tradition. Unfortunately, the author, John O'Donohue, died several years go."

Jane said, "I'm with Sallie on this. I actually read this *Celtic Spirit* from cover to cover, and now I'm ready to explore these places. I want to see Brigid's well."

Tour at Clonmacnoise

They chatted about *Celtic Spirt* until they reached Clonmacnoise, a monastery in County Clare. There, among the green fields, Seamus pulled into a lot near the ruins where the rivers met. For the next hour, a guide led the group through the doorways and around the grounds, sharing stories of monks who once lived at the monastery and kept scholarship alive during the Middle Ages. He explained that the monasteries were the centers of culture during that time. But Henry the VIII of England invaded and took the monasteries for his own, appointing a steward to manage the lands, shutting down and turning out the monks. That ushered in a very dark chapter in their history, he told them. British dominance had only ended a few years back.

When the tour concluded, Abigail asked the group to take a few minutes to journal before boarding the bus to their destination for the night. They spread out among the ruins of the monastery as the late afternoon sun illuminated the landscape with an almost mystical glow. Some sat on tombstones; others used them as a writing table. Abigail noticed Seamus stood, writing in his journal. Reagan sat cross-legged in the grass, sketching the rivers' convergence.

Abigail found a bench and began to write. She was glad that the trip seemed to be going well. She penned a few words and then the leprechaun appeared again, dancing out in front of her with his little hat. She tried to ignore him, but he started to speak.

"Glad ye came to me monastery, lassie. Gotta stay close to ye God, I say, to keep you on the track. Follow your Maker, yes, and ye will receive the desires of your heart. I see ye lookin' at our man Seamus, and ye know he's lookin' right back at ye. He likes you, he does. Now, love's a good thing, and don't ye forget it. I know the history of me island be a bit sad, they say. But tears feed the soul. Now, don't ye forget the deep learnings that come when yer oppressed. It may be easy for me to say, but the Irish be a happy people for the most part. They find the sunny side of the situation, though that Henry was a bitter lesson. I don't like that man. He shoulda let Ireland alone, but, like many rich people, he got greedy and took more than his share. That be the downfall of many a civilization, like that country of yours over there, a-grabbing way too much of the pie. Now, you get some sleep tonight, and I'll see ye in the morning, lassie."

Abigail scribbled quickly, trying to get it all down, even as she wanted to quit listening. Really, she felt amazed at what he'd said. She looked up, but he was gone. She checked her watch and shook her head. Time to call the group together. She couldn't read this response. They'd know she was crazy. In fact, she decided to nix a sharing time for today. Later, she'd give them a chance to catch up.

Seamus ushered them back to the bus for the short trip over to the coast and a little town south of Galway called Kinvarra. Abigail enjoyed the ride through the countryside. She worried a bit, wondering about Nikki's distant relations, but Seamus knew the place and they arrived in no time. He pulled up to the front of the inn, letting them pile out.

Nikki took the lead, albeit a bit timidly. She opened the door and the group followed closed behind. She walked up to the counter and said, "Hi, I'm Nikki Blain, from the States. We made it."

A buxom woman stepped out from behind the counter. "Nikki Blain? My dear, you're a sight for me eyes, ye are. Come here, lass, and let me give you a hug. Like a spirit from the past, just like my cousin Erin back in the day." She enfolded Nikki in her stout arms. Then she let her go, saying, "Oh my, where are my manners? Come in, come in." And she whisked the group into their dining room where the aroma of beef stew filled the small room. "It's time to eat."

After a wonderful Irish dinner, they checked into the inn for the night. Nikki's relatives led those who wanted to go for a sunset walk along the coast before turning in. Abigail thought they must've brought the whole town along to meet Nikki. She lagged behind with Seamus, feeling tired, content to be strolling with a fine man on a beautiful evening. Afterward, she succumbed to exhaustion and didn't even have time to reread the leprechaun's messages before falling asleep.

Reagan at Breakfast

Reagan examined the view out the window in the restaurant at breakfast the next morning. In the distance, she could see Kinvarra Bay. To the right, Dunlaugh Castle. To the left, little fishing boats moored along the docks. Had her ancestors sat in this same place in years past? A story her Irish grandmother once told her came to mind. Even now, she could hear her grandmother's voice.

"Back in the homeland, our people were starving. My grandfather's papa took the family to Galway Town to board a steamer for America. He sold everything they owned to buy passage."

Reagan looked beyond the castle, knowing that Galway would be the next city north along the western coast of Ireland. She tried to imagine leaving everything familiar.

"They had three children. The oldest, my grandfather, at ten, and then another boy at seven and a little girl who was four. And their mother was pregnant, with a huge belly. She became very sick two days into the voyage and her contractions started. The new brother, Ryan, was born and, as they were cleaning her up, the contractions started up again, and out came new brother number two, Dylan. She was so very sick after those twins. My grandfather took care of those babies for his mother, so she could get better."

Reagan knew all about "those babies." They were the ones who later convinced the family to buy a plantation in Georgia. Perhaps that was how she'd ended up with some West African DNA. For now, she found that fact most embarrassing. She looked over at where Welby and Charlie sat with George and Tom. Welby had kept an eye on her, but hadn't come close since Newgrange.

Reagan knew there was a part of the story her grandmother held back. Something she wouldn't say. But she didn't know what. She wondered about what happened in Georgia. She wondered about relations left behind in Ireland. There'd been a story about a treasure left behind. She tried to remember, but the details were fuzzy and she couldn't coax them out of the recesses of her mind.

She picked at the food on her plate. Usually, she liked to eat a full breakfast, but this morning she didn't have an appetite. She looked at the blood sausage and scrambled eggs, then passed them up to take a bite of a biscuit and a drink of coffee as she looked over at Welby again. Were some of her ancestors the slave owners of some of Welby's? Had her people really done that to people like him? That it was possible they had was disturbing. She felt a sense of shame, a sense of guilt, and a bit embarrassed. She didn't know this part of her family tree well, but she knew it lay there, a part of her roots, which meant it must be a part of her, as well. Had some of her people loved some of Welby's? Where did the African DNA come from? Why had nobody ever talked about that?

Welby on the Road

Welby shuffled along the path toward the bus with his suitcase, enjoying a full belly and looking forward to another day of touring. Next stop: Cliffs of Moher. He wondered if he'd be able to maneuver to sit by Reagan. He dropped off his suitcase by the cargo hold and walked up beside her. Hands off this time; he decided to use words. "Mornin', Reagan. How did the night go for you? Get all your beauty sleep?" He drawled his words, making it sexy. He figured Reagan would like that.

Sure enough, her big baby blues opened wide and took in his in a way that gave him a little twitch in his heart and his groin at the same time, and just about then, he figured out he was in big trouble. He carefully became a little bit aloof, raising his eyebrows with a shrug. "Looks like you got all the looks you need, baby," he said. "Age after beauty." He bowed and swept his arm in front of him, signaling her to step up into the bus first. His mama'd taught him to let the ladies go first. His uncle had explained that was so you got the benefit of the view at the same time you were being polite. He laughed. She turned and gave him a frown.

"You're okay," he told her with a gentle pat on her shoulder. "I'm not laughing at you."

Reagan took a seat about halfway back and he slid in beside her. He noticed Abigail whispering to Molly right after he sat down, and wondered if they were going to bust him soon. He turned to Reagan and, in a gentle, caring voice asked, "So, how are you today?"

Reagan batted her eyelashes a little at him as she said, "I'm okay. I'm okay. Something's bothering me, but I can't quite figure it out. I wish I knew more about my Irish ancestors. I know they boarded the steamer for America up in Galway, but I can't remember where they came from. Dingle rings a bell. I think we may be going to their town today. I wish I could remember."

Reagan looked so forlorn, Welby wished he could enfold her in his arms and just kiss her sadness away. But he wasn't going to push his luck, so he just nodded. "Keep thinking, Reagan. Those little mysteries are tucked somewhere in that beautiful head of yours. Give it time. They just need a little nudge."

Then George arrived and put an end to his fun. "Welby, you're sitting with me. Move on back." Welby gave Reagan a shrug and a wave, then followed George to a seat a couple rows back, with the guys. Seamus started gabbing. Welby leaned back and closed his eyes.

A while later, Seamus pulled the van into a big parking lot. Welby read the sign: Cliffs of Moher Visitor Center. Before they could go up to the cliffs, they had to go in this place. Reagan went off with the ladies, leaving Welby to shuffle around the visitors' center on his own. Seemed like a museum, and he liked museums. He started reading, going to each display, learning about the cliffs and the history. Then he came upon a climate change display. The sign said changing climate would be affecting the cliffs with more storms. He pushed a button on a replica of the country of Ireland, surrounded by oceans. Three lights lit up, illuminating the largest cities. "In a hundred and fifty years, Galway, Dublin and Cork could all be underwater," a recording said.

Suddenly, it all came rushing back to him. The cover-up, the fossil fuel people. Re-segregating the public schools in North Carolina. Snowing the American people about climate change. He remembered his anger and resolve to do something about it. But now here he was, going off the deep end on Reagan, a self-pronounced Steele supporter. Wasn't she what was wrong with America?

And how to solve the problems of America eluded him. His dream of blowing up the fossil fuel headquarters had come to naught.

Welby followed along, walking on a paved path toward the cliffs. In the distance, he could see water, seafoam with a gray sky. The wind picked up, white caps churning, water rolling in and crashing on the rocks. He loved the sea. They began to climb up toward the cliffs. He wondered how many people went up there to end it all. How easy would it be to just jump off and solve all problems once and for all? No fence, not much separation at all between the little path and the edge. He'd heard drowning was a good way to go.

But then Grand MaMa came back, haunting him again. "Marcus Welby Jones, you just get that thought out of your head right now. The good Lord didn't give you life for you to take it away. No, sir. That's not your right. That's not your job. Your job is to make the most of this gift you've been given. And look at you there, boy, you got a big whopping second chance and I expect you to rise to the occasion. Now, don't you even think about it."

Welby rolled his eyes. "Yes, ma'am," he muttered under his breath and hung his head like he'd done as a little boy when she caught him with his hand in the cookie jar. He'd long since learned not to mess with the Grand MaMa. But he also knew there were no easy answers to the dilemmas of his country—and of his own life.

They came to a fork on the path and Seamus offered them a choice. They could go to the lighthouse or walk up to the top of the cliffs. Always up for an adventure, Welby picked the cliffs to the left. Reagan turned right, going toward the tower with the rest of the women.

He enjoyed the sensation of wind whipping against his body. After being locked up for all those years, he appreciated the freedom. The path meandered along the edge of the cliffs. To the left, farmland stretched as far as his eye could see, but down and to the right, the churning ocean crashed into the rocks. He felt a little dizzy looking at the sea. He turned his attention to the lighthouse. There he saw people gathered with a man dressed up in some old-fangled clothes. He thought he saw Reagan's red jacket and blonde hair streaming out into the wind.

Was Reagan the problem or the solution? What did Abigail say the other day about that poet Rilke? Sometimes you just have to live the question. He liked women, but they caused problems and challenges. And what was he thinking? Falling for a Steele supporter? Not going to happen. But she was so beautiful.

They reached the end of the path. Here on the top of the world, on the edge of Ireland, he imagined that somewhere across the water would be the fishing cove where he'd spent his summers back in North Carolina. They turned around, but his thoughts were still focused on home. The farm fields to his right reminded him of the old farm place where Grand MaMa lived out her days. He felt a kinship here to the farm, to the land, to the genes of the Irish people, and also to the Gullah people and the West Africans. Planting seeds, being uprooted, replanting in different soil, mixing things up. The Irish Africans. The African Irish. The melting cauldron of America. He looked back to the lighthouse but couldn't see Reagan anymore.

Could there be connections here to heal the divide? That ocean had served as a passageway for his Irish ancestors, for his African forefathers, for himself. He stood suspended in time, feeling the circle of life. His old girlfriend would've chanted "Om" at a time like this. He didn't want people to laugh at him, but he did mutter an Om under his breath.

CHAPTER NINE
MOVING ON TO DINGLE TOWN

Listening to the Differences, Abigail Convenes a Circle

Seamus pulled the bus up to a park with picnic tables for a meal break on the road to Dingle. They ate box lunches among the trees. Afterward, Abigail asked them to write in their journals, about the cliffs, the day, and whatever might be surfacing. She gave them fifteen minutes, then brought them together for a time of sharing.

Today, she'd brought a listening stick. "When you have the stick," she said, "it's your time to speak; the rest of us will listen." She knew the practice could help keep the focus on the person talking and avoid interruptions. "We each have something to say and need to be heard. Remember, we're not here to argue, just to listen and try to understand one another."

Nikki led off. "Well, this has been so cool for me, visiting my relatives, meeting the people Grandma's always talking about. They're good people. They don't know how messed up I am. They treated me like I'm important and good. Aidan, Erin's son who runs the inn, invited me outside for a talk. He warned me that alcoholism is in our genes. He told me his story. He couldn't just have one, so eventually he stopped, went cold turkey, to get his life back on track. The family still gives him a hard time, always wanting him to drink up. Creates tension, he says, but he must stay sober. I'm so glad he told me that. But, whew, he talked politics and I wanted to hide. Why do they hate Steele so much?"

Welby grabbed the stick from Nikki and said, "What's not to hate about Ace Steele? A bigot and a construction worker. Just because he won a lottery and followed those get rich schemes to make his millions doesn't mean he has a clue how to run a country. Look at what he's done so far."

Reagan's nostrils flared. She walked across the circle and snatched the listening stick from Welby. "Stop that right now. Ace Steele is our president, and he deserves our respect. We Republicans put up with Dictator Rosales for eight years; now it's your turn. Give the man a chance. He's going to make our country good for the people again, whether you like it or not."

Charlie, sitting beside Reagan, tapped her on the shoulder and motioned for the stick. He said, "Yes, Steele's our man. We need someone speaking for the working man. He started out working construction, building skyscrapers, you know. He's going to put us back to work, brother. He's got a temper, but that's what I love about him."

Welby shook his head in disgust. "He's got you snowed, man. He's concerned about one person and one person alone, and that's himself. Haven't you been readin' the papers? He's out for himself. He says he'll help the working man, but he's in bed with all those rich billionaire Republicans. Maybe he started out blue collar, but now he's all about padding his own pockets with the rest of the white-collar kings. Dude, did you read that display at the Cliffs of Moher? In a hundred and fifty years, this whole island may be underwater. Climate change. The rest of the world came together to deal with the problem in Paris. But Ace? He leads the pack of those money-grabbing fossil fuel folk, hell bent on destroying not only our country, but the planet. How can you sleep at night, bro?"

Abigail interrupted, taking the stick from Charlie. "Welby, you didn't have the listening stick. The purpose of the stick is to help us listen. Reagan and Charlie, you took the stick, but you were responding, not sharing what's happening with you today. The point of the listening circle is to share your experience, not to debate. Talk about your experience on the trip."

An uncomfortable silence descended. Abigail wondered what to do. She noticed a twinkle in Seamus' eye. Had he enjoyed the argument? For her, it had brought ugly, deep divisions front and center. She felt nauseated. That type of debate rarely led anywhere productive. She didn't want a fracture in their group. Too late to avoid that, she realized. She appreciated that the MAMs didn't weigh in. Then Nikki solved the problem for her.

"Can I finish?" Nikki asked. Abigail handed her the stick. "I get it, Abigail, that you just want us to talk. But I think Welby helped me understand where my relatives are coming from," she said. "That must be what they're talking about. I don't read the papers. I just listen to Fox. I think I know what's going on, but I traveled a lot with the band. Maybe I don't know."

After a few more moments of silence, Katharine took the stick. "We are so divided these days. Some support President Steele, some think he has no business being president.

"The political divide needs healing, but we are not making progress. And now the politicians are fighting against themselves and can't pass much legislation. I wonder what will happen in the

November election.

Thank you all for speaking up. And thank you, Abigail, for this listening stick." Then Katharine looked out across the fields and said, "When I'm in a foreign country, for some reason, I can listen better. Here, I see the ocean. The Cliffs of Moher speak to me of creation, of the power of God in the created world, and how small we are in comparison to the universe around us. Out by the cliffs with the water churning below, I thought I heard the Earth say, "Wake up. Pay attention. Be real.'"

Tom took the stick from Katharine. "You guys are so deep. Working as a police officer all those years, I saw people at their best, but mostly at their worst. A lot of the guys on the force with me had the attitude that you just need to lock these no-goods up. Either you were a law-abiding citizen or you were a scoundrel, a cheat, a liar and a criminal. They just wanted to get them all off the streets. And if they had dark skin, they practically convicted them before they arrested them. So, part of me understands the focus on law and order and trying to clean up our streets. But, being an African-American, I hear Welby, too. It's not fair for the Black man in our country. And here we are in an all-white country, and they hate our president. That's something. Makes you think, don't it?"

Jane took the stick. "I've traveled a lot, and I find that that people around the world often know more of what's going on than I do. I suppose you could say I'm not a reader. Usually, they like Americans enough as people, but whew, have I gotten some earfuls about our government and our leaders."

Katharine grabbed the stick back. "Yes, that's so true. President Rosales was well-loved in other countries, but many of our presidents have been ridiculed. Did you see the protests in Europe when Steele went there last summer?"

Abigail frowned. "Tom, Jane, Katharine, you're not talking about your own experience here in Ireland." Abigail looked at her watch. "We're out of time. We need to get back on the road. Next time, please share your own experience *here*."

The theme of listening surfaced again and again for her. Abigail wanted each of them to listen to what they were learning about their roots, but she worried political discussions distracted them. "Thank you all for sharing," she said. "Nikki's getting in touch with her relatives left her with questions today. She wonders why they hate Steele. Families often contain political differences and that opens up debate within our self.

"We certainly have a variety of perspectives in our group on this trip. As we travel on, I encourage you to continue to listen to the landscape and to the voices inside of you. Continue journaling. Consider what you're learning about your roots." Then Abigail turned to Seamus. "Take us to Dingle! Could you also tell us a little about the road we're traveling on and the people who came before us?"

"Yes, ma'am," Seamus said. He took Abigail's arm and led the group back to the bus for the trip south along the coast.

Abigail smiled up at her new friend. "We lucked out, getting you as our guide."

"Aye, that you did." Seamus gave her a wink and a smile. "Best guide in all of Ireland, I be. The luck o' the Irish be with ye, for sure."

Abigail on the Bus

Abigail settled into her seat and relaxed, feeling great. They were seeing a lot of Ireland, and had had no major problems. She believed some good listening was happening. She wondered if her own Irish roots drew her to Seamus. A couple months ago, she hadn't thought she had a drop of Irish blood. Now here she was, learning about her own roots and turning over a new leaf, it seemed. Life never ceased to surprise her, just like God through the years. Whenever she got stuck in a rut, something would upset the whole apple cart, turning her upside down into something much better than she ever could have imagined. That's why she stayed close to her Creator. Never a dull moment. She closed her eyes as Seamus began talking. She loved the sound of his Irish brogue.

He narrated their journey. "Now we continue on some back roads down south to ease our way to the Dingle Peninsula. Ireland just started developing in the last hundred years, and many of the roads weren't really built for modern travelers. So they get a wee bit tight sometimes. But ye have a good driver in me, so no need for worry. It's the Americans who come over here and rent cars and vans that have the problem, they do.

"We be heading through the countryside now. In the past, most Irish people farmed the land, just like in your country. But that way of life be changing. We're a little behind America. The potato famine cleared out many a farmer, you know. Never should have shifted to a single crop, no. Of course, that was the British for ye, trying to get their cash crop. Not good for the people; they starved when the crop failed. We drive by these cottages, empty now." He pointed out the window to small, thatched-roof structures. "We call them famine houses. The people up and deserted them, either sailing for America up from Galway north of where we stayed in Kinvarra, or died. So ye still have the farmers in these parts, but then you have most of the young people moving to the cities. And we only have few of them. Dublin, Galway,

Cork, those be the big ones these days.

"But now we be heading off to Dingle, the little place by the sea. Some say it's like your Key West, sort of a beach community type place. You'll notice a different way o' bein' down in Dingle, you will. We'll be in the west-most point in Ireland. Tonight, we'll visit a tavern in town for some traditional Irish music. There they let the foreigners join in. Get ready for some fun.. Sit back and relax and I'll have you there in no time."

Abigail enjoyed looking at the farmland out the window for a while, then turned back in to watch Seamus driving and whistling an Irish tune. She felt a tug at her heartstrings. Something about him really called to her deep inside. She flashed back to high school days when she'd become interested in boys and developed her first serious crush. What she felt now felt strangely familiar. Seamus put a smile on her face and some new enthusiasm in her heart, but she also knew she wasn't an adolescent anymore. It felt so strange to be single, widowed. Maybe falling in love would help her. But with all those men back home who'd sought her out, why here? Why this man? In a few days, she'd return to Ohio. She needed to let this go. She focused on the path ahead. She could see Seamus, she could see the road. The words of an Iris Dement song came to mind, perhaps triggered by Nikki's singing. "Let the mystery be ...."

Dingling Down Reagan with Welby

Reagan changed into some jeans, grabbed her violin, and left the little room she shared with Priscilla. She liked this place. It did remind her of Key West and other beach towns she'd visited in the past. Down here on the southwest corner of Ireland, the people seemed more laid back. In the afternoon, when Seamus gave them a tour of the peninsula, she'd enjoyed hearing about the Druids, the monks, and the pilgrims who'd passed this way. They read an Oldham stone, with Druid markings. They checked out an old church made of stone they called The Oratory, that had survived intact nine hundred years. Like an upside-down ark, he'd said. That's the design of most churches. She'd never thought of that before. They went by some thatched roof famine cottages. She shivered, realizing that one could be the house of her ancestors abandoned when they left for America to avoid starving to death. They visited a modern school, where Irish girls learned the Gaelic language so later they could become teachers in the schools, to keep the culture alive.

She looked forward to Irish music night at the pub. Her fingers itched to fiddle in Ireland. Fortunately, her time would come soon. When she walked out of the bed and breakfast, there stood Welby by the van, his hand propped on his banjo case.

"Do they play banjos in Ireland?" she asked.

"We're soon to find out," he said. "I can't let you play alone."

She laughed. "I guess not."

Welby responded, "They planned ahead, made a packing list for everyone. Mr. George's got his bass guitar. Mr. Tom, his trumpet. Ms. Abigail brought a dulcimer, and they found a guitar for Nikki. They want us to keep on with our music. Say it will help our recovery. Now they're taking us to a pub? What d'ya think of that?"

"Yeah, it's strange they'd take addicts to a pub, but I guess it's for the music."

Welby looked at Reagan with soft eyes. She ignored a tug of something stirring within and shifted the focus elsewhere. "What about Charlie?" she asked.

"He just plays the spoons. Brought some from the kitchen. A little crazy, you know."

"No, Welby, spoons aren't crazy. That's part of Appalachian music, but what do you know?" She raised her nose just a little bit, walking right by him toward town, making sure to wiggle her hips good as she left to link up with Nikki and Abigail.

***

Welby: Strummin' on the Old Banjo

Welby'd watched Reagan as he eased his way along the quaint Irish street down to the pub for some traditional Irish music. He didn't quite know what to expect. Music had wrapped itself around his life when he was a little tyke. He'd found he could pick up the tunes easily, whether he knew them or not. Music helped express the sadness he felt over losing his mother, something he couldn't put into words. He also experienced the joy of love in a song, but this Celtic stuff never made his radar. He wondered if he'd be able to enjoy Irish music when he couldn't even sip a Guinness in the country that gave beer a good name.

George caught up with him, patted him on the back and asked, "How ya doin', Welby?"

"Doin' okay, man. Sure beats the pen. Travelin' the world? Not doin' bad, not at all," Welby said with a laugh, shaking his head.

"Yes, these women are something, bringing us halfway around the world to Ireland. Not on my bucket list, but who's complaining? Can't beat a free trip, no, sir," George said. "Have you noticed solar panels on some of the houses?"

"Yeah, man. Cool. They might need our services here, d'ya think?"

Welby asked. "Maybe we can drum up some business and come back?"

George laughed. "Speaking of drumming, I'm hoping someone in the pub will have a bodhran, the Irish drum. I played it once and I'd sure like to do it again."

In the pub, the musicians gathered in a circle, welcoming the Americans with great hospitality. The Irish folk led off with some jigs. Welby chorded it out, watching the guitar player. Sure enough, a woman played a bodhran, and she passed it to George a time or two. Like jammers everywhere, they passed the melody around the group. Once again Reagan impressed him with her ability to make her fiddle sing. Her fingers flew as she snapped the bow back and forth, putting him into a trance, casting a spell on him. She spun him plumb dizzy, and he had to stop playing for a while. But then the song came back, and he switched from chords to melody, finding his own fingers flying over the frets, matching the haunting melody that Reagan passed on. Tom led on the trumpet. Welby watched George pounding the bodhran, keeping them playing together. Welby felt the steady beat, the pulsating song, and lost himself in the community of it all.

After a while, the Irish musicians asked for the visitors to share their own music. Nikki sang a ballad or two. George and Tom led "When the Saints go Marching In." Welby wished he had the sax for that one. When his turn came around, he put down his banjo, pictured Whitney Houston and opened up his soul to sing her ballad from "The Bodyguard." As he neared the end, he watched Reagan's face, thinking maybe he'd touched her as he closed out, "If I should stay, I would only be in your way … I'll think of you every step of the way … and I will always love you …."Afterwards, the pub went silent.

That silence almost made him wonder how long it had been since he'd really sung a song, but he knew exactly. When they'd slammed the door shut in the pen five years ago, he stopped. No way would he sing in that sorry penitentiary, and he'd made up his mind to never sing when he got out, either. Didn't think he could feel it again. But here on foreign soil, where, truth be told, some of his ancestors might have been singing eons ago, he felt a shift, an urge to let his voice rip. That felt real good and made him happy. And others, too, it seemed.

Welby read admiration on the faces in the pub. He knew he had them hooked. He loved pulling at people's heartstrings. He made eye contact with each of the group leaders, one at a time, enjoying his gallery of support. Priscilla, Abigail, Katharine, Molly, all sitting there, hanging on his every word.

Molly spoke. "Welby, you been keeping a secret. You got some pipes going on there."

Welby shrugged. He gave Reagan a wink, blew a kiss, and said, "For all of you ladies."

Charlie ordered, "Hey, man, stop that."

Welby saluted Charlie, who put his spoons down. Maybe he had it goin' on for Reagan, too. Charlie's face turning red. He raised a fist and started to stand, motioning to Welby with a glare. But a man put a hand on Charlie's shoulder, urging him to sit down, and passed him a mug. Welby looked the other way, thankful for a peacemaker. Then he wondered what was in that mug. Wouldn't catch him squealing. No one seemed to notice. But would they really let him drink a beer like that? Nah, he decided, probably not.

Abigail asked to sing a song. She asked for the key of D. "Sing along," she said. Damned if Reagan didn't pick it right up on her violin. The song sounded Irish. Welby'd never heard it before. "My life flows on in endless song, above earth's lamentations... Since God is Lord of heaven and earth, how can I keep from singing?"

Welby found the chords and opened his voice again, harmonizing with Abigail. George joined in, and then Nikki crooned along with her Appalachian accent. For a few minutes, Welby felt lifted way above the moment, into a different place and time. Felt like back home in the church where he grew up, feeling God all around and the love of the people gathered. This shining emerald moment caught him singing again.

Then Grand MaMa spoke up again. "Mm hm. Mm hm. I been waitin' for this moment, Welby. God ain't finished with you yet. You got a song to sing, boy."

Welby wondered if anyone else heard. Seeing no evidence, he smiled and muttered under his breath, 'Yes, ma'am. Yes, ma'am. I think I will."

CHAPTER TEN
CORK, COBH, AND THE EASTERN PORT

Reagan does AA Ireland at Cobh
Reagan checked out the circle. AA Ireland? On foreign soil in the drinking capital of the world, AA? Abigail had said they'd throw in a few meetings. So here they were.

As she took her seat in the circle, she remembered the night before at the pub, when, in a few short hours, a circle of players became friends. She'd chatted with an accordion player from Russia, laughed with a fiddler from Finland, and accompanied an Irish singer and guitar player. A virtual United Nations. Welby's banjo had fit right in. And when he sang, "I will always love you," she'd had to fight the tears away. She'd danced to that song with Tyler, more than once. But she realized she could never go back to Tyler. On the other hand, Welby probably wasn't the answer either. Her daddy would never accept a Rosales supporter with a record.

***

The whirlwind trip was sailing by too quickly for Reagan. They'd traveled east from Dingle after breakfast, stopped at a national park for a hike in the late morning, and then enjoyed another Irish lunch at a restaurant before going on to Cork. After some shopping and a tour of the Waterford Crystal Factory, they landed at a hotel in the quaint port town of Cobh.

There had originally been an evening of Irish entertainment planned, but George volunteered to take the others to AA. Now they sat in a familiar AA circle with strangers, all with a common problem. Reagan pondered her own Irish roots. No one talked about addiction in her family, but she knew some liked to drink too much. Her grandmother had once complained about the drinking Reagan's daddy had done in college and how she'd worried if he'd even finish. Said he spent too much time at his fraternity house, drunk. Now and then, someone in the family would get picked up for OUI. But they managed to get off easy—that strings were pulled, she had no doubt— and everyone kept it quiet. Sometimes her parents argued when her daddy insisted on driving home after drinking too much. Was the addiction gene in her family tree? Had she inherited her curse from the Irish or had the addictive painkillers done her in? Maybe both?.

Her thoughts rambled while the group leader finished an introduction and led the serenity prayer. Reagan suddenly felt her own problems looming large. She wondered what she could do to change and heal her life. What couldn't she control? And how would she know the difference?

The leader interrupted her inner soliloquy. "Now, I know ye Americans be here t'night, and ye probably be askin' questions about AA Ireland, so I want to tell ye the story. After AA went to the States, back in 1946, they brought it over here. Ye all hear, I'm sure, o' the Irish love o' the drink. Perhaps ye don't hear so much about the Irish drunk? But in a country where we drink ale like water, quite a few struggle with addiction. 'Tis not healthy at all, you know. Aye, they say we carry a gene for alcoholism, many of us. In our DNA, ye know?

"So the story goes that an Irishman from Roscommon in the west of Ireland, Conor F., joined AA Philadelphia. On holidays back in Ireland, he wanted to start an AA group in Dublin, but ran into stone walls all around. They said the alcoholics lived in Northern Ireland and that Ireland already had a temperance society, Pioneer Association, if they drank too much. But then he met a lady, Eva Jennings, who introduced him to Doctor Norman Moore at Saint Patrick's Hospital in Dublin. Conor asked the good doctor to try AA on a patient he feared might be saddled for life. Doctor Moore told Conor, 'If you can help this man, I'll believe in AA one hundred percent.' Conor and that drunk set about to arrange the first closed meeting in Dublin two weeks later on November 18, 1946. Neither man was ever to drink again. Today, there are thirteen thousand AA members in Ireland with over seventy-five thousand meetings annually."

"Wow," Reagan exclaimed. "I had no idea. I thought you all knew how to drink over here."

"No, no," the leader said. "We suffer just like all of ye, we do. I pass."

Another spoke up. "My name is Ryan, and I'm an alcoholic."

"Hello, Ryan," the group answered.

"My family be drinking all the time. We be alcoholics, the whole lot of us. I'm the only one in AA and that's hard. They always want me to take a drink. They drink with breakfast, lunch, and supper; our way of life, they say. I'm so glad I have all of you. Thank you. I pass."

Reagan considered Ryan and all the Ryans she knew in the USA. None of them would ever be caught dead in AA, but now that she thought about it, probably quite a few of them needed it.

Nikki spoke up next, "I'm Nikki, and I'm an alcoholic and a drug addict."

"Hello, Nikki," the group responded.

"Out of high school, I traveled around with a rock band. Drugs and alcohol are just part of the way of life on that circuit. Before I knew it, I was hooked. I got busted and went to prison. It was there that I learned I have a disease. Now I'm learning I probably also have a genetic predisposition, just like Ryan said.

"We stayed with my relatives in Kinvarra a couple nights ago. One of them told me that a lot of our family have this problem, but they don't face it, like Ryan's. My cousin Aidan goes to AA. Even if it's in my DNA, I take responsibility for my choices and my ability to heal. I have to rely on God to pull me through, one day at a time. I pass."

Reagan listened to Nikki, thinking she could almost say the exact thing herself.

Then Charlie spoke. "It's not easy being here in Ireland. I messed up bad last night. I had a beer. How can you not have a beer at a pub? I just have to quit going to bars. That's what we call 'em in the States. I just messed up three years of sobriety. Today, I start over. With God's help and all of you, I can do this. One day at a time. I pass."

Welby asked, "Can I say something?"

The leader nodded. "Please do."

"I'm Welby and I'm a drug addict."

"Hello, Welby," they all said.

"All my life, until now, I've lived in North Carolina, what we call 'the South.' Down there, a Black man's got a bad rap, going back to slavery. Not a day goes by that I don't feel that. Although things opened up some with the civil rights movement, I still feel put down and spit out by the whites. So many Black men use drugs to ease the pain.

"But this is crazy, man, to hear all of you talkin' about your Irish alcoholic genes. I just found I got some Irish DNA myself. Do you think the white man gave me my disease? Gave me all that and now this? We're all in this together. One day at a time. I pass."

Reagan followed. "I'm Reagan, and I'm a drug addict."

"Hello, Reagan," the others said in unison.

She continued. "I'm with you, Welby. I got these Irish genes, too. In my family, alcohol and life go hand in hand. I never thought about that affecting me, but maybe that's what being Irish is all about for me. I pass."

George went next. "I'm George and I'm an alcoholic."

"Hello, George," the others responded.

"I don't think I have any addictive genes in my DNA, yet I got the disease. I don't blame it on my genes or the color of my skin. I take responsibility for my choices. Maybe I carry an alcoholic gene, but if so, my brothers didn't wind up like me. No, this is my own damn fault. But with God's help, I'm sober twenty years now. I pass."

The leader responded to George. "That's a very good point, George. In AA, we admit we made a mistake. We take responsibility for our addiction. Until we realize it's our own fault, we can't really begin to heal."

"But you don't know how they treat Black men in the USA," Welby said.

"Welby, it's your choice, man," George said. "Don't you get it? You can't blame your addiction on somebody else. You made that choice."

"But the doctors are prescribing too many pain meds, and then their patients get hooked. That's what happened to me. It wasn't my fault a drunk driver hit me and I needed pain meds. It was their fault," Reagan said.

"Well, you have a point there, but still, you made a decision to get illegal drugs at some point. You could have chosen withdrawal," George stated. "In AA, we take ownership of our mistakes and turn it over to God. Don't you think it's time, Welby? Reagan?"

Welby shrugged. Reagan wasn't convinced, either. She hadn't gotten into this situation because she'd asked for it. And now, realizing her Irish genes helped cause the problem as well, bolstered her feeling that it wasn't her fault.

The conversation continued for a good hour and then the leader closed it with the Lord's Prayer. As they left, Reagan watched George pull Charlie aside and heard him say, "Next time, you go home." Charlie'd broken the rules, but they gave him a second chance. George was going easy on him. She wondered why.

Reagan's mind raced on. She felt changes, shifts, new understanding. She itched to get back to her journal and write it all down. She needed to explore the idea that her addiction might really be her own fault.

Abigail and the MAMs do Cork

Seamus offered to take the MAMs and Tom out for a meal in Cork when the others left for the Cobh AA group. Molly wanted to debrief the trip and talk about how things were going. They selected a pub known for a traditional Irish food and music. On the road there, Seamus offered a few tidbits about the city. "And now, ladies and gentleman, we be entering Cork. In Gaelic, the name comes from the

Irish word 'craight', meaning marsh. This be a port town with water everywhere, including under the main streets which once were water ways. Founded eight hundred years ago, this city is a portal to the world, and to itself as well. Yacht clubs, music, even the first Ford factory on foreign soil you find here.

"Many an Irishman left this town for America. The Titanic made a last stop here before its fateful voyage. And did you know William Penn, Junior lived here, disgracing his father, a military man from London, by going pacifist on him, becoming a Quaker? Yes, he did. The lad who started Pennsylvania for ye. I bet ye didn't know he lived first right here in Cork.

"As a young man, he started feeling bad about his father's role in the colonization of Ireland. He decided to study war no more. A bright lad, yes," Seamus said. "Still find some of those Quakers around Ireland here and there. Some of my people, they are."

Abigail's eyes opened wide. She leaned back into her seat, even as she watched stars circling around Seamus. Seamus had Quaker roots? She knew most of the Irish belonged to the Catholic church. She felt the gates of her heart opening just a little more. She sat up and leaned forward. How could she get him alone? Perhaps later tonight? She entered the conversation, feeling like her life could begin again and knowing that it would.

"Seamus, tell us about these Irish peacemakers," she said. "And are you a Quaker as well?"

"Aye, that I am," he said. "We've been here, trying to make the peace, for centuries. Gave us a bit of work, they did, with the civil war, through my youth, right up until the '90s. We Friends always sent up peacemakers. Some came from the States as well. But tempers were strong. So glad they settled this for now. A lot of praying, and a lot of hard work."

Abigail wanted to know more but decided to wait. Instead, she asked, "Where are we going for dinner?"

"We be heading out to Oliver Plunket's place, where they have dinner and music every weeknight. They try to be like your Cheers place ... where everybody knows your name. We'll have some time to visit before the show starts. In fact, we're here now."

Soon they were seated in Oliver Plunket's in Cork, where a friendly waiter took orders, asking each of them their names. Once he completed the rounds, he departed, leaving them with time to catch up a bit on the whirlwind Irish roots tour.

Molly asked. "Is this trip helping our re-entry folks? What d'ya think?"

Sallie started laughing. "A trip to Ireland. Yep, that just about does it, don't you think? None of these four will ever go back to prison again."

Seamus interrupted. "Aye, once ye've been to heaven, you can't go back to hell, they say."

The man never ceased to amaze her. Abigail asked, "Is that an Irish saying?"

Seamus smiled. "Something like that, aye. Something like that me mother always told me. Whether it be Irish or just her good sense, I never knew."

"How do you measure success?" Katharine asked. "Do we do surveys? So many variables. We should hire a researcher. May be too late for this trip, but for the next one."

Abigail said, "Yes, we do have surveys, and probably they need improvement. Good idea, Katharine. We'll have to rely to some extent on anecdotal information, what our re-entry people tell us and write. But I think some significant stuff is happening. What do you think?"

Priscilla said, "Well, I see the most of Reagan, as we share a room. I think she's getting into her roots on this trip. Last night, she was so excited after playing her fiddle at that pub. We prayed together. I think she's really seeking God's help in healing."

"I'm bunking with Nikki," Jane said. "That experience with her cousin's son really hit home for her. To realize her Irish family struggles with addiction and that it may be related to her genes helps her. She was really happy they have AA here."

"I think we better keep an eye on Welby and Reagan," Tom said next. "I notice some energy flying between them. George has doused the sparks a few times. We changed the seating on the bus, but we need to monitor them carefully. We—they—are playing with fire."

"I don't think you need to worry about them," Molly said. "They're a hundred years apart on their political beliefs. Like oil and water. I don't think so."

"Opposites attract, ye know," Seamus said and winked at Abigail.

Tom nodded. "So true, so true. I know they argue about Steele and Rosales, but you must not be watching Welby watching her. Or Reagan checking him out. Jumping in the sack? First opportunity. Their sexual attraction is off the charts."

Molly laughed. "Tom, how do you know that? Really?"

"Remember, George and I are shacking up with Welby and Charlie. Men talk. Always have, always will. I know what I'm talking about."

Abigail said, "Okay, ladies, no sleeping on the job."

"Hear! Hear!" Jane lifted her Guinness mug and plopped it back down.

"Aye!" Sallie gave a salute. "And what's up with Abigail and Seamus?"

Abigail blushed; Seamus laughed. Sallie raised her eyebrows and Katharine smiled.

Seamus said, "Aye, ye can't stop love. Ain't no use in tryin'. You'll be fanning the flame, you will, if ye try to put it out. The wind blows where it will." And with that, he picked up his own mug. He put his other arm around Abigail and gave her a kiss on the cheek. "Here's to love. No, ye can't stop love. Ye can't. And don't ye be trying."

Abigail laughed, letting the warmth of Seamus send ripples into her heart space.

"Let the show begin," Seamus said, motioning toward the front of the room.

As if on cue, a man with scraggly red hair standing at the mic with a guitar hanging from his neck spoke up. "Good evening, ladies and gentlemen, and welcome to Oliver Plunket's, where everybody knows your name. Welcome to the MAMs Book Club traveling all the way from River City, Ohio, along with their man, Captain Thomas Mabra, just retired from the force. And their fearless guide, our good friend, Seamus O'Reilly. We'll start off here with a little jig for you, and please welcome our dancing friend, Gillian Murphy, over from Cobh way."

Abigail settled back in her chair to listen to the music and watch the dancing. For the next two hours, the band regaled those gathered with Irish jigs and ballads. Dancers kept popping out to kick along. Energy sizzled in the little bar. Abigail felt drawn into the joy of the Irish. She felt happy to know her people might come from a place just like this.

Toward the end of the night, they invited Seamus up on the stage to sing a few. He led with "When Irish Eyes are Smiling". As his rich tenor voice filled the room, Abigail fell just a little further under his spell. His Irish eyes landed on hers as he finished off, "and when Irish eyes are smiling, they'll steal your heart away." He punctuated the number with a little wink to her, sending a wee bit of his Irish magic into her soul. Then he surprised her by asking her up.

He introduced to her the crowd. "This be my new friend, Abigail Wesley, from River City, Ohio. She's going to sing the next number with me. I heard her a-singing this very song over in Dingle Town, so I know she owns the Irish pipes, she does. The rest of ye who know this song, please join in. It's a little tune called 'How Can I Keep from Singing?'"

Abigail felt goose bumps, along with a little stage fright. Although she'd sung regularly in church since her youth, this felt different.

Seamus seemed to sense her hesitation. "We're all family here. These be my nephews, Orion, Jupiter, and Mars. And my brother, Curtis, over there on sound. This be our living room. Just enjoy yourself, all of you, please."

Orion strummed a few chords, and Seamus began, with Abigail close behind. She found the alto to his tenor melody. She found the light in the dark room. She found a new partner and sang into the space of Oliver Plunket, wondering where this song and this evening and this trip might carry her. Ready to let it all happen. For the first time in many years, she felt fully alive. On the last verse, Seamus stopped singing to let Abigail close it out. She sang confidently. "Since love is Lord of heaven and earth, how can I keep from singing?"

After the last note, silence filled the crowded bar for just a moment before the MAMs began a standing ovation. Soon all of those around the room and at the bar were cheering as well. Jane held up her mug in a silent toast. Seamus surprised Abigail with a full hug and a kiss on the lips. The crowd cheered for more, but Orion closed the band down for the night.

When they returned to their bus, Abigail slipped in first, claiming a seat in the front, right behind Seamus. She perched on the edge of the seat by the middle aisle, not wanting to be displaced by any of the others.

Jane reached out to shake Abigail's hand as she entered. "You, my dear, are a star. We should be signing you up with a record label, then then you can finance our trips. What a voice."

Sallie followed and said, "Didn't I always tell you to do something with that voice of yours?"

"You guys." Abigail laughed. "I'm not all that, but thank you."

Molly bumped into Sallie. "Move along, please. This old lady needs to sit down." Abigail knew that since Molly'd completed her treatment for breast cancer, she received a clean bill of health, but still got tired a little more easily than before. "And sign me up for your fan club, Abigail. I'm with Jane. We need to find you a recording contract."

Next in, Priscilla continued the banter. "You can sing for God at my church. We need some more vocalists. Why don't you at least come as a guest soloist from time to time?"

When Katharine came in, she told Abigail, "I enjoyed your singing. You and Seamus make quite a pair." She giggled. "We'll have to get you two singing together again."

"I heard that," Seamus said as he followed Katharine in and closed the door. "That can be arranged. We will do more Irish music before we send you all back to the States." He started up the bus and drove them back to their lodging for the night.

Abigail felt excited. Her whole body tingled as she watched the man sitting at the driver's seat in front of her. He continued to surprise and delight her. She remembered the kiss, the way their voices combined into a beautiful space, and the twinkle in his eye when he'd introduced her. Taking a deep breath, she smiled. *What a night*, she thought. *What a night.*

A few minutes later, when Seamus pulled up to their hotel, he turned around and asked Abigail, "Can ye wait a minute? I'd like a word with ye, if ye have the time."

Abigail waited as the others filed out of the bus. Jane gave her a high five. Sallie gave her an a-okay sign, their longtime code for when things were good. Priscilla nodded and smiled as she passed by. Abigail wondered what Seamus wanted to talk about. Did he feel swept away, too? Her heart started beating faster in anticipation. She felt flushed, like a schoolgirl. She laughed at herself.

Soon Seamus joined her on the seat. "Thank you for waiting, Abigail. You're one fine lady, ye are. I'm finding myself wanting to know more about ye."

Abigail was nervous and couldn't quite find words. Finally, she managed a response. "What do you want to know? My husband died three years ago, but it feels like yesterday. You lost your wife, so you know what that's like, right?"

"Aye. Not a day goes by that I don't think of her." Seamus sighed and looked off into the distance. "But life goes on, though sometimes I hear her a-talkin' to me. She wants me to be enjoyin' my life. So here we are, Abby. I'm enjoying you quite a bit. I want to know everything about you. So tell me," he said. "I've got all the time in the world." He folded his hands on his belly and leaned back on his seat. "Tell me about you, Abby."

Abigail shrugged. "My life's rather simple. I went to college, married my college sweetheart, and he became a minister. We believed in living simply, as Quakers. We did farming as well. I became an environmentalist, not that it seems to be helping very much these days. We have two daughters and three grandchildren. What about you?"

"Ah. So now my little lady comes alive. I can imagine ye out there as a farmer's wife in the green fields. I like the picture, I do. See, there's so much more I want to know about ye, Abigail." Seamus yawned. "But it's late and we've got an early tour tomorrow to the castle. Perhaps we slip away into the enchanted forest for a bit while we're there and you tell me more about what's going on behind those blue eyes of yours." He laughed.

Abigail copied his yawn. "Sounds good. But tomorrow I want to hear your story, too. "

Seamus used his fingers to turn her chin toward him. "But I'm not leaving before I kiss you goodnight." He put his lips over hers and connected for a luscious moment. The sensation warmed Abigail's entire body all the way down to her toes.

"I'll look forward to walking with you in the enchanted forest at the Blarney Castle tomorrow," she said. Yes, and she might just be dreaming about him all night long.

Welby Sails

Welby woke up happy. The night before, Seamus had announced that he'd booked them onto a sunrise breakfast cruise at Cobh Harbor. They'd get a view of the southeastern coast before going north to Blarney Castle and then on to Dublin.

As their small cruise ship set sail into the sunrise, Welby thought about how he'd bad-mouthed Aunt Rosie for sending him up to Ohio. He owed her an apology. Always hard to eat crow, but he'd do it first thing when he returned to the States. He'd felt a time of reckoning at the AA group the night. He'd listened to George. He needed to own his mistakes and there were quite a few apologies he owed to the folk he wronged. Now he felt a new day dawning in more ways than one. For the first time in a long time, he started thinking about his old girlfriend, wondered if she still thought about him. He'd be apologizing to her, too, even though she'd probably found another man years ago, moving on without a backwards glance.

Seamus interrupted Welby's inner soliloquy just as he noticed Reagan bending over, picking up something off the deck. He smacked his lips and let out a whistle. She turned around and laughed. That woman would cause him big problems if he didn't just let her be. He did a one-eighty and faced the ocean again, listening to the information about the harbor.

Never one to mince words, Seamus continued to share information about the area. "The Irish never be too far from the sea, and many an Irish left off for America from this port back in the day. The Titanic docked here to pick up some ill-fated folk before heading up to encounter that iceberg. Those little boats be fishermen going out for their morning catch. We'll enjoy yesterday's catch for breakfast this morning. Ye'll be eating in just a little while. I'll stop my chattering so ye can catch a few photos of the sunrise, and then I'll meet back up with ye tell ye more."

Welby took his camera out of his bag. The generosity of their benefactresses continued to amaze him. He knew it was a cheap camera, but still. He stood and looked around for a good frame for a photo. There! A silhouette of Reagan with the sunrise on the horizon behind her. For some reason, she didn't have her camera up, but was gazing out across the water. Using the zoom, he snapped quite a few shots. She might be the painter in the bunch, but he was pretty sure that one of those photos would knock her pants off. His pulse raced as he imagined that sight. *Slow down, Welby,* he told himself. Then he focused on the big golden ball emerging from the water, bringin' it on, ushering in a brand-new day. "Hallelujah," he yelled.

"Don't tell me you got religion," Nikki yelled back.

"Oh, yeah," Welby replied. "Oh ,yeah. I got it all goin' on, babe. How can you keep from singing at a moment like this?" Then he laughed. "I think you got it all goin' on, too, sister."

After that, he relaxed into his seat for a little more to the history of the Irish, wondering once again about his people, where they'd lived and what they'd done. Then Ms. Abigail asked them to get out their journals and write about what all was going on in their heads. Welby searched deep within, and some serious stuff surfaced. He found himself connecting with the water, moving along the ocean, considering the passages of his life, considering the passages of his people from Ireland, from Africa to the USA, and then considering his own passage back as well.

Ms. Abigail rang her little bell. They went down to the lower level of the small boat to a table spread with food, the fish that Seamus promised, along with blood sausage and eggs, a food that seemed to grace every Irish breakfast. Potatoes and scones waited for them also, with some good Irish coffee. Welby filled up his plate and they sat around a long table to eat.

"Now," Abigail said, "if you're willing, share some of your thoughts this morning. We're about halfway through our journey. It's hard to believe that in three more days, we'll be heading home. We've seen the west coast, now the east. What do you make of all of this?"

Everybody got real quiet. Maybe nobody else would talk, but Welby wanted to share. Years back, he could rap as good at the next guy, Today, that voice came back. He stood up and said, "Be something big for me, this trip. I wrote a rap.

"You call me Black?

"You see my skin, shining, polished, oiled, the color of night.

"That make me bad? That give you fright?

"You call me Green?

"No, you don't, because you ain't read my DNA.

"But I spit into a bottle and I'm coming up Irish, they say!

"Listen to the past.

"You'll see my ancestors crossing those waters, just to be.

"Some bad DNA, Irish, African, yes! All me!

"They survived the Atlantic, survived famine and being sold.

"You see black and green make me precious, makes me something, makes me gold."

Welby sat and they all began to clap. He felt a little foolish, but they smiled at him.

George slapped him on the back. "Didn't know you had it in you, man."

Tom complimented him, too. "You got it goin' on, Welby. That's some bad rap."

Then Molly put her thumbs up. "You know, Welby, we hoped this trip would help you live into your future. We hoped it might offer you courage. Just when I began to think we were crazy, there you go and lay it all out. Yes. That's what I'm talking about. Exactly."

Welby tried dismissing their accolades. "It's not all that. Just a little rap. That's all."

"But, Welby, do you understand? You're making us happy," Abigail said. "Finding your roots is making you strong. That's exactly what we hoped."

Welby shrugged and then nodded. He looked at Reagan, but she didn't have anything to say. Nor did Charlie or Nikki. Maybe they thought he was showing off.

But then Nikki spoke up. "Welby, could I make a song out of that?"

"Only if you rap it. Don't be goin' all country on me," Welby teased.

Nikki laughed. "Right, I do rap. No worries. We'll work it out." She looked at her journal. "Something about Ireland just seems to make me want to sing." Then she started singing her morning composition:

"Shoreline... waters rippling... new day rising... I am here...

"Sober to enjoy the sun rising... Sober and happy... Full of good cheer.

"My Irish people be smiling, the leprechaun's starting to dance.

"I raise my sails for journey, nothing happens by chance."

That's just the chorus, I think," she said. "I pass."

"We're not in AA, Nikki," Reagan said.

Welby looked at Reagan with a snarl. What put a burr up her butt? Jealousy? "Reagan, stop," he told her, then turned to Nikki. "I like it. I like it. Very nice, baby."

Welby glanced back at Reagan. A little jealousy turned her into one ugly lady. But he had to admit, if she didn't like Nikki getting all his attention, that might not be a bad thing, not bad at all. He watched a shadow grow across her face. Was that a tear? Had he caused that? Boy, if he intended to make amends for the old stuff, he sure didn't want any new stuff hanging over his head. "Reagan, it was a joke. I didn't mean you to get all upset on me. I know you were jokin', too. AA chatter. That's all. You're funny. Don't cry, darlin'."

She choked out a few words. "It's not you, Welby. It's me."

"Do you want to talk about it?" Abigail asked.

"Everything hit me this morning," Reagan confessed. "I realized how badly I've messed up my life. Up to now, I blamed everybody but myself, thinking I'm better than the rest of you. I came from privilege, and I flaunt it. I'm a nurse, but I never planned to be working as a servant to the sick in that hospital for very long.

"Then this morning, I heard the words of Jesus. He said, 'The first shall be last and the last shall be first.' He said, 'Blessed are the poor in spirit, for they shall inherit the earth. If you want to be great, you should be a servant. It's harder for a rich man to get into heaven than for a camel to get into the eye of the needle.' That was a small pass in the desert— not actually a needle. Well, anyway, I don't know why all these verses came up to me. Maybe I heard a sermon once about them, but, before, it just sort of floated over me. I sat here thinking about my early ancestors, probably fleeing Ireland because they were starving. I thought about how poor we really all are. I'm just like the rest of you. And God loves us all. God forgives me. That's all,"

"Oh, baby," Welby said. "You told it, you did. You said it all. Go ahead and cry. Sometimes you just gotta get it all out."

Reagan sniffled. Jane passed her a tissue, and she dried her face.

Abigail said, "Thanks for sharing what's in your heart, Reagan."

Priscilla piped up. "Yes, honey, thank you for being so honest. You know, we all make mistakes. All of us fall short. But you're way ahead, being willing to confess your sins. I'll be praying for you."

Abigail said, "Anybody else? It's about time to go."

"Well, I guess I better speak my mind," Charlie said. He stood up, surprising the group. "I, too, have a confession to make. I've been proud of my Irish heritage. I've been downright proud of being a white man as well. Ever heard of the Aryan Nation? Ever heard of white supremacists? Well, I've been proud of all that.

"But this morning, I looked at the ocean and realized I'm just a drop. I understood that Reagan and Welby and Nikki and me are all part of that Irish sea. Welby is as black as night, but that doesn't make him so different. I'm ashamed. I'm sorry. Welby, will you forgive me?"

"Okay," Welby said. "If we Black folks refused to forgive you white folks, we'd be a sorry bunch. Why you think we go to church all the time, brother? It's not easy puttin' up with that white mess. It's not easy puttin' up with cops shooting our kids. It's not easy being put down, ignored, and called stupid. No sir, not easy. So, when someone apologizes? We appreciate you, just so long as you don't go back to that mess. Thank you, Charlie, for fessin' up and for wantin' to change. Thank you. I forgive you."

Abigail looked at her watch. "Oh, my. Thank you all, but I think we better stop."

Seamus agreed. "Gather your things so you'll be ready when we arrive back at the dock. We're heading on in now. We'll be on the bus to Blarney Castle in no time."

Welby made sure he had his stuff, and then gazed back over the harbor and on out to sea. He figured it would be a long time before he came this way again.

The words of his rap came back to him now. I be gold. His thoughts wandered back to a sermon years ago. We all are part of the royal priesthood, the priesthood of all believers.

Back there in that little white church down home, Welby'd heard God calling, but he'd shook it off. Now the voice came back. Ready or not, here I come! But this wasn't a game of tag — or maybe it was. Here God comes again. Oh, no. Here He comes. And then if Jesus didn't just appear again out there in a fishing boat. Welby remembered his words. "I will make you fishers of men."

Welby glanced around to see if anybody else saw the Lord out there. Nope, looked like they were all packing up and getting ready to get off the boat. Nikki seemed to be looking in that direction, but didn't pay Jesus no attention. She couldn't be hearing the guy. Right. First Grand MaMa, and now Jesus? Maybe those drugs had messed with his head.

CHAPTER 11
THE GIFT OF BLARNEY

The MAMs Do Blarney – Abigail Kisses the Stone

After the sunrise cruise, they returned to the hotel. The short drive gave Abigail time to think. So far, she considered the trip a success, although how much connecting with their Irish roots would make a difference for the men and women in their programs, she couldn't be sure. Certainly, Nikki'd enjoyed meeting her family in Kinvarra, and Reagan talked about her family history. Welby seemed to get it. This morning, they'd all seemed to have some spectacular moments on the boat.

She also considered her own hope for new perspectives on Celtic Christianity. She hadn't heard it yet. With another monastery and a retreat center to go, she hoped for something more. Today, they'd tour Blarney Castle, an iconic travel destination. Everyone could kiss the Blarney Stone and receive the gift of gab—even though most of them had gotten that years ago, she told herself jokingly.

Her last trip with her husband to Ireland floated into her mind. The children off to college, they'd finally had time for themselves. She remembered enjoying the gardens around Blarney Castle; laughing at the fairy gardens, going backward down some witch's stairs, admiring shamrocks, being spooked by the poison garden, enjoying native plants, kissing Jon in the enchanted forest.

Last night, she'd kissed Seamus, more than once. The first man since Jon. She took a deep breath. She'd never thought she'd love again, but her reservations seemed to be slipping away. Soon she would walk into the enchanted forest with this new man. Then, in a few short days, Seamus and Ireland would be a memory. What was she thinking?

She tucked her confusion away and became a leader. "Pack up. Get your bags to the bus in thirty minutes," she told the group. "We want to get there early, to avoid a line. We will tour the castle, kiss the Blarney Stone, and then you'll have an hour to explore."

The group scattered. Abigail went to finish packing. She whispered a prayer of thanks for the sunny skies and a cool breeze. They'd been blessed with good weather on this trip. Their week seemed remarkably dry on an island where rain often came daily.

Back on the bus, the MAMs sat in the front for a little catch-up. "So," Abigail started, "what have you liked so far about Ireland?"

"I always love traveling," Sallie said. "You all are my favorite part! And I love the ocean. Watching the waves at the Cliffs of Moher. Walking by the water in Kinvarra at sunset. Following the coast on the Dingle Peninsula tour, a view of the sea around every turn. This morning's sunrise breakfast cruise. Absolutely fabulous. So cool to be on an island."

"My favorite parts are the colorful little towns," Priscilla said. "Our guide said the government conducted a contest, to paint their houses cheerful colors for the tourists. Isn't that sweet?"

"I've appreciated our very knowledgeable tour guides," Katharine said. "The Newgrange visit, the Clonmacnoise Monastery, the Dingle peninsula tour, all very informative about the history and people of Ireland. I've been here several times, but I'm learning even more. Thank you, Abigail, for lining up such good guides and for finding Seamus."

Abigail blushed. "Yes, I found Seamus. He can take credit for the rest." She patted him on the back. He smiled. "And thank you, Jane. Are you enjoying the trip?"

Jane put her thumbs up. "A fine time with all of you ladies. I really enjoyed the night of music at the Dingle pub. Made me want to get out my guitar again. Quite a group of musicians we have here." Then she turned around. "What's up with Reagan and Welby back there?"

They all turned to look at once. Welby sat alone, in the first of the male rows. Reagan was sprawled out with her legs across the seat in the last of the female rows and had her arm propped on top, engaged deep in conversation with Welby.

"Oh, boy," Abigail said. "We have to keep George and Tom on that. Should we have them move now?"

Just then, Seamus pulled up to the front entrance of Blarney Castle. He opened the door, leaving their discussion hanging as they filed out for their trip to the stone.

"This is like a garden estate," Priscilla exclaimed as they entered the castle grounds.

"Yes, quite lovely," Sallie agreed.

Seamus ushered them toward the castle. "Ye want to get in line to kiss the stone first, and then ye can explore all the rest. If we wait, the line gets a wee bit long and then we'd be a-spendin' all of our time a-waitin', we would. Follow behind and I'll have ye there in no time."

Abigail walked over to Reagan and asked, "You've been here before?"

"Yes, several times," Reagan said.

"So you already got the gift of gab?"

"Right," Reagan said. "Silly, but I still kiss it every time."

"What's that all about?"

Seamus overheard. "Ah, the Blarney Stone. Ye want to know, eh?"

Abigail nodded, enjoying Seamus' responsiveness. He continued. "Well, with the Blarney Stone, we have many legends, and you can't be quite sure where the truth lies. Aye, and that's the way the blarney be, ye know." He laughed.

"One legend tells us that Cormac Laider McCarthy, the man who built this castle back in the fifteenth century, faced a lawsuit, so he sought help from the Goddess Cliodhna. She told him to kiss the first stone he found on the way to court, and so he did. When he pleaded his case with great eloquence, he won. He took that stone back to use in building the castle. So now they be a-sayin' that the stone helps you to deceive without offending.

"But some think the stone traveled to Scotland and then back to the emerald shore. Others tell ye that Robert the Bruce of Scotland gave it over to Cormac McCarthy for help at the Battle of Bannocburn. Yea, or this be the Stone of the Scone, always present for crowning kings and queens of the British Isles. The modern ones say it's all blarney. So ye just have to wonder."

Sallie asked, "What exactly is the gift of gab? What will I get? Tell me again why I should kiss this stone?" She laughed. Her belly shook and soon all the MAMs were laughing.

Seamus chuckled right along. "Were you a-listenin' to my story, lassie?"

Sallie said, "I heard the story, but I don't understand. This will help me win court cases? My church doesn't believe in suing people. So what do I have to gain?"

Seamus chuckled again. "Oh, I see, I see. What kind of religion is that?"

"Church of the Brethren," Sallie said. "A peace church, like you Quakers, you know?"

"Oh, yes, ye be one of us, then, aren't ye?" Seamus said. "A small world here. Abigail's a Friend, and yer a Brethren. Ye just never know who'll turn up, do ye?" Seamus stopped for a breath before saying, "What do ye get for kissin' the stone? Hard to say exactly. P'rhaps ye'll find ye can talk yer way out of a spot. Not that they'll always believe ye, mind." He chuckled. "Then again, they might just tell ye 'That's a crock o' blarney.'"

Sallie laughed. "Oh, yes. When I was a teacher, my students gave me that. Dogs ate homework, parents made them go to bed."

"Right," Seamus said. "So the stone be offerin' help for the tongue-tied. Ye know, it helped this auntie and that cousin and this grandpa over the years. Once ye get an Irish storyteller gabbing, it's like a snowball rolling down the hill. Yet sometimes, all ye need is to believe ye can do somethin' and then ye can. So it will help ye, if ye think it will."

"Oh, I see," Sallie said. "We call that a self-fulfilling prophecy. I'll kiss the stone. It might come in handy someday."

"Good, good," Seamus said. "Why come to Ireland and miss out on the blarney? Let's be on with it then. As we head up through the castle, ye can learn some medieval history. Read about the pictures on the wall. Before your country was born, McCarthy built this castle, in 1446."

The group wound its way among the stone ruins of the ancient building. Climbing stairs, traversing dark hallways, imagining former inhabitants, here, sleeping quarters there; a large banquet room depicted in an artist's rendering on the wall. Now and then, there were openings to the sky and portals to the gardens below. On the castle's top floor, they came to the line of tourists waiting to kiss the stone.

Seamus directed. "So watch now how this be done. Lie down, hold on to the bars, lean back and upside down, and give it a kiss. Who wants to go first?"

Reagan said, "I can show them how it's done." She stepped forward.

Welby said to George, "Does she think she's somethin' or what?"

"I heard that, Welby," Reagan said. "I've been here before. I'm just trying to help."

"Right, okay," Welby said. "Show us how to do it, baby." He took his hand and rotated it, bowing to Reagan and announcing. "Hear, hear! The queen of the castle will teach her minions how to kiss the rock. Watch closely, peasants. Let's see if she uses her tongue or brushes it with her cheek. Will she pucker up and keep the connection going long enough to feel that geological sensation? We don't know how—"

George interrupted. "Enough, Welby. That's enough."

Seamus broke the uncomfortable silence that followed. "Thank you, Reagan, for volunteering to go first. Show them how to do it. A bit awkward for first timers, for sure."

Abigail perused the stone courtyard. They stood next to a metal fence on the flat roof. Parapets decorated the wall. Never a fan of heights, she kept her distance from the short walls so she didn't have to look down and see just how high they were. In her experience, builders placed an important stone as a cornerstone on ground floor.

She wondered why they'd put this one at the top. She watched Reagan. First, she stretched out on a mat, hanging out over an opening, close to the stone. Then she grabbed two vertical metal bars and the guide encouraged her to slide a little closer to the wall. Reagan tilted her head back, reached her neck out a bit, and kissed the stone.

Abigail chuckled. She'd done this before, but had forgotten just how you get the gift of gab. People are crazy, silly, but so fun, she decided. She felt the warm touch of Seamus' hand on her arm, pulling her back while the others moved forward. The others pursued Blarney while Seamus pursued her. He whispered, "Ye be the one I want to kiss, my lady." And he totally surprised her by placing his lips firmly on hers, holding the connection just long enough to wake up some dormant sexual energy.

But then Welby yelled, "What's good for the goose is good for the gander. No kissin' allowed." Abigail grimaced, embarrassed.

George quickly told him to be quiet, and Seamus didn't seem ruffled. He told her, "Don't mind him." She took a deep breath and decided to ignore Welby and focus on the incredible man beside her. His soft blue eyes gently met hers, and he said, "Now that's the kiss I'm talkin' about. That's what I'm lookin' for. I like ye, Abigail. You're gettin' under me skin, ye are."

She smiled. The man literally took her breath away. Just like him, all she really wanted to do was to kiss, again and again. But she fulfilled her obligation and kissed the stone. Suddenly she felt energy pulse through her entire body. Seamus offered his hand to help her stand up and said, "Now ye've got the gift of gab. What have ye to say?"

She brushed her lips with her hand. "Just like that?"

"Aye, my sweet," Seamus replied. "Just like that."

"Wow." Words escaped her . Between the energy of the Blarney Stone and the energy of Seamus' kiss and eyes, she felt herself being lifted into a brand-new world. "Oh, wow," she repeated, taking Seamus's hand as they began climbing down the castle stairs into the garden. She looked at him, feeling another surge of energy as their eyes met. He caressed her soul without a word. "Later," she said. "I want to talk to you."

"Oh, yeah," he said. "Later, my dear."

Welby does Blarney

When their tour bus pulled up to Blarney Castle, Welby felt resigned to being alone. Reagan hung out in the seat in front of him, talking a little, but, clearly, he'd not won her over yet. Then Abigail explained they'd split the men and women up for the tours, but first they'd all kiss the stone. He stepped off the bus and gave Reagan a wink right before she headed to the front of the line. Perhaps with the gift of gab, he'd talk himself into her arms—if he could get her alone. He chatted with Charlie, biding his time.

"Done any buildin'?" he asked. "Looks like you got some muscles goin' on there."

"Tell me about it. I grew up building stuff with my old man and his construction company. Yeah, man, I done that. Every day, every day of my life, until I took a tour to the pen."

"Ever build a castle?" Welby laughed. "How'd they even do this way back then?"

"No, can't say I have. Built a stone house a time or two. We worked over in Texas. Man, they got hot summers. They like these limestone houses over there in the Hill Country. I don't care if I never go to Texas again. Wore me out," Charlie said.

"I bet it did," Welby said. "Probably keeps them cool, though. How d'ya think they cut these stones?"

"Good question, Welby. Ask Seamus."

Welby tried to imagine builders seven hundred years ago putting this castle together. Had they been slaves like his people? Sure did a good job, just like his ancestors did one helluva job with cash crops, making the damn masters the richest tyrants in the land. A few rich people controlling all the goods, making the rest of the people toil with sweat. Probably wasn't no different here.

As they climbed the castle steps, Welby started panting, and made a mental note to start working out again when they got back home. He hoped they reached the stone soon. Then Seamus pulled the group over for a little talk, giving Welby time to catch his breath.

Once again, Reagan started showing off. Why did he even care about this spoiled rotten lady, so full of herself? He decided to have some fun, but as soon as he got going, George cut him off. So he had to watch her as, lying on that mat, stretched out, head upside down, she kissed the rock.

Welby couldn't stop himself. "Oh, yeah. Show us, baby, how it's done. Mmm-hmm."

George interrupted him again. "Welby, I said enough."

Welby mumbled, "Sorry, sir." He turned his head away and tried to let it go. She was a pretty face, a nice body, a beautiful behind. And, yeah, deprivation could do things to a man. But consorting with the enemy? She stood for everything he hated. Just because they shared African and Irish blood didn't mean they had a future.

And he knew better. If there was one thing his ebony sisters hated, it was a brother going after a white thing. Betrayal of the first order.

"Good riddance, darlin'," he muttered aloud to the long-gone Reagan as he approached the mat. But when he stretched his legs out, all he could see was that damn woman stretched out as well. He could not get her out of his head. He grabbed the bars, kissed the stone, and wished for magic—a miracle, really.

Oh, man, he thought. *Oh, man.* He stood tall, but still felt upside down and out of whack. *What a trip. They brought me halfway around the world to kiss some stupid stone?* And then he remembered. *I've got this white Irish blood now. What did that mean?* He really needed a snort. This stuff made him crazy. No drugs, no women, traveling in a foreign land; he didn't even know himself anymore.

He turned around and spied that old guy, Seamus, kissing Abigail. His pent-up frustration got the best of him and he yelled, "What's good for the goose is good for the gander. No kissin' allowed."

George gave him a look, and Welby felt bad. He shouldn't have said it, but it just didn't seem right. Not fair at all, but par for a Black man. He apologized and hung his head, following George down the steps and back out of the castle. As they walked through the stone rooms—solid, but empty and sort of cold—he felt that ice inside. Felt himself freezing up, shutting down, clamming up, goin' within. Putting one foot in front of the other, he tried to get things right. But his world had spiraled out of control, leaving him upside down, inside out, and plumb confused.

George and Tom led the way. Welby, right behind, matched Charlie's stride, but didn't want to shoot the breeze. He'd seen Charlie's confederate flag ankle tattoo and his belly button swastika decor. *Charlie might say he's past all that now, but could he switch up so fast?* Next time they were alone, he'd ask if Charlie if he planned to cover up that racist tattoo.

They walked into the native plants garden and lo and behold if Welby didn't see a familiar old Black woman standing there with a frown on her face and shakin' her finger straight at him. He practically jumped out of his skin. He looked at Charlie to see if he saw her. *Charlie ain't seen nothing. How did she get over here?* Charlie seemed focused on the path ahead. Grand MaMa started in on Welby in her loud and demanding voice. Wasn't no getting away from her.

Welby stopped and waited while the rest of them went on. He folded his arms, tilted his chin, and he waited. She had thousands of lectures up her sleeve.

"Welby, Welby, Welby," she told him now. "You be some piece of work. What your problem, son? What kind of negative talk do I hear coming out of that big mouth of yours? What you doin' looking down? What you doin' bad-mouthing white people just 'cause they ain't treating you right? What you doin' going so glum on me? Didn't you just see Jesus, boy? One moment, the Lord's walking on water to be by your side and the next, you be actin' like your life's worthless. No, sir. I beg to differ. You be gold. You got it right earlier, and Jesus came to visit to let you know that, too. So you just shape on up now and take this second chance. You be on a trip of a lifetime. Make it all work. I'm countin' on you, boy. You represent our family and I want you to do us proud. You hear? You hear, Welby?"

Welby muttered, "Yes, ma'am." As soon as he did, she slipped off into the mist.

George called, "Welby? You back there? Stay up with the rest of us, please."

"I'm comin'," Welby answered. "I'm a-comin'." He broke into a little jog and hurried down the path. He thought about Jesus as he ran, about how they killed Jesus, and then he thought maybe he just needed to get over it. Grand MaMa was right. He needed to focus on the gold, the opportunity, the possibilities.

Reagan does Blarney

Reagan felt good. When she'd kissed the Blarney Stone, her body'd come alive, making her feel happy. She loved Ireland, but had felt somewhat down this visit. When her lips touched the stone, she felt brand new. She skipped down the stairs, ready to explore with the women.

"Can we go to the Rock Close trail?" she asked Jane. "It's an enchanted forest."

"Abigail's the boss," Jane said. "Seamus took the men, and we ladies are with Abby here. Can we get enchanted, Abby?"

Sallie sang, "Some enchanted evening—"

Abigail interrupted. "Please, no singing, Sallie. Sure, we'll follow this sign to the Rock Close Trail."

Sallie pouted. "Why can't I sing? What's life without a song?"

"Sallie," Abigail said, "we're not here on a choir tour, and besides—"

"I know," Sallie said. "I can't carry a tune. But how can I keep from singing?"

Abigail laughed, then Reagan. In seconds, ripples of laughter spread through them all.

"I love going out with the girls," Reagan said.

"Then let's get going, ladies," Abigail said. "Let's make the most of our time."

Sallie linked arms with Abigail and put Reagan on her other side. "We're off to see the wizard," she sang out in her slightly off-key, scratchy voice.

Abigail humored her and picked it up from there. "The wonderful Wizard of Oz."

Reagan laughed at them and sang, "Because, because, because … because of the wonderful things he does." She said, "Let's synchronize our steps like the munchkins." Together, they took a step to the left, then crossed their left legs over their right ones and took another step. Soon they were walking quickly, in sync, toward the Rock Close Trail. Not to be outdone, Nikki, Jane, and Molly hooked arms and followed suit behind. Priscilla and Katharine brought up the rear much more sedately, in character only with themselves.

When they arrived at the tunnel leading to the trail, Reagan appointed herself tour guide. She loved this part of the castle grounds and knew it like the back of her hand. She said, "Okay, ladies, here we go. Through the tunnel and into a fairy land, where magic dances and shamrocks shine. Here, the rocks hold clues of the past, witches still haunt, and fairies play."

They stopped at a waterfall. "Photo op, ladies," Reagan said. "Have you ever seen a greener place? No wonder we associate green with the Irish, huh? Notice the shamrocks. Can you believe it? They're actually growing here. It's magical."

"Cool," Sallie said. "Will you take my picture with my old buddy Abby?"

"You got the 'old' right," Jane quipped.

Reagan grabbed Sallie's camera. "You'll love this! There's a rainbow in the mist."

Sallie sang, "Somewhere, over the rainbow—"

"The glass is cracking," Jane yelled.

Sallie laughed and stopped her song. "Spoilsport."

"Let's go," Reagan said. "No bickering. And now, the witch's stairs. If you walk backwards down and then up the stairs with your eyes closed, your wish will come true."

"Break your neck and your dream comes true? Right. Not me," Sallie protested.

"I'm in, Reagan," Abigail said. "Worth a try."

"Let's take turns," Molly suggested. "We can guide another so we don't trip and fall. We need each other to achieve our dreams."

"Awesome," Reagan responded.

Abigail said, "Make a wish and share. Speaking your hope brings it alive."

"I thought you have to keep wishes secret," Sallie said.

Reagan said, "Whatever. Keep it secret if you think that will help."

"This trip changed me. I wish to fall in love and get married," Abigail announced.

"Hah! You mean Seamus is changing you," Sallie said. "You go, Abigail. Great to see you smiling again. I want to mentor another woman from prison. Thomaseena turned out so well."

"That can be arranged, I bet." Reagan smiled. "I want to get my life back together. I messed up royally, but after kissing the stone today? I am ready. I'll ask the witch to help, but really, I'm asking God, and I know God will help me."

Priscilla agreed. "Yes, it's God who will help us realize our dreams. I want to help my friends start another farm re-entry house in Columbus."

"Cool," Reagan said. "Anything else?"

"I'm with Priscilla," Molly answered. "My dream is to clone our triple bottom line businesses and take them national. I'm not sure how, but that's my wish."

Nikki spoke next. "I want to keep singing and writing songs, with a drug-free band."

"You go, girl," Reagan said. "I'll be your fan. You've got talent."

"Okay," Jane said. "If you're all dreaming on me, here's what I want. Somehow, we gotta cure the divide in our country. This has gone on long enough, ladies. Don't you agree?"

"For sure, Jane," Katharine agreed. "I thought we were the greatest country on Earth, but now our Congress seems stalled out. They can barely keep the country going, let alone lead us into the future. We need to reunite and get the job done."

"Yes, we do," Reagan said. "For me, I'm looking to President Steele to lead the way. Just pray for him. He's got this. Now, ladies, let's do the stairs, and let this old witch help us out."

"Good luck with that," Molly muttered, looking at Katharine as they all waited in line.

"Just wait," Reagan said. "Give him time. Give him four years. It's not an easy job."

Katharine chuckled nervously. "I don't see Ace Steele talking unity here."

"You got that right," Sallie said.

"Let it go," Abigail said. "Let's have some fun, ladies."

"Right-o, boss," Sallie said and laughed. "Maybe I will try this after all." She paired with Abigail and they took the lead. Reagan and Priscilla took a turn. Nikki and Jane came next. Molly and Katharine went last. While the pairs did the steps, Abigail suggested it would be a good time for the rest to journal. Reagan watched Abigail close her eyes and smile, then write in her journal, and thought she must be off somewhere in dream land.

Afterward, Reagan led them, saying, "Onward! To the fairy

houses. Let's go. Use your imaginations and you'll see fairies dancing in their neighborhood of tiny houses."

"Precious," Priscilla exclaimed.

When they came to another marker, Reagan pointed out, "Here is the Druid's Circle of stones. The Druids were medicine men."

"Is this a thin place?" Priscilla asked. "Where you can see through the veil to heaven?"

"I think so," Abigail said. "Maybe my husband Jon can hear us here. Could we pray?"

"Yes," Reagan said. "Let's hold hands."

The women formed a circle, joining hands. Reagan prayed. "Dear God, we thank you for this trip to learn about our roots, encounter new experiences, and dream. We pray you'll bless each of us and grant our wishes. May our dreams come true."

Her words brought a chorus of Amens.

Abigail looked up at the heavens and said, "I love you, Jon." Then she asked the others, "Do you think Jon would like Seamus?"

"For sure," Sallie said. "Seamus is a nice guy, and you know Jon would want you to be happy."

Reagan silently agreed, thinking about her own experience of the day. Much later, when they returned to the bus to drive to Glendalough, Reagan thought about the Druid's Circle, kissing the Blarney Stone, and the enchantment of Rock Close. She was excited that her life finally seemed to be coming back together. She would remember forever this day as a turning point, a bridge, a pivotal moment. She whispered, "Praise God."

CHAPTER 12
WICKLOW MOUNTAINS AND GLENDALOUGH

Riding North with Seamus – Abigail

The crew packed back into the bus, heading north according to schedule. Seamus distributed box lunches, saying, "Now eat up, then catch a little shut-eye, and I'll have ye up to the mountains by early afternoon. We'll stop for some sights, then move on to the monastery of Glendalough by three thirty. We'll visit the lakes and the ruins, if you like. Now, mates, relax and leave the driving to me." The bus clipped along the highway, traveling faster than they had in days.

Abigail munched on her sandwich, doubting she could sleep with her mind in high gear and her heart beating up a storm as well. She kept her eyes on Seamus, even as he focused on the road ahead. She wondered if he often developed relationships with his tourists. She felt a special bond with him, but wondered how he really felt. Flashing back to his kiss at the Blarney Stone, she decided he must be feeling this, too. Because they'd split the women and men from there, she never got to walk into the enchanted forest with him. She wanted to get him alone again. Abigail felt a stream of words surging up, words she wanted to share with Seamus. Would she remember them all when the time came? She laughed. *How could I have all these feelings for this man I've only known for three days? Was this for real, or just temporary Irish magic?*

Just as she closed her eyes, determined to nap, she heard a familiar voice. She looked up to see the little green guy perched right up in front, next to Seamus, but looking straight at her. Seamus paid him no mind. The leprechaun gave her a thumbs-up and a silly grin.

"What are you doing here?" she asked, somewhat indignantly. She felt self-conscious. One, because she sounded so upset, and, two, because she worried others could hear.

"Ah, I get around. Just popping up when ye least expect it, I do," the little man said.

"Why here? Why now?"

"Ah, my little lassie. I be here to congratulate ye on your new love.

Here ye are with us on the Emerald Isle and today ye kissed both the Blarney Stone and the good Irish man. Making connections with ye ancestors, with our green place, and now with the Irish himself. That's what ye be searching for, even if ye didn't know it. And it's more than just a passing fancy, don't ye think?"

Abigail did a second take as, without warning, he evaporated into thin air. A kiss from Seamus, a kiss of the Blarney Stone, and now another visit from the leprechaun? This trip to Ireland would be etched into her psyche for years to come. She watched the passing cars. They graduated from the little roads to a regular highway. She peered over Seamus' shoulder, trying to read the speedometer, but didn't ask.

"You okay?" Seamus asked. "I thought I heard you say something. And now you're checking my speedometer?" He laughed. "Never met a woman who didn't tell me how to drive. Trust me, Abby. I'm zipping along to get you where you need to be before the sun sets. Don't worry your pretty head. I'll deliver you, safe and sound."

Abigail smiled. "I'm fine. I just can't sleep. The others follow directions better than me." Sallie snored beside her; Priscilla and Nikki were out cold, across the aisle. She really didn't see anyone talking. Even Welby slept, in the seat behind Reagan.

Seamus chuckled. "Keep me company to pass the time for us both. Ye've been here before?"

"My husband and I took a day trip from Dublin when we visited Ireland," she answered. "We stopped in the Wicklow Mountains and Glendalough, a long time ago. Our bus driver talked about movie stars and famous people who lived there. A few fables about Saint Kevin. I wanted to know about the Celtic spiritual traditions, but he talked about the movies.'

"Aye. We like to brag about the movies. You Americans like Hollywood, so we tour guides give ye what we think ye want. Let's see … *P.S. I Love You*, filmed by a bridge up in the mountains. And the Guinness family owns land, and there hasn't been a working monastery for hundreds of years, so fable is what we have. But I'll talk up the Celtic Spirit for ye, Abby."

"Thanks, Seamus," Abigail said. "We only have two more nights. Tonight, at the Holy Well Retreat Center, and then tomorrow at the peace center, then to the airport."

Seamus sighed. "Don't remind me. Yes, we have two more nights, but three days. A lot can happen in a short time. Look where we've come already. Don't look so glum."

Abigail paused. She didn't know what to say, so she called on her new gift of gab. Taking a deep breath, she began, "Seamus, I feel very

124

attracted to you. I haven't even noticed a man since my Jon. But here we are on a one-week trip and I'm feeling so much. What will become of us when I fly home? What are you thinking?"

Seamus chuckled. "Slow down, my dear. Ye be asking so many questions. Before I can compose an answer, you're off to another. Let me tell ye, I be feeling the exact same way. I haven't looked at the ladies much since my wife passed on. I didn't care to try again. My lady was my life. But then I met you. I'm feelin' like a teenager, I am. My heart's a-beatin' and you're lighting up my soul. It's the luck o' the Irish I found you, lassie.

"Where are we headed? We'll figure something out, we will. That's what I be a-thinkin', if you want to know. Now I need to mind the road a bit, okay? We'll talk later."

"Yes," Abigail said. She didn't know why sometimes the cars raced each other, bunching up together, but it was one of these days. Seamus held his own until the cars dispersed. She watched him relax into an easier driving stance. He sure could drive. What other skills would she discover in him? She liked his ruddy complexion, his cute accent, and his gift with words. Yes, she liked this man. If it was meant to be, God would help them find a way.

Reagan in the Wicklow Mountains

Reagan opened her eyes, stretched, and pulled her cell phone out of her pocket. 2:10 p.m. She watched the fields rolling by, seeing the many shades of green and feeling genuinely good inside for a change. She loved the Irish mountains and watching the movies filmed there. As a teenager, she'd learned about the movie shoots in the Wicklow Mountains. Later, her dad gave them all to her. Many date nights with Tyler had ended in the den, with Irish landscapes and Tyler's hands making her feel good.

Seamus spoke. "We're almost to our first stop in the Wicklow Mountains. Wake up, mates."

People began to stir. She heard Welby mutter behind her. She thought she heard him ask, "What the?" She suppressed a giggle. Up front, she heard Sallie complaining to Abigail. Beside her, Priscilla opened her eyes.

"Oh, my, how long did I sleep?" Priscilla jerked up, pulled out her compact and freshened up, brushing her hair, then applying some blush and bright red lipstick.

"Two hours," Reagan said. "Almost to the Hollywood-famed mountains."

"Great," Priscilla said. "I watched those movies before we came. What about you?"

Reagan chuckled. "Me, too. Well, sort of." She'd watched them many times during those teenage love sessions with Tyler on the couch. What began there had led to so much more, until … Reagan frowned. She'd always thought Tyler would be her man for life. Was her daddy right when he said that he'd come back? She didn't think so. A drug addict would not fit with his political aspirations, even if she were in recovery. Until she'd gotten hooked on painkillers, she'd been the ticket to his dreams—along with her daddy as his father-in-law. It was a straight road to the top for him. But now, she'd kill his career before it began. Besides, she reasoned, he was probably out looking for a daughter of another Republican lawmaker to snatch for his planned journey to the presidency someday.

Come to think of it, maybe he'd never loved her in the first place. If he could dump her at the first roadblock, maybe she should be thankful for the accident and her drug problem. Had he just wanted her for his own gain? Like her counselor in rehab told her, sometimes good things come out of bad situations. This could be another silver lining in the stormy clouds of her life.

She remembered her recent dream. A young girl talked with her, telling Reagan that she was a servant girl, a follower of Jesus. The girl said to watch out for people with money. She shared her own story: a rich boss ravaged her mother, and she was conceived. That same rich man sent her away. Mother lost daughter, daughter lost mother. But the girl also said she met God and learned a better way. She said to always remember that Jesus said it's harder for a rich man to enter the kingdom of heaven than for a camel to get through the eye of the needle.

She'd had an Irish brogue, like Seamus. In her church back home, they always glossed over that camel scripture. Instead, they said God blesses the righteous with riches. One time, she asked her daddy about it. He said not to be worrying her pretty little head over it. "It's hard for everyone to get into heaven, not just the rich," he said. "God will welcome us, though. We're good people." But she'd wondered what it meant and why the rich would be excluded . She knew they worked hard for their money and deserved it, unlike all the welfare cheats who lived off the system or those minorities who played the race card to get ahead. Welby, for example. A bad Black man, using drugs, spending time in prison. Her rich people were better than him, yet she kept feeling attracted to him. The whole thing was much more complicated than she'd ever thought before. And, of course, she knew it was possible to find light and darkness in each person. Certainly, she knew her own dark side.

Seamus interrupted. "We be a-comin' up to our first stop now.

Let's get off the bus and I'll tell ye about these mountains, and then we'll cross the road to the Guinness family estate." He pulled the bus into a small lot, near some other cars. Once outside, he gathered them around the van and started to talk again. "Now, this soil is called peat. It's been created by years of cooking in God's good earth. Long ago, the Irish realized they could heat their cottages by burning this stuff. People still come up here to cut big squares out of the ground, taking it back to their cottages to burn in their little fireplaces. Now let's cross over the road for a photo op. I be willing to take yer picture with the Guinness family valley in the background."

"Oh," Abigail said, "maybe we could get a group shot!"

"Your wish is my command, darlin'," Seamus replied. "Let's be movin' along. I want to get ye to Glendalough before the sun goes down. We don't have all day, ye know."

Sallie teased him. "Oh, Seamus, don't you know we have all the time in the world? We're on vacation. I don't like to hurry when I'm on vacation. I like to take my time and enjoy what I'm doing. Don't rush me."

"We do have a time schedule to follow, and you know it. Enjoy the timelessness within this moment all you want, but get a move on," Abigail said.

Reagan laughed. She enjoyed these women. They spoke their minds and were down to earth, not as pretentious as women in her circles back home. Tyler's mom wouldn't be caught dead talking like that. She appreciated them, too, as another blessing for her, despite her mistakes. She was getting to see another side of life. Sure, she'd seen some poor folk in her nursing job, but that was different than just being with folks day-to-day, without illness intervening.

The group posed and yelled, "Cheese!" Seamus snapped several shots of them on a lookout, high above the Guinness family place. He pointed out how the lands were divided among the heirs. He continued chatting, leading them on to the *P.S. I Love You* bridge.

It was another familiar scene for Reagan. The stone bridge provided passage for mountain travelers. It was an architectural masterpiece of decorative stone masonry, with a traditional arch over the small mountain stream below. There was even a small waterfall. The arch made a perfect photo, framing the people and the green hills sloping off into the distance.

Reagan looked at the bridge and could almost see her dad snapping her picture. Back then, she'd climbed down on the boulders, posing with the waterfall behind her. Then she remembered Tyler, rerunning the scene from the movie so she could see the bridge and remember being there.

A lot of water under the bridge, she quipped to herself, since then. She asked Priscilla to take her picture with the bridge, thinking maybe she could paint it. She snapped a few pictures with her phone. After a little while, Seamus loaded them back up into the van and they started for Glendalough.

Welby walks the Glendalough Trail

Welby stretched his long legs out into the aisle, putting his hands behind his head and getting the lay of the land once Seamus pulled into the parking lot. There were a lot of cars, so he concluded it must be a popular spot. He wondered what drew them in such numbers. The green? He could almost see the mist lifting off the ground. Maybe it was that, too.

When Seamus offered a choice of a hike up to an upper lake or a tour of the monastery grounds and the lower lake, he chose the hike, hoping the walk would clear his mind. He was still struggling with his thoughts, trying to figure out the whys and, more important, what the recent visions he'd had really meant. All he'd gotten so far was the beginning of a headache.

The older and less agile folks opted for a guided tour of Glendalough, which included most of the MAMs except Jane and Abigail. Tom joined them to be with Molly. That left the groupies, as Welby liked to call them—Nikki, Reagan, Charlie and himself— along with Jane, Abigail, and George opting for the hike. Seamus led at a good pace. They scrambled to keep up on a steady incline. Up, up, up, they went, with great views of the valley below.

Reagan stayed right up behind Seamus. George held the space ahead of Welby. He could sort of see Reagan, but mainly he saw George's backside every time he looked straight ahead. So instead, he looked sideways, enjoying the trees which reminded him a little bit of home. Memories of his childhood—visiting Grand MaMa on the Sea Island in the summertime and playing in the sand for hours, building sandcastles, digging for oysters—filled his thoughts. At the end of those day, he'd walked through the woods to get back home. He'd felt so close to the earth. He'd missed that feeling when he returned to the city each fall. Homesickness for the Sea Islands wrapped around him while he tried to remember his last visit to the one place on Earth where he felt fully alive.

His heart pounded with the exertion of climbing. Breathing deeply, he basked in the sunshine and fresh air as his body surged forward. He planted one foot firmly in front of the other, on this Irish soil of his roots, following the pack toward the upper lake.

Seamus surprised him. The old guy didn't look physically fit. He heard George grunting from exertion and laughed. When Abigail started panting, Seamus called for a break.

He circled the group up. "Okay, we'll slow down a little, for Abigail." Seamus chuckled and gave her a wink. Welby figured Seamus would steal more kisses when no one was looking. He could feel the sexual energy between them, even at their advanced age. He wished for something like that for himself. He looked at Reagan and then away. As tempting as he found her, he still didn't understand how she could support Ace Steele.

Seamus continued, "I don't want you all to miss out on your history lesson just because you opted for exercise. So sit down and let me tell ye about this place."

Abigail and Jane took the one bench; Reagan and Nikki sat cross-legged on the ground as if getting ready to meditate. George asked to scrunch onto the bench with the ladies, complaining his knees couldn't handle sitting on the ground anymore. Welby reclined on his side in the grass, stretching out his long body and propping his head up with his arm, enjoying the eye candy of Reagan and Nikki nearby. He smiled. Charlie squatted behind Reagan and Nikki, making them laugh. Truth be told, he'd prefer Charlie's spot.

Seamus interrupted Welby's musings by beginning his lecture. "Glendalough," he said, "means Valley of the Two Lakes. We parked by the first lake. This trail heads up to the second lake. We may not make it all the way up, but we'll try. Depends on your stamina—and how much I talk, which you know I like to do a wee bit too much at times." Seamus chuckled.

"Ah, Glendalough, nice ring to it, don't you think? The word just rolls off the tongue. A fitting name for a beautiful spot. We're just an hour south of Dublin, here. Did ye know? Aye, we're headed back. We've almost come full circle." Seamus' eyes twinkled as he told them, "Life is a circle, don't ye know. But I digress."

He scanned the landscape and turned back to face the group. "Saint Kevin, a hermit monk who died about 618 A.D., started this monastery. Here about the grounds, ye'll find several churches, a round tower, and some other structures, dating all the way back to the seventh century. Yes, Glendalough began with Saint. Kevin, a descendent of one of the ruling families of Leinster. As a boy, he studied under three holy men: Eoghan, Lochan, and Eanna. As a young man, he came here to live at Glendalough. Legend tells us he lived in the hollow of a tree on his first trip. You just have to let your imagination figure that one."

"How do you live in the hollow of a tree?" Charlie asked.

"Like I said," Seamus answered, "use yer imagination." His eyes twinkled. "The Irish like a good tale. The folk probably lived in all kinds of places, before proper houses, ye know."

Charlie shrugged. "Sounds like Kevin was a little nature boy, huh?"

"Right-o," Seamus said. "They say he died early because he liked sleeping on stones, wearing animal skins, starving himself, and making friends with the birds and animals. Died in 618, not too long after he came back here with a small group of followers to establish the monastery. But Glendalough flourished for the next six hundred years. Read all about it in the Irish history books. Abbots died. Raids happened. By the eight hundreds, it rivaled Clonmacnoise. Remember the place we visited the first day? Glendalough and Clonmacnoise led as monastic cities of Ireland in the Middle Ages, until Henry the Eighth robbed the church wealth, taking over."

"Gotta watch the rich," Welby warned. "They'll rob you blind and hang you out to dry."

Seamus nodded. "Aye. and history repeats itself again and again."

"Watch what you say about rich people," Reagan said. "They aren't all bad. They make the world go around and create your jobs. I mean, look at our current president, serving the people, though he doesn't need to work at all."

Welby looked at Reagan. "Are you crazy, Reagan? Don't you read the paper? Don't you know what Ace Steele is really doing? He's draining the treasury with his fishing outings every other week. He spent up a year of the Secret Service budget in two months. Get real, Reagan. That man cares about nobody but himself."

Reagan stuck her nose up in the air. "Show some respect for our president. It's a big job. He needs time off to relax."

"Bet you said worse about Rosales," Welby shot back. "Did you show respect for President Rosales? He was our president, too, you know."

Abigail intervened. "Okay, stop. We're here to learn about Glendalough. We need to pray about our divide and listen to each other, I agree. But right now, we're learning about Glendalough. Let's hold that discussion for later." Abigail signaled Seamus. "Continue, please."

Seamus saluted her. "Yes, ma'am. At one time, this settlement included not only churches and monastic cells, but also workshops, guesthouses, an infirmary, farm buildings and houses. Most date back to between nine and eleven hundred. Now, let's continue with our little hike."

"How long is this *little* hike, Seamus?" Abigail asked.

"Ah, about five kilometers, a little more than three miles," he replied.

"Can you do that, Abby?" he asked.

"Yes, but it takes me a while. I don't run anymore," she replied.

"Well then, we better get a move on," Seamus said.

They wandered back into the woods, then alongside a lake. Welby didn't think it looked like the Sea Islands anymore, but he could appreciate the scene. The lake glistened in the afternoon sun, and he enjoyed the vista of hills and mountains around.

When the trail leveled off, he didn't have to hurry to keep up. As he relaxed into an easy stride, he began to think. He remembered the conversation about Steele a few minutes earlier, remembered Reagan's infuriating words. One minute, he felt so attracted to her; the next, she totally disturbed him with her political comments. Sometimes she seemed almost reasonable, but then not. He wondered why he couldn't just let her go,

"This is beautiful," Nikki exclaimed. "I could write a song about this."

"I want to paint it," Reagan said, snapping pictures with her iPhone.

Welby took out his phone and captured a few himself, but then he tucked it away so he could enjoy the landscape instead. What had Grand MaMa said? "Soak in the sun, boy. Soak in this good space of God's Earth. He made this all for you. You be richer than kings and princes, because you got creation to enjoy." So Welby soaked in the sun, feeling it warm his skin and his clothes, creating sweat on his back. The water reflected the sun and above, the blue sky displayed with white puffy clouds. He felt downright happy.

The Meeting

The leprechaun danced out onto the lower lake of Glendalough, one of his favorite hangouts. The humans flocked to this place as well, with cameras clicking. He understood. A thin veil here. A person would have to be dead to not notice the Other World here. Long ago, the first leprechaun had chosen the Emerald Isle because of its thin spaces, and here they'd remained ever since.

He skipped across the water, then perched himself on a rock to think. The tour would conclude soon. He had work to do.

Síocháin decided to call a meeting. He snapped his left fingers to summon Saint Brigid. She emerged from the center of the pond, lazily swimming over to join him.

"The top o' the morning to you, Saint B," he greeted her. "Could ye give me a hand?"

The fair young woman smiled. "For ye, Sir Síocháin? Yea, I come to do yer bidding. What need ye from me on this beauty of a midafternoon?"

"Oh, I just be a-meddlin' with these Americans, I am. A-tryin' to help them see day from night, ye know?" The little man clapped his hands. "Figured ye might tell them a thing or two."

"And what do ye wish we shall tell them, Sir Síocháin?"

"Hold ye horses there, Saint B. We need more help first." Síocháin clicked his fingers again. A large dark woman in a colorful gown and headwrap materialized a ways off on the shore among the nearby trees and walked toward them.

"Who be the lady drawing near?" Brigid whispered.

Síocháin answered by saying, "Hello there, Grand MaMa. So glad to see you this fine afternoon."

"Mmm-hmm," she drawled. "This better be good. You be wakin' me from my nap. What you be wantin' from the likes of me out here in this white people's land?"

Brigid looked the lady up and down. Síocháin gave Brigid a frown. "Not polite to stare, Saint B," he said. "You know better than that."

Brigid nodded, then rose out of the water, shook herself off, dried her hands on some leaves, and walked over to shake the lady's hand. "Blessed be to greet ye," she said. "I be Brigid, and by what name are ye called?"

"My name is Missus Mary Matilda Turner Jones," came the answer. "Grand MaMa will do. I believe we met up in the States a while back?"

"Aye, how quickly I forget. I be so very pleased to make your acquaintance again, Madam Jones," Brigid said while shaking her hand. "Forgive me, I be dripping from an afternoon dip."

Grand MaMa leaned back her head and laughed loud and long. "A lady after my own heart, my dear. If I weren't so old, I'd be right in there with you. Back in the day, nothing I liked better than an afternoon dip in a refreshing pool of water. And I'm not talkin' 'bout just getting my feet wet, neither. Pleased to meet up with you again, my dear." She turned to Síocháin, pointing at him with her long red, manicured fingernail. "Now tell me, who are you and why are we here?"

"Síocháin, ma'am," he replied, reaching for her hand. "Síocháin the Leprechaun. Remember me?"

Grand MaMa laughed again. "Are leprechauns real? Am I dreamin'?"

Síocháin was a bit flustered, but quickly regained his composure. "Yes, well. You've heard about us, I suppose. My clan's been in these parts for thousands of years, long before your tribe got yanked off the

African continent over there to do time with those ugly Americans. But save that for another day. We've got our job, ladies. I think you're just the ones to do it."

Brigid crossed her arms. "I don't believe ye ought to be a-meddlin', Síocháin. We must let the people find their own way. We're in the Other Place now. Their best may not be good enough, ye know, but let them figure out this life, please."

Grand MaMa interjected, "If there's something I can do to help my boy, Welby, I'll be the first to step in. What you got, Síocháin? My people need all the help they can get. Angels? Divine intervention? Whatever, we ain't picky. If a leprechaun can help, bring him on."

Síocháin laughed. "Thank you, Grand MaMa. Now, Saint B, just humor me for a few. Didn't ye yerself get yer own divine intervention back in yer Earth time, dear?"

Brigid smiled. "Yes, ye be right, Sir Síocháin. What do ye wish be accomplished here?"

"Okay. First, assignments. Grand MaMa, you're already on Welby. You stay there; he'll listen to you. I'm doing Abigail. Brigid? You get Reagan. Okay?" He crossed his arms and looked from Grand MaMa to Brigid and back. "Okay, ladies?"

"I done Welby since day one, not stopping now. Sure thing," Grand MaMa replied.

"Reagan?" Brigid asked. "I'm entering her pretty head. Such a rare lass with so much potential to be throwing it all out the door. Yes, I'm wanting to help her."

"Will we get our wings, Síocháin, if we do good?" Grand MaMa wanted to know.

Síocháin uncrossed his arms, threw his hands up above his head, and chortled. "Now, now, Grand MaMa, I'm not in charge of wings. Check with the producer of that TV show —what was it, *Touched by an Angel*? Or ask the director of *It's a Wonderful Life*. That's Hollywood. We're just trying to do good. Now, let's get down to business."

Brigid said, "Meddlin's a messy pastime, ye know. Be careful now."

"I know, I know," Síocháin said. "But here's what I want to do." He stood tall on his little stone perch, putting his arms around Brigid and Grand MaMa, whispering his plan. "So, ye have your assignments, but mix it up a little now and then. Grand MaMa, drop in on Reagan when the time's ripe. I plan on bending the ear of your lad, Welby. Saint B, let the Spirit guide."

In a distance, the MAMs clicked their photographs of the lower lake of Glendalough. The returning hikers joined them, capturing snapshots as well. The mist lifted off the water in the late afternoon sun while the scheming trio continued deliberations. Seamus herded his crew back to the bus. Síocháin, Saint Brigid, and Grand MaMa watched them go, then resumed conspiring to meddle for the good.

CHAPTER THIRTEEN
RETREAT AT THE HOLY WELL

Beginning the Retreat with Abigail

Abigail stepped back into the bus, ready to rest for a while. The hike had invigorated her, but she also felt tired and worried. She was concerned about having the energy to facilitate the retreat she'd planned for the coming evening and morning and thought maybe she should ask Jane to lead. But then she remembered the sisters at the retreat center's offer to help. She decided that, with coffee, she could do it. Only two days left. Adrenaline and caffeine would carry her through. As sometimes happened, her dreams loomed larger than her stamina. Her body weakened even as her heart kept dancing. She considered the man in the front who'd started to speak.

"All righty, ye lads and lassies, just lean back and take a snooze and I'll have you over to County Kildare within the hour. I imagine your bellies be craving some grub. It's first on my agenda as well when we get over there to the Holy Well Retreat Centre and Hermitage. I be a-knowin' the sisters there for some time now, and I can promise they'll serve a hearty meal with good Irish soda bread to fill ye up for the night."

When Seamus finished, Abigail asked for his microphone, wanting to explain the plans for the evening. The silent retreat would be a new experience for most of them and she wanted to prepare them. She just wished she wasn't so tired. She asked Jane quietly if she'd share. Jane had liked to talk about her experiences in a contemplative class after their archaeological adventure in Turkey. She'd had some powerful spiritual retreats in that silence.

"Now, before you take a nap," Abigail said, "I want to talk to you about what our plans are for tonight. Our next stop will be the Holy Well Retreat Centre and Hermitage near Kildare. The nuns created this new center just a few years ago. They've agreed to let us do a spiritual retreat there. People go there on hermitage for a time of prayer. They only have a few beds, but they've borrowed some cots to set up dorm rooms for us. One for the women, one for the men."

Abigail continued, "We will enter into a silent retreat tonight after dinner and continue through breakfast tomorrow. You'll have time to reflect on your trip. We'll give guidance on that. No talking. Silence can be a powerful experience. We Quakers have long believed that when you become quiet, it's much easier to hear the voice of God. Most religious traditions honor silence in some way. If you think about it, prayer should be a two-way conversation, but if we're always thinking and talking, how can God get a word in edgewise?" Abigail looked at Jane. "Jane, could you come tell us about your experience on a silent retreat?"

Jane reached out to take the microphone and then turned to face the others in the bus. "Silence is golden, or so they say." Jane waited for their laughter and it quickly came. "That's exactly what I thought the first time I went on a silent retreat when I took my contemplative class. I signed up to learn how to lead retreats. I didn't know they were going to teach me to lead silence." More laughter erupted.

"But, you know, that first time, I found it quite amazing. Once I had a good nap, I started following Spirit around, and the place came alive. I could hear the crickets. I could feel the people around me. We had prayer partners. I felt so close to them, even though we didn't speak. I'd just gotten divorced before that retreat, and it was weird, but I just felt so much love for him in the silence. You know, we're still friends."

Sallie asked, "Isn't that hard? You don't talk at all? I love to talk."

Jane replied, "Yes, but you start to realize words aren't all. The main thing is to connect with God, with yourself, and even to others on retreat. You'll find yourself present in a brand-new way. You start to sense life more deeply. At first, yes, it's hard. It's not normal. We're all used to talking. But when you close your mouth, you become so very much more aware. My life was rough back then. My husband couldn't stop drinking. I'd had enough. I couldn't stop him from destroying himself. The silent retreat helped me listen to my own pain, to feel God's love for us both. I knew I'd done the right thing when I listened in silence. I started to see new life for myself. It's hard to explain." Jane paused for a moment and then said, "Try it. See for yourself what I'm talking about. You'll like it."

Seamus reached for the microphone. "Silence is underrated, for sure. We Quakers practice silence all the time, but many people like to surround themselves with noise. When you shut ye trap, ye hear the birds sing, ye see the sunrise glowing off the trees, and ye realize miracles are springing up all around. It's deep. Can I join ye on this retreat, Abigail?"

Seamus kept surprising her. She smiled. "Absolutely. We'd love to have you."

Sallie laughed out loud. "She means she'd love to have you,

Seamus," she said, poking Abigail in the ribs. "Don't get me wrong, we all like having you around, but especially Abby."

Seamus gave Sallie a wink and an okay sign.

Abigail blushed. "Any questions about the retreat?" she asked.

"We can't talk at all?" Reagan asked. "What if we need something or get hurt?"

Abigail said, "Of course, if you have an emergency, you can talk. But you'll find most of what you want to say can wait. If you need to give someone a message, write it down. We'll explain more at the center. Until then, it's time for a nap."

Abigail watched Seamus driving and then allowed her eyes to close, hoping for sleep. When they arrived at the center, Sallie shook her awake. Hurriedly, she gathered her things to leave the bus.

A kind woman with a weathered, smiling face greeted them, introducing herself as Sister Angela. She guided them through the central hallway into a large room with windows. She instructed them to sit in a circle of chairs in the center of the room.

"Welcome to the Holy Well Retreat Centre," she said. "We're proud of our new center, just opened three years ago. We are sisters of the Holy Wells. This is a green building. We use zero fossil fuels to heat and cool it. We keep the tradition of Saint Brigid alive here. It's only a short walk to her well. We also have a labyrinth behind the building."

Abigail relaxed into the space, feeling a sense of peace permeating the room. In the center of circle, she observed a cross of overlapping shafts of wheat, with a single white candle burning in the center. The afternoon sunlight streamed through the window, illuminating the room.

"We want you to feel at home here," Sister Angela said. "First a tour, then dinner. After dinner, the retreat will begin. We're so glad you're here. Now, let's get on with it."

As she began the tour, she pointed out large copper columns outside. "Like I said, this is a fossil fuel-free, green structure. Those rods heat and cool the building."

George and Welby were particularly interested and started asking questions that Sister Angela told them she couldn't answer, but suggested they could ask the building manager such technical questions at dinner.

George mentioned their solar business. He said he wanted to learn more to see if they could build something similar back home.

Sister Angela said, "Oh, how exciting." Then she showed them the other rooms in the small building. "These are meeting rooms, so they're not usually used for sleeping, but we've turned them into makeshift accommodations for the night.

"Hmm," Sallie said. "We're sleeping on cots? Do you think they'll hold us?"

"Oh, my," Priscilla exclaimed. "Not the Hilton, is it? Is there room for my suitcase?"

Abigail felt embarrassed, and wanted to smooth things over with Sister Angela. She knew the retreat center didn't usually accommodate groups and she'd pushed to get them to take an overnight group. "It's my fault, guys. And it's just one night. You can handle it. I wanted you to experience this place and they don't usually do overnight groups."

Sister Angela said, "I didn't think this was a good idea, but we decided to try it once. The first may also be the last time. Let me know tomorrow if you think we should do it again."

She then took them outside to see three special hermitage rooms, used by those coming for a quiet time away. Molly and Tom were assigned one of these rooms for privacy. Although fitted with a single bed, they'd rolled in a rented cot to make it work for two. The MAMs decided Seamus should get his own room as well. They drew straws to see who got the third room. Abigail won.

"So, you're staying next to Seamus?" Sallie whispered. "Tell me all about it later."

"It's a silent retreat," Abigail whispered back. "Don't expect a story."

Sister Angela asked, "Do you want to share your conversation with the group?"

"No, sorry, Sister Angela." Sallie laughed. "We've been busted. We'll do better."

Jane asked, "Were you a schoolteacher? You sound like a nun I used to have."

Sister Angela laughed. "Oh, no. But I know what you're talking about, yes. I want us to respect each other. Now, let's eat."

She ushered the group into the small dining area. "Before we eat, let's pray." She crossed herself. Jane followed suit. Sister Angela led the prayer. "Bless this food to your service and our hands to your work. May you speak to the people gathered in the silence and may the Holy Mother accompany our friends. Keep us safe and growing in your love. In the name of Jesus, we pray." She crossed herself again and said, "Let's eat! Tonight, we have a traditional Irish favorite, Shepherd's Pie. Usually we eat vegetarian, so we do Irish food with a twist: meat-flavored tofu and vegetables, covered with mashed potatoes. There's always potatoes in an Irish meal, you know. Take salad, too, and a beverage. We're partial to tea. And there's a nice cherry tart for dessert."

Charlie and Welby headed directly for the table, followed by Tom and George, not waiting for the ladies this time. Abigail guessed they must all be fairly hungry.

Seamus hung back with Abigail. "Do you think we could have a chat tonight? Or must we maintain the silence, too, Abby?"

"Certainly, I'd like to talk with you. But since I'm leading the retreat, I'm not very comfortable about breaking the silence." Abigail paused and considered his request. They only had a couple days left. Would there be a way? Then she had an idea. She turned to Seamus. "As the retreat leader, I offer sessions with retreatants if they need a spiritual director. You could sign up for an hour of my time in the morning. How about that?"

"Yes, my love, I'll sign up to be directed by ye. Sounds like a right old plan." Seamus winked at Abigail and motioned to her to claim her food.

Abigail took a deep breath, enjoying the aroma of the steaming food. She felt amazingly rested after such a short nap. She'd heard that a twenty-minute nap could do wonders. A sense of peace and hope blossomed within her. The windows provided a view to outdoors, and everywhere she noticed signs of contemplative presence. She almost had to pinch herself. She glanced at Seamus and her heart started beating with joy. Seamus followed close behind her in line. They found a table together, just as Sister Angela began to talk again.

"Many of you know of Saint Patrick. You celebrate Saint Patrick's Day, and you drink. But in Ireland, we honor him for bringing us Christianity, not beer."

Charlie and Nikki snickered. Reagan's eyes opened wide. Welby nodded. Abigail noticed Sallie poke Jane in the ribs. The others seemed to be observing silence already.

"We call him the patron saint of Ireland. But Saint Brigid is also very important to us. She founded our order of nuns, and she shares her name with an earlier woman of the Celtic spiritual tradition that predates Christianity. We have many stories about Brigid. Sometimes the stories get mixed up in the minds of the people. It can be hard to separate the two.

"Saint Brigid's mother was a slave for a rich man who took advantage of her. His wife became angry when Brigid's mother got pregnant. She sent the young woman away, because she didn't want a sign of her husband's infidelity around. The rich man sold her as a slave to a faraway household. Like in your country, our people suffered losing loved ones to slavery.

"Brigid possessed an uncanny connection with animals and with people, too. Her heart went out to the hungry and the poor. She got in trouble often for helping them with food and possessions from her household where she served the wealthy. If I told you all the stories about her, we'd be here all night. But I encourage you to read a few things in our library and let her speak to you during the retreat. Now finish your dinner and we'll get the silence started."

Sister Angela served up her own plate of food, then joined Abigail and Seamus at their table,. "So, how can I help? Could I explain the labyrinth and Brigid's well?"

Abigail nodded. "That would be wonderful. I'll start off with a few thoughts and scripture and give them time to journal their intentions. I'll have them share a bit with each other before we go into the silence. Then could you end the session and describe the labyrinth and the well? Perhaps offer a closing prayer to take us into the silence?"

Sister Angela agreed. "You got it. Let me finish my meal, and we'll get started."

Abigail took another bite, savoring her shepherd's pie. She tasted the potato, thinking of how the potatoes long ago led to such suffering among the Irish people, decimating the population, between starvation and migration. She took another bite with a pungent carrot, and then munched on the crust. She thought about the goodness of Ireland and the many people living in the States with roots here. Seamus smiled at her. She felt the glow of his love and the flame within her own heart and gave thanks for their growing friendship. She relished the last bite, looking forward to their time ahead.

Reagan on Retreat

Reagan picked out a seat in the circle for the silent retreat introduction and plopped into it. An unexpected feeling of peace came over her. She remembered feeling this way as a child in church with her parents, studying the stained-glass windows. Later in college, she'd experienced this peace during prayer time with Intervarsity Christian Fellowship. She'd aimed to stay close to the Lord, and she always had until that car accident turned her world upside down, life became a struggle, and drugs helped her handle the pain.

Abigail distributed papers with an agenda and some questions. Reagan scanned it, then placed it on the floor. She enjoyed the sunset out the window that illuminated the grass at dusk, wondering just what you do on a silent retreat.

Abigail began to explain. "So, about the silence. I know for most of you, this will be a new experience. I encourage you to go with it. Follow the Spirit and your own inner guide. If you're tired, sleep. That may be exactly what you need. We often don't give ourselves time to rest. God can speak to us even during sleep. We need space to live fully.

"When traveling, we must let our spirits catch up with our bodies. We've traveled so far in these last few days, from Ohio to Dublin, from Newgrange to Kinvarra, from the Cliffs of Moher to Dingle Peninsula, from Blarney Castle to Glendalough, and now here. Listen to your heart and your own rhythms. Use your senses to observe. Go outside. Look. Listen. Touch. Smell. Taste.

"When you let go of words, you have more time to pay attention. Let your senses explore the world around you. Let God speak to you through nature."

Reagan listened to Abigail, and she spoke to her artist self. Paying attention was what artists do. When she painted, she observed very carefully She then strove to make her work a sensual experience, capturing the scene beyond the pure visuals. She decided she just might enjoy this silent retreat.

"In our Quaker tradition," Abigail continued, "we say each of us carry an inner light. That light will guide you. A silent retreat is a good time to listen to God within."

"Ah, yes. The inner light, that's what we be looking for." Seamus said. "The light shines in each person, ye know, not just we Quakers." He winked at Abigail.

Sister Angela smiled. "You Quakers aren't the only ones. We Celts love the silence, too."

"Righto," Seamus said. "All of us are from the same cloth when we listen to the Spirit."

Sister Angela responded, "Yes. We've had many Celtic spiritual writers here. And if they were here now, they'd tell you to slow down and listen. Listen to that light inside of you. Use your senses to experience the day fully."

"But don't you think some people get confused in the silence? I think God speaks through the scripture, in the church, through the preacher. There can be evil in silence. That's what they say in my church," Priscilla said.

"Trust God," Sister Angela said. "Trust and listen."

Nikki said, "I don't like silence. Sometimes I hear mean voices in the silence. I like to listen to music. I always have the TV on at home. I'm not going to like this."

Abigail said, "Nikki, you have headphones for your iPod, don't you? If you want to listen to music some, you can do that. I think God speaks through music, too. I would recommend instrumental pieces, though. If you hear mean voices, journal about it. Dialogue with them. Argue with them. Maybe this will help you understand how you can deal with the negative voices and let God transform your life. Listen for the Spirit. Let that inner light grow. Don't focus on evil, focus on the love."

Reagan thought about that, the light inside of her. For so long now, she'd felt only darkness. She went through the motions, but really didn't feel that sense of light that had seemed so clear to her in her younger days. Could she get that sense back? She hoped so.

Abigail nodded and then said, "We also want you to use this time to consider your dreams, as well as how you can let go of fear and move forward with courage."

Reagan's dream had gotten all trampled and hung out to dry. Could she dream again? Could she take courage and cast out her fear? She honestly didn't know.

Abigail said, "Life is a privilege and a gift. The poet Rilke once said, 'Being here is so much.' Take time for gratitude, as well. Make a list of your blessings. Certainly, there are always negative things in life, but you find much more happiness if you focus on the good."

Reagan loved that. "Being here is so much." She savored the thought, turning it over in her mind. The peace she'd felt earlier cascaded into something more. Looking outside, she watched the colorful sunset, but inside, she felt the sunrise of a new day. She wanted to return to an attitude of gratitude.

"Take a few minutes now to set your intention for the retreat," Abigail said. "Intentions are so powerful, so worthwhile. They make all the difference."

"I know you talked about this before, but I forgot. What's an intention?" Charlie asked.

"Good question," Abigail responded. "An intention is your goal, what you hope for during this silent retreat. Maybe you want to just relax and listen to God. Or maybe you want to listen for dreams for your future. Maybe you want to consider your roots. We brought you here because you have Irish DNA. What does that mean to you? Think about your Irish ancestors.

"Have you ever heard the expression 'If you don't know where you're going, you'll end up somewhere else'? On the other hand, if you have a clear idea of where you want to go, then that's where you'll go. An intention is like that destination, that hope you have for yourself."

"Okay," Charlie said. "Say I'm working on a project, building a house. I might say my intention for the day is to get two rooms painted?"

"Right," Abigail said. "Exactly. You got it."

Reagan pondered the question, feeling clarity forming within. She wrote: I want to slow down and listen to my inner light. I want to find courage to dream with God about my future.

She put her pen down and waited for the others to finish. After a few more minutes, Abigail told them to find a partner of the same gender, saying, "Share your intentions and pray for each other."

Reagan sought out Priscilla, the person she identified with most in the group. She knew that Priscilla attended an evangelical church like her own and belonged to the Republican party. Not that that made a difference on a silent retreat, but then again, she wondered if maybe it did. It was hard to lay aside labels. She wanted to be with someone from the party of God when she prayed.

Priscilla asked her about her intention. Reagan read aloud from her journal and then added, "It feels very peaceful here. I've never done a silent retreat, but I think I'll like this."

"Bless your heart," Priscilla responded. "I know God's going to speak to you in a powerful way. My intention is just to listen to God and pray. That's all. I want to pray a lot." Priscilla smiled. "Let's pray now. I'll pray for you, and you pray for me, okay?" She reached out and took both of Reagan's hands in hers and bowed her head.

Reagan felt comforted to hear Priscilla praying over her. And then she found words flowing from her as she prayed for Priscilla. Yes, she realized, she felt some inner light shining already.

When they came back together, Abigail explained the schedule. Tonight, they could stay in or walk the lighted labyrinth out back. In the morning, she recommended a visit to Brigid's Well. Sister Angela distributed a small map and assigned groups. Nikki and Reagan would go with Priscilla and Sallie at 9:00, and Welby and Charlie would go with Tom and George after they returned. Other than that, they were free until 11:30, when they'd meet to break the silence and share over lunch before traveling north to their next stop.

Sister Angela closed the session with a familiar Irish blessing. "May the road rise up to meet you. May the wind always be at your back. May the sun shine warm upon your face, and rains fall soft upon your fields. And until we meet again, may God hold you in the palm of His hand." The nun paused at the end of the blessing and looked directly at Reagan. "May God speak to your hearts during this time of silence. Allow the silence to nurture you. There is great freedom in this time."

Abigail added that if anyone wanted to talk over things during the retreat, she would be available tonight, and also early in the morning or right after breakfast. She held up a sign-up sheet listing the times, saying she'd leave it on the table.

George spoke up next. "Now, you're on your own for the silent retreat. We won't be staying in a group but stay either in the retreat center or on the grounds, except for when we visit Brigid's Well together. Remember. your ankle bracelets have a tracking device. I don't expect any problems. You've all been great, but remember that leaving the group is a violation of your parole. You could go back to prison. Don't go off the grounds. I'll be tracking you. Be good."

Reagan nervously glanced down. Would they send her to prison when she never went in the first place? She wasn't about to take any chances.

No one asked any questions, which Reagan thought strange. Sister Angela took a rubber mallet and walked over to a brass-colored bowl sitting in the center of the room. "May you be present to God, as God is always present to you. The great silence begins." She struck the bowl, and a ringing noise filled the room, then gradually dissipated.

Reagan listened while the sound faded, then gathered her journal and headed toward the labyrinth. She enjoyed the FARM labyrinth and wanted to try out this one before it got too dark. While the sunset cast amazing colors across the sky, she captured the scene on her cell phone, deciding the best way for her to listen would be to paint. She gave thanks for art supplies in the meeting room.

A slight chill filled the air, but she moved briskly, feeling her body warm with exertion. A short path led to the labyrinth. The design was different than the Living Vine Labyrinth, but she knew it would wind into the center and back, so she walked confidently, without fear. She paused to capture some photos of the scene, including the labyrinth with trees in the distance. She framed a picture including the beautiful sunset. Later, she hoped to memorialize this moment of entering the silence with paint on canvas.

She remembered her retreat intentions. Listen to that inner light. Find a path to the future. She stepped slowly on the path of the labyrinth, trusting that answers would come. She let go of thoughts, allowing her feet to carry her along into the center. She enjoyed the crunch of gravel beneath her feet. She felt comforted with the circling path as the rhythm and balance filled her body with peace. She even enjoyed the chill in the air. She noticed that the trees, illuminated by the sunset, were beginning to let go for winter. She circled closer and closer to the center. When she arrived, she decided to sit down, to listen.

Suddenly, a large Black woman walked up, stopping just a few feet away, looking at Reagan with an alarming intensity. Reagan closed her eyes. Was she hallucinating? Were drugs still messing with her head? She opened her eyes. The lady started talking.

"Mmm, mmm, mmm," she said. "I am Grand MaMa, a relative of your friend Welby there, and I came to give you some advice."

144

Where had she come from? Should I be afraid? What was a Black lady doing in Ireland, much less on the labyrinth at this remote retreat center? Do I speak? Ignore her? Reagan decided she'd observe the silence. She drew her fingers across her closed lips, hoping the lady would get the hint.

The woman threw back her head and laughed. "Okay, then, we'll do this your way." Then Grand MaMa looked deeply into Reagan's eyes. Reagan felt a ripple of warmth radiating through her whole body, taking the chill off the night. She felt dumbfounded. She actually felt a connection with this woman; a stranger no more.

The two of them shared a moment beyond this world, transfixed. Reagan felt light awakening in her heart as the sun finished its descent into the horizon, casting darkness across the labyrinth while the Centre's lights provided illumination.

Grand MaMa spoke again. "Reagan. Welcome to my people. You're one of us now. That is a good thing and don't you let nobody be scaring you away. We gonna love you hard, baby. Don't fear that good Black blood coursing through your veins. We got your back, and you're goin' have a good light. You trust that candle inside your heart, and you get to know that great-grandson of mine, too. He's not all bad, honey. He's got some of that spark I see in you. You two could help each other out. Be friends. Okay? You two are not so different as you think. That's a good thing. Now, you think on that a while. I must be goin'. Nice to meet you, chil'."

She walked off into the dark night. Reagan slipped down onto the earth for a moment. She pinched her arm. The pinch hurt, so she wasn't dreaming.

Oh, no, Reagan thought. *A lot of people who used drugs got brain damage. Is that my problem now?* But she reviewed the warmth of the exchange, pondering the words. Suddenly, she knew inside that Grand Ma Ma and her message were very real.

Welby. Grand MaMa told her to be friends with Welby. She'd been fighting that very urge within herself. Maybe she just needed to try it. Maybe God wanted her to cross the line. Maybe that's what love was all about.

Reagan needed to get that message recorded on canvas and in her journal, before the experience faded into oblivion. She walked quickly back along the winding path, heading for the art supplies. She found a photo on her phone of the trees, the labyrinth, and the sunset. She remembered the image of Grand MaMa, holding her hand, looking into her soul and telling her about her newfound DNA. She wanted to memorialize the moment, because somehow, Reagan sensed that experience was going to change her life.

A Time of Reckoning for Welby

Welby shuffled along the hallway, spotting Reagan through the window. He turned away. He was not going to let any woman get him off track, no, sir. This retreat might be freaking weird, but maybe he could hear the voice of God speaking if he just got down on his knees and prayed. Problem was his pride didn't want nobody seeing him doing that, didn't want nobody laughing at him. Earlier, he'd noticed a door ajar with a broom and a pail behind it. He hurried there, making sure the coast was clear before slipping into the closet for some reckoning.

A verse came back to him and he recited it quietly. "And whenever you pray, do not be like the hypocrites; for they love to stand and pray in the synagogues and at the street corners, so that they may be seen by others. Truly I tell you, they have received their reward. But whenever you pray, go into your room and shut the door and pray to your Father who is in secret; and your Father who sees in secret will reward you." Welby surprised himself. Those words rolled off his tongue perfectly, even after all those years. He told God, "I'm ready for my reward, anytime now." He laughed, knowing rewards came in the hereafter.

Welby dropped down to his knees. He felt tears welling up. Soon, he was bawling like a little baby and once the floodgates opened, he couldn't stop.

And then as quickly as it started, it stopped. He wiped off his face with the handkerchief in his pocket and stood, smoothing his hair, trying to compose himself. He peeked out of the closet, to make sure the coast was clear and then slipped back out into the hall. He felt all clean inside. It had been a long time since he got it all out like that. Right after sentencing, he'd done something similar, but this seemed different. Now he felt hope stirring. He'd done did his time. Now his future beckoned. These Irish folk were part of his own fabric. He laughed. His white blood connected him to the green people, this island, and the Celtic spirit stuff, too.

Welby rubbed his face with his hands. Did he just hear someone talking down the hall? This was a silent retreat. *Who's breaking the rules?*

Oh. My. God. Welby started to walk the opposite direction. He'd left the drug culture behind long ago and he wasn't about to start hallucinating now. He tried to escape down the hall, but the voice called him back.

"Welby, come here. Don't be a-fearin' me. I'm a leprechaun, is all."

Welby did a second take. There stood a small man, all dressed in green, wearing a green hat with a shiny buckle. He had a pointy nose and looked to Welby like something out of a cartoon book or an animated movie. Welby wasn't buying it. He backed away, heading the opposite direction. *Maybe I should just go to sleep now.*

He lay down and gave himself over to the cot. Not the most comfortable sleeping arrangement, but good enough for now. Better than the slammer, for sure, with the toilet in the corner and the bars all around for five long years.

But just as he slipped off into slumber land, he heard him again. "Welby, Marcus Welby Jones, how ye doing, Mister Jones?"

Welby opened his eyes and didn't have to look far. His visitor was perched on the corner of his cot, with his knees all tucked up, showing off little pointy black shiny shoes. Welby slammed his eyes shut. No, he would not be caught dead talking to spirits.

"Now, Welby, don't be a-fearin' me," he said a second time. "I don't want to haunt ye, I'm here to help. Your Grand MaMa sent me. She wants me to talk to ye, man to man."

Welby opened his eyes once again to look at this little guy. Maybe he should just listen.

He sat up in the bed, saying, "Pleased to meet you, sir. And what's your name?" Welby extended his right hand out to shake, offering his forefinger. Since he'd never shaken hands with a leprechaun before, he didn't quite know how to execute the maneuver when the other person's whole hand wasn't much bigger than his own thumb.

"Síocháin," the leprechaun said. "That's what they call me. Pleased to meet ye, sir. I've heard a lot about ye. I think we could be good friends. In every time and place, God sends some messengers to lead the way. I believe ye have a call, Marcus, I do."

"I go by Welby," Welby said. "And I'm not all that. I'm an ex-con, you know?"

"Oh, sorry. Welby, yes. I know yer past, but I'm talking about yer future. It's shining bright, very bright."

Welby was doubtful. What did this guy mean? What did he know?

"Welby, ye need some leaders over there in yer country these days. Remember Martin Luther King, Junior? I'm looking for someone like him. I think yer the man."

"MLK never messed up like me," Welby said. "People don't listen to ex-cons."

"Give yourself credit, Welby. Everybody makes mistakes, even him. That doesn't mean God can't use ye. Have you read yer Bible lately? All kinds of screwups in those old days, and yet some of them became God's main players. Don't just say no, just think about saying yes."

"What do you want me to do?" Welby asked.

"I'm not telling ye what to do. Ye need to figure that out. I recommend prayer. And get to know Lady Reagan, too. I see ye look her up and down, but take a look inside. You two be like night and day, but we need opposites together to find a way. She be a leader, too. Together, ye will have much to say. Mark my words, Welby."

Welby shook his head. "You're bona fide crazy. That woman ain't gonna look at a Black man like me. You're crazy, man."

"Marcus Welby Jones, stop that right now." The leprechaun held out a pointy finger, waving it back and forth. "Now ye be talking pure garbage. Because I already see her eyeing ye when ye not be a looking."

Welby didn't think so. He wanted to argue more, but the man disappeared into thin air. He was done trying to figure it all out, He went to sleep.

***

Sunlight streamed into the room as Welby opened his eyes. It took him a moment to remember where he was. He made out Charlie next to him and George and Tom over by the other wall. Padding down the hall, he noticed it was already 7:00 according to the clock on the wall. He must have hit the pillow hard not to hear the other guys coming to bed.

He recollected himself, as the memories of the night before rolled in. He needed coffee. Perhaps with a little caffeine, he could make use of this morning. He wanted to write in his journal.

Sister Angela had showed them the breakfast food the night before and said to help themselves. Now he heated up water for oatmeal, then stirred it into the bowl. He poured a cup of coffee and pulled up a chair to the table. The closet. The leprechaun. What a night. He began to write. Could he really be the next MLK, Junior? What does a leprechaun know about civil rights leaders? And how did he meet Grand MaMa? He couldn't even imagine the two of them together, let alone having a conversation. Laying that aside, he concentrated on turning over a new leaf. Seemed becoming an MD was out of the question. An electrician, maybe. A civil rights leader, unlikely. Maybe silence could help him figure it out. Maybe he could try that labyrinth Reagan walked last night.

He didn't really feel crazy, just that some crazy things happened to him. He wanted to keep his head clear. Letting go of thoughts seemed a good thing. He remembered the labyrinth instructions, "Release, receive, re-enter." He entered the path and released it all up to God, questions and all. Not trying to figure it all out, he just walked slowly, methodically, putting one foot in front of the other. And gradually he felt peace slipping over him. The pristine early morning air enveloped him with a goodness he couldn't explain. A gentle rhythm settled him while he walked, circling into the center.

Now, receive. He waited in the center, feeling open. Nothing happened, but Welby felt extremely patient, and so he sat quietly, waiting for something to transpire.

Welby reminisced. First, he thought about the little green man's ideas. Then he traveled way back to the day he got arrested. He remembered his mission to make the country right by blowing up the fossil fuel headquarters. He'd wanted to blow those racists off the face of the earth. But even then, he knew better. Those drugs had messed him up real bad.

Still he felt an urge to do something. He realized he'd been going about it all wrong.

Martin Luther King, Junior, now, that man knew how to do it right. Dare he follow in his footsteps? Dare he make a difference in a good way? What would that look like? Would Reagan really help him in the quest?

Welby had no idea. But a seed had been planted. He didn't know if he could become a preacher man, a civil rights leader, or a counselor of other Black men like himself, trying to find a new path. But he felt a light come on and, for the first time in a very long time, he knew his life was something good. Maybe he couldn't solve the problem of Black and white, maybe he could only make a few ripples in the pond, but he now knew he had a purpose. When he stood up to walk out of that labyrinth, he felt God walking with him in a new way, in a different way, in a way that added a spring to his step and a smile on his face and hope in his heart.

"Oh, boy, look at me now, Grand MaMa," he muttered into the fresh air. "Look at me now."

Retreat Wrap: The Encounter, The Well, and Moving On

Abigail enjoyed silent retreats. She never knew exactly where the path would lead, but she'd learned years ago to trust the Spirit to guide. Here at the Holy Well Retreat Centre, she sensed new light streaming. The night before, she'd slipped out to walk the labyrinth while the moon shone brightly. Now she remembered the trees, the night sky, and the moon, the light shining through it all.

This morning, she lit the candle in the center of the circle where they'd gathered the night before and spent her morning meditation time alone with the shafts of wheat forming St. Brigid's cross. She knew very little of this Irish saint but wanted to learn more. She spent the next hour perusing a few books about Brigid in the library before her appointment with Seamus. She became entranced with the stories of Brigid, a Celtic Goddess and the other Brigid, an early Christian, a lover of animals and the poor, a slave, an intuitive, a worker of miracles. She loved the way the woman bridged the Celts from their indigenous spiritual understandings onto their Christian path. Two women merged into one in the memory of the people. Where did the Celtic Goddess end and the Christian woman begin? It was hard to tell after centuries of storytelling and imagination.

She believed Brigid held a key, not only for the ancient and traditional Irish, but also for the modern people looking for a bridge across cultures. She laughed to herself, realizing that the saint's name sounded like "Bridge." Not being Catholic, Abigail never prayed to a saint, but she longed to connect with Brigid.

Tempus fugit. It was time for her rendezvous with Seamus already. Not wanting to overthink this thing with Seamus, she trusted her inner light to guide her, in the Quaker way. She knocked on Seamus' door.

"Come in." Seamus said. "And good morning, my love." He closed the short distance between them, embracing her and planting a kiss on the cheek. "Have a seat, dear. Would you like a cup 'o tea?"

"Yes, that would be nice," Abigail responded. "I like this practice of having tea. You honor the tea and the moments you spend with it."

"Ah, yes," Seamus said. "It's always time for tea, for sure. We Irish do love a break with a warm cup o' liquid in our hands. Just a minute and I'll be right back." He started toward the kitchenette, then turned back. "Caffeine or herbal?"

"Do you have Lady Grey?" Abigail asked. "I love the citrus-flavored teas."

"Yes," Seamus said. "My favorite, too."

Abigail raised her eyebrows at that. Could they even have their favorite tea in common? "Really?" she questioned with a nervous laugh, realizing she sounded doubtful.

"Ah, yes," Seamus replied quickly. "I've always loved the ladies, so whenever Lady Gray's an option, I pick her. Don't get me wrong, I like the citrus taste in my tea, too. And I like that song." Seamus paused and then sang in his beautiful tenor voice, "Love be a lady tonight." He handed her a cup.

Abigail laughed. "Oh, okay. I get it." She cradled the warm cup in her hand, settled into a chair, and wondered where their conversation might lead.

"So how's the silence been treatin' ye?" he asked.

"I'm following the Light," Abigail responded. "The moon, a candle, the sun, Brigid … an illuminating time. You're my only appointment, by the way. No one else signed up. What about you?"

"I be a-thinkin' about you, my love. The first time I be a-thinkin' about another woman since my wife passed on. Not an easy thing, ye know? What do we do, an ocean apart? What does the good Spirit say? That's what I'm about, my love."

Abigail smiled at his blue eyes. "And?" she asked. "Is the Spirit speaking?"

Seamus winked. "Always. Always, my dear, but I make too much noise. I'm too busy telling the Spirit what I want, which is to keep us together."

"Let's listen together," Abigail said. "Let's take five minutes of silence and then write a little to see what we hear. Okay?"

Seamus nodded, so Abigail set her watch for five. "Close your eyes," she told him.

"When I open my eyes, will I get a surprise?" He held out his hands.

"You silly oaf. No. Okay, we're starting over." She reset the timer. "Are you ready?"

"Yes, set the clock, and I'll be a good lad and listen to the Lord," he said

Together, they welcomed the silence. Abigail felt goose bumps on her arms as she slipped into the heart of God, loving that silence that embraced her with love. Letting go of thoughts, she just absorbed the light of the Spirit, focusing on her breath and letting the light permeate her body, imagining it coursing through her veins, filling her with love. Five minutes later, her phone chimed, startling her from the silence. She reset it for five more, telling Seamus to journal while she pulled her own journal out of her backpack and began to write. Seamus followed suit. When her phone chimed again, she put her pen down.

"So," she said, and then asked, "What did you hear?"

"A bridge," he said. "I saw a bridge. You spoke of Brig-id. And perhaps that inspired me, I'm not sure. But I see our relationship as a bridge, between the two of us, between Ireland and the States, between a man and a woman. We can meet in the middle, we can be light for others. We will find a way, my lady. I do believe we will. That is our call." Seamus finished talking and asked Abigail. "What about you?"

"Hm," Abigail said. "I like that, a bridge. It does connect with what I've been hearing. This is what I wrote: Abby, now is your time to embrace life fully. You've met a wonderful man. Don't stop here. Don't let the ocean keep you from exploring your relationship more. Possibilities dance on particles of dust, illuminated now by light of a new day. You are stardust, living in a radiant moment. Let love guide. Take Seamus' hand. Walk into the future, together."

Abigail stopped. Her voice caught in her throat. Tears streamed from her eyes. She felt naked, exposed, vulnerable.

"Ah, such sweet words. How wonderful, my love," Seamus said. He scooched in beside Abigail on the couch. Handing her a handkerchief, he enclosed her with his arm and reached down to clasp his hand in hers. "Yes, my love. That's what I be a-wantin', too. Let's cross that bridge and walk into the future, together."

***

Abigail's watch rang again a half an hour later. She didn't want this moment to end.

Seamus broke the silence. "Who'd be callin' at this hour?"

"It's time for the women to go to the well," Abigail told him.

"Ah, yes, the women at the well. No room for a man, eh?"

"No, but I'll see you after."

Abigail smiled, giving him a wave as she closed the door behind her. She walked the short distance back to the Centre, where the others gathered in the atrium. Sister Angela presided, pointing to a chair for Abigail in the circle. The silence continued.

The moment felt powerful to Abigail as she joined the MAMs, her friends who accompanied her through the ups and downs of life. She reminisced on all they shared: books, travels, the FARM and Sun Power House projects. She felt so blessed to be part of this circle.

She observed her friends. Katharine looked downright serene. Sallie seemed less boisterous, not laughing for a change. Molly's face looked reflective as she wrote in her journal. Jane sat very still with her arms folded; she was hard to read. Nikki seemed edgy and fidgeting. Sometimes silence is disturbing, Abigail knew. Reagan appeared relaxed. One chair remained open. Who was missing? Ah, Priscilla. There she came.

Sister Angela passed a sheet of paper to each of them. On one side, there was information about St. Brigid. On the other were instructions for the visit to the well.

Abigail perused the information about Brigid. It echoed what she read earlier in the library. The word "peacemaker" jumped out. She'd felt tensions in their small group. Charlie, Nikki, and Reagan loved Ace Steele. Welby's disdain for the man seemed equally strong, a view shared by some of the MAMs.

The split in their small group reflected their country as well. She prayed for reconciliation. Feeling the deep significance of this trip for her own life, she hoped that the trip would lead them toward a path of peace, for not only the recovery people in their midst, but for the larger communities back home. Bridging the divides across race, culture and economic lines would be no small feat. Most political rhetoric on both sides seemed focused on division.

She turned the paper over and read instructions for the walk.

***

After a few minutes, Sister Angela rose and walked toward the door. The others followed. Abigail hurried ahead and held open the door as they filed past, streaming out into the sunny morning. It was such a simple act she offered, holding the door open and sharing smiles, but it felt good to provide service. The affirmative grins she received in return only added to the gratitude and joy of her morning.

Abigail fell in behind, putting one foot in front the other. Turning off her thoughts, she enjoyed the view of the countryside as she walked.

Finally, a makeshift arch of sticks framed an entrance. Abigail was captivated by the enchanted march of time, sensing continuity as their silent procession passed under the opening and into the courtyard of the well. They gathered in the small area, not much larger than her backyard at home.

On the right side, a statue of Brigid towered holding a flame towered over them. Abigail remembered that the Sisters of Brigid kept the flame burning, a service to all in a day before matches, stoves, and lighters. They'd tended the fire so that others could use it when needed. She remembered the eternal flame at the retreat center as well. Sort of like the Olympic torch, Jane had commented earlier.

Abigail picked up leaves as mementos of her visit. She didn't see a well. But then Sister Angela gathered them at the back of the arbor, arranging them around a circular stone structure about three feet high, in need of repair. They looked down into water that held reflections of the trees above. She guessed the well was about three feet across. A large stone cross stood above the water. There was an open area in the wall, perhaps a place to sit or rest a bucket. Lower in the wall, a small hole; perhaps a drain for overflow. Abigail gazed into the water and now the faces of her friends sparkled in reflection with the early morning sun.

They joined hands and stood as one, women at the well, circling the mystery where living water sprung forth, continuing to bring life.

Abigail felt the fullness of the moment. She felt Spirit moving, forging a bond, connecting them to women of the past and extending them into life to come. St. Brigid provided that bridge. In the silence, time stopped. For several minutes, they held on to each other, enjoying mystery.

Then Sister Angela bowed her head and squeezed her hand. Abigail prayed a silent prayer and then passed the squeeze on to Molly. She watched as the squeeze made its way around the circle. When it came full circle, Sister Angela nodded and broke her clasp on the hands she was holding. She walked away to sit on a bench by the well. Slowly, the others dispersed into the tree-lined compound.

Abigail took out her journal and found a place to sit on the grass. She wanted to capture the moment, to remember later. She wrote about Seamus, about Brigid, about her feelings and about her hopes. She wrote about her morning vision, a bridge of reconciliation uniting the people of her country. For a moment, her bright vision obscured the fog of division.

She heard a voice. "Abigail. Come ye, fine lady, for a drink." A woman dressed in a dark cloak held a bucket by the well. Abigail looked around at her friends to see if they'd heard, but they all seemed busy with their own reflections. Abigail maintained the silence, but decided to walk over to the woman and listen.

The woman dipped a cup into the well, drew it out, and offered it to Abigail. Abigail self-consciously looked around before smiling and accepting the cup. She cradled the small ceramic bowl with her fingers, then lifted it to her mouth, sipping the offering. The water cooled her throat and then its energy surged through her body. She drank more. Startled, she locked eyes with the mysterious lady. Very strange, but very holy. No wonder pilgrims flocked to this site over the centuries. Did others encounter this woman here, the spitting image of the statue across the way?

The lady spoke again. "Abigail, ye be the keeper of the flame. Ye Quakers tend inner light, I hear. My order tended the flame so necessary for the heat and the cooking. But now ye use other means; ye know so much more. But ye still need that inner light. Tend the light. Let it shine for the people."

Abigail nodded as tears spilled down her cheeks.

"Ye see the bridge across the creek, there? Focus on the bridge. I heard ye speak about it earlier. It's a good thing ye be doing, encouraging yer people to listen. In yer circles, listening to one another, you will find the path of illumination. Ye build powerful connections to be a beacon into peace for yer future."

Abigail took a moment to write the lady's words in her journal, wanting to be able to savor the message in days to come. She longed to communicate in some way, without breaking silence. She extended her

154

hands to the woman who received them, interlocking fingers, sharing warmth and compassion. Energy surged again from her eyes, fueling Abigail. She leaned in, giving Abigail a long, all-encompassing hug. Abigail squeezed back, enjoying the warmth. When they separated, the lady's eyes twinkled as she smiled her farewell and slipped away into the surrounding field, disappearing as she walked.

Abigail blinked, staring into space. *Did I just hallucinate?* Before she could give it another thought, Sister Angela joined her at the well, calling the others back. She pulled a large ceramic cup out of her satchel and squatted down to submerge the cup in the well, filling it with water. Once again, they stood in a circle around the well.

She took a sip and then passed it on to Priscilla, who took a quick taste, as if trying to avoid taking too much. If she even took a drink at all. Abigail couldn't tell. *Probably worried about parasites*, she thought. *Will I get sick? I've already drank quite a lot of it. Or did I? If a ghost gives you water, is it real? It tasted real. Living water?* She remembered Bible verses. Jesus told the woman at the well that he gave living water, from which you never thirst. Now she understood exactly.

The other women seemed to have no qualms about drinking the water, passing it around the circle. Abigail couldn't quite help but make a connection with the Lord's Supper. *Not grape juice, or even wine, but certainly holy water.* Once again, she enjoyed standing with her circle, imagining the thousands of pilgrims who came here seeking healing or a message of hope from the well. She felt a sense of solidarity with those former people, with her friends, with the people of the Earth, and with the people back in the States, struggling with the great divide these days. When the cup came to Abigail, she cradled it in her hands for a moment, then lifted it in toast to the statue of St. Brigid. After the silent tribute, she took a long drink from the cup. Once again, the water seemed alive. It tingled her tongue and danced down her esophagus. The energy surged through her body, refreshing first her mouth and digestive system, and then awakening even her pores as she felt her heart beating with new joy. Living water. She wished she could bottle that and take some home. But instead she passed the cup on to Jane and stood still, a little dizzy from the whole experience. She watched the cup finish its way around the circle. Sister Angela drained it, tucking it back into her satchel and then signaled for the group to follow.

They fell into line, walking the perimeter of the small compound one more time. Abigail gazed beyond to the graveyard that contained remains of Brigid and some Druids and famous Celtic lords of former times. As they passed by the shrine, Jane pulled out some euros, placing them in a donation box. Abigail took a last look at Brigid holding the flame, framed by three stone arches, presiding over running water below.

***

A few hours later, they prepared to move north for their last two days of the trip. She knew Seamus had planned a special treat of a visit to the Giant's Causeway and a meal in Belfast, before taking them to the Shalem Centre of Peace for the night. She could hardly wait. But first, they must break silence and share their experiences of the retreat. She felt both curious and anxious. She hoped they'd enjoyed the experience.

She finished packing and pulled her suitcase out by the front door, then joined the circle for the closing session. Sister Angela waited by the large singing bowl. Abigail noticed small, unlit candles circling a cross made of shafts of wheat and placed in the center of the chairs. In the center of the cross, encased in glass, a large candle burned.

She heard the rattling of suitcases as others brought theirs to the entrance, creating quite a din after the silence of the past day. Abigail enjoyed silence and was sorry to see it end. Seamus winked at her and then went to put the suitcases into the bus to prepare for departure.

Five minutes later, he returned and took the last seat in the circle. Sister Angela struck the wooden baton on the large copper singing bowl.

She let the sound fade before she spoke. She smiled and looked at each of them around the circle before speaking. "Now we break our silence," she said. "We conclude this sacred time, as you prepare to move on in your journey together. Now we have a time to let you share out of your experience. I know for many of you, this was your first time with the silence. Let's start by talking about that. What was it like? How did it affect you? Did you like it?"

She looked expectantly around the circle and Abigail did as well. She wondered what the others would say. She didn't have to wait long.

Welby spoke first. "I liked it," he said. "Funny how you can hear God when you quit talking. I didn't think I would like it, but I did."

Sister Angela nodded. "Yes, God often speaks in a still, small voice. When we're so busy talking and playing on our cell phones, tablets, computers, listening to TV, and to podcasts, sometimes it's hard to hear that quiet voice. But in the silence? Yes, sir. I agree with you."

Priscilla spoke next. "Yes, there's a quality of stillness here. It felt so holy. I didn't expect that. Very nice, actually," she said.

Abigail was happy. As a Quaker, she knew that their form of

worship seemed strange to many Christians. Sitting in silence for worship each Sunday didn't seem right to many. But here, she appreciated so much that others were finally getting it.

Jane let out a long sigh. "Nice to be able to talk again, I'd say. But I liked it, Sister Angela. A very relaxing, soft space. You wouldn't think it would do all that, just by quitting talking. I found myself thinking deep, and I don't do that very often."

Silence followed. Sister Angela seemed comfortable with that, letting it fill the room. Abigail glanced at her watch several times. They had miles to go on a trip all across Northern Ireland. But then she remembered Ireland wasn't all that big in the first place. She tried to let go of her anxiety. Wasn't that what the silence was all about?

Nikki spoke next. "I don't know that I liked it very much," she said. "I started feeling bad things in the silence. I started thinking about what I've done. Not good, you know? I just kept writing it all down. My journal reads like a bunch of trash from this retreat."

Abigail was surprised when Sister Angela just nodded.

"Good. Good," Sister Angela said.

"No, it's not good," Nikki replied. "It's bad. It gave me nightmares. That's not good."

"Well, no," Sister Angela said, "but, you see, that's the stuff that needs to be cleaned out. When you slow down and listen, bad stuff surfaces. I'm glad you wrote it all down. Now, let it all go. Don't let it control you. Accept God's forgiveness. Let the nightmares go, Nikki."

Nikki's face lit with an incredulous grin. "Really? Just like that?" she asked. "But how do I let it go? I've been having those nightmares for years."

"Ah," Sister Angela said, "yes, that takes time."

George piped up. "Nikki, that sounds like the twelve steps. You're confessing your sins and asking for forgiveness. Maybe you need to make amends? Maybe you need to forgive yourself?"

Silence again, and Abigail felt a shift. She knew that some of these people spent quite a lot of time with the Twelve Steps in AA.

Nikki'd brought it back home, at least on behalf of those who attended the program.

"Let's not turn this into another AA meeting," Charlie whined.

"But maybe that's exactly what you need, man," Welby said.

Charlie shrugged.

Jane said, "Yes, it's the twelve steps, but it's also what happens when you meditate. When I took that class on leading contemplative small groups and retreats, I had to do a lot of reading ... and you know that's not all that easy for me. You read any book on meditation and it'll tell you the same thing. You've got to go through the darkness to get to the light. You've got to deal with your own stuff, your own sin. We Catholics go to confession. We know how to confess. You might make fun of us, but it's very important to us. All that sin clouds up your life, turns you dark. And it's not just your own sin, but it's the sins of others gathering into your life. So you've got to forgive yourself, but you've also gotta forgive others. That can keep you behind bars more than anything else, if you don't let go of that pain."

Abigail sighed. She knew the silence was powerful and here they went off the deep end into something very real. When Jane quit talking, the silence was palpable. Once again, Sister Angela let it be. Abigail decided she loved this lady. Maybe she'd send her an honorary Quaker award when she returned to the States.

Sister Angela said, "So, you see, the Spirit works in the silence. I hope that helps you, Nikki. You were just doing some necessary clearing. The best way out is through. Don't curse the darkness. Look at it, accept it for what it was, and let it go. Forgive. Make amends. Let God love you now. You'll be okay, girl." She nodded. "Thanks for sharing, honey."

And then she asked another question, a very simple one. "What did you learn?" She made eye contact with each of the people around the circle. "What did you *hear* on this retreat? We don't want to be here too long, but I'd like each of you to share a few sentences, if you will. And as you do, please take one of the small candles and light it off the candle in the center and set it back down, as a symbol of the light of God shining within you. Our response to each other will be the Light of God shines within you, flame on."

Sister Angela walked into the center and claimed a small candle. She lit it, then set it back down. "You give me hope. When we created this retreat center a few years back, there were skeptics. When I see and hear you all learning and finding God right here, I feel so very happy." Then she said, "Let's respond." She led them in saying, "The Light of God shines within you, flame on." She continued, "Now, let's just go around the circle, to save time. I don't want to rush you, but ...."

"But you do," Sallie laughed and completed the sentence, but then quieted down to share. "Well, for me, this was a very nice time. I needed some sleep, so I did." Sallie put her hands on her belly and leaned back, then pushed her glasses up onto her nose. "I did need to rest. But I woke up this morning, feeling good. I really loved going to Brigid's Well and getting some of that living water. That was so cool, thinking about people coming there for over fifteen hundred years."

Molly said, "You know, for me, this was a good time to consider past and future. I think back to us starting the FARM, just a couple years ago, to my breast cancer, to Sun Power House, and now this trip and our focus on our roots. It's a lot. God is moving with us. I don't know where we'll end up, but we're moving, we are. Just think about it. It's really something."

"I know," Tom said. "I was thinking about all that, too. When I retired from the police force, I thought I wanted to get a place down in Florida and just relax. But Molly's the boss. At first, I was mad." He looked at her with a lopsided grin, "Sorry, dear," he apologized.

"I know," Molly said. "You told me. I felt sort of bad, but—"

"No, you didn't." Tom laughed. "Fess up, Mol'. You never feel bad about telling me what to do. Don't pretend."

"Okay," Molly admitted. "Okay, you're right."

"But anyway," Tom said, "when you take time to be still, you see the big picture and it all just opened up for me. I watched the trees out here and at Brigid's well. And you know, those trees have air roots, as Mol' likes to call them. A tree is really just a mess of roots into the sky, and then you know there's all kinds of roots down underground, maybe three times as much as the growth you see up above. And you think about all of us being here on this planet, and how we're all connected. Molly and Welby with their Irish DNA. Priscilla and Reagan with some of our African DNA. And these trees, they were here on this Earth long before any of us. And we are all connected. We need each other, you know. Now is not the time for division. We've got common roots and we gotta grow into the sky together."

Molly looked at Tom, her eyes open wide. "Tom," she asked, "what happened to you? Never in all my days have I heard a speech from you like that. This silence is magic, holy. Tom, really?" She paused. "Did you really think all that? Wow."

Tom put his hands up in surrender. Abigail wasn't sure exactly why he did, but she wouldn't argue. Letting Molly define him?

Then Welby said, "You know, I heard some serious stuff on this retreat. You'll probably all think I'm goin' crazy if I tell you."

"You're not crazy," Sister Angela said. "No, you're not. Of course we want to hear it."

Welby grinned sheepishly. "Well, okay. Here goes. But don't forget I warned y'all in advance." He leaned forward and put his big hands on his knees and then sat straight up. "I guess at first, I was like Nikki. I had my sins to deal with and I made short work of them by going into the closet to pray. Nobody needed to tell me I messed up, and when I went into the silence, the first thing I knowed was I gotta 'fess up. Yes, sir, I went down on my knees, and I just poured my heart out, and I cried. I admit it. I cried. That's the way we do down where I come from. I did it right, in the closet. Right, Sister Angela?"

"Yes, but don't be bragging about it too much, or you'll be just like the hypocrites."

"Yes, ma'am," Welby said. "I'll stop all that now. Just so you know, Nikki, I got a whole lot of that bad, too, and I'm working on letting it all go when I get down on my knees to pray."

Nikki nodded and smiled at him.

"After all that, I got wore out and went to bed early, but damned if I didn't see a little leprechaun in the hall and on my bed. Now, here's where it gets crazy. He told me he wants me to be the new MLK. Can you believe it? No, I didn't think so. Just tell me I'm crazy. It's okay. I know it's true." Welby hung his head.

George replied, "Welby, that's not crazy at all. I've just been thinking myself we need a whole slew of new Martin Luther King, Juniors these days. Are you being called up for the job?"

Welby surprised Abigail when he agreed with George. "I think so. I do think so. I told you y'all would think I gone plumb crazy, but I do believe that's what the good Lord wants me to do. I pass."

Seamus thanked the group for letting him join along and said he'd had a particularly bright morning talking with the spiritual director, pointing at Abigail. Everyone laughed. Priscilla said she appreciated time to pray. Katharine said she'd liked visiting the well. She said she'd visited other Irish wells on a tour once. George said he'd talked to God for the first time in a long time.

Then even Charlie spoke up. He'd been quiet until then. Abigail didn't know what he'd say. "This silent retreat got me going. When you set this all up last night, I thought you were all crazy. Not just you, Welby. It's the whole lot of you." He laughed. "I never heard nothing like this in all my life. Silent retreat? Crazy! And leprechauns. Welby, that's plumb crazy, too."

Welby shrugged, raising his hands with a smile.

Charlie smiled back and continued. "But when I actually went into the silence? Wow. I heard something, for real. You know what? I started to see our country coming back together again. I saw Ace Steele shaking Alejandro Rosales' hand. I saw a right-wing political talk show host sitting down with a Democratic president and laughing over some grub. And I saw Welby, here, and Reagan, sitting side by side and not arguing, but—"

"Right," Welby interrupted. "Not goin' down in this lifetime."

"He's joking," Nikki said. "Can't you take a joke, Welby?"

But Charlie didn't laugh. "I'm dead serious, man."

Reagan's eyes opened wide, and Abigail looked at Sister Angela, wondering how to respond. Sister Angela knew exactly what to say. "In the silence, sometimes we move beyond either/or to both/and. The paradox, sometimes called bridge thinking. Your presidents, Steele and Rosales, seem light years away from each other. But in the sacred silence, you never know where the answers will come from. You just know that they will. Both/and. Everything is possible."

Reagan reached behind her chair and pulled out a picture. She held it on her lap so everyone could see. It was a beautiful rendering of the labyrinth at sunset, with an African-American woman standing at the labyrinth, laughing.

"What's that?" Welby said. "Where'd you see her? Reagan, you seein' ghosts?"

Reagan laughed a little bit. "Well, you saw a leprechaun; at least I saw a human. This lady came to the labyrinth last night. She said she knew you. Have you ever seen her before?"

Welby got quiet. He looked at the floor, cradling his head in his hands. Then he looked up at Reagan.

"Oh, man," he said. "That's my Grand MaMa, my great-grandmother."

"What?" Reagan said. "What? You actually know that woman?"

"Oh, yes," Welby replied. "That old lady's been haunting me ever since I got to Ohio. She visited me at the monastery the other day, and before that, at the castle. Don't get me wrong, she's a nice person. If there was ever a person in this world who loved, she's the one. But she's been dead since I was a little boy. Now she's haunting you, too, Reagan? I can hear that laugh. That lady loved to laugh."

Silence again. Abigail felt energy passing between Reagan and Welby. Curiosity got the best of her. "Reagan, did the woman have a message for you?"

Reagan looked at the painting and then at Welby, as if to ask for permission. Then she said, "I think she laughed because I wouldn't talk to her. Silent retreat, you know? She didn't respect the silence." Reagan laughed, and the rest of the group joined her.

Reagan cleared her throat. "Actually, she welcomed me into the family. Now that I'm Black, you know? She was very friendly. It was weird. Very weird."

"Amen, sista. Say that again. We all part of one big family, right? That's Grand MaMa for you. Sure enough sounds just like something she'd say." Welby paused and looked straight at Sister Angela. "What's going on here, Sister? Is this place haunted or what?"

"Well, well, well," Sister Angela replied.

"That's a deep subject," Jane quipped. "We were just there this morning."

Everybody laughed again. Abigail thought the group needed the comic relief. Always, debriefing silent retreats brought stories, but these were really something. Unusual. Then she laughed at herself. What would they think if she told them about her visits from the leprechaun, and Saint Brigid? Maybe she'd leave that for another day. Or then again, maybe this was the perfect time. But before she could bring it up, Sister Angela started talking again.

"We call it 'thin space' here in Ireland. The veil between this world and the next becomes very thin at times. If you read Irish folklore, you'll hear many stories like yours. So, relax, Welby. It's okay, Reagan. These things happen here. For centuries, the little people, the leprechauns, have lived in this place. Many of the old Irish believe the spirits of the departed inhabit a place. You're not the first person, and you won't be the last. What's important is what you do with the message. What are you going to take away from this retreat?"

Reagan's eyes grew large again. "Oh," she said. "It's deep, very deep. To see myself connected with the African-Americans in our country? That's something. That's really something. After me and my people have spent a lot of time distancing ourselves, now to realize I'm one of them? My whole family, actually. And that they want to welcome me, after the way we've treated them. I don't know about all this." She looked at the picture of Grand MaMa laughing. "But her? I like her. She's something real good."

Welby looked at Reagan and Abigail saw a light come on in his eyes. She'd seen Welby looking Reagan up and down before, but this was different. She saw a gentleness, she saw something more. And then she noticed the light in Seamus' eyes for her. He winked. She smiled. And then she decided better late than never. She might as well spill the beans.

"Okay, folks. Here goes." She stopped and looked around. "I didn't tell you about this before because I thought you might think I was crazy. But now that Welby and Reagan have shared, I guess I better come clean as well."

She looked at Welby. "That leprechaun? He's been talking to me, too. Since before I left home even. He visited me in my living room. He's been in the bus. He popped up over at Newgrange. I didn't see him here, though."

"And you think I'm crazy, seeing Steele and Rosales together back home?" Charlie asked.

Sister Angela frowned. "Let's listen." Then she asked. "What did he say, Abby?"

"Well, it's all good. He's encouraging me to enjoy life, to listen, to love. He's a nice little guy, actually. I don't know much about leprechauns, I admit. He's the first one I've ever met."

That led to more laughter and Abigail laughed as well.

"Yes," Sister Angela said. "The leprechauns are good little people. Sometimes tricksters, but it sounds like you got an uplifting one."

Abigail nodded. "And there's more. I saw Brigid at the well."

"Oh. My. God," Reagan said. "You saw Saint Brigid? What did she look like? What did she say?"

Abigail smiled. Sharing the story seemed much easier than she imagined. "Well, she looked like the lady in the statue. I kept thinking the rest of you could see her, but I guess not. She offered me water from the well. Wow. That was something. Wait. I wrote down what she said. It was really heavy."

Abigail pulled her notebook out of her backpack and began to read. "Do you see the bridge over the creek there? Keep focusing on that bridge. I heard you talking about it earlier. I love the way you've been encouraging all your people to listen on this trip. The listening circles, so important. Each person, with their inner lights, will illuminate your way. There are powerful connections building among you that will become a beacon into peace for your future."

Charlie spoke up. "Okay, I'm beginning to have some doubts. You *are* crazy. Leprechauns, Welby's great grandmother, Saint Brigid? I think there's some thin space between you all and sanity, that's what I think. You're losing it, man."

"No, Charlie," Reagan said. "Just listen. This is really something. You know Brigid's been talking to me, too. She talks to me about the way of Jesus. Do you think God is trying to get us to do something? This is big."

Sister Angela smiled. "Yes, God wants you all to do something. You've all got a mission in this world. That's why we're here. And listening on a silent retreat helps you hear your call. I think you've all got some work to do. I'm so glad you could be here with us. So glad you hear the voice of God, and Brigid, our leprechauns, and Grand MaMa. Now it's up to you to answer. Let's pray before you move along." She looked at Abigail. "Could you close us out, Abigail?"

Abigail nodded, grabbed the hands of those to either side of her and motioned for the others to do likewise. Then, she prayed, "Dear God, you have brought us together in this circle, in this time. Thank you for the voices from Brigid, the leprechaun, and Grand MaMa. Thank you for speaking to us during this silent retreat. As we go forth, help us to continue to think about our call in this world. Help us to be Light. Help us to build bridges. Help us work for peace and keep the legacy of Saint Brigid alive. In the name of Jesus, we pray. Amen."

CHAPTER FOURTEEN
HEADING NORTH

Those Surprising Little Green Men

Welby remembered the counselor back home who'd tried to draw him out years ago. Struggling to name his feelings had felt like crawling out of a swamp. Impossible. Back then, he always seemed to be sinking into some sort of mess that he couldn't get a handle on. Now he'd discovered clarity.

Now that he'd had some time to figure it all out, he wanted to start praying hard about his future. Because back there in the closet, back there on the labyrinth, back there with that little green man, he'd suddenly begun to feel the sadness he'd carried for so long begin to lift. He could actually feel happiness starting to seep in.

Seamus interrupted his thinking. "A change of plans, we have now. I'll be a taking ye on a tour over to Dublin town to visit the National Leprechaun Museum. Since the little men decided to haunt our Abigail and Welby, I thought ye might want to know ye be in good company. My friend Laura will give ye a tour. And then we be heading on up Belfast way for a Black Cab Tour. We'll also slip in a visit to the coast before we bunk at Shalem Centre. Now I need to make up some time, so hang on for a quick ride up to Dublin."

Welby felt a smile forming on his lips. A Leprechaun Museum? This could be fun. Perhaps he wasn't really going crazy, or if he was, his Irish forefathers and mothers had paved the way for his insanity years ago.

"Are you serious?" Sallie called. "Is there really a Leprechaun Museum?"

Seamus picked his microphone back up. "Aye. A national museum devoted to them. Opened in 2010. Designed by Tom O'Rahilly with help from some Italian designers. They dedicated it to our Irish folklore and mythology and to our oral tradition of storytelling. Claims to be the first leprechaun museum in the world. And 'tis probably so, for where else in the world would you find a leprechaun?"

"Do the leprechauns live there?" Sallie asked.

Seamus laughed. "Well, we'll just have to find out, won't we? Wait and see."

Welby felt drowsy and closed his eyes. Soon he was sound asleep.

At least until Charlie tugged on his arm. "Wake up, man. Quit snoring. We're at the museum."

Welby rubbed his face. What museum? Oh, the leprechauns. *Leprechauns, here I come.*

"Now, ye all just line up here and wait a few minutes. I got ye tickets for the next tour. I'll park the bus and be back to collect ye," Seamus said as he handed George the tickets.

Welby followed the group into a small triangular lobby that looked something like a movie theater back home. A woman sat behind a glass window. A sign read 16 euros. He laughed. Twenty bucks a head for this show?

Welby started to read the signs on the wall, waiting for their turn. Okay, so they have a night tour in the dark. Probably trying to scare somebody, just like he'd jumped out of his skin when he encountered that little man back at the Holy Well Centre. He pulled his coat tighter just as the lady ushered them into the next room where the tour would begin. He felt the warmth of a heater and paused to take the chill off. Back home, it was colder. He knew he shouldn't complain at the fifty degree weather, but his blood liked the hot sun of the South.

They crowded into a little room with mirrored doors at one end and leprechaun stuff displayed behind the glass in little cubicles all around. Soon, he figured, they'd enter the enchanted kingdom of the little green men. In the meantime, he would check out the displays.

Yep, definitely a museum of leprechauns. Everywhere he looked were little figurines, dolls, and displays. He stopped beside the photo of a rather stern-looking man. The First President of Ireland, Douglas Hyde, the sign read. A quote from Hyde, who'd died in 1949, proclaimed: Every hill, every crag and gnarled tree and lonely valley, has its own strange and graceful legend attached to it.

He liked that. Grand MaMa would approve. She'd say the same thing, if she had the chance.

He sidled up to a portrait of a grey-haired lady. Underneath her picture, another quote: They go by in a cloud of dust, they are as many as the blades of grass. They are everywhere... This is the news I have been given by some who have seen them and some who have known their power.

He guessed that referred to leprechauns, although it didn't say. Lady Gregory, a dramatist and folklorist, died 1932. She seemed to be talking to him from behind the glass.

"Look at this," he heard George telling Molly. "What's this about?"

George stood in front of a sign saying something about the

166

leprechauns. "The leprechauns didn't have civil rights, either. We've got something in common with these little guys. This man wants a government of leprechauns, saying it would be better than what they've got."

Welby stood alongside and read: *Some of my best friends are leprechauns. But they have been denied civil rights. They may not sit in Parliament, join the guard or own property.*

Was this real or a joke? The plaque credited it as being from the Irish Times back in 1946.

"Is that for real?" he asked George.

"Hard to tell," George said.

The guide interrupted them. "Hi. I'm Laura, and I'll be taking ye on the tour. Now, before we start, I want to know if there are any Americans here?"

Sallie said, "I'm from America. And so are all my friends here with me."

"Okay," Laura said. "Then I need to say thank you. You Americans made leprechauns very popular. Back in the nineteenth century, we had the potato famine here and many of the Irish left for America. And everywhere they went, they took our stories. And so the leprechauns became well known from the tales they told. But did ye know that the leprechauns here stayed underground and tried to hide from the people? When they did appear, they'd be a-wearin' brown to hide themselves from being seen.

"And ye've heard tell 'bout how the grass is always greener? Those who went to America wanted their children to know about the beauty of Ireland, and so the stories they told were of a land where all the skies are blue and the grass so many shades of green, and so beautiful that before long, even the leprechauns were dressed all in green, as well.

"Step through the door to the left of the mirrors, walk through the tunnel, and I'll meet you in the next room."

Someone pushed open the door. They walked through a circular tunnel of wooden slats. At the end of the corridor, a round, shiny blue mirror shrank their reflections, making them look like little people. From there, they entered the next room, which held several large chairs.

Abigail got the idea that they should all pose, so Welby climbed up into one of the high chairs and smiled as she snapped his photograph. If you get your picture taken in an over-sized chair, you look like a little person. Welby the Leprechaun; that's what he'd look like, having his picture taken in the oversized chair. Maybe it would be fun to click up that kind of magic.

In one corner, Reagan and Nikki cuddled up with Charlie on a big, upholstered chair. Welby laughed, but didn't appreciate that Charlie put his arms around the women for the shot.

Laura joined them, ushering them into a small room with a bed, a table, and a bench. Welby made himself at home on the bench.

"This room is about as big as many of the cottages where the people lived in days gone by," Laura explained. "And they didn't have TV, radio, or computers back then. But they had stories. Many a night, they would sit around and share the tales of the little people." To illustrate, she launched into a leprechaun tale.

Welby tuned her out and thought about the slave houses back in the South. Nobody lived in them anymore, so they seemed haunted. They were little places, like this little room. When he returned his attention to Laura, she was finishing up her story. He had a hard time understanding her Irish accent, and hadn't listened to the story, but the rest of the group seemed to enjoy her enough.

"This is so cool," Sallie told the tour guide. "I love these stories. Thank you."

Welby rolled his eyes as Laura led them into yet another room, where she told more stories. They walked through a passageway decorated with a painted forest and entered into a room with a big map of Ireland in the center. A special projector illuminated the ancient civilizations of Ireland. A recorded voice explained how the early people created Newgrange and the Hill of Tara, aligned with the heavens, and how legends emerged.

"Wow," said Reagan. "A map of Ireland. Look, that's where we were. Newgrange."

Laura nodded and told another story. While the rest of the group seemed enthralled with the legend, this one put Welby to sleep.

The tour ended at a customary gift shop. In the corner, a little stuffed leprechaun perched on a bench for photo ops. This time, Welby posed with the ladies. Abigail passed out green hats to Reagan and Nikki, and then to Welby. He placed the hat on his head, doubting it could turn him into a leprechaun. Then Abigail handed him a beard. Welby dutifully stretched the elastic around his head. With Reagan on one side and Nikki on the other, Welby wrapped his arms around both of them.

"Say cheese," Abigail instructed, and then counted, "One, two, three."

***

Once Seamus returned, Welby walked out to the bus. The strange little museum had given him more questions than answers. Of course, it might have helped if he'd listened to the stories.

Seamus pointed the bus north. He picked up the mic and asked, "So what did y'all think of our National Leprechaun Museum? Did you enjoy that stop?"

Welby decided to listen, rather than complain, not wanting to put a damper on their fun.

"I loved that, Seamus," Sallie said. "Thank you. Weren't the stories humorous? My kindergarteners would love those tales. Makes me wish I were teaching again. I'd tell them about the leprechauns and then we could imagine them lurking about. It was a lot of laughs. Glad we went."

Molly said, "Did you see that about discrimination against the little people? Was that a joke? George said they were lobbying for their rights. Did the leprechauns get a bad rap?"

Seamus chuckled. "I can't say for sure on that one, Molly. Remember, we Irish boast the gift of blarney, we do. They may have been pullin' your leg. I'll have to ask Laura about that."

"I love the way they explained the history with the map, showing the ancient societies, focused on the seasons and the sun," Katharine said. "Ireland's history is rich with so many archaeological sites, the ancient Druids, magic, and Saint Patrick's Christian missionary work. I got the impression that the leprechauns were remnants from an earlier time."

"I asked Laura where the leprechauns originated," Abigail said. "She said there are a lot of theories, but they aren't really sure. Maybe there were actually short people at one time, or maybe it's part of the magic and the fairy understandings from their early religion."

"My grandmother talked about them," Reagan said. "The museum reminded me of her. She made us think they were all around when I was a little girl."

"I liked it, too," said Nikki. "It was fun. Thanks for taking us, Seamus."

Charlie weighed in from the back. "A bunch of blarney, if you ask me. Just trying to get your money. A tourist trap."

Seamus laughed. "Yes, well. That, too, Charlie, so it is. And the thing with the storytelling of the Irish is it brings some joy and some answers to life. You're never quite sure what's real and what's a fabrication, but that's okay. The museum shares that with the tourists, ye see?"

"I get it," Charlie said. "It's just not for me."

Welby nodded, again keeping silent. He hadn't liked the museum. But it spooked him that he could still hear the words his small visitor had shared back at the retreat center. Maybe what he'd been told was real. Maybe not. He didn't know.

Black Cab Belfast

Abigail's thoughts twirled around the leprechauns and Seamus as she sought the seat closest to Seamus. She still couldn't quite believe she'd found a Quaker in Ireland. And not only a Quaker, but a singer and a storyteller, too.

"Where are we going now?" she asked. "To the Giant's Causeway? First the little people, then the giant? You Irish do have the stories, don't you?"

"Aye, for sure," Seamus replied. "Me mum had a story for every occasion. By the time I graduated school, I'd heard them all a hundred times. She could never remember what she'd already told me. My brother and I would finish the stories, imitating her exaggerations. She'd laugh and slap our behinds."

"Do the Irish people go to that museum, or is that just for the tourists?" Jane asked. "I've heard that Ireland is all about the tourists these days. It's a big money-maker for the entire country."

"Well, Jane, you're right about that," Seamus said. "I don't imagine the Leprechaun Museum would have been built without the tourists in mind. It's for you foreigners. But I think most of the Irish people have visited it, too, by now. We are the keepers of our past, and the leprechauns have kept the Irish people laughing through some hard times."

"Did you say we have another stop before the causeway?" Abigail asked.

"Aye, my love. We be heading up Belfast way for another tour before we go on up north. Belfast, the capital of Northern Ireland, tells another part of our story here. Because, you see, we've been a country divided, just like yours. Between the north and the south, the Catholics and the Protestants. It's a different story, with the same culprits. The King of England messed everything up. He stole many of the Africans away from their happy homes, selling them into slavery in the USA. He took over our monasteries and messed up our people, too. Ah, the people in power, always taking advantage of the little guy, aren't they?"

"I don't know much about the Irish conflict," Abigail said. "You had a long civil war?"

"Aye, we did. We call it 'the troubles' and so it was, a whole lot of trouble for my people. Only now are we putting it behind and trying to put our country back together again."

Sallie said, "Humpty Dumpty sat on the wall. Humpty Dumpty

had a great fall. All the king's horses and all the king's men couldn't put Humpty Dumpty together again."

Seamus laughed; Jane rolled her eyes. Sallie reprimanded her. "Okay, Jane. Roll your eyes all you want. It's true, isn't it, Seamus, that the king's men couldn't put it together again?"

Seamus responded. "Well, no, they couldn't. Not for a long time. You'll hear all about it soon. Ask the tour guide in Belfast about the king's men. He'll give you an earful."

"Is that where that nursery rhyme came from?" Sallie asked.

"Funny you should ask," Seamus said. "I've heard tell that goes back to King Richard III of England way back in 1493. You see, he had a hump on his back, and it was a story they made up about the king, not the country."

"Is there anything you don't know?" Abigail asked him.

Seamus laughed again. "Oh, 'tis my country, love. Of course I know about my country and the kings and queens of England. But a lot of my knowledge stops right here. It's my job, you know? Whatever you focus on, you become the expert, right?"

"Okay, that makes sense," Abigail said.

"Northern Ireland," Seamus said. "It's a different country up there. At one time, the whole island belonged together. But back in 1948, the southern part established themselves as the Independent Republic of Ireland. They govern themselves, but Northern Ireland belongs to Great Britain. So the troubles started long ago. There are only six counties up here in the north, and twenty-six in the south. Ye see, the king didn't keep very much of our land."

"Do the people in the north want to be independent?" Sallie asked.

"Well, by then, it was the Parliament. I don't want to spoil the story for ye. You'll get an earful, more than ye want, probably, from my chap Ryan up there in Belfast. But just so you know, the north tends to have the Protestants, and the Republic is more Catholic. But all that's changing these days, too. And then ye have the Loyalist, or Unionists, the ones who side with the Brits. And the Nationalists, or Republicans, those are the ones who want to be independent. And you still will see all of these in the north. Some still want to get out of the Commonwealth.

"Oh, and your euros aren't good up there. We'll have to stop and convert to the British pound. Your dollars won't buy as much right now. The value goes up and down, but right now, the pound's way ahead of the euro and further yet ahead of the dollar. Economics, ye know?"

Abigail still had much to learn about Ireland, and only one more day. Perhaps she needed to come back. She certainly hoped to. Could she live here? Could she give up living in the States? She didn't know. Perhaps they could go back and forth. Was she getting ahead of herself? Did Seamus do this with all his tourists? He'd said no, but again she wondered.

"How far is it to Belfast?" she asked.

"Oh, a good two and a half hours. So you might want to read a book or take a long nap, or then again, maybe we could just have a good chat." Seamus hung up the microphone and turned to Abigail, jumping in as if he'd read her thoughts. "Now, dear, do ye want me to come visit you sometime soon? I've got some vacation coming up. Actually, I'm on vacation more than I'm on the clock these days. Even back before I lost my wife, I'd been cutting back. Trying to ease into retirement slowly. After I lost her, I needed something to keep me going, so I picked up more tours. But we're coming up to the slow season now. The tourists don't like to be around when the temperature dips, ye know. It gets a wee bit cold here in the winters and the rains come. My job slows down until March or April when it starts to pick up again. So, Abigail, I could come for a long visit, if ye'll have me."

Abigail felt nervous. She'd only known the man for a few days. A moment ago, she wondered if he was playing her, but ... had he just invited himself to her home? She wasn't sure she was ready for that. Questions swirled in her mind. *What would the neighbors think? Would we have separate beds?*

Her emotions bounced her back and forth, up and down as more questions flooded in. *Invite him to the US? Move to Ireland? Do I trust this man? How do you date a man from another country? Moving right in seems a little abrupt, but then maybe you have to write a different script in the later part of life. Why wait? It's not like young love where we have our whole future to imagine.*

"Cat got your tongue, Abby?" Seamus asked. "Maybe I misread you."

Abigail looked over to see if Jane and Sallie were listening. She didn't want her friends to hear their discussion, but they seemed to be snoozing already.

She searched for the right words, then settled on honesty. "This is all so quick, Seamus. I really like you a lot, and I know you like me, too. But can we trust these feelings to last? Is it too soon? How do we do this?"

Abigail stopped. She needed to leap if she wanted to enjoy her future. God knows she'd grown very tired of lonely nights. She didn't want to die alone.

She cleared her throat and summoned courage. "I'd love for you to visit, Seamus. Yes, I would. I'd love to show you my home and introduce you to my people."

"I'd like that, I would," Seamus replied.

Abigail smiled, looking with Seamus at the road ahead. The miles seemed to be speeding by, just like the days of her life.

"Seamus," she said. "My husband and I planned to travel in retirement. Now those ideas are just gathering dust in my desk drawer. Have you seen the States? Want to travel with me?"

Seamus chuckled. "Well, love. I've never been to yer country. All new to me, ye see. Just the holiday for an old tour guide like me. Listen to other tour guides spinning tales? Yes. I'd love that. Ye know, me wife and I made plans of our own. We hoped to visit that land of yers, we did. But after the children, then came the grandchildren, and my work. Everything got delayed. Before we knew it, me love came up sick."

"Just like us, then." Abigail said. "You had your travel plans as well." Abigail started getting excited. "How soon could you come? For Thanksgiving? Christmas?" With Seamus, perhaps the sun would be shining brightly again.

"Let me think on this, Abby dear. I must talk to my kids, ye know? They like me around for the holidays. But after Christmas? They might be happy putting me on a plane. One less thing to worry about in their busy lives."

Abigail could hardly contain her excitement. "You could come the day after Christmas. My children will still be in town, so you could meet my family. Then we could go to Florida, to the beach."

"Abby," Seamus said. "I'd love that, I would. And I'd love you to meet all of my family as well. Maybe that could be arranged before you leave. Would you like to meet me clan, Abby?"

"Yes," Abigail replied. "Of course. When?"

The traffic picked up, drawing Seamus' attention. Abigail leaned back, enjoying the view, not only of the Irish countryside, but also of the man. With this funny, kind Quaker man in the driver's seat, she would enjoy traveling again. But first, Belfast. Maybe learning about the troubles would help her gain insight for the divided USA. She closed her eyes and relaxed.

***

Seamus' bright tenor voice bugled out into the quiet bus. "It's time to get up. It's time to get up. It's time to get up this afternoon."

Abigail woke abruptly and laughed. Her heart warmed over this jolly Irish man, so familiar to her now, after such a short period of time.

"All right now, we're coming up to the taxicabs for our Black Cab Tour. Our drivers will teach us about the Troubles of Ireland. We have ye divided into three groups now. The men will be with Paddy O'Ryan and the women will be divided between my friends Ryan O'Mallory and Colin Russell. The cabs will fit five of ye, four in the back on two seats facing each other, and one seat in the front beside the driver."

Abigail collected her belongings, spilling out with the others onto the sidewalk of a busy Belfast street. A row of cabs waited at the curb. Seamus locked up the bus and then shook hands with the drivers and assigned them to the cars.

Seamus sent the men with Paddy, but assigned himself to Abby's car. He opened the door for her to sit in the solo seat beside the driver, and climbed into the back with Sallie, Nikki, and Jane. On the one hand, she got it. He wanted to give her the best seat. On the other hand, in this case, she sure would like to be riding back there with him. Maybe she could switch at the next stop.

Abigail couldn't think of Belfast without thinking of bombings, but it looked like a modern city now. Still, she felt fearful. The cabs looked like they'd been around the block a few times, too. The city was more dingy than Dublin, yet as they drove through the neighborhoods, the buildings were well-kept, much better than some of the Ohio towns she knew.

Ryan started out chatting up the group and continued nonstop for the next hour and a half. He explained the troubles in his own life. Born into a Catholic family in 1971, he'd grown up in fear, never knowing which people he loved might be killed next.

"In 1920, England divided Ireland," he said. "They kept Northern Ireland under their control but formed an independent state in the south. Tension continued through the years. The troubles began in 1969. So ye see, I was born right into it. It was all I ever knew."

At their first stop, Ryan parked across the street from a long building with a series of murals. As they got out of the car, he pointed at a mural and talked about the subjugation of the Catholics. "The young people went to prison, but they refused to wear the clothes of criminals, so they wore none at all. They were treated like animals, really. They spread their excrement over the walls. They went on hunger strikes."

"Ewww," Sallie said. "How could they do that? *Why* did they do that?"

"Yes, I know. I wondered, too," Ryan responded. "But you see, they had no choice. If they left the stuff in the corner of the cell, it would draw maggots. The prison guards didn't empty their pots. That was the best they could do. Of course, those people who stayed in those cells ended up with a lot of mental health issues that lasted for years."

He pointed out the Irish flag made of green and orange, with white, the color of peace, in between. "That's what we want, but it's not all there," he said. "In 1998, they made the peace, but, you see, Ireland is still divided, the northern part still with Great Britain. We wanted it to be all together. But we wanted an end to fighting more. So that's what we have.

Abigail thought the civil war had ended. She didn't know that the people didn't feel at peace. She wanted to learn more.

"As an adult, I don't follow religion anymore. I believe we're all the same. I'm non-sectarian. But back when I turned of age and went to get a job, they asked me if I was Protestant or Catholic. Of course, I grew up Catholic. People knew. I had to tell them. Then they told me, 'No job for you.' And that's how it was. But now we can have a better life and raise a family and not live in fear. And that's what I want for my children. I teach them to like all people. They can't put down either side in my house. I don't allow it.

"Back then, though, the Unionists killed the Republicans for fun. One time, we had a funeral possession and, all of a sudden, a car with two young men drove into the procession. The people pulled the men out of the car and would have torn them apart, but the IRA wouldn't let that happen. Instead, they took them away. Because if the people had beaten them and killed them on the spot, it would have been just what they wanted: to show that the Catholics were evil. Turned out those were two military members, ordered to stir up trouble."

Ryan led the group back to the cab and drove around the block to another mural. This time, they stayed in the car. "That's Bobby Sands," he said. "This was their place to meet." He told about people being shot right there, people he knew. "One time, a policeman came to the building and knocked. When they didn't open the door, he broke in and killed three people, including Paddy, someone everyone loved. That policeman was crazy, with a mental health problem, but, still, he killed the people, ye know, and that doesn't make it right."

He read aloud Sands' quote, "'Our revenge will be the laughter of our children.' One time, I was at a soccer game with me wife. Everyone was having a good time, laughing, and I told her, 'This is the life, ye know, to hear the laughter of our children.'"

Seamus took Abigail to the side and put his arm around her. "He tells a one-sided view of the troubles. Bobby Sands killed people. The IRA did much bombing. That story he told about the funeral has other versions. The crowd tore the clothes off the men and started to beat them, then the IRA took them away and executed them. I'll tell ye the rest later. I just wanted ye to hear the Catholic side, because back home you hear only the BBC."

As they walked back to the car, Abigail whispered to Seamus, "Can I sit in the back with you?"

"Aye, my love," He gave her a squeeze and opened the front door of the cab, motioning to Nikki. "Yer turn for the front, Nikki. Then Jane, at the next stop." He opened the back door for Abby. She scooted over into the middle of the back seat, leaving the window seat for Jane. She settled in, happy to be close to Seamus for the ride.

They stopped again in a small memorial park where a mural depicted those who died during the Troubles, with names and dates. "You'll see members of the IRA on this side, civilians on the other," the guide explained.

"They killed five-year-olds?" Sallie asked. Abigail knew she was thinking of her students.

"Yes," Ryan said. "Now the police say there was a riot going on and that it was an accident. But we lived here; there was no riot that day."

They stood in the quiet afternoon, considering the faces of the children and adults killed. Abigail felt the loss, the pain, and wondered how people weathered such suffering.

Behind the garden, Ryan pointed out the Peace Wall, scheduled to come down in 2019. "Now," he said, "it's sad that the house over there needs a screen to protect itself from debris thrown over the fence. But the Protestants still throw things at the Catholics over the wall."

Abigail tried to imagine having to screen in her own porch for protection.

Their tour continued on to the Protestant part of town, not too far away. "Still segregated, you see." He showed a memorial to one of their own slain. "That man's no hero," he complained. "He killed Catholics and also turned to drugs in his later years. The Protestants have a saying: 'Kill All Pigs'. Catholics are pigs, they say. They write KAP on the buildings."

He pointed out some graffiti, but Abigail read KAT, not KAP. She wondered if it had worn, or if it really meant something else, because nearby, a building sported a mural of a quilt made by the Protestant women proclaiming: Women's voices matter, Equality for all, Love, Peace, and Friend.

Abigail thought of the Grandmothers for Peace group the MAMs had started after their trip to Ephesus and about how women everywhere want peace. She took some pictures of the quilt to post to their website and found herself wanting to know more about these women. She hoped they'd have time to talk it all over later, maybe at the Shalem Centre for Peace.

Ryan told them they were out of time, and he'd be taking them back. Abigail sat quietly, thinking, imagining, wondering. So much pain in this city, in the life of this man. Finding a path to peace was never an easy task, it seemed.

Seamus instructed Jane, "Your turn for the front seat, Jane. Then he opened the back door for Abigail and gave her a quick hug. "Hard to hear about the troubles, my love, eh? It's not a pretty story."

Abigail frowned. "No, it's very disturbing. How do people do this to each other? Why?"

"I know. If the people would all just become Quakers, we'd have peace, eh?"

Abigail smiled. "I loved the women's quilt in the Protestant section. If only women could rule the world."

"Aye," Seamus responded. "But we have some female leaders that don't make the peace either. What's the solution? Here, you know the troubles never really go away."

Abigail let the thought go. She didn't want to try to solve the problems of the world right then. She just wanted to enjoy. She took a deep breath and let a smile spread across her face. She definitely wanted Seamus to be a part of her life.

Soon they were back in the bus, and Abigail thought they were finally going straight to their evening destination, but Seamus pulled into a little house on a quiet street instead. "And now, ladies and gentlemen, I want you to meet a very good old friend of mine for another look at the Troubles, Sir Ethan Johnson. He's approaching ninety this year. Lives on the Protestant side, he does. And he'll give ye something to think about. He's seen it all. Like a good Irishman, he loves to talk up a storm. Just listen. Take notes. Later, we can talk about it."

Abigail felt tired as she climbed out of the bus and walked up to the door of the little brick house. Seamus knocked and a woman answered, then invited them inside. They crowded into the living room where a frail man sat on a plump cushioned chair. Beside him on a table rested a crown. A British flag hung from a pole in the corner of the room. On the walls, pictures of stern men in military uniforms from various eras presided. Abigail shivered.

"Welcome, welcome," Sir Ethan said. "Good to see ye again, Seamus. Thank ye for bringing another group to hear from an old man what really happened to my homeland. I come from a long line of loyal Brits, dating way back. We line our genealogy up with the kings and queens of England. And then come these Irish nationalists. All they needed to do was to go along with the crown, but, instead, they wanted to overthrow our queen. We are good God-fearing Presbyterians, always ready to serve our country, loyal through and through. Like ye say in America, God, guns, and apple pie? A similar thing, ye know?"

"I never heard that, never mind say it," Sallie whispered to Abigail.

Abigail nodded, somewhat embarrassed, although also agreeing with her friend. She noticed Charlie seemed all ears. Reagan and Priscilla were standing near, leaning in and smiling. Maybe what he said resonated with them, if not with Abigail and Sallie.

"The mother country gave the Irish most of the island, but that wasn't enough. So then you have these northern parts, still under Great Britain. In Northern Ireland, a civil rights movement started up to give the Nationals their due, and soon street fighting broke out. They formed gangs and started shooting innocent people. Over half the people killed during the Troubles were innocents, not members of official organizations or militias."

Abigail mulled that over for a moment. Over half the casualties were innocent people? Obviously, there *were* two sides to this story. It was hard to imagine what that level of conflict would be like. While there was conflict in the States, but open warfare seemed the exception, rather than the rule, although it crossed her mind that Black people might say it was more violent than she thought it was. She looked at Welby. He stood over in the corner, but his eyes were locked on Ethan, engaged, and carefully watching.

"When the IRA started shooting our people, what could we do but shoot back? If they just would have stayed in their place, there would have been no trouble. None at all. So that's the way war happens. One side starts it, the other defends, and then you start going back and forth. And the problem here was it wasn't just the police, but the young people took it on as a personal vendetta and started shooting people right and left. The IRA were no knights in shining armor, like some pretend. No, they killed innocents to make a point. They kidnapped good people just out shopping on the wrong side of town.

"My own son joined the Ulster gang. After some of his friends got killed, he went out one night and shot a Catholic in revenge. Never could live with himself after that, he couldn't. He served time for his crime, but that wasn't enough. He took his own life a few years back. Nothing could make him right again after that. But he just did what the others did, ye know? He blamed himself, but that's war. He was a good boy."

Ethan stopped, closed his eyes, and took a deep breath. Abigail looked around the room. Everyone seemed spellbound. This storyteller spoke from his heart. A moment later, Ethan opened his eyes and lifted his frail hand with a sigh. His fingers shook as he pointed to a picture of a young man on the wall standing by the British flag. "That's my William."

Priscilla closed the distance between them and patted the man on the shoulder. "I'm so sorry," she said.

Ethan continued, "So, you see, we Loyalists, you might view like the older son in the Prodigal Son story. We always did the right thing, paid our dues, worked hard, loved God and the Queen. Yes, we did our best to follow the narrow path, and then these Catholic Nationalists rose up and attacked us. We had to fight back. We still need to protect our neighborhoods from them."

"No, you can't let them take over, can you?" Charlie said. "My dad always taught me to stand up and defend what's mine. And always to love and fight for our country."

Oh, my, Abigail thought. *Charlie understands the old man. Maybe that attitude explains a whole lot of the tension in the USA today.* Around the room, she saw smiles–Priscilla, Reagan, Nikki, Jane, and frowns — Sallie, Molly, Welby. The others' faces were neutral. George and Tom stood with their arms crossed, impassively listening.

"We have the peace now, but they had to put a wall up to keep the two sides from killing each other. And twenty years later, we still have a divided Belfast. We stay on our side, the Catholics stay on theirs, and still they fight. Not as much, but the Catholics throw a missile over the wall, and so our boys throw one back. That's the way it is.

"Loyalists are law-abiding citizens. We follow the rule of law. We serve our country. We may be across the channel, but we're a part of our mother land, Great Britain. We wouldn't have it any other way."

What he said made sense to Abigail. A law-abiding citizen. She could understand his point of view. She looked back at the pictures of military men hanging about the room and saw more. A twinkle in one's eye, a slight smile at the curve of another's lip. Courage and resolve. She knew there were always two sides. What she'd just learned made the whole conflict just a little clearer in her mind. She continued to ponder the situation long after they boarded the bus to drive north to the coast.

Giant's Causeway

As they left downtown Belfast, Reagan opened her journal. She needed to process this stuff, and writing had never let her down. So much happened and it was so good. She started to write:

It all started when I kissed the stone. So many legends about the power of that old rock to transform a person. In some strange way, it worked for me. After I kissed it, I felt a spring in my step that I haven't felt for a very long time. I led the ladies through the fairy garden, telling them what I remembered from earlier visits.

St. Brigid visited me in a dream and said it's all about taking care of the poor and loving all people. I want to learn more about this lady who tried to be a peacemaker for her people.

Then came Grand MaMa, Welby's great-grandmother. She made me feel like I have a new family. And she wants me to get to know Welby? Maybe if I look at him as a brother. That would be good for now. Maybe we could be friends. I think he could teach me about his people, and I could teach him about mine. We aren't all bad, even though he thinks we are.

The road started getting bumpy as they drove through the countryside. Reagan tucked her journal away and focused on Ireland out the window. She looked forward to views of the northern coast. She worried they might arrive after sunset, but Seamus had promised her there would be good light.

She pulled her iPhone out of her bag and clicked on Google Maps. She set her destination to the Giant's Causeway and viewed the landscape. She perused the geological formations and then decided to read about it. She hoped to get some good photographs to paint later. That would make a great Christmas present for her parents.

She'd decided on this trip to become an artist full time. She felt something ignite deep within when she picked up her paint brush. Nursing was a job. Painting was her lifeblood.

She checked out Wikipedia and learned, among a whole host of things, that the Giant's Causeway had been created by an ancient volcanic eruption.

She thought about an ancient volcano spewing molten lava over the land and wondered if that had been what formed the whole island in the beginning. She hoped to capture that in her painting. She then read about the volcanic origins, but found the geological history rather complicated. Ireland actually formed when the North American and European continents collided four hundred and twenty million years ago. *Wow. Maybe the world wasn't really created in 4,000 B.C.* She picked up her pen again:

Life is always so much more than I imagine. Here I am, in the place of my people, but, actually, this land came from the soil on which I now live. The connection astounds me. North American and European soil formed this place. The molten lava birthed something new. Just think what change may be possible for me.

Reagan remembered the Black Cab tour and the Troubles, as they called them. Then she considered the troubles back home—and on this trip, for that matter. Ireland might have the Catholic/Protestant split, but the United States had a whole lot more of a problem in many ways. She sighed. She'd just wanted to enjoy the day.

Reagan watched houses and farmland flying by outside the window. She'd never been to Northern Ireland before, but it didn't look so different from the south.

Seamus grabbed the microphone. "Now, in less than hour, we'll arrive at our first stop. We be going up to what some say is the most beautiful part of Ireland now. In the summer, more people live up here, ye know? We come to the beach and play. Some of the smaller houses we pass are empty at this time of year, but come summer, the people move back in.

"Our first stop will be the Carrick-A-Rede rope bridge in County Antrim. The bridge links the mainland with Carrick-A-Rede, a small island. That name means the Rock of the Casting. Now, if ye don't like the high places, ye may not want to go across the bridge. But it's not very long and it's very safe. They close it when the winds a-blowin', so if it's open, ye know it's a safe thing to do..

"During the Troubles, those in the south didn't come up here. If ye came up to the border to Northern Ireland, the guards would search ye. But now the tourism is all opening up again. Belfast is doing all they can to attract the tourists. It's a pretty place to come and enjoy the sun. Ye'll see, very soon now."

Reagan checked her camera battery and then turned around to see what the guys were doing in the back of the bus. Ever since Grand MaMa told her to become friends with Welby, she'd been watching him more. Early on, he'd kept his eye on her, but then he'd turned cold, maybe because she put him off. Honestly, she did look down on him. She didn't think he was very smart. Most Blacks weren't, from her experience. Not too hard to look at, though. He played a mean saxophone and made the banjo sing. And he'd talked a good line on solar at the farmers' market. And hadn't George said Welby learned stuff so fast, they were training him to be an electrician? Maybe she'd pegged him wrong.

Welby seemed engrossed in a conversation with George and didn't notice Reagan's stares, but Charlie did. He gave her a wink. She smiled back, always enjoying male attention. But Charlie was too working class for her. She needed an educated man. But not a politician like her dad; she'd like to escape that world of parties and pretense.

"I see the ocean," Sallie yelled. "We're here."

"Aye, we're getting close," Seamus said.

Reagan tried to capture the beauty with her camera. The water glistened in the late afternoon sun. The blue sky, broken only by white wispy clouds, created a perfect picture. Below, foamy waves rolled in. She checked the results in the viewfinder. Nope, the bus moved too fast. The picture blurred.

Once they'd arrived, Seamus said, "We'll have to walk down quite a way to get to the bridge. If ye don't want to go the whole way, that's fine. Remember, first, we walk down, and then ye gotta walk back up and that's the hard part."

Welby walked up to Reagan and asked, "How are you today?" The expression his face told her he wanted an answer.

Reagan thought for a moment. *How am I? What do I want to tell him?* But then she relaxed and laughed. "I'm fine. Beautiful place here. I want to paint this."

Welby nodded. "Do you try to imagine if your people came here in years gone by? Do you feel a connection to this land? Is this your homeland?"

Reagan considered his question. "Hmm … I know my people came from farther south in Ireland. I don't think traveling was so easy back in those days. I've honestly never thought about it."

As they made their way down, the coast unfolded with breathtaking beauty. Reagan stopped again and again to take pictures.

"You might not make it to the bridge at this rate," Welby told her.

"Am I slowing you down?" Reagan asked. "You can go on if you want."

"No, it's good," Welby responded. "I'm happy staying by your side, baby."

Reagan grimaced. She didn't want to lead him on. She might be willing to be his friend, but anything more was out of the question. "Welby, why do you suppose your Grand MaMa said I should become your friend?"

"She told you that?" Welby laughed. "Why she be meddlin' in my life? She be long gone. That woman. I have no idea. She loves me hard. Maybe she thinks I ought to partner up with you. Really, she told you that?"

"Yes," Reagan said. "She did. I've been trying to figure it out. No offense, but I don't think we fell off the same tree. We're like night and day."

"Black and white," Welby added. "But we *are* part of the same tree. You got some of that good Black blood. I've got some of your green DNA. We're family, sista. Just call me 'brother.'"

Now Reagan laughed. "Now, there's something. I never thought I'd be a sister to a Black man. I guess you're right. We do share family trees, don't we? Somewhere, way back there."

"Actually, Reagan, you know the cradle of civilization was Africa. So all the humans emerged from the jungles there, way back when," Welby said.

"Don't go there, Welby. Those are lies. That's not in the Bible."

"Have it your way then," Welby told her. She knew he wasn't convinced. And she remembered her science classes very well, so she also knew quite a few people agreed with him.

She felt growing concern about the way her party put down the scientists these days. As she learned about organic farming at the FARM and the way the climate was changing, she started to realize that some of the political people were just trying to deregulate to make money. She wished they'd address the big issues that would cause problems for the future of life on Earth. She lobbied hard for unborn babies, and she'd realized recently that she needed to start lobbying for the environment of those babies as well.

Welby dragged her out of her thoughts. "Some beauty here, for sure," he said.

"For sure," she echoed. She stopped to capture the waves rolling into the black rock. "Do you think that's volcanic rock?" she asked him. "It's black. I think I remember from Hawaii they said the black rocks were from the lava."

"I have no idea," Welby said. "No money for high falutin' travel in my family, honey. Never been out of the country 'til now. Although I saw quite a bit of the country on the road as a truck driver, I don't remember black rocks. Maybe you could ask Seamus."

"Mmm-hmm," Reagan said. She tried to imagine what Welby's life might have been, growing up. Different than hers, for sure.

The group slowed as they approached the rope bridge. Now she could take in the view of the small bridge, suspended over water. She'd worried about walking on a rope, but a path of wooden slats reached across to the little island. The ropes stretched out along the top of each side for a handrail and crisscrossing ropes on the sides protected walkers from falling into the water.

"Welby," she asked, "would you take a picture of me out on the bridge?"

"Okay, beautiful, sure thing. Just tell me how to work your camera," he replied.

She showed him how to focus, where to push the button, and handed the camera to him.

The others caught up with Welby and Reagan. "Group shot," Sallie exclaimed. "Welby, could you do the honors for us, too? Get that green water, the brown cliffs and that blue sky," Sallie said. "We want a beautiful backdrop, even if we're not all that."

Seamus interrupted, saying, "We need to move along. The sun's sinking. I want you to get to the Giant's Causeway before dark. Take your pictures, walk across the bridge, and head back on up."

Welby looked at the cameras they'd dropped at his feet. "I promised to get Reagan's picture, ladies. Then I'll get yours."

Reagan took a few steps onto the bridge. She heard Welby snapping a shot. "Hey, I didn't say to take a picture yet," she yelled back.

"Oh, baby, that's the best part. You'll love it," Welby responded.

Reagan said, "I'll delete it." Then she flashed Welby a big smile and said, "Now."

Welby snapped a few pictures in landscape, then tilted to portrait, moving the camera around, framing her with different parts of the sky and water.

"You're good," Reagan said.

"Yes, I'm real good," Welby called back. "You have no idea."

George said, "Watch it, Welby. You're crossing the line."

Reagan complained, "I asked him to take my picture, George,"

"Okay, looks like he got enough for your modeling portfolio. Now move on. You heard Seamus. We need to hustle across the bridge and then head back up to the bus," George said.

Next, the MAMs posed for their group shot and Welby patiently took a picture with each of their cameras.

"Thank you, Welby," Sallie said. "You've captured us for posterity, an important job."

"You're welcome," Welby said. And then he threw in a compliment. "Never a problem to take pictures of beautiful women."

Reagan stopped on the bridge, watching Welby handling the photo shoot. For a moment, she'd forgotten she was on the bridge. Now she needed to finish her walk across. Her heart started to thump. Her hands felt clammy. She looked a long way down at the water between the slats. The bridge swayed as she took a step. The rope railing felt unsteady in her hands. She closed her eyes for a moment and stopped.

"Reagan, get a move on," George told her.

She opened her eyes. To her left, water stretched as far as her eyes could see, and waves rolled into the rocky cliffs below. To her right, more water. Straight ahead, land. The little island awaited. With determination, she put one foot in front of the other, focusing on *terra firma* in the distance. The bridge continued to sway. She felt nauseated, yet she walked on. She thought she might never arrive at the other side. She quit looking down. She didn't look left or right, but kept focused on the land ahead. And soon enough, she stepped off the swaying nightmare, feigning composure. Soon she would need to return. She began to pray.

Welby joined her on the island and handed her camera back.

"Thank you, Welby," she told him.

"The pleasure's all mine, Reagan," he said. And then his voice went quiet. "Check out that first shot and give it to me before you delete it. You got one nice behind."

She looked at him and felt energy sizzle between them. Startled, she looked away and tried to distract herself by taking more pictures.

When it was time to go, Welby led the way back across the bridge. Somehow, watching him walk first helped calm her. The bridge held his muscled frame well. If it could hold him, it would hold her. Comforted, she followed behind.

When they reached the end of the bridge this time, Reagan noticed Nikki and Priscilla sitting on a rock, chatting. "Aren't you crossing the bridge?" she asked.

Nikki laughed nervously and covered her eyes with her hands. "I don't like heights," she said.

"No," Priscilla said. "I am so not doing that. No, that's not for me, honey. But did you have a good time?"

Reagan thought about the question. She felt very good about crossing the bridge. She was glad she'd ventured out, even though it wasn't quite in her comfort zone. "Yes," she answered. "It was a little scary, but something I'll remember for a long time, you know? It's important to face your fears, ladies."

"Okay, have it your way, Reagan," Nikki said. "But I'll never be a daredevil."

Priscilla gave her a side hug and said, "It's sometimes a good thing to be cautious, Nikki."

Reagan shrugged and then George told everyone to get a move on.

Threatening clouds now covered the sky, portending rain. Reagan snapped more pictures. The clouds added depth. She decided it had been a perfect afternoon. "Hey, guys," she called. "Let me get a picture of you men."

She took pictures of them smiling, then making funny faces.

Seamus interrupted their play when he announced, "Everybody on the bus. Next stop, the Giant's Causeway. We'll take their shuttle bus down to the water. Ye can take yer pictures. Then we'll head over to Shalem Centre, where they're expecting us for dinner by seven. We need to hurry now."

The rest of the afternoon passed in a blur. Rain began shortly after they arrived at the Giant's Causeway, making photography difficult. She managed to get a few shots, but soon tucked her camera away to keep it dry. Instead, she heightened her scrutiny of the landmark.

Little square columns, some no higher than a foot and others standing up to fourteen feet high. She'd expected more height. She thought it strange that a volcano would birth such structures. Most things in nature were more irregular and rounded, but these columns stood squarely proportioned, almost like wooden beams on end. She wondered exactly how the columns had been formed, geologically, and decided she'd look that up.

They didn't stay long in the pouring rain. As the Giant's Causeway shuttle bus made its way back up to the car park, the driver told an Irish legend about the origin of the basalt columns: Two giants, one from Ireland and one from Scotland, faced off across the water. One of them built a bridge to get closer for a real fight, but the other broke it down, forming the columns.

After writing a few lines, Reagan tucked her journal back in her bag. Out the window, rain streamed down. She loved Ireland. The magic, the mystery, the meanings all stirred up together.

CHAPTER FIFTEEN
SHALEM CENTRE: THE RETREAT
BEGINS

Seamus Brings Abigail Home

Back on their bus, Seamus said, "And now we're off to Ballycastle and Shalem Centre. I'm taking you home."

"You live there?" Sallie asked.

"In a matter of speaking, yes, I do. They say home is where the heart is, and my heart belongs to the Shalem Centre."

Abigail perked up. "Did you grow up here? I didn't realize you were from Northern Ireland. I thought you said you were from Cork?"

"Well," Seamus said, "I am from Cork, yes. But when the Troubles came, my wife and I received an invitation from the Quakers to come up here to Shalem Centre for some peace talks. We Quakers always are looking to make peace, we are. We came here to pray for peace. They brought both sides together here to try to talk it all out at this peace center."

"Did people get shot there, too?" Abigail asked.

"No, no. Shalem Centre was a safe zone. Everyone left it alone," Seamus said. "A beautiful space where both sides had a place. Like Jesus himself, welcoming all.

"After the Peace Agreement, we bought a little cottage up here so we could spend our summers close by. Like ye going to the beach. Then, I worked as a tour guide here and back south. We joined the Shalem Centre Community, too."

"You live at Shalem Centre?" Abigail asked.

"No," Seamus answered. "I stay in my cottage, but I participate in the activities of the Shalem Center Community when I'm up here, and I support it financially."

Abigail took the microphone and said, "So, group, our tour of Ireland will end at Shalem Centre. Seamus and his friends have planned a retreat for us there. After that, Seamus will take us back to the Dublin airport for an afternoon flight home. Explain the retreat, Seamus, please."

"Let me say we'll be doing things in the way of the Shalem Centre, bringing ye all together to listen to each other, to consider the things that make for peace. We'll go to the Croi, the chapel. We will process your trip a wee bit. Trust me, we've got a good plan. Not all easy; there are always some rough spots, when ye try to make peace, ye know?"

Charlie called, "Do we get to eat soon? It's almost bedtime."

Abigail looked at her watch. It *had* been a long time since their box lunches on the way to the museum. Storm clouds and rain had morphed into a misty night somewhere along the way.

"Aye," Seamus said. "Yes, sir. We'll be pulling up to the center in just a wee bit here. We'll show ye to yer rooms after dinner. We'll be a little late, but they'll wait. I called them a few minutes ago."

Good as his word, a minute later, Seamus turned down a little lane. The headlights illuminated a sign announcing the center.

Abigail had looked at pictures of Shalem Centre on the internet, but she didn't quite know what to expect. It was a rather modern-looking building, at least from what she could see in the dark. As she stepped out of the bus and walked toward the door, she pulled up her hood to keep her hair dry. The door slid open automatically, opening into a spacious foyer. Looking across the way, she saw more doors, leading back outside, it appeared. There was an office on the right and, on the left, a table with a sign with a sign welcoming them. A sign-in sheet lay next to it.

Delicious aromas filled the air. Her stomach grumbled. A man reached out to shake her hand, welcoming her to Shalem Centre. A thin woman with gray hair instructed them. "Come this way," she said. "First things first. We want you to eat. Welcome to Shalem Centre."

Abigail wanted to sit with Seamus, so she let the others go ahead and waited while several young men helped him unload suitcases. While Seamus went out to park, Abigail looked over some books in the reception area. He soon returned and said, "Let's get some food," motioning her toward the dining room.

Seamus suggested they sit at a table with an older couple after they'd made their meal selections.

"Hello," the woman said. "My name is Erin O'Reilly, and this be my husband, Michael. Welcome to Shalem Centre."

Abigail smiled and said, "My name is Abigail Wesley, and this is Seamus."

Seamus laughed. The woman followed suit. "Oh, yes, we know Seamus. He's one of us, ye see," she told Abigail. "So glad you could come. My husband and I are volunteers. We live in Australia, so we came over to help out a bit. We've been here before and decided to volunteer three months this time."

"That's a long way to come," Abigail said.

"Aye," Erin agreed. "But we're retired. We like to travel, and we love Shalem Centre."

Seamus said, "Shalem Centre runs with the help of volunteers like Erin and Michael here. We couldn't do it without them. The young people, they come for a year. Maybe when they're trying to figure their lives out, ye know? Most of the volunteers are eighteen to twenty-five. Some of the older volunteers work here three to six months, sometimes longer."

"Oh, okay," Abigail said, thinking she might enjoy that. "How do you apply?"

"Look at their website. They have an application," Erin said. "We love it here. I highly recommend it. This is a great place to live and work."

"So you might come over for a spell, Abby, and help out?" Seamus' blue eyes twinkled.

"Yes, I just might," she replied.

"All in due time," Seamus said. "Let's give ye a chance to get acquainted with the place first. Now Erin came in yer youth, didn't ye?"

Michael and Erin started to laugh. "Yes," Erin replied. "So I did. We sent our daughter over as well. She met Seamus' son at a youth meeting. One thing led to another, and they got married a few years back."

"Oh," Abigail said.

"We call it the land of match makin' and mayhem," Seamus explained. "More than a few young lasses and lads have found their mates in this place."

"So do you have grandchildren?" Abigail asked.

"Aye. Thanks for asking," Erin replied. She displayed a picture of a young family on her phone. There she saw a young version of Seamus next to a woman who shared features with both of their tablemates, and two very cute cherubs, with rosy cheeks and red hair, stood in front of them.

"Seamus," Abigail exclaimed. "Your son, your grandchildren, they're adorable."

"Aye," Seamus nodded. "That be my son, Patrick, with his love, Marie, and their two little ones, the twins, Callie and Corky. Those two can give you a run for your money, they can."

"Where do they live?" Abigail asked.

"Oh, they live up Dublin way," Seamus responded. "Working in the big city, ye know. High tech. Your American firms employ a lot of our people, and for good money. Both Marie and Patrick work for one. They can work at home or in the office. They prefer to put the wee ones in the creche and work at the office. Can't get much done with those two around."

Abigail marveled at this information.

"Now finish up," Seamus said. "Looks like our crew's getting restless over there."

Abigail scanned the room, noticing more than a few strangers, but also familiar faces. Welby sat with Reagan, Tom, and Molly, looking like two couples on a date. She wondered who'd let Reagan and Welby together. They appeared to be happy, she observed. Perhaps they'd put their past friction aside.

Abigail changed the subject. "Who are all these people? Is there another group here?"

Michael answered, "No, no. We have a lot of volunteers who help run the place."

Seamus brought ice cream partially covering a brownie, all smothered with caramel sauce. "Here's a sundae for ye to top off your first meal here. What do ye think?"

"Great meal," Abigail said. "You all do a great job here." Then, changing the subject again, she asked, "What are we doing tonight?"

At that moment, a ruddy young man stood up and introduced himself. "Hello to the MAMs Book Club and friends. My name is Matey O'Brien. I'll be helping Seamus here with your retreat this weekend. I hope you enjoyed your meal.

"Now, in just a little bit, we'll be checking you in to your rooms. The women will stay over in the People's Village, the men upstairs in this building. After that, we will close the day out with eventide in the chapel, the Croi, as we call it." He looked at his watch.

"As you finish, go on back where you came in and check in at the table to get your room keys. Take your luggage to your rooms. We will help, if needed. Any questions?"

"Do we get our own rooms?" Charlie asked.

"I believe we doubled ye up," Matey replied. "Ask me again when you check in."

"Is that water over there?" Abigail asked as Seamus led them to their accommodations. She thought she could hear waves breaking and saw water behind the fence, to the right of the sidewalk where they walked.

"Aye. We be up on top o' the cliffs right here, we are. In the morning, ye'll see quite the view. The best place in all of Ireland, some say."

The short walk led to a building where doors opened into a large foyer. On the left, a long hall on the right, Abigail noticed another dining area. The modernity impressed her.

"Now, yer rooms be in this wing," Seamus said. He consulted a piece of paper and gave them their room numbers. "Get situated, then meet me in the foyer in ten minutes, and we'll head to the Croi."

Abigail opened their room. Inside, there were two single beds on one wall, and another across the room. Each bed had its own nightstand with three drawers. She noticed windows, now dark, on each of the two exterior walls. A small bathroom opened off the interior wall. Pulling her suitcase over to one of the beds, she proclaimed, "Nice room."

"Yes," Sallie, who'd been assigned to room with her, agreed. She plopped down, sprawling out on the bed. "And comfortable. I'm ready to hit the hay. What a workout today. I need my beauty sleep."

"Not so fast," Abigail said. "We need to go to church first."

"Can't that wait 'til morning?" Sallie asked. "I'm all for church, but at nine at night?

Reagan, the third roommate, slipped into the bathroom.

"Here, they go to the Croi morning and night, nine and nine. It's part of the rhythm of their life. We need God, Sallie, and regular worship helps. Seamus loves the worship here."

"I worship a lot better when I'm not falling asleep. Do I have to go?" Sallie asked.

Abigail looked at the bathroom door. "Well, normally, I'd say no, but with Reagan here, I think you should. Be a good role model."

Almost on cue, Reagan opened the door. "I'm ready," she announced.

The three of them went back out to find Seamus. When the others joined them, Seamus led them out the front door and across a sidewalk; it was a short distance to the Croi.

"We've arrived in the heart of it all," Seamus announced. "Now, we call this the Croi which means 'heart' in Irish. And, like the human heart, this building has four chambers. We'll be going into one to pray tonight, and we'll use another chamber tomorrow. Four separate spaces, parts of the whole. This building is also shaped like the womb and the inner ear. Everything here has meaning. A place to meet, to listen, to feel the love."

Abigail loved that they called the chapel "The Heart." She loved its circular rooms. Chairs lined the exterior wall of the little room where Seamus led them for worship. In the center, a simple round table held a candle, a cross, and an open Bible. Red cushions lay around the altar. A few people were already gathered in the space, so they took the seats among them. She noticed Matey in the corner, perusing some books and checking his watch. Abigail silenced her cell phone, noticing they'd arrived only a couple minutes early.

Matey spoke. "Welcome to the Croi. We're glad you're here. If you could open the worship booklet to page forty, we'll use this order of welcome worship tonight." And then he read, "As we gather for worship in the Croi, the heart of this Community, we acknowledge symbols of faith and hope found here at the Shalem Centre worship. A burning candle to remind us of Christ, the light of the world, a turf cross, a symbol of Christ's love for us and reminder of our Celtic heritage, and an open Bible, telling the story of God's love for all creation."

He continued, "It is often difficult to leave home. To leave the familiar and comfortable and come away to a strange place – to strangers. We come tonight to this place in fear and excitement, in hope and in expectation.

"Now join me," he said, and together they read aloud from the worship book, "We have left one community, but have come to another."

Matey continued the leader part by himself. "You are all very welcome here to worship and to this community of which you are a part – a member. Look around for a moment at each person and begin to discover who is here." He paused. "Greet the person beside you."

Abigail turned to Seamus as he put his arm around her and kissed her on the cheek. "It's scriptural, ye know. Greet one another with a brotherly kiss?" Abigail smiled. Then he turned to the stranger on his left, and she took Sallie's hand and gave it a squeeze. Her eyes connected with Sallie's, and she felt a spark, that light of friendship they shared.

Matey said, "Let's affirm together ... Read the next line from the book."

In unison, they said, "We are all very welcome."

"Now, turn to 'We are Gathered" in the song book and let's sing."

As the song concluded, Matey said, "A reading from the third chapter of Colossians, verses twelve through fifteen. 'As God's chosen ones, holy and beloved, clothe yourselves with compassion, kindness, humility, meekness, and patience. Bear with one another and, if anyone has a complaint against another, forgive each other; just as the Lord⁻ has forgiven you, so you also must forgive. Above all, clothe yourselves with love, which binds everything together in perfect harmony. And let the peace of Christ rule in your hearts, to which indeed you were called in the one body. And be thankful.'"

Matey continued reading the service as printed in the worship guide. "This is the Shalem Centre of Peace. We hope you feel welcome and at home here. Shalem is the adjective form of the word Shalom. The Hebrew greeting means peace, but so much more. It implies an inner state of wholeness and health. The name is appropriate to describe what happens here. We are community. To be a community is to be a family, at home with one other. We form not only a community, but a family. Like your body, made up of many different limbs and organs, we all need each other."

The worship went on for a while longer. When it was finished, they left the Croi silently. Abigail felt a sense of deep inner peace and connection, not only with Seamus, but with the whole group. She took the Croi with her into the dark night.

"I'm glad I went to the Croi," Sallie told her. "Thanks for making me go."

Abigail put her arm around Sallie and pulled her in close. "I'm glad, too, girlfriend. Another special moment for us. Thanks for being here, Sallie."

Sallie and Abigail walked back to the People's Village, arm in arm, yoked together in a friendship that spanned the years, anchored in the heartfelt moment of the night at the Croi.

The Trio Reconvenes

In the morning, before the sunrise, hints of color and light twirled in the mist, gently lifting off the sea. An orange and pink sky met the waves just below the cloud line. As the music of dawn spread out across the water, Síocháin's feet pranced at land's edge. He completed a jig and jumped up onto a cliff to think. Long ago, his people gave the dance to the Irish, but now, centuries later, he wanted to give so much more. He believed leprechauns had gotten a bad rap in storybooks over the years. The Irish liked to spin a tale. Often as not, his little people showed up in the stories as tricksters hiding out in the glens, deceiving, and tripping up the humans. What folks didn't understand, they attributed to evil spirits. But he'd always been taught to be good. That's what he wanted to do right now.

Síocháin jumped the fence, heading toward the Shalem Centre of Peace. He stopped on a bench overlooking the water and sat. Then he clicked his fingers and waited for company. He didn't have to wait long until St. Brigid dropped out of the clouds and lazily floated down, landing on the seat beside him.

"The top o' the morning to ye, my good friend Síocháin. What ye be wanting from me this fine morning?" she asked.

"Well, time's a-runnin' out on the Irish soil for these 'Mericans. I'd like to finish our assignment today," Síocháin responded.

"And what ye be thinking here?"

He clicked his fingers again and a now-familiar woman started to materialize on the bench across from them.

"Fine lady Grand MaMa," Brigid exclaimed. "It pleases me to see thee again."

High above the Irish Sea, in the backyard of the Shalem Centre, the three spirits met again, putting their heads together.

"You better have woke me up for some good reason, boy," Grand MaMa said.

Síocháin started to laugh. "Now what ye got better to do than meddle down here, Grand MaMa?"

"I done appeared to Miss Reagan like you wanted, and I think I got her goin' on a better track. And you done scared my boy Welby out of his britches, so don't you get smart with me, you young whippersnapper."

Brigid tried to suppress a giggle, but it slipped out and then she started to laugh. Once she started, she couldn't stop. She stood and then she sat and she laughed and laughed and laughed.

When her laughter had stopped, Síocháin asked, "Are you done?"

Brigid nodded, covering her mouth as if to keep another giggle from slipping out.

"I don't see the humor myself," Síocháin said.

"No?" Brigid asked. "Síocháin, you know I love ye, but for such a small man, ye sure can disturb the humans here. I've never heard someone put ye in yer place before." She turned to Grand MaMa and offered her hand. "I must congratulate ye, dear ma'am."

"Okay, then, ladies. If you're so high and happy, you tell me. What should we do?"

"Leave them alone, boy," Grand MaMa said. "We done meddled enough. They'll get the job done. Just let them be. They're here in this place of peace. They can do this on their own."

Brigid nodded. "I must agree with the wise lady. Let us trust the young ones to discover their truth. The Centre will help."

"But we know so much more; we owe it to them. They need our wisdom to find the straight and narrow," Síocháin replied.

"Now, Síocháin, the problem is, ain't no humans really figured it all out. You see, my people in the long view of history over there in America, and you see a people so sad, so displaced. How you aim to fix that up now? You can't do it; it can't be done. I'm a realist. I been watchin' what goes on there and, if anything, it's gettin' worse."

Brigid disagreed. "Now, now, I beg to differ. Yes, ye be in a sad state of affairs over there. And here on our own island, we find despair as well. While we have peace from the Troubles, many of our people still think in terms of Protestant and Catholic, Brits and Irish, Loyalists and Nationalists. It's a hollow peace, but Shalem Centre makes a difference."

"How that Shalem Centre be makin' a difference now?" Grand MaMa wanted to know.

"For many years," Síocháin said, "the Centre's been in the peace business. Here, they bring people together to listen to each other, and to realize they are all complicit in the Troubles. All of us cause problems from time to time, ye know?"

Instead of trying to argue more, Síocháin snapped his fingers and the sounds of an Irish jig filled the morning air. He rose from his chair and skittered out in front of the two ladies and began to dance. He kept his arms straight down, glued to his sides, while his feet shot up in straight kicks. He twirled around and raised his knees, one at a time. Behind him, the sun emerged for a moment, illuminating the sea. And then the big ball lifted just a little more and slipped behind the line of low-lying clouds on the horizon.

Soon Síocháin stopped dancing. He said, "The sun goes away. The clouds come. Always rain, sometimes snow. Me mother always told me ye can't quit dancin' just because we all got ourselves a problem. No, she would say, keep dancin' and ye will find your way. Ladies, let's get close to God and figure this out. How can we bring hope? Faith? Love? At Shalem Centre, they say, 'if God is to be found, God will be found in the space between.'"

"Okay," Brigid said. "Let us remember our good Lord who prayed that all would be one. He said when two or three be gathered in his name, there ye find Him, too. You're in the right, Síocháin. I believe He bringeth a new day. I always pushed through troubles when I took my time on Earth. I want to help, but how do ye solve this one? I don't know."

Grand MaMa looked up at the clouds and then at her new Irish friends. "Now, we got a sayin' back in America. 'When the goin' get tough, the tough get goin'.' I think that's all that's needed here. We see from beyond. We got a better view than them. We can see their conflicts, but since we also got to look straight into the face of God, we know those divisions ain't nuthin' but malarkey. If there's anything we can give 'em, it's just that sense of unity, that prayer of Jesus, that they all might be one. That's all. Let them figure it all out and take it from there."

Síocháin clicked his fingers. "Ye speak the truth, Mrs. Jones, ye do. Let's be on with it. The message so simple, so clear. The humans will know, when God is near."

Considering Roots with Reagan

Too early, Sallie's off-key voice rang out, "Rise and shine." Reagan rolled over. She didn't want to get up. She was comfortable in the ample bed. The comforter on top felt so soft, nicer than the quilts back home. She snuggled up to her pillow, enjoying the warm caress of the fluffy, downy coverlet.

"Reagan," Abigail said. "We let you snooze, but now you're out of time. We need to leave for breakfast soon. Are you taking a shower? Sallie and I are done in the bathroom."

"No, not today," Reagan said. She might feel better if she showered, but she preferred a few more minutes in bed.

"You have five minutes," Abigail said. "Get a move on."

Reagan resented being stuck in this situation without freedom. While it was nice to be traveling Ireland again, at the moment, she felt like a caged bird. She scooted out of bed, finding her jeans, a green short-sleeved top, and a brown sweater. When it came to dressing in Ireland in October's changeable weather, layers were the wise choice. .

"Reagan," Sallie called. "We need to leave. Are you done in there?"

Reagan finished up, gave herself a smile in the mirror, and then opened the bathroom door. She dropped her makeup bag into her suitcase, grabbed her camera, and followed Abigail and Sallie out the door.

"You've got to see this," Sallie said. "You will not believe where we are." She walked up to the automatic glass doors which opened to second set of doors, which opened as well. "My genie, at your command," Sallie quipped. As Abigail laughed, Sallie dramatically bowed in front of them and announced, "I present to you ... the Shalem Centre of Peace on the Irish Sea."

Reagan stepped out of the building and looked at the vista spreading across the lawn behind the building where she'd spent the night. She turned on her camera and started clicking.

"I went for an early walk and discovered this. Can you believe it?" Sallie asked Abigail. "Did Seamus tell you about the beauty of this place?"

Abigail said, "Well, yes. I knew we'd be on the coast, but I wasn't sure how close."

Reagan couldn't stop taking pictures. To the left, she framed a peninsula with some houses, keeping nearby bushes in the foreground. She captured waves rolling in. She pointed her camera through the fence, using briars for texture, and the sea in the distance. Walking on toward the main building, she focused on a clearing and benches, high above the water. Then she leaned closer and thought she spied three luminous beings chatting on the benches. Quickly, she

196

reviewed the images on her camera's screen. Nothing. She looked again, and the figures were gone. Again, she worried about her mental state. She'd always worried about lingering effects of the drugs she'd taken. She brushed the thought aside, taking pictures of a white cross, standing in yet another clearing, water churning below. Then she noticed an island across the water and captured that in her lens as well. Sallie and Abigail stood chatting, giving Reagan more time for her photos.

"What a sacred space," Abigail said. "Now I understand why Seamus loves this place so much. I feel so close to God in nature. Here, you step out of the building, and you got it."

"I know," Sallie said. "Thank you for bringing us here, Abby. I'm so glad I met you. Who'da thought that joining a romance reading club would give us all of this?"

Abigail responded, "I know. And then there's Seamus …."

Sallie smiled. "Speaking of."

Reagan watched Abigail's head turn. There came Seamus walking out of the main building toward the ladies. He announced, "Breakfast is served. We're waiting for you."

"Are we late?" Abigail asked.

"Yes, but we'll forgive ye, we will. But hurry before the porridge disappears," he recommended.

***

Matey stood, asking for a time of silence, which seemed to span five seconds at the most. Then he thanked them and talked to them about their day. "We'll start off this morning with Quaker worship in the Croi at nine, and then you'll have a time to collect yourself before we head down to the meeting room at the end of the hall over in People's Village at ten. We'll be doing an ice breaker and then what we call a mapping exercise. After that, we'll give you time to create until lunch. After lunch, we'll head to the Croi for some storytellin', and then we'll see where you lead us from there. We like to find bridges here. You'll be a-meeting each other in some new ways as you map, do art, and share stories. It's the sort of thing we do at Shalem Centre."

When Matey sat down, Nikki blurted, "What's Quaker worship?"

"A silent meeting," Katharine explained. "Abigail's Quaker, and Seamus, too."

"Oh," Nikki said. "Is that why they hooked up?"

Katharine laughed and raised her eyebrows. "Maybe. Time will tell."

"You don't talk in Quaker worship?"

"No, not much," Katharine said. "Quakers believe that silence helps you hear the quiet voice within. Now, it depends on the meeting. Sometimes they speak a little if they hear God. And in some meetings, they'll sing songs and pray together at the end, as well."

Reagan had never done silence before this trip. But after the silent retreat at the Holy Well Retreat Centre, she started to appreciate the value of not speaking. Maybe she would like this Quaker worship.

They filed into the round room again, taking seats against the wall. Unfamiliar folks already sat waiting, and a few more strangers joined them.

Seamus took up a small book and read from it briefly and then said, "We will sit in silence for twenty minutes. Listen for God within ye."

He picked up a small wooden stick and struck a small brass bowl. The sound reverberated off the walls, fading into silence, as Reagan shut her eyes and let waves of peace roll through her and around.

Reagan had wanted to learn to meditate, but never found time. Now time was all she had. The silence resonated with her heart. When Seamus hit the brass bowl again, it startled her.

He read a short prayer to close the service.

After a few minutes to freshen up, they walked down a long corridor to the meeting room, joining the others already sitting in a semicircle in large upholstered green chairs. Windows on the right side of the room framed views of the coast. Reagan plopped down into an empty seat between Molly and Nikki and stared at the ocean vista through the glass, mesmerized. Once again, she saw three luminous figures. Looking more closely, she recognized them now. Grand MaMa, St. Brigid, and ... a leprechaun?

"Do you see that?" she asked Nikki, pointing out the window.

"Yeah," Nikki responded. "Ain't that view something?"

"No," Reagan said. "I mean, yes. But do you see anything else out there?"

"Looks like it's going to rain. Some storm clouds over the water?"

"Yeah," Reagan said. Nodding, she ventured another peek. The trio stood together. St. Brigid smiled at her. The leprechaun gave her a thumbs up. Grand MaMa lifted a finger to the heavens, then put her hands together like she was getting ready to pray. Then she raised her hands up over her head, wiggling her fingers; her smile seeming directed right at Reagan. Reagan understood loud and clear that Grand MaMa felt just as grateful and mesmerized by this place as she did. She knew something big was about to happen. Just as Matey began to open the session, she glanced over at Welby, for some reason not surprised to find him staring at her. She felt a twinge in her gut.

Matey interrupted her internal soliloquy. "Now, mates, we start our session. I know ye all know each other pretty well, but we like to start off with some ice breakers. For strangers, it's to help ye get to know each other, but for groups well acquainted like yours, well, it just helps loosen ye up a little and feel hospitable in this space."

They participated in getting to know each other by listing their favorite music, movie, food, and then sharing in small groups.

After a few minutes, Matey called a halt and had the groups report on their findings, starting with music.

Welby found fellow soul mates with Molly and George who chose soul music. Nikki, Charlie and Jane were all into country/pop music. Sallie stood alone with a child's song. And then a big surprise came with Tom and Katharine mooning over classical music.

"Now, if we had more time, we'd play some of your tunes. I encourage you to do that later. Music brings us together, eh? The music of life, full of diversity and beauty," Matey said. "Let's do the same thing now, with the movies. Find your like-minded souls."

This time, the group divided up quickly with most of the women forming a romance group, although Jane joined Charlie in a horror film duo, and Molly and Tom preferred comedies. Welby and Katharine liked foreign films. Welby's choice surprised Reagan. This time, George stood alone. "Documentaries," he announced. "They teach me so much about life."

After that, Matey got them talking about food. Here, more borders were crossed. Reagan found herself with Welby, his sweet potato pie to her pumpkin; not too far removed. Sallie joined them with green tomato pie, which she said tasted a whole lot like apple pie. "My dad's pie won an award at the State Fair one year. Mmm, so good, with early pickin's from the garden."

Welby and Reagan laughed. "Ever do fried green tomatoes?" Welby asked Sallie.

"Oh, yeah. We love those, too," she responded.

Over in one corner, Charlie and Tom huddled with Jane and Nikki. "We love a good, juicy steak," Tom said. In another corner, Abigail, Molly and Priscilla sang the praises of salads and fresh veggies. Finally, George and Katharine were fans of casseroles. George liked Mexican cornbread the best and Katharine liked broccoli with chicken, but they were comparing notes, and both loved the church potlucks.

Matey stood quietly as the group reported and then he asked a pointed question. "So what did you learn here?"

Reagan looked at Welby and Sallie, not the folks she would normally pair with herself. George and Katharine, also a surprise. And before that, Katharine and Welby.

"Surprising," Reagan answered. "A lot of unusual matches."

"What do you mean?" Matey probed.

"Well," Reagan said, "this brings us together in new ways. I mean, we're all different, some more than others." She laughed. "Yet here we are together."

"I know a steak lover when I meet one," Charlie weighed in.

"But did you expect Welby and Katharine to connect over foreign films?" Reagan asked.

Priscilla said, "God made us all different. Similar and different. Isn't that special?"

"Right," Welby said. "Tell that to the Ku Klux Klan."

"Okay," Matey said. "Yes, Welby, sometimes differences lead to violence, wars, discrimination."

"It all seems so simple here to see how we're alike and different. It shouldn't be a big deal," Sallie said.

Reagan quietly agreed. And she also knew Welby was right. She wished she had time to journal on this, but Matey moved on.

"Now," he said, "this morning, I want you talk about the big picture in the USA today. We've learned at the Shalem Centre we each have a story. But then there's a larger narrative too. And sometimes it's good to stand back and really look at that. That backdrop stands behind the drama of our lives and our world, but often, we don't bring it out into the open. This morning, we're going to talk about it.

"Abigail, could you repeat what you told me about this?"

Abigail said, "Well, I think it's clear that we're rather divided in our country. This last election showed it pretty well. We have conservatives and liberals, usually that's the Republicans and the Democrats. During eight years of President Rosales, the Republicans blamed him for everything, even though he helped us recover from a financial crisis. Things were going pretty well, from my point of view. To me, it seemed racist when they didn't go along with him on anything. Then we had a woman, Marcy Smith, run for president. She wasn't liberal enough for the young people. Boy, did the Republicans smear her up. And the young people went for Marsh Tull, who was be more of a Socialist. Steele enters the scene and excites the white working class who aren't faring so well. He gets people mad about immigrants. And then he gets elected.

"Ace Steele brought out a whole lot of ugly. Riots in the south over an abortion clinic. the Women's March and a Me, Too movement because there were many allegations about politicians and celebrities and the way they've treated women over the years."

"Okay," Matey said. "I want to stop you here. You hear Abigail's bias coming through? We all have a bias, born from our experiences.

At Shalem Centre, it's all about story. So Abigail's talked about some of that, and I want to hear from some of the rest of you, too.

"We will break this down as a difference between liberals and conservatives. Always, there are other viewpoints, so you can make up other categories if you wish, okay? Just as earlier you chose your favorite songs, movies and foods, now you'll be sharing about your favorite political perspective. Remember that some of the people you paired up with earlier now may be in a different camp. Just different preferences."

Silence followed. Reagan saw heads nodding. She didn't know what to say; her perspectives had broadened and shifted on this trip.

"My assistants, Amanda and Riley, will write it all down. We want to map what divides you. Before you can build a bridge, you've gotta know what you're trying to cross."

Katharine said, "Well, like Abigail said, the big divide in the USA would be between the liberals and the conservatives."

"What does that look like?" Matey said.

"We got ourselves a blue donkey and a red elephant," Welby said.

"A donkey and an elephant?" Matey asked, smiling.

"The liberals, the Democrats, go by the blue donkey. The conservatives, the Republicans, go with the red elephant," Welby clarified. "You know, the political party symbols."

"Oh, okay," Matey said.

Amanda took a blue marker and drew a donkey. Riley grabbed a red one and created an elephant. Reagan marveled at their handiwork, happy to see artists in the room.

"So you have red and blue, an elephant and a donkey?" Matey asked. "What's going on here? Are they having a fight?"

"Well," George said. "The two parties always disagree about something. But lately, they don't talk to each other. They just blame all the problems of the country on the other party."

Amanda took up a black marker and made a little caption box coming from the donkey's mouth. "It's your fault, Mr. Elephant." Then Riley followed suit with, "Donkey, you're the problem."

"You got that right," Tom said. "It's a blame game and we're all stuck in the middle."

"Do we have conservatives and liberals both in the room?" Matey asked.

The group nodded.

"Let me ask the conservatives, why are you on the elephant's side?"

"We believe a person's got to work hard to make it in our world," Jane said. "We're the party of good people making our country strong with creative entrepreneurship."

"We don't want no illegal immigrants taking all our jobs. For Republicans, it's law and order all the way. Arrest them and deport them, we say," Charlie said.

"Well, they can enter our country legally. The businesses like the cheap labor, but they need to quit sneaking in. They need to do it the right way," Jane said.

"We believe in God," Reagan said. "We don't believe in abortion or homosexuality. You must let people choose the schools they attend. Public schools don't work, so we must allow experimentation. We believe in private schools. We shouldn't have to pay for public schools if our kids aren't attending. The educational funds should help us, too."

"Okay," Sallie said. "So you believe in personal choice when it comes to schools, but not when it comes to women's bodies or sexual orientation? I don't get it."

Reagan gave Sallie a hard stare. "It's about what God wants. God doesn't want us killing babies or doing unnatural things. That doesn't have anything to do with educational choice. How did the vagina become a magical canal that leads from a place of no rights to a place of being a protected population?"

Matey interrupted. "Sallie, let's just listen to the Republicans right now."

"The NRA belongs to us," Charlie said.

"NRA?" Matey asked.

"National Rifle Association," Nikki said. "The right to bear arms."

"That's right," Charlie agreed. "Them Democrats want to take all our guns away."

"I believe in gun control, but not gun abstinence," Jane said. "We have a right to bear arms. We Republicans are reasonable folks."

Molly squirmed in her chair. Abigail's and Sallie's eyebrows went up. Reagan could tell they weren't happy, but they kept quiet. On the other hand, Priscilla smiled.

"Free enterprise," Jane said. "We shouldn't saddle the businesses with regulations. For a strong economy, we need to let the businesses make money."

"Strong national defense," Charlie said. "We fund our military to make us strong. The liberals want to turn us into wimps without guns."

"Okay, good," Matey said. "Now, are there some Democrats in the room?"

"I think we've got a majority," Molly said.

"Not so fast," Priscilla said. "Please add that the Republicans are the party of God. God's in our camp. Real believers are Republicans. You won't find a Democrat in my church; they're not on the narrow path anymore."

"Stop," Molly said. "You can't say that. Do you listen to Jesus? Do you really read your Bible?"

Matey interjected, "Priscilla, just talk about your party. Please, no put-downs, okay? Molly, wait. You'll get your turn."

"That's hard," Priscilla said. "The Democrats are leading us straight to hell."

Molly crossed her arms and frowned at Priscilla. Tom patted her on the shoulder. Sallie's mouth hung open and Abigail didn't look very happy. Reagan didn't like the conflict brewing in the room, but she agreed with Priscilla.

Matey spoke again. "Priscilla? Did you hear me? Focus on what you like about your own parties. Now we're going to listen to the Democrats. And I'd like the Republicans to just listen. The Democrats listened to you, now it's your turn. What do the Democrats like about their party?"

Priscilla rolled her eyes and crossed her arms. Reagan felt her disgust. She patted her on the back and whispered, "You got that right, girlfriend."

Matey frowned at Reagan. "Please, no side conversations. Democrats, tell me the positives about your party."

"Where do I begin?" George started. "They elected the first Mexican-American president a few years back. They're the party for the people, for the ninety-nine percent."

"We care about the Earth," Abigail said. "Environmental regulation, addressing climate change, pollution. Keeping the natural resources safe for the humans. It's a little scary right now because, with the Republicans in charge, they want to let businesses pollute everything. We already have so much climate change, cancer, and environmental problems. The Democrats believe taking care of the Earth is good for business and the people."

Reagan watched as Amanda started writing stars under the donkey. For the people, 99%, caring for the earth, protecting the environment, addressing climate change, cancer. She'd never quite thought of it that way before.

Matey spoke. "Okay, again, please remember to just focus on the positives in your own party, not what the Republicans are doing."

"The New Deal? All Democrat," Molly said. "The Democrats care about the workers. They want livable wages. They try to raise the minimum wage so people have enough money to live on. The Republicans think low wages are better for the businesses."

Matey interrupted, "Just the positives, Molly."

"Okay. Democrats are pro-women. We believe in equal pay for equal work."

Welby spoke. "The Democrats care about minorities and immigrants. We want a fair and just country. We want everyone to vote. Republicans don't want minorities to vote."

"We don't want voter *fraud*," Reagan corrected. "We want to make sure that people aren't cheating at the polls."

"Right," Sallie said sarcastically. "That's not true. You want to try to keep people who disagree with you out of the voting booths."

"No, I believe it's okay for them to vote. They just need proper identification. Only legitimate citizens should vote," Jane said.

Matey said, "I hear a lot of contention here."

"You got that right," Reagan said. "We don't like each other very much."

"Okay, I understand. But let's remember, we're listening to the liberals now. Just the positives."

Abigail said, "I believe the Democrats have the Christian agenda. In the Bible, Jesus favored the poor more than the rich. Hard for a rich man to get into heaven, he said. And he said we'll be judged on how we help the poor. Democrats look after the poor. We want a safety net to help people out. Social Security and welfare—not to make people dependent, but to help those who can't take care of themselves. That's important. We favor universal health care. We're the only developed country without decent, affordable health care for its people."

"Socialists. Damn Commies," Charlie said in an angry tone.

"My granny always told me Jesus was a Socialist," Welby said. "I voted for Marsh Tull. He cared for all the people. Socialists believe in the common good. Jesus was for everybody, too. Sometimes, the Democrats aren't different than the Republicans. A lot of Democrats didn't like that woman, Marcy Smith, who ran for president."

"Well, we're a capitalist nation," Abigail said. "I don't see that changing. But if you want a government for the people, by the people, we Democrats look after the people, rather than just letting the corporations do whatever they want—which is make money. The role of government is to make sure they don't abuse the people and the planet in the process."

Reagan looked at the list of positives under the donkey now and realized that her party didn't have a monopoly on the good. There were about as many items there as on her side. A safety net, the environment, concern for the poor. St. Brigid's words came back. For the first time in her life, she wondered if God really was a Republican?

"Schools," Sallie said. "The Democrats believe a strong public education system is important for our future. This gives each child a chance to succeed. Private education favors the rich. Schools should be good, regardless of location and wealth. Most teachers are Democrats."

"That's not true," Reagan said. "I know a lot of Republican teachers."

Sallie rolled her eyes.

"A strong economy and taxes to support the government," George said. "If you look at the figures, the economy does better under the Democratic administrations, because they focus on policies to benefit all people. When the people are good, the businesses succeed as well."

"Okay," Matey said. "That's a good start. Now tell me what these liberals and conservatives have in common. Remember earlier, you all paired together in different ways over the songs, movies, and foods. You have similarities alongside your differences. It's part of being human."

Reagan watched as Amanda and Riley posted the red and blue sheets on the wall, then picked up purple markers and waited.

"Nothin'," Welby said. "Ain't got nothin' in common."

"You got that right," Charlie said. "Let's quit wasting our time. We don't speak the same language. We don't talk to each other."

"Now, Charlie," Matey said, "I've watched you talking with the people here. I think you're exaggerating a little. Think a little harder. What do these two groups have in common?"

Charlie's eyes lit up. "White," he exclaimed.

"You got white and Black Democrats, but Black Republicans are few and far between," Welby said. "You talkin' white, probably Republicans."

"White?" Matey asked. "Can you explain that a little more?"

"Well, you know our colors are red, white, and blue. The Republicans got the red. The Democrats got the blue. So I guess we both got the white."

"Oh," Matey said. "Your flag."

"And our colors in general," Charlie said.

"We say that about our Irish flag, you know. We have the Orange for the Protestants, the Green for the Catholics, and white in the middle, the color of peace."

"Hmm," Katharine said. "I never thought about it that way before."

"Good deal, Charlie," Matey said. "What else?"

Silence filled the room. Reagan wanted to say something, but she couldn't think of single thing they had in common.

"We share the same country, the land?" Molly said.

"Okay," Matey said. "Good, good. What else?"

Reagan watched Amanda and Riley with their purple pens, waiting. "Competition," she said. "Do you see, we're always in races against each other. We like to compete."

"Yes, the American way," Jane said. "Survival of the fittest. We love our sports teams, free enterprise, the polls. It's a democracy. We fight for the people's vote."

Reagan tried to wrap her brain around the commonalities.

"Two hundred-plus years of stability, with liberty and justice for all," Sallie said.

"Well, it's in our Constitution, Sallie," Tom said, "but do Republicans believe in justice for all? To me, it seems like they just want to keep the Black man down."

"That's not true," Katharine pointed out. "What about Condoleeza Rice? Colin Powell? These were Republican cabinet members."

"Diversity," Molly said. "There are a variety of people from all walks of life in both parties, different ages, colors, creeds. I've known quite a few African-Americans who are Republicans. Tom and George's brother, Leo, went there for a while."

Katharine said. "I don't know many families that don't have a mix of Republicans and Democrats. I know mine does. That's part of why I've been Independent most of my life. I try to listen to both sides."

"Any of the rest of you? Welby? Nikki? Abigail?" Matey asked.

More silence, but then Welby spoke. "Everybody wants the best life for themselves and their family. Maybe not concerned about everybody else, but all looking for the best life."

"Good observation," Matey said. "Look at all your similarities. Do you see how your differences melt away as you find your commonalities? It might be over music, films, food, or just other aspects of being human and life in your country. Good work. I want you to keep thinking about this. At Shalem Centre, we always seek common ground."

Reagan liked that idea. She'd never thought about things this way before.

"Now," Matey said, "you have an hour until lunch. What I want you to think about now is your story. How did you grow up and what made you become a Republican or a Democrat, a conservative or liberal or progressive? What's important to you? What are your hopes for your country and government? We have some art supplies, some paper, and pens. You can write or do some drawing, painting even. After lunch, bring your creations to the Croi. Okay?"

Again silence until Reagan broke it. "Can I paint?"

"Yes," Matey said, looking at Amanda. "We have some paints, right?"

"Sure thing," she replied. "Watercolors, acrylics, canvases, and blot paper."

Reagan stood, hurrying to the table with the supplies. She picked up the largest canvas and grabbed a set of acrylics. When her thoughts gathered, she needed to get it out. The impulse to create overwhelmed her at times. She checked her watch, gauging her time. She would sketch ten minutes, then spend the rest of the hour painting.

Her story. First, her beginnings: the house of her childhood, where she had a swimming pool, a silver spoon, a doll house, a two-story playhouse in the back yard, a three-room suite of her own. On the ground floor of her life, she'd had it all. She sketched it in the left-hand bottom corner. Then she drew a quick representation of college in the top left, directly above her childhood home. Moving around the canvas, to the right she drew the car crash that flipped her life upside down. A wheelchair, a nursing degree, pills, handcuffs, rehab and then—the FARM. And as she began to draw the FARM, she drew a seedling, something new growing.

What to put in the center? Something spiritual. The sun? White light? Green? A cross? What might grow from that seedling? A vegetable, a flower, some fruit? Her future was a big question mark, so perhaps she could just leave it at that.

She picked up the paintbrush, filling in color from the hints of images in her sketch. A large house, a little house in the backyard, the pool. A little girl with long braids playing with a doll house. She moved up the canvas to paint a campus building. Then she painted herself, this time standing on the sidewalk, holding books, chatting with a friend. Blue skies, green grass.

Moving on to the center on the top, she painted a collision in bright red. Pain surged through her body, and she relived the impact, then the days and nights of anguish. Changes. With no time to linger, she moved on. She painted herself in a wheelchair, then as a graduate with a diploma. Next she stood as a nurse on the hospital floor, taking meds from the locked box, popping a pill. Handcuffs, rehab … the FARM, the seedling. She stopped, letting out a sigh.

When she could, she continued. In the center, she painted an illuminating sun. She so much wanted to let the light bring her whole life back into sunshine. She added Tyler's proposal and the ring to the left of her college engagement. She added in her parents. She stopped again, watching her life unfolding on the canvas in front of her. She painted a question mark next to the seedling. There was still so much unresolved. Her idyllic life had given way to pain, criminal behavior, and now a chance for new life. Life wasn't fair. From silver spoon to what?

"Five minutes," Matey announced. "Finish up. We'll be heading to lunch soon."

Reagan added finishing touches. She painted sunlight over the seedling. She added swoops of grey, suggesting movement around the canvas, up from her childhood home, to college, through the crash, graduation and then the rest, down to the seedling. She took a thin paintbrush and added black lines to define some of her images a little more. And then she stopped and leaned back. Not perfect, but it captured the essence of her life. The yellow center, always shining, said it all. In these past few weeks as she'd begun to experience hope and healing, she'd also begun to think she could rediscover happiness.

Welby Considers Life

Welby sat in a chair, looking out at the sea, with his hand posed to write. His story, the story of his life. How could he explain what it was like growing up in the South? He searched for words, considering the various experiences of his life. The world he grew up in he knew was light years away from Reagan's. He could see her over across the room, painting a house with a swimming pool and a playhouse in the back. His swimming pool had been the Atlantic Ocean, and his playhouse a woods full of trees. His people were the downtrodden; his aunt's and uncle's pockets were mostly empty. No silver spoon at his house. They'd been lucky to have enough spoons to go around some days.

And yet the voices in his head spoke of something else. He could hear his Grand MaMa and his aunt, too. They'd never let him think he didn't have what he needed. No, truth be told, they were all about telling him to be grateful to God to be alive, for the chance to live, and for the food to keep him going, no matter how meager it might be. Looking back, he had to hand it to them. They'd made do with so little, and they'd tried to help him think big. That he'd messed it all up along the way, was on him, not on them. They tried their best to help him get his feet planted firmly on his way in a difficult world that didn't really have much room for a Black boy from North Carolina.

Reagan kept filling up her canvas, while Welby sat contemplating. Around the room, everyone seemed busy. Why couldn't he get started? What could be so hard about writing your life? He saw George sitting at a table, writing nonstop. Nikki sat in a chair facing the window, gazing at the sea, but he could tell she was composing a song because she hummed quietly and wrote and then hummed some more. The MAMs sat at a round table, and they all seemed to be writing. Sallie laughed and said something to Abigail, who smiled. Then Molly shushed them. Even Charlie, over in the corner, sat intently writing in his journal.

Welby told himself to get with it. He picked up his pen and started to let the memories flow. He started with the Sea Island and the summertime in the South. He wrote about his mom and his granny, his aunt and his uncle. He wrote about the ocean, and the faith and hope they tried to instill in a little Black boy. He wrote about the day he left the island for good and about his teenage years in Raleigh, and then his truck-driving career. Wine, women, and song, and then the drugs, too. He had it all. He knew it all. He didn't let no one tell him anything back then.

Then, splat, it all came crashing to a halt when that pig stopped him on the road and took him to the slammer for five long years. Welby stopped writing again and gave a long sigh. Looking back, looking forward, looking deep within. He penned a few sentences about the slammer. He didn't want to go back there at all, even to think about it for a moment. He put down his pen and saw Reagan looking at her watch.

"Five minutes," Matey announced.

Welby picked up his pen again and tried to squeeze out just a little more. It had been a long time since he just let it all flow. What did it all mean? They kept talking about roots and DNA, and now he'd just toured the place of his Irish ancestors. He felt important for the first time in a long while. He remembered all that his family had told him over the years, and now he thought about the Irish people who also had a hard row to till, coming to America. Strong, hearty stock. He paged back to the poem he'd written about that. Green and gold. Yep, he'd got it all.

He wrote the last line down in his journal, then went on, expressing his learning from the earlier days: I be Black, I be green, I be gold. You see, there's something really good about being Black. My people are as dark as night and they've been swimming in that darkness ever since they got kidnapped from their native land, chained to boats for the Atlantic passage. Somehow, they made it across the ocean. Somehow, they survived twelve generations of slavery, suffering downright evil stuff from the hands of their white owners. Strong stock I got here. I'm made of strong, tough stuff. And my people love so hard. My people stay close to God, too. Ain't too many Black atheists, they say. No, you can't do this African-American thing without staying close to the Almighty. Nope. Can't do it alone. Now, we might fall off the path from time to time and pretend we can make it on our own, but when we get honest with ourselves, we know we're dependent on God the Father to pull us through, and he does. Look at us. How could we make it through all that without Him on our side?"

Matey said, "Time to go. Let's head over to lunch. Bring your stuff with you. We'll gather in the Croi to share after we eat."

Welby tucked his journal and pen in his backpack. Whew, once he opened the flood gates, it sure all started to come out. He hadn't even had time to get to the green and gold part.

He noticed Reagan cleaning up and putting away her paints over on the other side of the room, and he closed the distance quickly with an offer to help. Regardless of what she might think about politics or the USA, she was still one beautiful woman, and he didn't like to stand in the wings when there was a plane to catch.

"Reagan, wow," he said. "You sure can paint. I can see your life there spread out on the canvas. That's good. That's real good."

Reagan blushed. Did he sense a little insecurity there? What did she have to be nervous about?

"No, I'm serious," he told her. "That rocks."

She pushed her long blonde hair behind her ear. "Thanks," she said. "Do you understand the yellow?"

Welby looked at the painting. In the center, he saw a splatch of yellow, looking a little like the sun, which seemed to radiate out in all directions. He wanted to be able to read it, he wanted her to know he got her. But did he really? Night and day, black and white. So different, her and him. How could he possibly understand her, much less figure out what all that yellow in the painting meant?

"Illuminating," he said. "Very bright."

Reagan nodded. She pointed to a little plant beginning to grow.

"It's the sun, shining," Welby said. "It's the light, helping life grow."

She nodded again.

Then all of a sudden, Welby got it. Saw the center, saw the light, saw the truth as loud as day. Maybe they weren't so different after all.

"You got God in the center, Reagan, don't you. You got the redeemer of the world shining into your life, showing you out. Yes, ma'am."

Reagan's face lit up with something more. Welby sensed that light in the center behind her eyes as they sparkled. Her eyes connected with his, and he felt sparks. "Yes, Welby," she said, gazing deep into his eyes. "You got me. God does, too. Through it all."

Matey called to them, "You two, hurry it up. Let's get a move on. Lunch is waiting."

Welby didn't like that man very much at that instant. He didn't like the fact that their moment got broken up that way. Then he liked George even less when he came and took him by the arm and led him away from Reagan and out of the room. He gave her a backward glance of desperation and hoped she could read him as well as he felt he read her.

Welby didn't talk much at lunch. He sat with George and Tom, and they seemed to want to rein him in again. They carried on about their childhoods and their preacher dad, sharing the memories of getting in trouble and getting whipped. And they laughed about their escapades and their first girlfriends. Welby only wanted to think.

Welby stole a look at Reagan, sitting across the room, almost as quiet as he was. She picked at her food and didn't seem to be following the conversation between Charlie and Nikki, who chatted away. He wondered how they got away with sitting together like that. Probably because they were the privileged white ones. He thought about yelling, "Discrimination," but then he got sidetracked thinking about her.

Welby felt encouraged by the way things had been between them earlier. He chewed on his hamburger and contemplated his own childhood. He thought about his cousins and how they'd accomplished things with their lives. Went to college. Doctor, lawyer, preacher, he remembered now. He wondered what had pulled them apart, why he hadn't looked them up. He'd gone to Raleigh, and they stayed behind. Smart, all of them. Reading, writing, arithmetic, all part of everyday life in his aunt's and uncle's home until he went over to live with his dad when he was eleven. He got that good start, too. He should catch up with them sometime. He wondered where they were and what they were all doing—and if they'd even want to talk to him.

"You okay?" George asked. "You seem awful quiet."

"Just thinkin'," Welby said. "A lot of water under the bridge, you know? Brings up a lot of memories, this story-telling stuff."

"For sure," George said. "Well, you heard me and Tom here. I guess we're going to get to tell it all pretty soon."

"Yeah," Welby said

"What's next?"

"Storytelling at the Croi," Tom said. "I'm not sure exactly. I reckon we're going to find out."

As if scripted, Matey stood up and told them to finish up lunch and that they'd would reconvene in the Croi at 1:30 sharp.

A few minutes later, Welby walked through the open door of the little brick building. Shaped like a womb, the human heart, the inner ear? *These people got it going deep*, he thought.

CHAPTER SIXTEEN
SHALEM CENTRE: STORYTELLING IN THE CROI

Abigail and the MAMs Tell It

Abigail walked to the Croi in step with Seamus. He reached out and took her hand as they approached the small stone building.

"So what's next?" she asked him. "We tell our stories? Will that solve everything?"

"Ah, my lady, how can I tell ye what no one knows? There's power in the story, there is. Time and again in this little building, we've come to better understand each other. But the thing isn't solved here, no. We're still talking, people still disagree. But here, in the Croi, we provide a little space for the meeting of hearts. That makes a difference, it does. Maybe not the solution, but a beginning, a bridge. Ye must be patient. Let the stories unfold. We'll see."

They walked past the little round prayer room and went into a larger room, another chamber of the heart, Abigail supposed. They took seats and soon the session began.

Matey picked up a Bible. "You know the Sermon on the Mount? Up on the mountain, Jesus gave us a blueprint for how to live. Back in his day, they didn't have Republicans and Democrats, but sounds like they had their own disputes. Could someone read this, Chapter Five, verses twenty-one through twenty-four? Listen to this."

"I'll do it," Tom said and took the Bible from him and started to read. "'You have heard that it was said to those of ancient times, 'You shall not murder'; and 'whoever murders shall be liable to judgment.' But I say to you that if you are angry with a brother or sister, you will be liable to judgment; and if you insult a brother or sister, you will be liable to the council; and if you say, 'You fool,' you will be liable to the hell of fire. So when you are offering your gift at the altar, if you remember that your brother or sister has something against you, leave your gift there before the altar and go; first be reconciled to your brother or sister, and then come and offer your gift.'"

Matey said. "Anger, retaliation, Jesus addressed it all. Who will read verses thirty-eight through forty-two?"

Priscilla said, "I will. 'You have heard that it was said, 'An eye for an eye and a tooth for a tooth.' But I say to you, do not resist an evildoer. But if anyone strikes you on the right cheek, turn the other also; and if anyone wants to sue you and take your coat, give your cloak as well; and if anyone forces you to go one mile, go also the second mile. Give to everyone who begs from you, and do not refuse anyone who wants to borrow from you.'"

Abigail decided to say something. "I listen to that and wonder how Christians can support war or refuse to talk to people who disagree with them. Jesus sets the bar high, doesn't he?"

Matey nodded. "Aye, that he does. And another ... could someone read verses forty-three through forty-seven?"

Reagan stepped up. Abigail wondered why. She seemed poised, confident. She started reading clearly, with expression, "You have heard that it was said, 'You shall love your neighbor and hate your enemy.' But I say to you, love your enemies and pray for those who persecute you, so that you may be children of your Father in heaven; for he makes his sun rise on the evil and on the good, and sends rain on the righteous and on the unrighteous. For if you love those who love you, what reward do you have? Do not even the tax collectors do the same? And if you greet only your brothers and sisters, what more are you doing than others? Do not even the Gentiles do the same? Be perfect, therefore, as your heavenly Father is perfect.'"

When she sat down, Matey said, "So, Jesus lays it all out. Don't let the sun go down on your anger. Make peace. Deal with your own faults before you try to criticize another. And love your enemies. Keep this in mind when you tell your story. We've all got roots. We've all got stories. Experiences shaped us as we grew. One more passage here. Could someone read it for me?"

This time, Welby stood and took the book from Reagan. Abigail noticed something passing between them. She couldn't be sure, but there seemed to be an energy flow there. Something about their eyes, the look he gave Reagan, the look she gave him back.

Welby stood in the center and read. Now and then, he glanced up, looking at each person in the circle, and then focusing on Reagan. *Yep,* Abigail thought, *I sure do see something.*

He read the selection marked,: "'Do not judge, so that you may not be judged. For with the judgment you make you will be judged, and the measure you give will be the measure you get. Why do you see the speck in your neighbor's eye, but do not notice the log in your own eye? Or how can you say to your neighbor 'Let me take the speck out of your eye,' while the log is in your own eye? You hypocrite, first take the log out of your own eye, and then you will see clearly to take the speck out of your neighbor's eye.'

Now there's a message for us. Jesus got a sense of humor goin' on there, don't you think?" Welby held an imaginary log up to his eye and stumbled around. Then he stood straight and looked at Matey. "We got to deal with our own stuff first. Jesus knew what he was talking about." Welby handed the Bible back to Matey.

"Thanks, Welby," Matey said. "Righto, chap. Righto. And now the way this will go is ye each will have fifteen minutes to talk. We'll do four, take a break, and four more. Another break, then finish up. If it's okay, we'll be recordin' the stories so ye can go back and listen later.

"If ye could, spend the first five minutes talkin' about your childhood and then five on when ye became an adult. The last five will bring us up to date on your life right now. And please, include your political perspective, how ye came to believe what ye believe. Okay?"

"How can I tell the story of my life in fifteen minutes?" Reagan whined.

Matey laughed. "Good question. Ye can't. But the short version, okay? A summary, so to speak. Would ye like to go first? I'll help ye keep it short by ringing a bell after five minutes and after ten, so ye will know where you're at and when to finish up."

"No, I don't want to go first," Reagan said.

Abigail decided to be a good role model. She raised her hand. "I'll start."

"Good," Matey said.

So Abigail began to tell her story. She began with her childhood, growing up in a happy family on a Mennonite farm in Indiana. Her mom cooked and cleaned and taught her to take care of a house. Her dad farmed and preached. She told about circuit-riding preachers in her family tree. She talked about the practice of nonviolence, and how when the wars came, the Mennonite men were conscientious objectors. She explained how she was taught that, as Christians, they were in "in the world, but not of it." And how Christians shouldn't participate in the evil of the government that chose to go to war.

Abigail heard a bell, and realized she'd been talking five minutes already.

"When I went to college," she said. "I decided to get a science degree. I loved the farm and how things grow. I always wanted to stay close to nature. Before I got married, I taught biology in high school. Then I married a Quaker pastor and continued to teach for a while, but after our two children were born, I stayed home and looked after them. Eventually, I went back to teaching, and then worked for an environmental agency. I began to participate in politics. You see, I think as a Christian, I should try to make my government do better, so that's why I'm a Democrat. They support policies to help people. They don't fund defense as much."

She talked more about those times. The bell rang again. She finished up. She said, "My parents didn't do politics, but my husband taught me different. The Quakers have the American Friends Service Committee, to keep us abreast of political issues. They ask us to write letters and engage. It's been rough since my husband died. The MAMs helped pull me through. It's hard to be a widow. I've really enjoyed this trip and meeting Seamus." She looked at Matey. "I'm done."

"Okay, then," Matey said. "Let's give her a round of applause."

Matey started to clap. When the applause died down, Matey said, "Thanks, Abigail. Who's next?"

The group fell back into listening again. Listening, then applauding, as the stories began to unfold. Katharine shared about growing up on a farm in Minnesota in a good strong Lutheran community, where people didn't talk much about their feelings, they just worked hard. She mentioned Garrison Keillor and "Prairie Home Companion" and said that was her life. She learned the value of hard work, went to college, and excelled, ending up with a scholarship to get a Ph.D. at the University of Chicago. She explained how she became a political moderate. She liked conservative candidates in both parties that worked for the public good. In her job at Mainline College, she focused on developing young minds.

After a round of applause for Katharine, Molly shared her story, growing up African-American. "Well, actually, I'm a hybrid," she explained. "My people have some Shawnee blood, going back to when they first moved up to Ohio on the Underground Railroad. Story is that the Shawnee took in my great-great-grandfather, Ezariah Smith, and gave him a squaw for his wife. He carried with him the Gullah tradition, which has been passed down through the generations. The Gullah people are the West Africans, kidnapped into slavery, who maintained their culture on the Sea Islands off the coast of America on the plantations. Quite a story there. When you have time, I'll tell you more. Ezariah farmed the rice fields, that was all he knew. Well, that and making horseshoes. The Shawnee gave him some land, and later the white man tried to take it away, but Ezariah made some friends by keeping all the horses in the area clad in shoes. So, instead, he stayed put and farmed the land, as did my family for many generations. I grew up on the farm, too, just outside River City. So maybe my growing up wasn't all that different that these other farm girls here.

"When I went to school, I started realizing that my skin made me different. Mama and Papa protected us from all that out there on the farm, but eventually, it became clear as day. Ohio had more than a few white supremacist groups. I didn't see it as a child, but I knew that some of the white people didn't like me. My other Black friends mostly lived in a segregated neighborhood in town. It was the time of the Civil Rights Movement, just as I was starting high school. Things were unfair for my people. They killed Martin Luther King, Junior, and then things started to open up some. That's why my family always sided with the Democrats. And still, things were unfair, even with the Democrats.

"In college, I majored in sociology. I wanted to help my people. I provided assistance to them in my job at the city in community development. Breast cancer stopped me," she said. "All of a sudden, I realized life can be very short. Now I try to live each day fully." She turned to Tom, sitting beside her, and kissed his cheek. "He's my rock," she said. "I couldn't make it without him. And you MAMs keep me sane. I'm indebted to you all."

Abigail started the applause for Molly. Abigail could feel the love as they remembered.

Next Sallie talked about growing up on a dairy farm in Ohio. She learned how to work, but also to have fun. In college, she explained she'd concentrated on having fun, so her grades weren't the best. "I went to the Quaker school, Earlham, because we Brethren are pacifists, too. There, I met Abigail. We did some politics at that time, and I became a Democrat, like Abby.

"After college, I worked for the Brethren Voluntary Service in Maryland with immigrants, then I came back to Ohio to teach. Never got married, but that's okay. And, really, I never got too involved with political things. I focused on my children at school. Kindergarteners kept me busy. They don't worry about things like politics, so I didn't, either."

After Sallie, Matey said, "Good. We just started and already, four of ye've told us your life. Before we take a break, let's reflect. Were there any similarities, common threads here?"

For the first time, Abigail spotted a large loom on the side of the room. Amanda sat hunched over it, weaving.

"What's she doing?" Abigail asked Matey

"I meant to tell you about that. Amanda is about weaving a tapestry for ye, a symbol of your community. Each a separate thread, but all woven together as one."

Michael walked up to the front of the room, holding a large a sketch of a tree. Depicted under the soil were roots, as large as the tree above ground.

Matey explained. "What we see in each other is just the surface. We don't see all that made us who we are. But here ye see the tree and so much more underneath. Our roots make us, too. They come out in our stories, yes. Any questions?"

Silence ensued. He asked his original question again. "So what did you hear from Abigail, Sallie, Molly, and Katharine here? Similarities? Differences? What's in their roots?""

"Farming," Sallie said. "Three of us grew up on farms, close to the earth. Hard workers, we are. A sturdy breed."

"Yes," Matey said. "Michael, write that down?"

Michael took a marker and wrote the word farming by the roots on the tree.

"I noticed that their families shaped their beliefs. Where they grew up made a difference. Like Katharine there grew up in a conservative community, so she became a conservative, whereas Abigail and Sallie came from pacifists, so they went for the liberal party that didn't focus on wars. And Molly, too. She went with her family and the belief that the Democrats were more for African-Americans." Matey finished summarizing and nodded at Michael.

Michael wrote, family, community, pacifist, conservative, African-American, liberal.

Amanda kept weaving. Abigail watched her choosing a variety of colors. In between, she wove a shade of brown. Perhaps an earth cloth, a root cloth?

"Okay, now," Matey said. "Take a break and come back in fifteen. We put out some tea and scones. Have a bit of tea and chat it up. We'll regather soon."

Rather than stay for tea, Abigail and Seamus decided to take a walk. "I be a-learnin' more about ye every day, Abigail," Seamus said. "I think I could spend the rest of me life just listening to ye talk, I could." He took her hand and led her toward the water. "I don't want ye to be a-going home. I don't. I'm going to be a-missing you."

Abigail reached out for Seamus, circling him in a hug. She absorbed the warmth of his body, felt him closing in as she felt her heart jumping and leaping into the day. She felt loved. "I don't want to leave you, either, Seamus. I don't want to go home," she whispered as their time stood still. In the distance, she heard waves crashing into the cliffs below. She heard Seamus' heart beating, too, strong and sure. She held him tight, synchronizing her heartbeat with his.

Reagan Tells it All

Reagan felt something growing inside for Welby. Ever since he got the light on her canvas, she couldn't get him out of her mind. When they took a break, she followed him to the tea table, and then outside. They walked quietly. He commented on the ocean. She said something about the sky. They didn't say much. She could almost feel Welby's arms around her. Of course, George would stop that in a flash. She looked back toward the little chapel, noticing Seamus holding Abigail. She imagined the same with Welby and started to cry.

"What's wrong, baby? What's up? You okay?" Welby took a cloth handkerchief out of his pocket and handed it to her.

"It's just a lot," she said. "Too much." How could she explain to him these new feelings forming in her heart? She couldn't explain it even to herself.

"Oh, yeah, baby. We just never know what's comin' down, do we? You and me? Night and day, black and white. Different colors ain't supposed to be communicatin', not in my hometown. Yet here we are, in the land of our forefathers, learning about our roots and finding each other. That's something. Now you goin' make me cry, too, baby."

Reagan's mouth dropped open as Welby gave voice to the words forming in her head. She really wished she could put her arms around him. Instead, she covered her mouth with her hand and whispered, "Oh. My. God. Welby," she said. "Oh. My. God. Do you read minds?"

Welby broke out in a deep laugh which rumbled from his diaphragm. Reagan felt foolish, but then Welby stopped laughing. He gently placed his hand on her arm. "No, baby. Well, maybe, sometimes. But you see, Reagan, I get you. I do."

"Oh. My. God," she whispered again.

Of course, George spotted them and interrupted their moment before it could play out. "Come on back, you two. Watch it, Welby!"

Welby dropped his hand, breaking the touch. Reagan felt herself jolted out of an encounter she'd never anticipated, but one she'd like to visit again.

When they returned to the circle in the heart's chamber, she sat by Welby. No one made her move. In the tight circle of chairs, she could feel his warmth, and she liked that—a lot. When Matey asked for a volunteer, she felt bold and ready to speak. She collected her painting, then pulled her chair back out of the circle to stand in the opening where everyone could see her and her art. She turned to face Welby, gazing right into his eyes as she began.

Reagan told them all of it. She told of her beginnings, the silver spoon, about having everything. She described in detail her childhood home, the luxury, the pampering, the fun. A playhouse, a swimming pool, a doting daddy, and rooms of toys. "But," she said, "my daddy made me go to college and get a real job. You see that sun in the center here?" She pointed to the yellow light emanating out from the center of her painting. "I stayed close to God growing up and following the right path. My family taught me to be good. I grew up in church, singing and playing the violin for the Lord. I enjoyed Irish dancing, too. Daddy got elected time and time again. All his good friends came to our house. I met the leaders of our community, all great Republicans."

When she heard the bell, she turned to college talk. "I always wanted to be an artist," she explained, "but Daddy said I couldn't make any money doing that. He had enough money to keep me living high off the hog the rest my life. Oh, well. In my family, Daddy was the boss. I decided to major in art and nursing. That way, I figured I could work as a nurse, until I married, to keep Daddy happy. He seemed proud when I took on two majors." Reagan stopped and gave Welby a smile. "It wasn't always easy. I used to say art feeds my soul, but my nursing degree would feed my body. Then I went and fell in love with someone just like my daddy. We planned to marry after I worked a couple years. Well, Tyler wanted to get his political career off the ground a little, too. Personally, I would have been ready to tie the knot right away and quit working so I could stay home and have babies and paint.

"But, bam, everything came to a screeching halt when some no-good drunk slammed into me head-on one night on the way home from class. That turned my life inside out and upside down." She pointed at the crash on the canvas, and then at the light in the center. "God got me through," she said. She gave Welby a little smile. He winked back. Her heart fluttered.

"That was when the nightmare began. See the black cloud?" She pointed again to the painting. "Pain, a wheelchair, long nights. They didn't know if I'd ever walk again. I prayed so hard. They give you so much pain medicine in the hospital. Pretty soon, I got so I really liked it. Eventually, they cut me off the meds, but, working practicums in the hospital, I found ways to steal the pills I craved. It wasn't always easy and *it* was very wrong. But I was hooked." She looked down, embarrassed. "I got very good at sneaking," she said.

The bell rang again. She needed to finish up. She turned toward Amanda, just as she picked up a black and red piece to weave into the fabric. *She's got that right,* Reagan thought. A black cloud, a red crash, both depicted on her canvas she held out for them to see.

"And so," she said, "one day, I got caught. I was sneaky, but not that good. They handcuffed me at the hospital and took me to jail. Daddy bailed me out. I went to treatment, then to the FARM. I blew it, and I'm sorry. I'm thankful for a second chance. Thank you all."

Reagan pointed at the little plant in the corner of her painting. "See God's light shining, in spite of me? See that little plant growing? That's the new me. I don't know who I'm becoming yet, but I'm absorbing the light of God. No more pills. I look forward to a new day." She caught Welby's eye. He gave her a big grin and started to clap, the others quickly joining in. She listened to their applause, smiling as tears streamed down her face. She pulled Welby's handkerchief out of her pocket and wiped her face dry. She mouthed "Thank you" to Welby and then told the group, "I pass."

When she sat down, the tears kept coming. She tried to listen as George talked about getting hooked on drugs and going into treatment, too, about getting his life back together and the shame he felt, being from a preacher's family with the others being outstanding citizens and all.

"The Sun Power House gives me focus and an outlet for my business skills," he said. "I like giving back to men who struggle like I did. I became a Republican for a while, being a businessman. But when Rosales started running for president, I came back to the Democrats with the rest of my family."

After George, Tom explained his early life, then how he found love with Molly and his calling as a cop. "I've always sought to be a role model for African-American youth. Too many of them go to jail instead of college. God is my light, especially in the hard times, like when Molly got cancer, and when I saw so much racism at work and in our community."

Reagan learned a lot from their stories. She hadn't realized, growing up, that there were good African-Americans. That's not what she'd heard.

Priscilla finished off the set. Reagan enjoyed her soft, southern drawl. She talked about how she was raised in a good Southern Baptist church in Tennessee and how her mama and papa taught her to follow the good book and do the right thing. She talked about a woman's role and how she never strayed very far from that straight and narrow path.

"I've always been a good girl," she said. "But I got attracted to a man a few years back named Moses Sun who I thought was a man of God. He worked with those right wing, good Christians in Colorado. A think tank, he called it.

"Some of you probably don't know about our trip to Turkey. We went on an archaeological dig. That's a long story I can tell another time. Moses followed us overseas. He stalked us. We dug up scrolls from the first century. He wanted to stop us from sharing them with the world. He shot Katharine at our press conference and nicked Abigail's granddaughter, Emily, too. Whew, that was hard. But you MAMs let him confess his sins. Now he stands with me most days. He got better. I'm a Republican, because that's how I was raised, in the church and all. We're God's party because we don't believe in killing unborn babies. We want people to work hard and be good. All that, you know."

Reagan liked listening to Priscilla.

Matey asked for comments.

"Seems drugs and alcohol can be a problem on both sides of the tracks," Jane said. "My ex-husband was an alcoholic. Rich as the devil, drunk as a skunk, most days."

Reagan watched Michael write "drugs and alcohol" on the board.

"Redemption and new life," George said. "We fell down, but we got back up."

Priscilla said, "Bless your hearts. God forgave you. Yes, new life."

Michael wrote "forgiveness, redemption and new life."

Matey pointed to the roots. "See all that? Lots of story here. A lot of water under the bridge that grew you into the people you all are today."

Reagan saw the connections. For once, while she felt strongly connected to the Republicans, she could see the light in the Democrats as well. She liked how George saw good in both parties. Maybe she could, too.

Welby Preaches Light

Welby watched Reagan walk out of the heart chamber and longed to go with her. Before she left, she whispered to him that she needed to go to the bathroom. He took it as a message not to follow. He checked out Amanda and the tapestry she was weaving. He reviewed the drawing with the tree and all the words Michael had written among the roots. A few people remained in the room. He imagined they each had tree roots under their feet.

He opened his journal to review what he'd written and to prepare for his turn. If he planned to be the next Martin Luther King, Jr., he wanted to do the man proud, even if it was just by telling his story.

When the others came back, Welby was ready, but he waited. He leaned back and listened to Jane's story. She'd become a carpenter, then a businesswoman, and made a boat load of money. Yep, she was a Republican. He'd nailed that one. But there was something about that woman he liked. She seemed down to earth. He applauded hard with the rest. She explained the way her party helped the businesses with tax breaks.

Charlie went next. Welby knew a little bit about him, but not much. His negative opinions about Charlie came from his political views, which were diametrically opposed to his own. He gave the man his full attention, though, ready to hear what made Charlie tick.

"I came from a good family," Charlie said. "My parents believed in the value of hard work. Spare the rod, spoil the child and all that. My dad built a construction company from the ground up. He taught my brothers and me how to do it all.

"We belong to the Republican party, like many businesspeople, hunters, and those who work. It was a no-brainer for us. We liked to have some fun after we worked hard. Country music, some drinking. We love the NRA and our guns. The NRA helps us keep that right to bear arms. It's constitutional, you know? The American way.

"We know what happened down South in the Civil War. The Northerners messed with our way of life. We had a good gig, making money off the land, but the damn Yankees ruined it. In the good ol' days of the Confederacy, King Cotton raked in good money with cheap labor in the fields. Damn Yankees."

Okay, Welby thought. *So at least he admits it was all about making money. But doesn't the Good Book say the love of money is the root of all evil?*

Charlie continued. "Back in high school, we liked to party hard. After I graduated, I often drank more than I worked. I got my first DWI the night I turned twenty-one. The second came a year later. Then one night I ran into a car and killed a little boy."

Now it felt like they were in an AA meeting; Charlie seemed to be slipping into that familiar cadence. "I hit the bottom. Went to jail. I deserved it. I know I did. My family didn't want anything to do with me. I let them down. I knew better, but alcohol took over my life." Charlie looked up. "But the good Lord gave me a second chance. I got sober. I've apologized to all the people I hurt. I even talked with the family of that little boy I killed. They set that up in prison. Victim-Offender Mediation, they called it. Man, that was the hardest thing I ever done. But it helped. Helped them, I think, too. My family is talking with me again. I hope someday my dad will hire me back on.

"But I'm not perfect. I'm an alcoholic. I take one day at a time. I wish I could tell you that I've been sober ten years, ever since I went to prison, but I can't. I still want a drink. And I messed up my sobriety at that pub this week. But I only had one drink, and I didn't get drunk—because of all of you. Thank you.

"I'm Charlie and I'm an alcoholic, starting over again. I pass."

The room was quiet. Welby watched Michael writing on the roots. "Hard work, construction, alcoholism."

The silence bothered Welby, but he got it. He surveyed the room. Sallie's mouth hung open, Priscilla's eyes were wide, and even Reagan seemed to be a little perplexed. Nikki looked angry. She'd crossed her arms and was giving Charlie a disdainful look.

Welby tried to imagine the guilt that killing a kid would bring, but he couldn't. Then he reminded himself that he'd once almost blown up a whole building. How many people would have been inside? He could've been just as guilty as Charlie—or even more so. And Charlie'd come through it. He was making amends. He deserved applause like the rest of them, so Welby said, "Thank you, Charlie. Thanks, man. You put it out there."

Welby started to clap. *I'm clapping for Charlie? What is it about this place?* It took a while, but soon the others joined in, clapping loud and hard and long. Welby figured that while nobody else in the room had killed a person, they'd all made mistakes.

Charlie began to cry. Then, embarrassed, he covered his face with his hands.

"It's okay, man," George told him. He patted him on the back. "It's all good. Thank you for sharing. You're going to make it through, brother."

Charlie nodded and looked around the circle. "Thank you," he said. "That means a lot."

Then Nikki said, "We got Reagan's beautiful painting. Some of you are writers. For me, it's easier to sing what I have say." She looked at a guitar leaning against the wall. "Can I use that?" she asked Matey.

"Sure thing," he replied and picked it up, strummed a few notes, tinkered with the tuning pegs, and handed it to Nikki.

Nikki began to sing. "I was born into poverty. Couldn't ever seem to make ends meet. Family tried to help me see the future. All I wanted was food to eat.

"Making excuses on the playground, why my clothes were ripped and torn. Holes in my shoes and in my mittens. Got to wondering why I was born."

Then she belted out a chorus. "I'm a traveling girl. Looking for the light up ahead. Rambling through dark nights of laughter. Trying to find a better way instead.

"Saw the light in church when I was seven. Got baptized and all clean inside. My family trusted God for the next meal. I went along for the ride."

She had a verse for her teenage years. She explained the Party of God, as she called it.

"My ma don't have teeth no more, but still follows the narrow way. Taught me abortion is an evil and to follow God's party, the Republican way."

She sang a verse for her singing career, a verse for the road, a verse about drugs, one for her family, and she even gave Ace Steele his own verse.

Welby didn't agree with everything she said, but he had to hand it to her as a songwriter. The song gave him a peek inside Nikki's world, and he understood, which surprised him. He'd never thought Republicans were anything but a bunch of greedy bigots. But here was someone who grew up dirt poor like him. Nikki wasn't a greedy bigot. And he couldn't call Reagan one, either. And not Nikki, not Priscilla, not Jane. Charlie, maybe.

Maybe Welby clapped a little longer than the others because it was his turn next. The time of reckoning was upon him. He walked to the front of the room, carrying his journal for a prop. He would pretend to read, but he planned to speak from his heart all the way.

Once he began talking, it flowed. He explained growing up as a little Black boy in the South where he was to be seen and not heard. He talked about the put-downs from the white people where his auntie worked and the challenges he faced when his mother died and his being called a bastard, even though he had a father. He shared that he couldn't explain that his mom didn't want nothing to do with that man, or the rest of his family, for that matter. And he told them about the saving grace of Sea Island in the summers, time spent with his cousins and his Grand MaMa, how she'd made him read and practice his arithmetic, so that when he went to the school the rest of the year, he would know what he was doing. He talked about church and coming to God and even preaching as a young teenager. He talked about how his teachers liked him and told him he could do most anything. He'd believed them back then and planned to be a doctor, like his mom had named him.

"But then the court said he had to go with his father, and they took him away from his auntie and uncle. He started raising up his father's children in Wilmington, and he lost his dreams. In high school, he got hooked on girls. After he graduated, he wanted to impress them, so he took up truck driving, which paid the bills and for the dates. He experimented with recreational drugs for fun. He quit church and turned his back on God. He got way off track.

"Over time," Welby said, "I became one very angry dude. You see, some rich fossil fuel folks tried to re-segregate the schools in Wake County, North Carolina. Eventually, the people figured it out and voted it back. I got involved in politics. I started reading about those fossil fuel kings who are stacking the legislatures against not just the Black people, but also against the planet while advertising that climate change doesn't exist. I wanted to stop them.

"Once Rosales got elected, I thought things would change, but they didn't let him do nuthin'. The Republicans fought him every step of the way.

"I got frustrated. I got down. I decided to take matters into my own hands. I set out to blow up a company's headquarters. Instead, I got pulled over for speeding. The officer found drugs in my glove compartment, and they sent me to prison for five long years. I'm glad they didn't find the explosives buried in my cargo, though. I lucked out there. But here's the difference: Reagan goes to rehab, I go to the slammer, for pretty much the same thing.

"I came up north, and here I am. I'm changing right now. My people in Africa gave us a concept called *Ubuntu*. That means we're all in this together, all part of one common humanity. Jesus prayed that we might all be one. But we got division, brother. We got arguments, sister. Political parties, neighborhoods, North, South, Black, white, brown, yellow. We fight. Religion says to love but causes many people to hate. They say more wars have been fought in the name of God than any other reason. That's crazy.

"I'm just one sorry drug addict from North Carolina, thinkin' I'm better than the next guy. Thought I could solve this thing. But I can't without you. I need you. I've got those logs in my eye. You see them. You hear them. I can't tell you about your specks; I've got logs.

"We've got serious stuff coming down on this planet. We've got to figure it out. It didn't start with us, but it's on us now. We gotta come together. Our sin brings us to our knees. Our wounds knit us together.

"You look at roots on that tree there. Michael wrote it all down. Our stories, our experiences shape us into the people we are. But can you see the light of God shining there? Can you feel that love of the Spirit that makes us grow, that keeps giving us breath, that makes us grow roots, that makes us strong? Can you see our roots all growing together now?

"We came to Ireland to explore our roots. And what did we learn? We learned we're all connected. Even without this green and Black blood we got goin' on, we're still knit tight. I'm Nikki's sister and Charlie's brother. Our family tree started eons ago, and if you go back far enough, we're all related, all children of God.

"Now, families fight and siblings bicker, but at the end of the day, we're all one big family. We better start lookin' after each other, don't you think? We're on this planet together." Welby looked at Reagan. He'd seen her start to cry about halfway through his story, and now he saw she hadn't stopped

"Don't cry, baby," he said.

"In our stories, in our roots, in our lives, we find a bridge to each other and the future. God's light keeps shining down on all of us in this room, on this planet. We're in this together. We're royalty, heirs of the kingdom of this miraculous world, all created by one God."

Reagan started the clapping. Her tears continued to flow, but she smiled as well. Welby felt her love and, with it, a door opening into a brand-new day.

Over in the corner, Amanda finished her tapestry.

Matey asked, "So what else did you learn about roots here from this last group?"

Reagan spoke first. "The light of God shines on us all, making those roots grow." She gave Welby glance and a smile.

Priscilla nodded. "Amen, sister. You can say that again."

"Connections," Abigail said, looking at Seamus. "We're all connected."

"Aye," Seamus agreed. "The voices of our ancestors join us here today and applaud our understanding. Here in this place, new light is streaming. We do them proud."

"Saint Brigid," Reagan said. "She tried to bring them all together in her day."

"Grand MaMa," Welby said. "She calls us to be the best we can be. Told Reagan to be my friend." Welby hooked his arm around Reagan and she took a deep breath. He felt her absorbing his love. Miraculously, George didn't say a single word.

"The leprechaun," Abigail said. "Síochán told me to listen. Oh, my gosh. Look how much we've heard."

"Spooky," Nikki said.

"No, Nikki," Seamus said. "It's God. We're on holy ground, sacred space. The thin space of me country. The lowered veil catches light from the other side to show us the way,"

Matey turned to Amanda, who was pulling her handiwork off the loom. "Could you bring that over?" he asked.

Amanda held the tapestry up for all to see. Their colors came together. Green and brown repeated throughout. In the center, gold shone brightly.

"That's beautiful," Priscilla exclaimed. "It's like us. Woven together in love."

"I love it," Reagan said. "It's our community blanket, weft and waft of DNA. And gold in the center! That's what Welby said. We're all gold."

"Thank you, Amanda," Matey said. "Nice work. We want you to take this back to America as a symbol of your time here at Shalem Centre, a symbol of your community and how your stories connect you with each other."

"Now," he said. "we've had quite an afternoon. Next, you have some time to relax. After dinner, we'll return to the Croi for a final circle and prayer time to close off your retreat. Thank you for sharing. I feel honored to be with ye and to know each of ye."

The group filed out of the room, but Reagan and Welby stayed in their seats. No one seemed to notice.

Once they were alone, his lips found hers. He kissed her gently, moving his hands along the ridges of her back, then cradled her head, smoothing her hair and held her cheeks. He broke away, only to kiss her again.

And Reagan kissed him back. She took her hands and rubbed them along his scalp, feeling the texture of his hair and playing with the softness. She touched his cheeks, moved her hands down along his broad shoulders, feeling the muscles in his back.

Here on holy ground, in sacred space, Welby sealed the deal. He would never be the same again.

CHAPTER 17
WRAPPING IT UP AND HEADING HOME

Listening Up and Going Home with Reagan

The light of the October evening sparkled off the water below the path where Reagan and Nikki walked toward the Croi for the final session at Shalem Centre. In the morning, they would go back to Dublin for the flight home.

"I don't want to leave," Reagan said. "I want to stay here forever."

"Me, too," Nikki said. "I never thought I'd get to visit Ireland. It feels like home."

They stopped and put their arms around each other and held on while also gazing out to the sea. Reagan pointed to the south. "They say that's Scotland over there. Can you see it? Scotland or clouds?"

"I don't know," Nikki replied. "Hard to tell."

"Maybe we can come back," Reagan said.

"Unlikely for me," Nikki said. "Unless I break through in the music business. They did start up *American Idol* again." She laughed.

"Or *The Voice*. Don't stop dreaming, Nikki. You have to believe in yourself. You're talented."

"So are you, Reagan. You're an artist. Promise you won't give that up, okay?"

"No, ma'am. Painting is my life. I won't stop," Reagan said.

They walked back to the Croi. Reagan spied an empty seat by Welby and sat down. Suddenly she realized it wasn't Ireland or America that she considered home. It was Welby.

***

Matey asked them to share first about their time at Shalem Centre and then about the experience of the entire trip. Everybody got a turn. Most of it they'd said before. Reagan sat mesmerized, not so much by the individual words, but by the whole. Their community blanket lay on the table in the center. They were all woven together now.

When it was her turn, she talked about changes. "I used to just view you in terms of your political parties, your religion, your color, your money—or lack of it. Now, I see you as royalty, 'gold' as Welby says. It's like a whole new world view."

Sallie said, "We need to bottle this and take it back to the States. How can we get others thinking this way?"

"Good question," Matey said. "Good question. As you prepare to go home, what will you do differently? What will you take along? How will you 'bottle it' and keep using it?"

Abigail spoke up. "When we planned this trip, we hoped everyone with Irish roots would get a sense of where they came from. We thought that might help give you a different view of yourself, to help you appreciate the past and also the possibilities of your future. That happened, but much more. I think we need to do more of this. Traveling to a different place can open up a whole new vista."

"Aye, and a whole new love," Seamus said, sitting close to Abigail. "I find it time and time again when the groups come. In this thin space, they catch a glimpse of heaven. But ye can do this in America, too. Remember that the grass is just as sacred and green there, too."

"Can you come show us, Seamus?" Abigail asked. "We need to take you home with us."

Seamus laughed. "I'd be much obliged. In fact, if they got an extra seat on the plane, maybe I can hop on board tomorrow."

Reagan felt the love passing between Seamus and Abigail. She could see it, she realized, because she felt the same with Welby.

George spoke up next. "I never thought Ireland would be all of that. I came along for the ride. But you know, there's something here. Especially, I like the way you do things here at Shalem Centre. That's what I want to take home. Bringing people together to share stories. Could we bring the families of all Sun Power House guys together for a story weekend?"

"Great idea," Molly said. "But let's not leave out the FARM." She turned to Matey. "Would you lead a retreat for us in Ohio?"

"It's a possibility, but you know old Seamus could do this just as well."

Reagan looked at Seamus and asked, "Are you really coming home with us?"

"I just might," he replied.

Departure Dublin Airport with Abigail

The next morning, they rose before dawn for breakfast, leaving the Shalem Centre in the dark. Abigail felt tears welling in her eyes as she rode quietly behind Seamus on the bus. She cried because the trip was ending and she had no idea what would come of her newfound relationship with Seamus. But she also cried because she felt so incredibly happy for all that transpired during their short time in

Ireland.

As if he could read her mind, Seamus reached back and touched her head with a gentle caress. "Ah, my love, it's not the end, ye know. For us, it's just the beginning. I can feel it in my bones."

Abigail nodded and sniffled. When she finally managed to compose herself, she asked, "Are you really going to get on the plane?"

Seamus didn't answer right away. She didn't like the pause.

"Ah, I thought p'rhaps I could join you. But I dialed up the airlines last night and it's just not to be, my love. But I'll come and visit ye, I will. Don't worry, we will be together again soon."

He said all the right things, but still she cried. She wanted to believe him. But the thought of being alone again made her cry more.

Sallie came and sat beside her, putting her arm around her and pulling her close. "Abby, it's okay. We've had a wonderful trip. You met a man. We're going home, but we're taking memories. I heard Seamus. He's going to come visit. You have nothing to worry about. Just look at all that's happened in a little over a week."

Abigail nodded. She took the tissue Sallie handed her and dried her eyes. "Thanks, Sallie," she replied. "You're right."

"Damn right, she is," Seamus inserted from the front seat. "Abigail, I am not going to let you go. No, a love like this doesn't come along but once in a lifetime. Well, or maybe twice for the likes of us."

Abigail could hear the wink in his voice, even though she couldn't see his eye in the darkness. She felt comforted by both Sallie's arm and Seamus' words. She felt loved. She took a deep breath and let out a sigh. The tears stopped. She felt fragile, emotional, but loved.

She rested her head on Sallie's shoulder and felt her eyes grow heavy. Before long, she slipped into a deep slumber.

She woke with a start. "What happened?" She turned to Sallie and then to Seamus.

"You just had a nice nap," Sallie replied and laughed. "We're at the airport, dear."

Seamus stood and announced, "Last stop, Dublin airport. We made good time, but don't tarry now. Ye need to get checked in and go through security. Wait until you're through to use the facilities now, okay? I don't want them to leave any of ye behind. "It's been a real pleasure meeting all of ye, and I'll hope to see ye again across the pond before too long." He looked at Abigail, and this time she could see his wink. She felt herself blushing, even as her heart warmed at the thought of Seamus in the USA.

Seamus pulled her aside. "Abigail, my love. I will come to the States soon. I will. We can talk. We can keep in touch until I see ye again. I wish we didn't have to part, but we'll be together again. This is just the beginning."

Then he put his lips on hers. She didn't care who might be watching. She enfolded him tightly in her arms and absorbed the beauty of the kiss. She kissed him back with an intensity to match his own. They stood as one. It was a connection that would carry her until she could see him again.

Welby Reckoning with Future

A month later, Welby sat in his bedroom at Sun Power House, getting ready for church. He found himself praying harder and harder these days. Ever since he'd returned from Ireland, he took his responsibilities very seriously. Abigail had found him a spiritual director who helped him sort things out and decide on his direction. Although he knew he could be a good electrician, and he planned on finishing that up, where he really felt the call came was in the church, as a minister. In his free time, he started reading a biography of Martin Luther King, Jr. It still sounded a little farfetched, even to him, but he wanted to speak up, he wanted to lead, he wanted to guide the people into hope for this time.

He'd talked to George about his feelings for Reagan. He laid it all out asked George what he should do. He told Welby that if it was meant to be, it would happen. He encouraged Welby to take it slow, to give it time. He even talked to the FARM Board, and they agreed to let Reagan and Welby spend time together, if they agreed to keep it platonic for now. They wanted them to work on friendship, before planning a future together. Welby'd never tried platonic before, but he found he enjoyed getting to know Reagan differently. He worked at it very hard. She planned to introduce him to her family. That made him nervous. But Seamus offered to do a storytelling experience for them, and they were making plans for that time.

To become a pastor, Welby hoped to attend seminary, but that would require finishing his college degree. George helped him sign up to take college classes online, while completing his electrician apprenticeship at Sun Power House. Welby still regretted the wasted days of his life, but now he felt a new light, a new beginning.

George knocked on his door. "You ready, man?"

"Yes, sir," Welby said. "I'm ready."

Reagan Reborn

When Reagan returned to the FARM, a whole new world opened up for her. The shift in her life was profound. She began painting with new fervor in bold, bright colors. Her skies deepened into amazing blues. She relished the autumn colors and painted landscapes glowing with gold, burning with red, and shouting exuberance with orange. As the trees flashed brilliance and relinquished the year's leaves, she let go of her old self, flaming into a new season.

In her new life, she wanted to combine everything. She wanted her nursing to be connected to her art. She wanted her art to be connected to her politics. She wanted to let God's light shine through it all. She kept thinking she'd do some kind of art therapy. She wanted to help people heal through creative processes. She took her time to mull it over to find the right combination, because she was determined that the healing would not just be for individuals healing from their own physical and mental problems, not just from addictions and trauma, but also would involve the divisions and the pain in the heart of the country stemming from political venom. She'd been entered into a program for nurses with substance abuse problems back home when she went into rehab. Now the FARM staff helped her reapply for Ohio's program, the Alternative Program for Chemical Dependency/Substance Use Disorder Monitoring. She was on track to become a nurse again. and that felt really good.

And then there was Welby. Every day, her heart opened more and more to that incredible man. Although their relationship continued in platonic form, the conversations and the love she felt growing between them was unlike anything she'd ever experienced. She looked forward to the storytelling session planned for next month, when Seamus would be in Ohio. Her family would meet Welby for the first time in the context of their stories. She could hardly wait.

She knew Welby felt a call to become a minister and planned to attend seminary. She hoped to play a supportive role in his new calling as a modern-day prophet. Together, they could also speak truth to reunite the country. As they bridged the gap between them, they could lead the way for the Republicans and the Democrats to come together as well.

But first, she needed to finish her year out at the FARM. She wanted to finish healing herself. She needed this time. And the MAMs were planning another trip to Gullah Land. She could hardly wait to see the Sea Island of Welby's youth. Perhaps she could learn something about her own ancestors as well. She wanted to know what happened. Somehow her blood got mixed generations ago, and she felt ready to hear the story.

Reagan took out her painting supplies. She wanted to paint a bridge. She wanted to paint something about hope. She wanted to paint something about the USA coming back together. She sketched a bridge in the center, penciled in herself and Welby hugging at the midpoint. She sketched in the sun. She imagined the Light of God filling up her canvas with joy. She sat back down and waited for inspiration. She knew God's love would show the way.

Abigail and the MAMs, Home Again

On a chilly November night, Abigail headed for Molly's and a book club meeting. Although Seamus hadn't ended up getting a seat on their flight home, he was scheduled to arrive the next day at the airport in Columbus. Not a day passed that they didn't talk on the phone or by Skype since she'd gotten back. Thirty long days had passed since she kissed him good-bye in the Dublin airport. She counted every one of them, just as she now counted down the hours to his arrival tomorrow.

Molly welcomed Abigail at the door. "Want anything to drink?" she asked as Abigail shrugged off her coat and handed it to Molly.

"Just some ice water. Thanks," Abigail replied, taking a seat on the couch. It felt good to be home, good to be with her friends in a place she came time after time over the years. "I'm so thankful for you, Mol. Just think. What if you never started this book club? Just think of all that's happened. From our early meetings to the Butterfly House in Canada? From *In Search of Paul* to Turkey and Thecla; our archaeological dig? And now all this with the DNA and the Emerald Isle and Seamus? I owe it all to you, girlfriend."

Molly smiled. "Hold that thought while I get your water." Molly slipped into the kitchen and hurried back with a glass of ice water. "But it's not me," she said. "It's a God thing. Yes, I played a role, but all this never could have happened without God leading us out. We are so blessed. I'm so blessed having you all in my life. I can't imagine how I'd have gotten through that breast cancer ordeal without my MAMs."

Abigail replied. "You're right and so am I. You started this, sister."

The doorbell rang and Molly jumped up to answer. In came Sallie and Jane.

"How's it going?" Jane said. "Are you ready to rumble?"

"Rumble?" Sallie laughed. "I'm ready to sit down and relax. You guys wear me out."

Molly took drink orders, and, while she was in the kitchen, the doorbell rang again. This time, Jane did the honors, opening the door to Priscilla and Katharine. "Hi-de-ho!" Jane called in welcome, and then she pulled a bottle of wine out of her bag and joined Molly in the kitchen. She returned quickly with wine glasses for all.

"Hear! Hear!" she announced. "I propose a toast to us. Before we discuss our new book about Gullah Land, let's celebrate." She poured each of the MAMs a glass and then took up hers. "To a wonderful trip to the Emerald Isle and to the MAMs." She connected her glass with Molly's and then each of the others in turn before taking a sip.

"To an amazing trip and new love," Abigail said.

Glasses clinked again, the MAMs laughed and then Sallie toasted, "Yes, to Seamus and Abigail, Welby and Reagan, and the bridges we're creating."

Priscilla lifted her water and said, "To all the saints who spoke to us there. May we continue to listen." She clinked her glass to Abigail's and to each of the MAMs in turn.

Katharine toasted, "May the living water continue to inspire us, and the spirits, too." She lifted her glass with a soft chuckle.

"And now, we turn to the future, and prepare for another trip, this time to the American South. Gullah Land, here we come," Molly said, raising her glass high. "To the FARM, to Sun Power House, to us! Hear! Hear!"

Abigail lifted her glass to her friends and took a drink, savoring the wine, the moment, and the future. "To our next adventure!"

AFTERWORD

Thank you for reading my book! You may contact me at nancy.flinchbaugh@gmail.com and follow me on Facebook at Nancy Flinchbaugh, Author.

For more information on the MAMs Book Club, check out my website at SpiritualSeedlings.com. There you can find links and information about the MAMs' adventures in my first two novels, *Revelation in the Cave* and *Revelation at the Labyrinth*. You will also find a listing of over ninety books read by the MAMs Book Club Springfield, with study guides in which Molly, Jane, Abigail, Priscilla, Katharine, Sallie, and I offer comment on each of the books (spiritualseedlings.com/the-mams-book-club/). Join the MAMs Book Club Facebook Group to interact and discuss books.

The books in the Bibliography are ones mentioned in the book and/or served as background information for me in writing.

I wrote *Revelation in the Roots: Emerald Isle* as a lifelong peacemaker and mediator grappling with the racial and political divisions in the United States of America. If you, like me, long for ways for us to transcend our differences and work together to build a better tomorrow, I encourage you to check out Braver Angels and Everyday Democracy.

Braver Angels: braverangels.org

Braver Angels is a citizens' organization uniting red and blue Americans in a working alliance to depolarize America. We try to understand the other side's point of view, even if we don't agree with it. We engage those we disagree with, looking for common ground and ways to work together.

Everyday Democracy: everyday-democracy.org

Everyday Democracy supports organizing across the country by bringing diverse groups of people together, helping them structure and facilitate community dialogue on pressing issues, and training them to use a racial equity lens to understand longstanding problems and possible solutions.

If you are concerned about climate change and want to keep Galway, Cork, and Dublin from sinking into the sea, I heartily recommend joining Citizens' Climate Lobby. These are good people working hard to build bipartisan support for a climate solution.

Citizens' Climate Lobby: citizensclimatelobby.org

Citizens' Climate Lobby is a non-profit, non-partisan, grassroots advocacy organization focused on national policies to address climate change. Our consistently respectful, non-partisan approach to climate education is designed to create a broad, sustainable foundation for climate action across all geographic regions and political inclinations.

If you want to explore contemplative practices, I encourage you to read my book *Awakening: A Contemplative Primer on Learning to Sit*. If you want to become a contemplative leader, check out the Shalem Institute for Spiritual Formation.

Shalem Institute for Spiritual Formation: Shalem.org

Shalem offers in-depth support for contemplative living and leadership.

And finally, Corrymeela, a peace center in Northern Ireland would be a great place to serve, pray and learn as a volunteer, to discover more about how to live well together in this ever-changing, diverse global community.

Corrymeela: Corrymeela.org

In our increasingly divided world, Corrymeela is a movement of people rallied around one inspirational idea: 'Together is better'. Every year they welcome over 8,000 people from all walks of life to their beautiful Ballycastle home and into their programs in communities around Northern Ireland.

BIBLIOGRAPHY

Alexander, Michelle. *The New Jim Crow.* (New Press, 2012).

Coates, Ta-Nehisi. "The Case for Reparations" in *Atlantic Monthly* (2014).

Crane, Jeanne. *Celtic Spirit: A Wee Journey to the Heart of it All* (2012).

Crossan, John Dominic. *In Search of Paul.* (HarperOne, 2005).

Flinchbaugh, Nancy.
Revelation in the Cave (2012).
Revelation at the Labyrinth (eLectio Publishing, 2017).
Awakening: A Contemplative Primer on Learning to Sit (Higher Ground Books and Media, 2020)

Haley, Alex. *Roots: The Saga of a Family.* (Doubleday, 1976).

Helm, Matthew. *Genealogy Online for Dummies, 8th Edition.* (For Dummies, 2017).

McColman, Carl.
366 Celt: A Year and a Day of Celtic Wisdom and Lore. (Hampton Road Publishing, 2008).
An Invitation to Celtic Wisdom: A Little Guide to Mystery, Spirit, and Compassion. (Hampton Road Publishing, 2018).

O'Donohue, John
Anam Cara: A Book of Celtic Wisdom. (Harper Perennial, 2015).
Beauty: The Invisible Embrace. (Harper Perennial, 2015).

Ó Tuama, Pádraig, *Daily Prayer with the Corrymeela Community,* (Canterbury Press Norwich, 2017).

Smolenyak, Megan. *Hey, America, Your Roots Are Showing: Adventures in Discovering News-Making Connections, Unexpected Ancestors, and Long-Hidden Secrets, and Solving Historical Puzzles.* (Citadel Press, 2011).

Stevenson, Bryan. *Just Mercy: A Story of Justice and Redemption.* (One World, 2015).

Wilkerson, Isabelle, *The Warmth of Other Suns: The Epic Story of America's Great Migration.* (Vintage, 2011).

About the Author

 Nancy Flinchbaugh is a Christian contemplative who writes as spiritual practice. Recently retired, she wrote this book to continue her life work of peacemaking and building bridges across racial and political divides. Her other books include the first two novels in the MAMs series *Revelation in the Cave* (2012) and *Revelation at the Labyrinth* (eLectio Publishing, 2017), in addition to a memoir, *Letters from the Earth* (Higher Ground Books and Media, 2018), and *Awakening: A Contemplative Primer on Learning to Sit* (Higher Ground Books and Media, 2020). She enjoys nature, gardening, bicycling, traveling, leading contemplative experiences, community building, and writing books with purpose. Nancy is a member of First Baptist church and mother of two wonderful sons, Luke and Jacob. She lives in Springfield, Ohio, empty nesting with her husband, Steve, and cat, Emily Rose. Learn more about her work at spiritualseedlings.com and nancyflinchbaugh.com. Connect with her on Facebook at Nancy Flinchbaugh, Author.

Made in the USA
Middletown, DE
11 January 2022

57987551R00137